Dear Reader,

This collection of books contains some of my personal favorites, and it's a thrill to see them in print again.

Coltrain's Proposal was an idea that grew out of *That Burke Man,* because the redheaded doctor seemed perfect for a "Long, Tall Texan." It didn't take more than ten pages to convince me that I had a tiger by the tail. Coltrain promptly took over the book and apparently wrote it himself, because all I remember is staring saucer-eyed at the screen while the plot developed. Of course, he did get something wrong; he forgot that Burke's wife, Jane, had mentioned talking to "Copper" Coltrain's mother, who was long dead in *his* book. But, all in all, I was pleased with the book, and I hope you will be, too.

Beloved was a honey of a book to write. Tira wasn't my usual sort of heroine (she was a knockout), but Simon was a textbook beast, so she sort of had to be a beauty. I had fun watching him eat crow for six chapters. Most of my longtime readers will tell you that my heroes don't even begin to get human until the heroine takes them in hand. They eat crow a lot, actually, and I do so love to see a man in the wrong grovel! (Please do not mention this to my husband and son, who could eat live rattlesnakes in a temper and have never heard of the term "grovel." They would probably think it had something to do with the stuff you use to pave driveways.)

"Paper Husband" was the culmination of a dream. I got to do a duet with my all-time favorite Harlequin author, Margaret Way, and "Paper Husband" was my contribution to the project. Margaret knows more about sexy, masterful, exciting heroes than I have learned yet, and I had to buy two copies of each one of her books because I reread them so often. I love the idea of marriages of convenience, and having the reluctant bridegroom fall in love with the not-perfectly-gorgeous heroine. So often, the most beautiful people have rough exteriors or a lack of conventional good looks, and they blossom with a little attention!

Thank you for your continuing loyalty and friendship, and for taking time to write to me. I'm still painfully slow with snail mail, but you can e-mail me at my Web site, www.dianapalmer.com, and you'll get an answer within a month or so. Don't forget to visit www.eHarlequin.com, also, and see what's new with all our authors!

Love,

Diana Palmer

DIANA PALMER

LONG, TALL TEXAN
Weddings

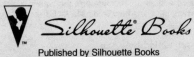

Published by Silhouette Books

America's Publisher of Contemporary Romance

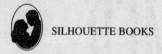 SILHOUETTE BOOKS

LONG, TALL TEXAN WEDDINGS

Copyright © 2001 by Harlequin Books S.A.

ISBN 0-373-48487-9

The publisher acknowledges the copyright holder of the individual works as follows:

COLTRAIN'S PROPOSAL
Copyright © 1995 by Diana Palmer

BELOVED
Copyright © 1999 by Diana Palmer

PAPER HUSBAND
Copyright © 1996 by Diana Palmer

CONTENTS

Books by Diana Palmer

Silhouette Desire

The Cowboy and the Lady #12
September Morning #26
Friends and Lovers #50
Fire and Ice #80
Snow Kisses #102
Diamond Girl #110
The Rawhide Man #157
Lady Love #175
Cattleman's Choice #193
‡The Tender Stranger #230
Love by Proxy #252
Eye of the Tiger #271
Loveplay #289
Rawhide and Lace #306
Rage of Passion #325
Fit for a King #349
Betrayed by Love #391
‡Enamored #420
Reluctant Father #469
Hoodwinked #492
His Girl Friday #528
Hunter #606
Nelson's Brand #618
The Best Is Yet To Come #643
*The Case of the Mesmerizing Boss #702
*The Case of the Confirmed Bachelor #715
*The Case of the Missing Secretary #733
Night of Love #799
Secret Agent Man #829
†That Burke Man #913
Man of Ice #1000
The Patient Nurse #1099
†Beloved #1189
‡The Winter Soldier #1351

Silhouette Special Edition

Heather's Song #33
The Australian #239
Maggie's Dad #991
†Matt Caldwell: Texas Tycoon #1297
‡The Last Mercenary #1417

Steeple Hill Love Inspired

Blind Promises

‡ Soldiers of Fortune
† Long, Tall Texans
* Most Wanted Series

Silhouette Romance

Darling Enemy #254
Roomful of Roses #301
Heart of Ice #314
Passion Flower #328
‡Soldier of Fortune #340
After the Music #406
Champagne Girl #436
Unlikely Lover #472
Woman Hater #532
†Calhoun #580
†Justin #592
†Tyler #604
†Sutton's Way #670
†Ethan #694
†Connal #741
†Harden #783
†Evan #819
†Donavan #843
†Emmett #910
King's Ransom #971
†Regan's Pride #1000
†Coltrain's Proposal #1103
Mystery Man #1210
†The Princess Bride #1282
†Callaghan's Bride #1355
‡Mercenary's Woman #1444

Silhouette Books

Silhouette Christmas Stories 1987
"The Humbug Man"

Silhouette Summer Sizzlers 1990
"Miss Greenhorn"

Abduction and Seduction
"Redbird"

To Mother with Love 1993
"Calamity Mom"

Montana Mavericks
Rogue Stallion

Montana Mavericks Weddings
"The Bride Who Was Stolen in the Night"

†A Long, Tall Texan Summer

Lone Star Christmas 1997
†"Christmas Cowboy"

†Love With a Long, Tall Texan

MIRA

Once in Paris
Paper Rose
Lord of the Desert
The Texas Ranger

COLTRAIN'S PROPOSAL

To Darlene, Cindy, and Melissa

Chapter 1

The little boy's leg was bleeding profusely. Dr. Louise Blakely knew exactly what to do, but it was difficult to get the right pressure on the cut so that the nicked artery would stop emptying onto the brown, dead December grass.

"It hurts!" the little boy, Matt, cried. "Ow!"

"We have to stop the bleeding," she said reasonably. She smiled at him, her dark eyes twinkling in a face framed by thick, medium blond hair. "Maybe your mom could get you an ice cream after we've patched you up." She glanced at the white-faced lady beside them, who nodded enthusiastically. "Okay?"

"Well..." He grimaced, holding his leg above where Lou was putting pressure to bear.

"Only a minute more," she promised, looking around for the ambulance she'd asked a bystander to call. It was on the way. She could hear the siren. Even in a small town like Jacobsville, there was an efficient ambulance service. "You're going to get to ride in a real ambulance," she told the child. "You can tell your friends all about it on Monday at school!"

"Will I have to go back?" he asked, enthusiastic now. "Maybe I could stay in the hospital for a whole week?"

"I really think the emergency room is as far as you're going to get this time." Lou chuckled. "Now pay attention while they're loading you up, so that you can remember everything!"

"I sure will!" he said.

She stood up as the ambulance pulled alongside the police car and two attendants jumped out. They started loading the boy onto a stretcher. Lou had a brief word with the female EMT and described the boy's injuries and gave instructions. She was on staff at the local hospital where he would be taken, and she planned to follow the ambulance in her own car.

The police officer who'd been citing the reckless driver for hitting the small boy on the bicycle came over to talk to Lou. "Good thing you were having lunch in the café," he remarked with a grin. "That was a bad cut."

"He'll be okay," Lou said as she closed her medical bag. She always had it in the car when she left the office, and this time it had paid off.

"You're Dr. Coltrain's partner, aren't you?" he asked suddenly.

"Yes." She didn't add anything to that. The expression on the officer's face said enough. Most people around Jacobsville knew that Dr. Coltrain had as little use for his partner as he had for alcohol. He'd made it all too evident in the months she'd been sharing his practice.

"He's a good man," the officer added. "Saved my wife when her lung collapsed." He smiled at the memory. "Nothing shakes him up. Nor you, either, judging by what I just saw. You're a good hand in an emergency."

"Thanks." She gave him a brief smile and went to her small gray Ford to follow the ambulance to the hospital.

The emergency room was full, as usual. It was Saturday and accidents always doubled on weekends. She nodded to a couple of her patients that she recognized, and she kept walking, right behind the trolley that was taking young Matt to a treatment room.

Dr. Coltrain was on his way back from surgery. They met in

the hall. The green surgical uniform looked sloppy on some of the surgeons, but not on Coltrain. Despite the cap that hid most of his thick red hair, he looked elegant and formidable.

"Why are you here on Saturday? I'm supposed to be doing rounds today for both of us," he asked sharply.

Here he goes again, practicing Coltrain's First Law...jump to conclusions, she thought. She didn't grin, but she felt like it.

"I wound up at a car accident scene," she began.

"The hospital pays EMTs to work wrecks," he continued, glaring at her while hospital personnel came and went around them.

"I did not go out to—" she began hotly.

"Don't let this happen again, or I'll have a word with Wright, and you'll be taken off staff here. Is that clear?" he added coldly. Wright was the hospital administrator and Coltrain was medical chief of staff. He had the authority to carry out the threat.

"Will you listen?" she asked irritably. "I didn't go out with the ambulance...!"

"Doctor, are you coming?" one of the EMTs called to her.

Coltrain glanced toward the EMT and then back at Louise, irritably jerking off his cap and mask. His pale blue eyes were as intimidating as his stance. "If your social life is this stale, Doctor, perhaps you need to consider a move," he added with biting sarcasm.

She opened her mouth to reply, but he was already walking away. She threw up her hands furiously. She couldn't ever get a word in, because he kept talking, or interrupted her, and then stormed off without giving her a chance to reply. It was useless to argue with him, anyway. No matter what she said or did, she was always in the wrong.

"One day you'll break something," she told his retreating back. "And I'll put you in a body cast, so help me God!"

A passing nurse patted her on the shoulder. "There, there, Doctor, you're doing it again."

She ground her teeth together. It was a standing joke in the hospital staff that Louise Blakely ended up talking to herself every time she argued with Dr. Coltrain. That meant that she talked to herself almost constantly. Presumably he heard her from time to time, but he never gave a single indication that he had.

With a furious groan deep in her throat, she turned down the hall to join the EMT.

It took an hour to see to the boy, who had more than one cut that needed stitches. His mother was going to have to buy him a lot of ice cream to make up for the pain, Lou thought, and she'd been wrong about another thing, too—he did have to stay overnight in the hospital. But that would only give him status among his peers, she thought, and left him smiling with a cautionary word about the proper way to ride a bicycle in town.

"No need to worry about that," his mother said firmly. "He won't be riding his bike across city streets anymore!"

She nodded and left the emergency room, her bag in hand. She looked more like a teenager on holiday than a doctor, she mused, in her blue jeans and T-shirt and sneakers. She'd pulled her long blond hair up into its habitual bun and she wore no makeup to enhance her full mouth or her deep brown eyes. She had no man to impress, except the one she loved, and he wouldn't notice if she wore tar and feathers to the office they shared. "Copper" Coltrain had no interest in Lou Blakely, except as an efficient coworker. Not that he ever acknowledged her efficiency; instead he found fault with her constantly. She wondered often why he ever agreed to work with her in the first place, when he couldn't seem to stand the sight of her. She wondered, too, why she kept hanging on where she wasn't wanted. The hunger her poor heart felt for him was her only excuse. And one day, even that wouldn't be enough.

Dr. Drew Morris, the only friend she had on staff, came down the hall toward her. Like Coltrain, he'd been operating, because he was wearing the same familiar green surgical clothing. But where Coltrain did chest surgery, Drew's talents were limited to tonsils, adenoids, appendices and other minor surgeries. His speciality was pediatrics. Coltrain's was chest and lungs, and many of his patients were elderly.

"What are you doing here? It's too early or too late for rounds, depending on your schedule," he added with a grin. "Besides, I thought Copper was doing them today."

Copper, indeed. Only a handful of people were privileged to call Dr. Coltrain by that nickname, and she wasn't numbered among them.

She grimaced at him. He was about her height, although she was tall, and he had dark hair and eyes and was a little overweight. He was the one who'd phoned her at the Austin hospital where she was working just after her parents' deaths, and he'd told her about the interviews Coltrain was holding for a partner. She'd jumped at the chance for a new start, in the hometown where her mother and father had both been born. And amazingly, in light of his ongoing animosity toward her, Coltrain had asked her to join him after a ten-minute interview.

"There was an accident in front of the café," she said. "I was having lunch there. I haven't been to the grocery store yet," she added with a grimace. "I hate shopping."

"Who doesn't?" He smiled. "Doing okay?"

She shrugged. "As usual."

He stuck his hands on his hips and shook his head. "It's my fault. I thought it would get better, but it hasn't, has it? It's been almost a year, and he still suffers you."

She winced. She didn't quite avert her face fast enough to hide it.

"You poor kid," he said gently. "I'm sorry. I suppose I was too enthusiastic about getting you here. I thought you needed a change, after...well, after your parents' deaths. This looked like a good opportunity. Copper's one of the best surgeons I've ever known, and you're a skilled family practitioner. It seemed a good match of talent, and you've taken a load off him in his regular practice so that he could specialize in the surgery he's so skilled at." He sighed. "How wrong can a man be?"

"I signed a contract for one year," she reminded him. "It's almost up."

"Then what?"

"Then I'll go back to Austin."

"You could work the ER," he teased. It was a standing joke between them. The hospital had to contract out the emergency room staff, because none of the local doctors wanted to do it. The job was so demanding that one young resident had walked out in the middle of the unnecessary examination of a known hypochondriac at two in the morning and never came back.

Lou smiled, remembering that. "No, thanks. I like private practice, but I can't afford to set up and equip an office of my own just yet. I'll go back to the drawing board. There's bound to be a practice somewhere in Texas."

"You're fit for this one," he said shortly.

"Not to hear my partner tell it," she said curtly. "I'm never right, didn't you know?" She let out a long breath. "Anyway, I'm in a rut, Drew. I need a change."

"Maybe you do, at that." He pursed his lips and smiled. "What you really need is a good social life. I'll be in touch."

She watched him walk away with grave misgivings. She hoped that he didn't mean what it sounded like he meant. She wanted nothing to do with Drew in a romantic way, although she did like him. He was a kind man, a widower who'd been in love with his wife and was still, after five years, getting over her. Drew was a native of Jacobsville, and knew Lou's parents. He'd been very fond of her late mother. He'd met up with them again in Austin—that's where Lou had met him.

Lou decided not to take Drew's teasing seriously because she knew about his devotion to his wife's memory. But he'd looked very solemn when he'd remarked that her social life needed uplifting.

She was probably imagining things, she told herself. She started out to the parking lot and met Dr. Coltrain, dressed in an expensive gray vested suit, bent on the same destination. She ground her teeth together and slowed her pace, but she still reached the doors at the same time he did.

He spared her a cold glance. "You look unprofessional," he said curtly. "At least have the grace to dress decently if you're going to cruise around with the ambulance service."

She stopped and looked up at him without expression. "I wasn't cruising anywhere. I don't have a boat, so how could I cruise?"

He just looked at her. "They don't need any new EMTs..."

"You shut up!" she snapped, surprising him speechless. "Now you listen to me for a change, and don't interrupt!" she added, holding up her hand when his thin lips parted. "There was an accident in town. I was in the café, so I gave assistance. I don't need to hang out with the ambulance crew for kicks, Doctor! And how I dress on my days off is none of your—" she almost turned blue biting back the curse *"—business,* Doctor!"

He was over his shock. His hand shot out and caught the wrist of her free hand, the one that wasn't holding her black medical bag, and jerked. She caught her breath at the shock of his touch and squirmed, wrestling out of his grip. The muted violence of it brought back protective instincts that she'd almost forgotten. She stood very still, holding her breath, her eyes the size of saucers as she looked at him and waited for that hand to tighten and twist...

But it didn't. He, unlike her late father, never seemed to lose control. He released her abruptly. His blue eyes narrowed. "Cold as ice, aren't you?" he drawled mockingly. "You'd freeze any normal man to death. Is that why you never married, Doctor?"

It was the most personal thing he'd ever said to her, and one of the most insulting.

"You just think what you like," she said.

"You might be surprised at what I think," he replied. He looked at the hand he'd touched her with and laughed deep in his throat. "Frostbitten," he pronounced. "No wonder Drew Morris doesn't take you out. He'd need a blowtorch, wouldn't he?" he added with a meaningful, unblinking blue stare.

"Maybe so, but you'd need a grenade launcher," she retorted without thinking.

He lifted an eyebrow and gave her a look that held mingled contempt and distaste. "You'd be lucky."

The remark was painful, but she didn't let him see that. Her own eyebrows lifted. "Really?" She laughed and walked off to her car, happy to have seen him stiffen. She walked past his Mercedes without even a glance. Take that, she thought furiously. She didn't care what he thought about her, she told herself. She spent most of her free time telling herself that. But she did care about him, far too much. That was the whole problem.

He thought she was cold, but she wasn't. It was quite the reverse where he was concerned. She always jerked away when he came too close, when he touched her infrequently. It wasn't because she found him repulsive but because his touch excited her so much. She trembled when he was too close, her breathing changed. She couldn't control her shaky legs or her shaky voice. The only solution had been to distance herself physically from him, and that was what she'd done.

There were other reasons, too, why she avoided physical involvement. They were none of his business, or anyone else's. She did her job and avoided trouble as much as possible. But just lately, her job was becoming an ordeal.

She drove home to the small dilapidated white house on the outskirts of town. It was in a quiet neighborhood that was just beginning to go downhill. The rent was cheap. She'd spent weekends painting the walls and adding bits and pieces to the house's drab interior. She had it all but furnished now, and it reflected her own quiet personality. But there were other dimensions to the room, like the crazy cat sculpture on the mantel and the colorful serapes on the chairs, and the Indian pottery and exotic musical instruments on the bookshelf. The paintings were her own, disturbingly violent ones with reds and blacks and whites in dramatic chaos. A visitor would have found the combinations of flowers amid those paintings confusing. But, then, she'd never had a visitor. She kept to herself.

Coltrain did, too, as a rule. He had visitors to his ranch from time to time, but his invitations even when they included the medical staff invariably excluded Louise. The omission had caused gossip, which no one had been brave enough to question to his face. Louise didn't care if he never invited her to his home. After all, she never invited him to hers.

Secretly she suspected that he was grieving for Jane Parker, his old flame who'd just recently married Todd Burke. Jane was blond and blue-eyed and beautiful, a former rodeo star with a warm heart and a gentle personality.

Lou often wondered why he'd ever agreed to work with someone he disliked so much, and on such short acquaintance. He and Dr. Drew Morris were friends, and she'd tried to question Drew about her sudden acceptance, but Drew was a clam. He always changed the subject.

Drew had known her parents in Jacobsville and he had been a student of her father's at the Austin teaching hospital where he'd interned. He'd become an ally of her mother during some really tough times, but he didn't like Lou's father. He knew too much about his home life, and how Lou and her mother were treated.

There had been one whisper of gossip at the Jacobsville hospital when she'd first gone there on cases. She'd heard one of the senior nurses remark that it must disturb ''him'' to have Dr. Blakely's daughter practicing at this hospital and thank God she didn't do surgery. Lou had wanted to question the nurse, but she'd made herself scarce after that and eventually had retired.

Louise had never found out who ''he'' was or what was disturbing about having another Blakely practice at the Jacobsville hospital. But she did begin to realize that her father had a past here.

''What did my father do at this hospital, Drew?'' she'd asked him one day suddenly, while they were doing rounds at the hospital.

He'd seemed taken aback. "He was a surgeon on staff, just as I am," he said after a hesitation.

"He left here under a cloud, didn't he?" she persisted.

He shook his head. "There was no scandal, no cloud on his reputation. He was a good surgeon and well respected, right until the end. You know that. Even if he was less than admirable as a husband and father, he was an exceptional surgeon."

"Then why the whispers about him when I first came here?"

"It was nothing to do with his skill as a surgeon," he replied quietly. "It's nothing that really even concerns you, except in a roundabout way."

"But what...?"

They'd been interrupted and he'd looked relieved. She hadn't asked again. But she wondered more and more. Perhaps it had affected Dr. Coltrain in some way and that was why he disliked Lou. But wouldn't he have mentioned it in a whole year?

She didn't ever expect to understand the so-controlled Dr. Coltrain or his venomous attitude toward her. He'd been much more cordial when she first became his partner. But about the time she realized that she was in love with him, he became icy cold and antagonistic. He'd been that way ever since, raising eyebrows everywhere.

The remark he'd made this morning about her coldness was an old one. She'd jerked back from him at a Christmas party, soon after she'd come to work in his office in Jacobsville, to avoid a kiss under the mistletoe. She could hardly have admitted that even then the thought of his hard, thin mouth on hers made her knees threaten to buckle. Her attraction to him had been explosive and immediate, a frightening experience to a woman whose whole life had been wrapped around academic excellence and night upon night of exhaustive studying. She had no social life at all—even in high school. It had been the one thing that kept her father's vicious sarcasm and brutality at bay, as long as she made good grades and stayed on the dean's list.

Outside achievements had been the magic key that kept the

balance in her dysfunctional family. She studied and won awards and scholarships and praise, and her father basked in it. She thought that he'd never felt much for her, except pride in her ability to excel. He was a cruel man and grew crueler as his addiction climbed year after year to new heights. Drugs had caused the plane crash. Her mother had died with him. God knew, that was fitting, because she'd loved him to the point of blindness, overlooking his brutality, his addiction, his cruelty in the name of fidelity.

Lou wrapped her arms around herself, feeling the chill of fear. She'd never marry. Any woman could wake up in a relationship that damaging. All she had to do was fall in love, lose control, give in to a man's dominance. Even the best man could become a predator if he sensed vulnerability in a woman. So she would never be vulnerable, she assured herself. She would never be at a man's mercy as her mother had been.

But Copper Coltrain made her vulnerable, and that was why she avoided any physical contact with him. She couldn't give in to the feelings he roused in her, for fear of becoming a victim. Loneliness might be a disease, but it was certainly a more manageable one than love.

The ringing of the telephone caught her attention.

"Dr. Blakely?" Brenda, her office nurse, queried. "Sorry to bother you at home, but Dr. Coltrain said there's been a wreck on the north end of town and they'll be bringing the victims to the emergency room. Since he's on call, you'll have to cover the two-hour Saturday clinic at the office."

"I'll be right over," she promised, wasting no more time in conversation.

The clinic was almost deserted. There was a football game at the local high school that night, and it was sunny and unseasonably warm outside for early December. It didn't really surprise Lou that she only needed to see a handful of patients.

"Poor Dr. Coltrain," Brenda said with a sigh as they finished the last case and closed up the office. "I'll bet he won't be in until midnight."

"It's a good thing he isn't married," Lou remarked. "He'd have no home life at all, as hard as he works."

Brenda glanced at her, but with a kind smile. "That is true. But he should be thinking about it. He's in his thirties now, and time is passing him by." She turned the key in the lock. "Pity about Miss Parker marrying that Burke man, isn't it? Dr. Coltrain was sweet on her for so many years. I always thought—I guess most people here did—that they were made for each other. But she was never more than friendly. If you saw them together, it was obvious that she didn't feel what he did."

In other words, Dr. Coltrain had felt a long and unrequited love for the lovely blond former rodeo cowgirl, Jane Parker. That much, Lou had learned from gossip. It must have hurt him very badly when she married someone else.

"What a pity that we can't love to order," Lou remarked quietly, thinking how much she'd give to be unscarred and find Dr. Coltrain as helplessly drawn to her as she was to him. That was the stuff of fantasy, however.

"Wasn't it surprising about Ted Regan and Coreen Tarleton, though?" Brenda added with a chuckle.

"Indeed it was," Lou agreed, smiling as she remembered having Ted for a patient. "She was shaking all over when she got him to me with that gored arm. He was cool. Nothing shakes Ted. But Coreen was as white as milk."

"I thought they were already married," Brenda groaned. "Well, I was new to the area and I didn't know them. I do now," she added, laughing. "I pass them at least once a week on their way to the obstetrician's office. She's due any day."

"She'll be a good mother, and Ted will certainly be a good father. Their children will have a happy life."

Brenda caught the faint bitterness in the words and glanced at Lou, but the other woman was already calling her goodbyes and walking away.

She went home and spent the rest of the weekend buried in medical journals and the latest research on the new strain of bacteria that had, researchers surmised, mutated from a deadly scarlet fever bacterium that had caused many deaths at the turn of the century.

Chapter 2

Monday morning brought a variety of new cases, and Louise found herself stuck with the most routine of them, as usual. She and Coltrain were supposed to be partners, but when he wasn't operating, he got the interesting, challenging illnesses. Louise got fractured ribs and colds.

He'd been stiff with her this morning, probably because he was still fuming over the argument they'd had about his mistaken idea of her weekend activities. Accusing her of lollygagging with the EMTs for excitement; really!

She watched his white-coated back disappear into an examination room down the hall in their small building and sighed half-angrily as she went back to check an X ray in the files. The very worst thing about unrequited love, she thought miserably, was that it fed on itself. The more her partner in the medical practice ignored and antagonized her, the harder she had to fight her dreams about him. She didn't want to get married; she didn't even want to get involved. But he made her hungry.

He'd spent a lot of time with Jane Parker until she married that Burke man, and Lou had long ago given up hope that he would ever notice her in the same way he always noticed Jane. The two of them had grown up together, though, whereas Lou had only been in partnership with him for a year. She was a native of Austin, not Jacobsville. Small towns were like extended families. Everybody knew each other, and some families had been friends for more than one generation. Lou was a true outsider here, even though she *was* a native Texan. Perhaps that was one of many reasons that Dr. Coltrain found her so forgettable.

She wasn't bad looking. She had long, thick blond hair and big brown eyes and a creamy, blemish-free complexion. She was tall and willowy, but still shorter than her colleague. She lacked his fiery temper and his authoritarian demeanor. He was tall and whipcord lean, with flaming red hair and blue eyes and a dark tan from working on his small ranch when he wasn't treating patients. That tan was odd in a redhead, although he did have a smattering of freckles over his nose and the backs of his big hands. She'd often wondered if the freckles went any farther, but she had yet to see him without his professional white coat over his very formal suit. He wasn't much on casual dressing at work. At home, she was sure that he dressed less formally.

That was something Lou would probably never know. She'd never been invited to his home, despite the fact that most of the medical staff at the local hospital had. Lou was automatically excluded from any social gathering that he coordinated.

Other people had commented on his less than friendly behavior toward her. It puzzled them, and it puzzled her, because she hadn't become his partner in any underhanded way. He had known from the day of her application that she was female, so it couldn't be that. Perhaps, she thought wistfully, he was one of those old-line dominating sort of men who thought women had no place in medicine. But he'd been instrumental in getting women into positions of authority at the hospital, so that theory wasn't applicable, either. The bottom line was that he simply did not like Louise Blakely, medical degree or no medical degree, and she'd never known why.

She really should ask Drew Morris why, she told herself with determination. It had been Drew, a surgeon and friend of her family, who'd sent word about the opening in Coltrain's practice.

He'd wanted to help Lou get a job near him, so that he could give her some moral support in the terrible days following the deaths of her parents. She, in turn, had liked the idea of being in practice in a small town, one where she knew at least one doctor on the staff of the hospital. Despite growing up in Austin, it was still a big city and she was lonely. She was twenty-eight, a loner whose whole life had been medicine. She'd made sure that her infrequent dates never touched her heart, and she was innocent in an age when innocence was automatically looked on with disdain or suspicion.

Her nurse stuck her head in the doorway. "There's a call for you. Dr. Morris is on line two."

"Thanks, Brenda."

She picked up the receiver absently, her finger poised over the designated line. But when she pressed it, before she could say a word, the sentence she'd intercepted accidentally blared in her ear in a familiar deep voice.

"...told you I wouldn't have hired her in the first place, if I had known who she was related to. I did you a favor, never realizing she was Blakely's daughter. You can't imagine that I'll ever forgive her father for what he did to the girl I loved, do you? She's been a constant reminder, a constant torment!"

"That's harsh, Copper," Drew began.

"It's how I feel. She's nothing but a burden here. But to answer your question, hell no, you're not stepping on my toes if you ask her out on a date! I find Louise Blakely repulsive and repugnant, and an automaton with no attractions whatsoever. Take her with my blessing. I'd give real money if she'd get out of my practice and out of my life, and the sooner the better!" There was a click and the line, obviously open, was waiting for her.

She clicked the receiver to announce her presence and said, as calmly as she could, "Dr. Lou Blakely."

"Lou! It's Drew Morris," came the reply. "I hope I'm not catching you at a bad moment?"

"No." She cleared her throat and fought to control her scattered emotions. "No, not at all. What can I do for you?"

"There's a dinner at the Rotary Club Thursday. How about going with me?"

She and Drew occasionally went out together, in a friendly but not romantic way. She would have refused, but what Coltrain had said made her mad. "Yes, I would like to, thanks," she said.

Drew laughed softly. "Great! I'll pick you up at six on Thursday, then."

"See you then."

She hung up, checked the X ray again meticulously, and put it away in its file. Brenda ordinarily pulled the X rays for her, but it was Monday and, as usual, they were overflowing with patients who'd saved their weekend complaints for office hours.

She went back to her patient, her color a little high, but no disturbance visible in her expression.

She finished her quota of patients and then went into her small office. Mechanically she picked up a sheet of letterhead paper, with Dr. Coltrain's name on one side and hers on the other. Irrelevantly, she thought that the stationery would have to be replaced now.

She typed out a neat resignation letter, put it in an envelope and went to place it on Dr. Coltrain's desk. It was lunchtime and he'd already left the building. He made sure he always did, probably to insure that he didn't risk having Lou invite herself to eat with him.

Brenda scowled as her boss started absently toward the back door. "Shouldn't you take off your coat first?" she asked hesitantly.

Lou did, without a word, replaced it in her office, whipped her leather fanny pack around her waist and left the building.

It would have been nice if she'd had someone to talk to, she thought wistfully, about this latest crisis. She sat alone in the local café, drinking black coffee and picking at a small salad. She didn't mingle well with people. When she wasn't working, she was quiet and shy, and she kept to herself. It was difficult for strangers to approach her, but she didn't realize that. She stared into her coffee and remembered every word Coltrain had said to Drew Morris about her. He hated her. He couldn't possibly have made it clearer. She was repugnant, he'd said.

Well, perhaps she was. Her father had told her so, often enough, when he was alive. He and her mother were from Jacobsville but hadn't lived in the area for years. He had never spoken of his past. Not that he spoke to Lou often, anyway, except to berate her grades and tell her that she'd never measure up.

"Excuse me?"

She looked up. The waitress was staring at her. "Yes?" she asked coolly.

"I don't mean to pry, but are you all right?"

The question surprised Lou, and touched her. She managed a faint smile through her misery. "Yes. It's been a…long morning. I'm not really hungry."

"Okay." The waitress smiled again, reassuringly, and went away.

Just as Lou was finishing her coffee, Coltrain came in the front door. He was wearing the elegant gray suit that looked so good on him, and carrying a silver belly Stetson by the brim. He looked furiously angry as his pale eyes scanned the room and finally spotted Lou, sitting all alone.

He never hesitated, she thought, watching him walk purposefully toward her. There must be an emergency…

He slammed the opened envelope down on the table in front of her. "What the hell do you mean by that?" he demanded in a dangerously quiet tone.

She raised her dark, cold eyes to his. "I'm leaving," she explained and averted her gaze.

"I know that! I want to know why!"

She looked around. The café was almost empty, but the waitress and a local cowboy at the counter were glancing at them curiously.

Her chin came up. "I'd rather not discuss my private business in public, if you don't mind," she said stiffly.

His jaw clenched, and his eyes grew glittery. He stood back to allow her to get up. He waited while she paid for her salad and coffee and then followed her out to where her small gray Ford was parked.

Her heart raced when he caught her by the arm before she could get her key out of her jeans pocket. He jerked her around, not roughly, and walked her over to Jacobsville's small town square, to a secluded bench in a grove of live oak and willow trees. Because it was barely December, there were no leaves on the trees and it was cool, despite her nervous perspiration. She tried to throw off his hand, to no avail.

He only loosened his grip on her when she sat down on a park bench. He remained standing, propping his boot on the bench beside her, leaning one long arm over his knee to study her. "This is private enough," he said shortly. "Why are you leaving?"

"I signed a contract to work with you for one year. It's almost up, anyway," she said icily. "I want out. I want to go home."

"You don't have anyone left in Austin," he said, surprising her.

"I have friends," she began.

"You don't have those, either. You don't have friends at all, unless you count Drew Morris," he said flatly.

Her fingers clenched around her car keys. She looked at them, biting into the flesh even though not a speck of emotion showed on her placid features.

His eyes followed hers to her lap and something moved in his face. There was an expression there that puzzled her. He reached down and opened her rigid hand, frowning when he saw the red marks the keys had made in her palm.

She jerked her fingers away from him.

He seemed disconcerted for a few seconds. He stared at her without speaking and she felt her heart beating wildly against her ribs. She hated being helpless.

He moved back, watching her relax. He took another step and saw her release the breath she'd been holding. Every trace of anger left him.

"It takes time for a partnership to work," he said abruptly. "You've only given this one a year."

"That's right," she said tonelessly. "*I've* given it a year."

The emphasis she placed on the first word caught his attention. His blue eyes narrowed. "You sound as if you don't think I've given it any time at all."

She nodded. Her eyes met his. "You didn't want me in the practice. I suspected it from the beginning, but it wasn't until I heard what you told Drew on the phone this morning that—"

His eyes flashed oddly. "You heard what I said?" he asked huskily. "You heard...all of it!" he exclaimed.

Her lips trembled just faintly. "Yes," she said.

He was remembering what he'd told Drew Morris in a characteristic outburst of bad temper. He often said things in heat that he regretted later, but this he regretted most of all. He'd never credited his cool, unflappable partner with any emotions at all. She'd backed away from him figuratively and physically since the first day she'd worked at the clinic. Her physical withdrawal had maddened him, although he'd always assumed she was frigid.

But in the past five minutes, he'd learned disturbing things about her without a word being spoken. He'd hurt her. He didn't realize she'd cared that much about his opinion. Hell, he'd been furious because he'd just had to diagnose leukemia in a sweet little boy of four. It had hurt him to do that, and he'd lashed out at Morris over Lou in frustration at his own helplessness. But he'd had no idea that she'd overheard his vicious remarks. She was going to leave and it was no less than he deserved. He was genuinely sorry. She wasn't going to believe that, though. He could tell by her mutinous expression, in her clenched hands, in the tight set of her mouth.

"You did Drew a favor and asked me to join you, probably over some other doctor you really wanted," she said with a forced smile. ''Well, no harm done. Perhaps you can get him back when I leave.''

''Wait a minute,'' he began shortly.

She held up a hand. ''Let's not argue about it,'' she said, sick at knowing his opinion of her, his real opinion. ''I'm tired of fighting you to practice medicine here. I haven't done the first thing right, according to you. I'm a burden. Well, I just want out. I'll go on working until you can replace me.'' She stood up.

His hand tightened on the brim of his hat. He was losing this battle. He didn't know how to pull his irons out of the fire.

''I had to tell the Dawes that their son has leukemia,'' he said, hating the need to explain his bad temper. ''I say things I don't mean sometimes.''

''We both know that you meant what you said about me,'' she said flatly. Her eyes met his levelly. ''You've hated me from almost the first day we worked together. Most of the time, you can't even be bothered to be civil to me. I didn't know that you had a grudge against me from the outset...''

She hadn't thought about that until she said it, but there was a subtle change in his expression, a faint distaste that her mind locked on.

''So you heard that, too.'' His jaw clenched on words he didn't want to say. But maybe it was as well to say them. He'd lived a lie for the past year.

''Yes.'' She gripped the wrought-iron frame of the park bench hard. ''What happened? Did my father cause someone to die?''

His jaw tautened. He didn't like saying this. ''The girl I wanted to marry got pregnant by him. He performed a secret abortion and she was going to marry me anyway.'' He laughed icily. ''A fling, he called it. But the medical authority had other ideas, and they invited him to resign.''

Lou's fingers went white on the cold wrought iron. Had her mother known? What had happened to the girl afterward?

''Only a handful of people knew,'' Coltrain said, as if he'd read her thoughts. "I doubt that your mother did. She seemed very nice—hardly a fit match for a man like that."

"And the girl?" she asked levelly.

"She left town. Eventually she married." He rammed his hands into his pockets and glared at her. "If you want the whole truth, Drew felt sorry for you when your parents died so tragically. He knew I was looking for a partner, and he recommended you so highly that I asked you. I didn't connect the name at first," he added on a mocking note. "Ironic, isn't it, that I'd choose as a partner the daughter of a man I hated until the day he died."

"Why didn't you tell me?" she asked irritably. "I would have resigned!"

"You were in no fit state to be told anything," he replied with reluctant memories of her tragic face when she'd arrived. His hands clenched in his pockets. "Besides, you'd signed a one-year contract. The only way out was if you resigned."

It all made sense immediately. She was too intelligent not to understand why he'd been so antagonistic. "I see," she breathed. "But I didn't resign."

"You were made of stronger stuff than I imagined," he agreed. "You wouldn't back down an inch. No matter how rough it got, you threw my own bad temper back at me." He rubbed his fingers absently over the car keys in his pocket while he studied her. "It's been a long time since anyone around here stood up to me like that," he added reluctantly.

She knew that without being told. He was a holy terror. Even grown men around Jacobsville gave him a wide berth when he lost his legendary temper. But Lou never had. She stood right up to him. She wasn't fiery by nature, but her father had been viciously cruel to her. She'd learned early not to show fear or back down, because it only made him worse. The same rule seemed to apply to Coltrain. A weaker personality wouldn't have lasted in his office one week, much less one year, male or female.

She knew now that Drew Morris had been doing what he thought was a good deed. Perhaps he'd thought it wouldn't matter to Coltrain after such a long time to have a Blakely working for him. But he'd obviously underestimated the man. Lou would have realized at once, on the shortest acquaintance, that Coltrain didn't forgive people.

He stared at her unblinkingly. "A year. A whole year, being reminded every day I took a breath what your father cost me. There were times when I'd have done anything to make you leave. Just the sight of you was painful." He smiled wearily. "I think I hated you, at first."

That was the last straw. She'd loved him, against her will and all her judgment, and he was telling her that all he saw when he looked at her was an ice woman whose father had betrayed him with the woman he loved. He hated her.

It was too much all at once. Lou had always had impeccable control over her emotions. It had been dangerous to let her father know that he was hurting her, because he enjoyed hurting her. And now here was the one man she'd ever loved telling her that he hated her because of her father.

What a surprise it would be for him to learn that her father, at the last, had been little more than a high-class drug addict, stealing narcotics from the hospital where he worked in Austin to support his growing habit. He'd been as high as a kite on narcotics, in fact, when the plane he was piloting went down, killing himself and his wife.

Tears swelled her eyelids. Not a sound passed her lips as they overflowed in two hot streaks down her pale cheeks.

He caught his breath. He'd seen her tired, impassive, worn-out, fighting mad, and even frustrated. But he'd never seen her cry. His lean hand shot out and touched the track of tears down one cheek, as if he had to touch them to make sure they were real.

She jerked back from him, laughing tearfully. "So that was why you were so horrible to me." She choked out the words. "Drew never said a word...no wonder you suffered me! And I was silly enough to dream...!" The laughter was harsher now as she dashed away the tears, staring at him with eyes full of pain and loss.

"What a fool I've been," she whispered poignantly. "What a silly fool!"

She turned and walked away from him, gripping the car keys in her hand. The sight of her back was as eloquently telling as the words that haunted him. She'd dreamed...what?

For the next few days, Lou was polite and remote and as courteous as any stranger toward her partner. But something had altered in their relationship. He was aware of a subtle difference in her attitude toward him, in a distancing of herself that was new. Her eyes had always followed him, and he'd been aware of it at some subconscious level. Perhaps he'd been aware of more than covert glances, too. But Lou no longer watched him or went out of her way to seek him out. If she had questions, she wrote them down and left them for him on his desk. If there were messages to be passed on, she left them with Brenda.

The one time she did seek him out was Thursday afternoon as they closed up.

"Have you worked out an advertisement for someone to replace me?" she asked him politely.

He watched her calm dark eyes curiously. "Are you in such a hurry to leave?" he asked.

"Yes," she said bluntly. "I'd like to leave after the Christmas holidays." She turned and would have gone out the door, but his hand caught the sleeve of her white jacket. She slung it off and backed away. "At the first of the year."

He glared at her, hating the instinctive withdrawal that came whenever he touched her. "You're a good doctor," he said flatly. "You've earned your place here."

High praise for a man with his grudges. She looked over her shoulder at him, her eyes wounded. "But you hate me, don't you? I heard what you said to Drew, that every time you looked at me you remembered what my father had done and hated me all over again."

He let go of her sleeve, frowning. He couldn't find an answer.

"Well, don't sweat it, Doctor," she told him. "I'll be gone in a month and you can find someone you like to work with you."

She laughed curtly and walked out of the office.

She dressed sedately that evening for the Rotary Club dinner, in a neat off-white suit with a pink blouse. But she left her blond hair long around her shoulders for once, and used a light dusting of makeup. She didn't spend much time looking in the mirror. Her appearance had long ago ceased to matter to her.

Drew was surprised by it, though, and curious. She looked strangely vulnerable. But when he tried to hold her hand, she drew away from him. He'd wanted to ask her for a long time if there were things in her past that she might like to share with someone. But Louise was an unknown quantity, and she could easily shy away. He couldn't risk losing her altogether.

Drew held her arm as they entered the hall, and Lou was disconcerted to find Dr. Coltrain there. He almost never attended social functions unless Jane Parker was in attendance. But a quick glance around the room ascertained that Jane wasn't around. She wondered if the doctor had brought a date. It didn't take long to have that question answered, as a pretty young brunette came up beside him and clung to his arm as if it was the ticket to heaven.

Coltrain wasn't looking at her, though. His pale, narrow eyes had lanced over Lou and he was watching her closely. He hadn't seen her hair down in the year they'd worked together. She seemed more approachable tonight than he'd ever noticed, but she was Drew's date. Probably Drew's woman, too, he thought bitterly, despite her protests and reserve.

But trying to picture Lou in Drew's bed was more difficult than he'd thought. It wasn't at all in character. She was rigid in her views, just as she was in her mode of dress and her hairstyle. Just because she'd loosened that glorious hair tonight didn't mean that she'd suddenly become uninhibited. Nonetheless, the change disturbed him, because it was unexpected.

"Copper's got a new girl, I see," Drew said with a grin.

"That's Nickie Bolton," he added. "She works as a nurse's aide at the hospital."

"I didn't recognize her out of uniform," Lou murmured.

"I did," he said. "She's lovely, isn't she?"

She nodded amiably. "Very young, too," she added with an indulgent smile.

He took her hand gently and smiled down at her. "You aren't exactly over the hill yourself," he teased.

She smiled up at him with warm eyes. "You're a nice man, Drew."

Across the room, a redheaded man's grip tightened ominously on a glass of punch. For over a year, Louise had avoided even his lightest touch. A few days ago, she'd thrown off his hand violently. But there she stood not only allowing Drew to hold her hand, but actually smiling at him. She'd never smiled at Coltrain that way; she'd never smiled at him any way at all.

His companion tapped him on the shoulder.

"You're with me, remember?" she asked with a pert smile. "Stop staring daggers at your partner. You're off duty. You don't have to fight all the time, do you?"

He frowned slightly. "What do you mean?"

"Everyone knows you hate her," Nickie said pleasantly. "It's common gossip at the hospital. You rake her over the coals and she walks around the corridors, red in the face and talking to herself. Well, most of the time, anyway. Once, Dr. Simpson found her crying in the nursery. But she doesn't usually cry, no matter how bad she hurts. She's pretty tough, in her way. I guess she's had to be, huh? Even if there are more women in medical school these days, you don't see that many women doctors yet. I'll bet she had to fight a lot of prejudice when she was in medical school."

That came as a shock. He'd never seen Lou cry until today, and he couldn't imagine her being upset at any temperamental display of his. Or was it, he pondered uneasily, just that she'd learned how not to show her wounds to him?

Chapter 3

At dinner, Lou sat with Drew, as far away from Coltrain and his date as she could get. She listened attentively to the speakers and whispered to Drew in the spaces between speakers. But it was torture to watch Nickie's small hand smooth over Coltrain's, to see her flirt with him. Lou didn't know how to flirt. There were a lot of things she didn't know. But she'd learned to keep a poker face, and she did it very well this evening. The one time Coltrain glanced down the table toward her, he saw nothing on her face or in her eyes that could tell him anything. She was unreadable.

After the meeting, she let Drew hold her hand as they walked out of the restaurant. Behind them, Coltrain was glaring at her with subdued fury.

When they made it to the parking lot, she found that the other couple had caught up with them.

"Nice bit of surgery this morning, Copper," Drew remarked. "You do memorable stitches. I doubt if Mrs. Blake will even have a scar to show around."

He managed a smile and held Nickie's hand all the tighter. "She was adamant about that," he remarked. "It seems that her husband likes perfection."

"He'll have a good time searching for it in this imperfect

world," Drew replied. "I'll see you in the morning. And I'd like your opinion on my little strep-throat patient. His mother wants the whole works taken out, tonsils and adenoids, but he doesn't have strep often and I don't like unnecessary surgery. Perhaps she'd listen to you."

"Don't count on it," Copper said dryly. "I'll have a look if you like, though."

"Thanks."

"My pleasure." He glanced toward Lou, who hadn't said a word. "You were ten minutes late this morning," he added coldly.

"Oh, I overslept," she replied pleasantly. "It wears me out to follow the EMTs around looking for work."

She gave him a cool smile and got into the car before he realized that she'd made a joke, and at his expense.

"Be on time in the morning," he admonished before he walked away with Nickie on his arm.

"On time," Lou muttered beside Drew in the comfortable Ford he drove. Her hands crushed her purse. "I'll give him on time! I'll be sitting in *his* parking spot at eight-thirty on the dot!"

"He does it on purpose," he told her as he started the car. "I think he likes to make you spark at him."

"He's overjoyed that I'm leaving," she muttered. "And so am I!"

He gave her a quick glance and hid his smile. "If you say so."

She twisted her small purse in her lap, fuming, all the way back to her small house.

"I haven't been good company, Drew," she said as he walked her to the door. "I'm sorry."

He patted her shoulder absently. "Nothing wrong with the company," he said, correcting her. He smiled down at her. "But you really do rub Copper the wrong way, don't you?" he added thoughtfully. "I've noticed that antagonism from a distance, but tonight is the first time I've seen it at close range. Is he always like that?"

She nodded. "Always, from the beginning. Well, not quite," she confessed, remembering. "From last Christmas."

"What happened last Christmas?"

She studied him warily.

"I won't tell him," he promised. "What happened?"

"He tried to kiss me under the mistletoe and I, well, I sort of ducked and pulled away." She flushed. "He rattled me. He does, mostly. I get shaky when he comes too close. He's so forceful, and so physical. Even when he wants to talk to me, he's forever trying to grab me by the wrist or a sleeve. It's as if he knows how much it disturbs me, so he does it on purpose, just to make me uncomfortable."

He reached down and caught her wrist very gently, watching her face distort and feeling the instinctive, helpless jerk of her hand.

He let go at once. "Tell me about it, Lou."

With a wan smile, she rubbed her wrist. "No. It's history."

"It isn't, you know. Not if it makes you shaky to have people touch you..."

"Not everyone, just him," she muttered absently.

His eyebrows lifted, but she didn't seem to be aware of what she'd just confessed.

She sighed heavily. "I'm so tired," she said, rubbing the back of her neck. "I don't usually get so tired from even the longest days."

He touched her forehead professionally and frowned. "You're a bit warm. How do you feel?"

"Achy. Listless." She grimaced. "It's probably that virus that's going around. I usually get at least one every winter."

"Go to bed and if you aren't better tomorrow, don't go in," he advised. "Want me to prescribe something?"

She shook her head. "I'll be okay. Nothing does any good for a virus, you know that."

He chuckled. "Not even a sugarcoated pill?"

"I can do without a placebo. I'll get some rest. Thanks for tonight. I enjoyed it."

"So did I. I haven't done much socializing since Eve died. It's been five long years and I still miss her. I don't think I'll ever get over her enough to start a new relationship with anyone. I only wish we'd had a child. It might have made it easier."

She was studying him, puzzled. "It's said that many people marry within months of losing a mate," she began.

"I don't fit that pattern," he said quietly. "I only loved once. I'd rather have my memories of those twelve years with Eve than a hundred years with someone else. I suppose that sounds old-fashioned."

She shook her head. "It sounds beautiful," she said softly. "Lucky Eve, to have been loved so much."

He actually flushed. "It was mutual."

"I'm sure it was, Drew. I'm glad to have a friend like you."

"That works both ways." He smiled ruefully. "I'd like to take you out occasionally, so that people will stop thinking of me as a mental case. The gossip is beginning to get bad."

"I'd love to go out with you," she replied. She smiled. "I'm not very worldly, you know. It was books and exams and medicine for eight long years, and then internship. I was an honor student. I never had much time for men." Her eyes darkened. "I never wanted to have much time for them. My parents' marriage soured me. I never knew it could be happy or that people could love each other enough to be faithful—" She stopped, embarrassed.

"I knew about your father," he said. "Most of the hospital staff did. He liked young girls."

"Dr. Coltrain told me," she said miserably.

"He what?"

She drew in a long breath. "I overheard what he said to you on the telephone the other day. I'm leaving. My year is up after New Year's, anyway," she reminded him. "He told me what my father had done. No wonder he didn't want me here. You shouldn't have done it, Drew. You shouldn't have forced him to take me on.''

"I know. But it's too late, isn't it? I thought I was helping, if that's any excuse." He searched her face. "Maybe I hoped it would help Copper, too. He was infatuated with Jane Parker. She's a lovely, sweet woman, and she has a temper, but she was never a match for Copper. He's the sort who'd cow a woman who couldn't stand up to him."

"Just like my father," she said shortly.

"I've never mentioned it, but one of your wrists looks as if it's suffered a break."

She flushed scarlet and drew back. "I have to go in now. Thanks again, Drew."

"If you can't talk to me, you need to talk to someone," he said. "Did you really think you could go through life without having the past affect the future?"

She smiled sweetly. "Drive carefully going home."

He shrugged. "Okay. I'll drop it."

"Good night."

"Good night."

She watched him drive away, absently rubbing the wrist he'd mentioned. She wouldn't think about it, she told herself. She'd go to bed and put it out of her mind.

Only it didn't work that way. She woke up in the middle of the night in tears, frightened until she remembered where she was. She was safe. It was over. But she felt sick and her throat was dry. She got up and found a pitcher, filling it with ice and water. She took a glass along with her and went back to bed. Except for frequent trips to the bathroom, she finally slept soundly.

There was a loud, furious knock at the front door. It kept on and on, followed by an equally loud voice. What a blessing that she didn't have close neighbors, she thought drowsily, or the police would be screaming up the driveway.

She tried to get up, but surprisingly, her feet wouldn't support her. She was dizzy and weak and sick at her stomach. Her head throbbed. She lay back down with a soft groan.

A minute later, the front door opened and a furious redheaded man in a lab coat came in the bedroom door.

"So this is where you are," he muttered, taking in her condition with a glance. "You couldn't have called?"

She barely focused on him. "I was up most of the night..."

"With Drew?"

She couldn't even manage a glare. "Being sick," she corrected. "Have you got anything on you to calm my stomach? I can't keep down anything to stop the nausea."

"I'll get something."

He went back out, grateful that she kept a key under the welcome mat. He didn't relish having to break down doors, although he had in the past to get to a patient.

He got his medical bag and went back into the bedroom. She was pale and she had a fever. He turned off the electronic thermometer and checked her lungs. Clear, thank God.

Her pulse was a little fast, but she seemed healthy enough. "A virus," he pronounced.

"No!" she exclaimed with weak sarcasm.

"You'll live."

"Give me the medicine, please," she asked, holding out a hand.

"Can you manage?"

"If you'll get me to the bathroom, sure."

He helped her up, noticing the frailty of her body. She didn't seem that thin in her clothing, but she was wearing silky pajamas that didn't conceal the slender lines of her body. He supported her to the door, and watched the door close behind her.

Minutes later, she opened the door again and let him help her back into bed.

He watched her for a minute and then, with resolution, he picked up the telephone. He punched in a number. "This is Dr.

Coltrain. Send an ambulance out to Dr. Blakely's home, 23 Brazos Lane. That's right. Yes. Thank you.''

She glared at him. ''I will not...!''

''Hell, yes, you will,'' he said shortly. ''I'm not leaving you out here alone to dehydrate. At the rate you're losing fluids, you'll die in three days.''

''What do you care if I die?'' she asked furiously.

He reached down to take her pulse again. This time, he caught the left wrist firmly, but she jerked it back. His blue eyes narrowed as he watched her color. Drew had been holding her right hand. At the table, it was her right hand he'd touched. But most of the time, Copper automatically reached for the left one...

He glanced down to where it lay on the coverlet and he noticed what Drew had; there was a definite break there, one which had been set but was visible.

She clenched her fist. ''I don't want to go to the hospital.''

''But you'll go, if I have to carry you.''

She glared at him. It did no good at all. He went into the kitchen to turn off all the appliances except the refrigerator. On his way back, he paused to look around the living room. There were some very disturbing paintings on her walls, side by side with beautiful pastel drawings of flowers. He wondered who'd done them.

The ambulance arrived shortly. He watched the paramedics load her up and he laid the small bag she'd asked him to pack on the foot of the gurney.

''Thank you so much,'' she said with her last lucid breath. The medicine was beginning to take effect, and it had a narcotic in it to make her sleep.

''My pleasure, Dr. Blakely,'' he said. He smiled, but it didn't reach his eyes. They were watchful and thoughtful. ''Do you paint?'' he asked suddenly.

Her dark eyes blinked. ''How did you know?'' she murmured as she drifted off.

She awoke hours later in a private room, with a nurse checking her vital signs. ''You're awake!'' the nurse said with a smile.

"Feeling any better?"

"A little." She touched her stomach. "I think I've lost weight."

"No wonder, with so much nausea. You'll be all right now. We'll take very good care of you. How about some soup and Jell-O and tea?"

"Coffee?" she asked hopefully.

The nurse chuckled. "Weak coffee, perhaps. We'll see." She charted her observations and went to see about supper.

It was modest fare, but delicious to a stomach that had hardly been able to hold anything. Imagine being sent to the hospital with a twenty-four-hour virus, Lou thought irritably, and wanted to find Dr. Coltrain and hit him.

Drew poked his head in the door while he was doing rounds. "I told you you felt feverish, didn't I?" he teased, smiling. "Better?"

She nodded. "But I would have been just fine at home."

"Not to hear your partner tell it. I expected to find your ribs sticking through your skin," he told her, chuckling. "I'll check on you later. Stay put."

She groaned and lay back. Patients were stacking up and she knew that Brenda had probably had to deal with angry ones all day, since Dr. Coltrain would have been operating in the morning. Everyone would be sitting in the waiting room until long after dark, muttering angrily.

It was after nine before he made rounds. He looked worn, and she felt guilty even if it couldn't be helped.

"I'm sorry," she said irritably when he came to the bedside.

He cocked an eyebrow. "For what?" He reached down and took her wrist—the right one—noticing that she didn't react while he felt her pulse.

"Leaving you to cope with my patients as well as your own," she said. The feel of his long fingers was disturbing. She began to fidget.

He leaned closer, to look into her eyes, and his hand remained curled around her wrist. He felt her pulse jump as his face neared hers and suddenly a new thought leapt into his shocked mind and refused to be banished.

She averted her gaze. "I'm all right," she said. She sounded breathless. Her pulse had gone wild under his searching fingers.

He stood up, letting go of her wrist. But he noticed the quick rise and fall of her chest with new interest. What an odd reaction for a woman who felt such antagonism toward him.

He picked up her chart, still frowning, and read what was written there. "You've improved. If you're doing this well in the morning, you can go home. Not to work," he added firmly. "Drew's going to come in and help me deal with the backlog in the morning while he has some free time."

"That's very kind of him."

"He's a kind man."

"Yes. *He* is."

He chuckled softly. "You don't like me, do you?" he asked through pursed lips. "I've never given you any reason to. I've been alternately hostile and sarcastic since the day you came here."

"Your normal self, Doctor," she replied.

His lips tugged up. "Not really. You don't know me."

"Lucky me."

His blue eyes narrowed thoughtfully. She'd reacted to him from the first as if he'd been contagious. Every approach he'd made had been met with instant withdrawal. He wondered why he'd never questioned her reactions. It wasn't revulsion. Oh, no. It was something much more disturbing on her part. She was vulnerable, and he'd only just realized it, when it was too late. She would leave before he had the opportunity to explore his own feelings.

He stuck his hands into his pockets and his eyes searched her pale, worn face. She wasn't wearing a trace of makeup. Her eyes held lingering traces of fever and her hair was dull, lackluster, disheveled by sleep. But even in that condition, she had a strange beauty.

"I know how I look, thanks," she muttered as she saw how he was looking at her. "You don't need to rub it in."

"Was I?" He studied her hostile eyes.

She dropped her gaze to her slender hands on the sheets. "You always do." Her eyes closed. "I don't need you to point out my lack of good looks, Doctor. My father never missed an opportunity to tell me what I was missing."

Her father. His expression hardened as the memories poured out. But even as they nagged at his mind, he began to remember bits and pieces of gossip he'd heard about the way Dr. Fielding Blakely treated his poor wife. He'd dismissed it at the time, but now he realized that Mrs. Blakely had to be aware of her husband's affairs. Had she not minded? Or was she afraid to mind...

He had more questions about Lou's family life than he had answers, and he was curious. Her reticence with him, her broken wrist, her lack of self-esteem—they began to add up.

His eyes narrowed. "Did your mother know that your father was unfaithful to her?" he asked.

She stared at him as if she didn't believe what she'd heard. "What?"

"You heard me. Did she know?"

She drew the sheet closer to her collarbone. "Yes." She bit off the word.

"Why didn't she leave him?"

She laughed bitterly. "You can't imagine."

"Maybe I can." He moved closer to the bed. "Maybe I can imagine a lot of things that never occurred to me before. I've looked at you for almost a year and I've never seen you until now."

She fidgeted under the cover. "Don't strain your imagination, Doctor," she said icily. "I haven't asked for your attention. I don't want it."

"Mine, or any other man's, right?" he asked gently.

She felt like an insect on a pin. "Will you stop?" she groaned. "I'm sick. I don't want to be interrogated."

"Is that what I'm doing? I thought I was showing a belated interest in my partner," he said lazily.

"I won't be your partner after Christmas."

"Why?"

"I've resigned. Have you forgotten? I even wrote it down and gave it to you."

"Oh. That. I tore it up."

Her eyes popped. "You what?"

"Tore it up," he said with a shrug. "I can't do without you. You have too many patients who won't come back if they have to see me."

"You had a fine practice..."

"Too fine. I never slept or took vacations. You've eased the load. You've made yourself indispensable. You have to stay."

"I do not." She shot her reply back instantly. "I hate you!"

He studied her, nodding slowly. "That's healthy. Much healthier than withdrawing like a frightened clam into a shell every time I come too close."

She all but gasped at such a blunt statement. "I do not...!"

"You do." He looked pointedly at her left wrist. "You've kept secrets. I'm going to worry you to death until you tell me every last one of them, beginning with why you can't bear to have anyone hold you by the wrist."

She couldn't get her breath. She felt her cheeks becoming hot as he stared down at her intently. "I'm not telling you any secrets," she assured him.

"Why not?" he replied. "I don't ever tell what I know."

She knew that. If a patient told him anything in confidence, he wouldn't share it.

She rubbed the wrist absently, wincing as she remembered how it had felt when it was broken, and how.

Coltrain, watching her, wondered how he could ever have thought her cold. She had a temper that was easily the equal of his own, and she never backed away from a fight. She'd avoided his touch, but he realized now that it was the past that made her afraid, not the present.

"You're mysterious, Lou," he said quietly. "You hold things in, keep things back. I've worked with you for a year, but I know nothing about you."

"That was your choice," she reminded him coolly. "You've treated me like a leper in your life."

He started to speak, took a breath and finally, nodded. "Yes. Through no fault of your own, I might add. I've held grudges."

She glanced at his hard, lean face. "You were entitled," she admitted. "I didn't know about my father's past. I probably should have realized there was a reason he never went back to Jacobsville, even to visit, while his brother was still alive here. Afterward, there wasn't even a cousin to write to. We all lost touch. My mother never seemed to mind that we didn't come back." She looked up at him. "She probably knew..." She flushed and dropped her eyes.

"But she stayed with him," he began.

"She had to!" The words burst out. "If she'd tried to leave, he'd have..." She swallowed and made a futile gesture with her hand.

"He'd have what? Killed her?"

She wouldn't look at him. She couldn't. The memories came flooding back, of his violence when he used narcotics, of the threats, her mother's fear, her own. The weeping, the cries of pain...

She sucked in a quick breath, and all the suffering was in the eyes she lifted to his when he took her hand.

His fingers curled hard around hers and held them, as if he could see the memories and was offering comfort.

"You'll tell me, one day," he said abruptly, his eyes steady on her own. "You'll tell me every bit of it."

She couldn't understand his interest. She searched his eyes curiously and suddenly felt a wave of feeling encompass her like a killing tide, knocking her breathless. Heat surged through her slender body, impaling her, and in his hard face she saw everything she knew of love, would ever know of it.

But he didn't want her that way. He never would. She was useful to the practice, but on a personal level, he was still clutching hard at the past; at the girl her father had taken from him, at Jane Parker. He was sorry for her, as he would be for anyone in pain, but it wasn't a personal concern.

She drew her hand away from his slowly and with a faint smile. "Thanks," she said huskily. "I…I think too hard sometimes. The past is long dead."

"I used to think so," he said, watching her. "Now, I'm not so sure."

She didn't understand what he was saying. It was just as well. The nurse came in to do her round and any personal conversation was banished at once.

Chapter 4

The next day, Lou was allowed to go home. Drew had eaten breakfast with her and made sure that she was well enough to leave before he agreed with Copper that she was fit. But when he offered to drive her home, Coltrain intervened. His partner, he said, was his responsibility. Drew didn't argue. In fact, when they weren't looking, he grinned.

Copper carried her bag into the house and helped her get settled on the couch. It was lunchtime and he hesitated, as if he felt guilty about not offering to take her out for a meal.

"I'm going to have some soup later," she murmured without looking at him. "I'm not hungry just yet. I expect you are."

"I could eat." He hesitated again, watching her with vague irritation. "Will you be all right?"

"It was only a virus," she said, making light of it. "I'm fine. Thank you for your concern."

"You might as well enjoy it, for novelty value if nothing else," he said without smiling. "It's been a long time since I've given a damn about a woman's comfort."

"I'm just a colleague," she replied, determined to show him that she realized there was nothing personal in their relationship. "It isn't the same thing."

"No, it isn't," he agreed. "I've been very careful to keep our association professional. I've never even asked you to my home, have I?"

He was making her uneasy with that unblinking stare. "So what? I've never asked you to mine," she replied. "I wouldn't presume to put you in such an embarrassing situation."

"Embarrassing? Why?"

"Well, because you'd have to find some logical excuse to refuse," she said.

He searched her quiet face and his eyes narrowed thoughtfully. "I don't know that I'd refuse. If you asked me."

Her heart leapt and she quickly averted her eyes. She wanted him to go, now, before she gave herself away. "Forgive me, but I'm very tired," she said.

She'd fended him off nicely, without giving offense. He wondered how many times over the years she'd done exactly that to other men.

He moved closer to her, noticing the way she tensed, the telltale quickening of her breath, the parting of her soft lips. She was affected by his nearness and trying valiantly to hide it. It touched him deeply that she was so vulnerable to him. He could have cursed himself for the way he'd treated her, for the antagonism that made her wary of any approach now.

He stopped when there was barely a foot of space between them, with his hands in his pockets so that he wouldn't make her any more nervous.

He looked down at her flushed oval face with curious pleasure. "Don't try to come in tomorrow if you don't feel like it. I'll cope."

"All right," she said in a hushed tone.

"Lou."

He hadn't called her by her first name before. It surprised her into lifting her eyes to his face.

"You aren't responsible for anything your father did," he said.

"I'm sorry that I've made things hard for you. I hope you'll reconsider leaving."

She shifted uncomfortably. "Thank you. But I think I'd better go," she said softly. "You'll be happier with someone else."

"Do you think so? I don't agree." His hand lowered slowly to her face, touching her soft cheek, tracing it down to the corner of her mouth. It was the first intimate contact she'd ever had with him, and she actually trembled.

Her reaction had an explosive echo in his own body. His breath jerked into his throat and his teeth clenched as he looked at her mouth and thought he might die if he couldn't have it. But it was too soon. He couldn't...!

He drew back his hand as if she'd burned it. "I have to go," he said tersely, turning on his heel. Her headlong response had prompted a reaction in him that he could barely contain at all. He had to distance himself before he reached for her and ruined everything.

Lou didn't realize why he was in such a hurry to leave. She assumed that he immediately regretted that unexpected caress and wanted to make sure that she didn't read anything into it.

"Thank you for bringing me home," she said formally.

He paused at the door and looked back at her, his eyes fiercely intent on her slender body in jeans and sweatshirt, on her loosened blond hair and exquisite complexion and dark eyes. "Thank your lucky stars that I'm leaving in time." He bit off the words.

He closed the door on her puzzled expression. He was acting very much out of character lately. She didn't know why, unless he was sorry he'd tried to talk her out of leaving the practice. Oh, well, she told herself, it was no longer her concern. She had to get used to the idea of being out of his life. He had nothing to offer her, and he had good reason to hate her, considering the part her father had played in his unhappy past.

She went into the kitchen and opened a can of tomato soup. She'd need to replenish her body before she could get back to work.

The can slipped in her left hand and she grimaced. Her dreams of becoming a surgeon had been lost overnight in one tragic act. A pity, her instructor had said, because she had a touch that few surgeons ever achieved, almost an instinctive knowledge of the best and most efficient way to sever tissue with minimum loss of blood. She would have been famous. But alas, the tendon had been severed with the compound fracture. And the best efforts of the best orthopedic surgeon hadn't been able to repair the damage. Her father hadn't even been sorry....

She shook her head to clear away the memories and went back to her soup. Some things were better forgotten.

She was back at work the day after her return home, a bit shaky, but game. She went through her patients efficiently, smiling at the grievance of one small boy whose stitches she'd just removed.

"Dr. Coltrain doesn't like little kids, does he?" he muttered. "I showed him my bad place and he said he'd seen worse!"

"He has," she told the small boy. She smiled at him. "But you've been very brave, Patrick my boy, and I'm giving you the award of honor." She handed him a stick of sugarless chewing gum and watched him grin. "Off with you, now, and mind you don't fall down banks into any more creeks!"

"Yes, ma'am!"

She handed his mother the charge sheet and was showing them out the door of the treatment cubicle just as Coltrain started to come into it. The boy glowered at him, smiled at Lou and went back to his waiting mother.

"Cheeky brat," he murmured, watching him turn the corner.

"He doesn't like you," she told him smugly. "You didn't sympathize with his bad place."

"Bad place." He harrumphed. "Two stitches. My God, what a fuss he made."

"It hurt," she informed him.

"He wouldn't let me take the damn stitches out, either. He said that I didn't know how to do it, but you did."

She grinned to herself at that retort while she dealt with the mess she'd made while working with Patrick.

"You don't like children, do you?" she asked.

He shrugged. "I don't know much about them, except what I see in the practice," he replied. "I deal mostly with adults since you came."

He leaned against the doorjamb and studied her with his hands in the pockets of his lab coat, a stethoscope draped around his neck. His eyes narrowed as he watched her work.

She became aware of the scrutiny and turned, her eyes meeting his and being captured there. She felt her heart race at the way he looked at her. Her hands stilled on her preparations for the next patient as she stood helplessly in thrall.

His lips compressed. He looked at her mouth and traced the full lower lip, the soft bow of the upper, with her teeth just visible where her lips parted. The look was intimate. He was wondering how it would feel to kiss her, and she knew it.

Muffled footsteps caught them unawares, and Brenda jerked open the sliding door of the cubicle. "Lou, I've got the wrong... Oh!" She bumped into Coltrain, whom she hadn't seen standing there.

"Sorry," he muttered. "I wanted to ask Lou if she'd seen the file on Henry Brady. It isn't where I left it."

Brenda grimaced as she handed it to him. "I picked it up mistakenly. I'm sorry."

"No harm done." He glanced back at Lou and went out without another word.

"Not another argument," Brenda groaned. "Honestly, partners should get along better than this."

Lou didn't bother to correct that assumption. It was much less embarrassing than what had really happened. Coltrain had never looked at her in that particular way before. She was glad that she'd resigned; she wasn't sure that she could survive any physical teasing from him. If he started making passes, she'd be a lot safer in Austin than she would be here.

After all he was a confirmed bachelor and there was no shortage of women on his arm at parties. Nickie was the latest in a string of them. And according to rumor, before Nickie, apparently he'd been infatuated with Jane Parker. He might be nursing a broken heart as well, since Jane's marriage.

Lou didn't want to be anybody's second-best girl. Besides, she never wanted to marry. It had been better when Coltrain treated her like the enemy. She wished he'd go back to his former behavior and stop looking at her mouth that way. She still tingled remembering the heat in his blue eyes. A man like that would be just plain hell to be loved by. He would be addictive. She had no taste for addictions and she knew already that Coltrain would break her heart if she let him. No, it was better that she leave. Then she wouldn't have the anguish of a hopeless relationship.

The annual hospital Christmas party was scheduled for Friday night, two weeks before Christmas so that the staff wouldn't be too involved with family celebrations to attend.

Lou hadn't planned to go, but Coltrain cornered her in his office as they prepared to leave that afternoon for the weekend.

"The Christmas party is tonight," he reminded her.

"I know. I'm not going."

"I'll pick you up in an hour," he said, refusing to listen when she tried to protest. "I know you still tire easily after the virus. We won't stay long."

"What about Nickie?" she asked irritably. "Won't she mind if you take your partner to a social event?"

Her antagonism surprised him. He lifted an indignant eyebrow. "Why should she?" he asked stiffly.

"You've been dating her."

"I escorted her to the Rotary Club meeting. I haven't proposed to her. And whatever you've heard to the contrary, she and I are not an item."

"You needn't bite my head off!" She shot the words at him.

His eyes dropped to her mouth and lingered there. "I know something I'd like to bite," he said deep in his throat.

She actually gasped, so stunned by the remark that she couldn't even think of a reply.

His eyes flashed back up to catch hers. He was a bulldozer, she thought, and if she didn't stand up to him, he'd run right over her.

She stiffened her back. "I'm not going to any hospital dance with you," she said shortly. "You've given me hell for the past year. Do you think you can just walk in here and wipe all that out with an invitation? Not even an invitation, at that—a command!"

"Yes, I do," he returned curtly. "We both belong to the hospital staff, and nothing will start gossip quicker than having one of us stay away from an annual event. I do not plan to have any gossip going around here at my expense. I had enough of that in the past, thanks to your philandering father!"

She gripped her coat, furious at him. "You just got through saying that you didn't blame me for what he did."

"And I don't!" he said angrily. "But you're being blind and stupid."

"Thank you. Coming from you, those are compliments!"

He was all but vibrating with anger. He stared at her, glared at her, until her unsteady movement made him realize that she'd been ill.

He became less rigid. "Ben Maddox is going to be there tonight. He's a former colleague of ours from Canada. He's just installed a massive computer system with linkups to medical networks around the world. I think it's too expensive for our purposes, but I agreed to hear him out about it. You're the high-tech expert," he added with faint sarcasm. "I'd like your opinion."

"My opinion? I'm honored. You've never asked for it before."

"I've never given a damn about it before," he retorted evenly. "But maybe there's something to this electronic revolution in medicine." He lifted his chin in a challenge. "Or so you keep telling me. Put your money where your mouth is, Doctor. Convince me.''

She glared at him. ''I'll drive my own car and see you there.''

It was a concession, of sorts. He frowned slightly. ''Why don't you want to ride with me? What are you afraid of?'' he taunted softly.

She couldn't admit what frightened her. ''It wouldn't look good to have us arrive together,'' she said. ''It would give people something to talk about.''

He was oddly disappointed, although he didn't quite know why. ''All right, then.''

She nodded, feeling that she'd won something. He nodded, too, and quietly left her. It felt like a sort of truce. God knew, they could use one.

Ben Maddox was tall, blond and drop-dead gorgeous. He was also married and the father of three. He had photographs, which he enjoyed showing to any of his old colleagues who were willing to look at them. But in addition to those photographs, he had information on a networking computer system that he used extensively in his own practice. It was an expensive piece of equipment, but it permitted the user instant access to medical experts in every field. As a diagnostic tool and a means of getting second opinions from recognized authorities, it was breathtaking. But so was the price.

Lou had worn a black silk dress with a lace overlay, a demure rounded neckline and see-through sleeves. Her hairstyle, a topknot with little tendrils of blond hair slipping down to her shoulders, looked sexy. So did her long, elegant legs in high heels, under the midknee fitted skirt. She wore no jewelry at all, except for a strand of pearls with matching earrings.

Watching her move, Coltrain was aware of old, unwanted sensations. At the party a year ago, she'd worn something a little more revealing, and he'd deliberately maneuvered her under the mistletoe out of mingled curiosity and desire. But she'd evaded him as if he had the plague, then and since. His ego had suffered a sharp blow. He hadn't felt confident enough to try again, so antagonism and anger had kept her at bay. Not that his memories of her father's betrayal hadn't added to his enmity.

She was animated tonight, talking to Ben about the computer setup as if she knew everything there was to know about the machines.

"Copper, you've got a savvy partner here," Ben remarked when he joined them. "She's computer literate!"

"She's the resident high-tech expert," Copper replied. "I like old-fashioned, hands-on medicine. She'd rather reach for a machine to make diagnoses."

"High tech is the way of the future," Ben said coaxingly.

"It's also the reason medical costs have gone through the roof," came the predictable reply. "The money we spend on these outrageously expensive machines has to be passed on to the patients. That raises our fees, the hospital's fees, the insurance companies' fees..."

"Pessimist!" Ben accused.

"I'm being realistic," Copper told him, lifting his highball glass in a mock toast. He drained it, feeling the liquor.

Ben frowned as his old colleague made his way past the dancers back to the buffet table. "That's odd," he remarked. "I don't remember ever seeing Copper take more than one drink."

Neither did Lou. She watched her colleague pour himself another drink and she frowned.

Ben produced a card from the computer company for her, and while he was explaining the setup procedure, she noticed Nickie going up to Coltrain. She was wearing an electric blue dress that could have started a riot. The woman was pretty anyway, but that dress certainly revealed most of her charms.

Nickie laughed and dragged Coltrain under the mistletoe, looking up to indicate it there, to the amusement of the others standing by. Coltrain laughed softly, whipped a lean arm around Nickie's trim waist and pulled her against his tall body. He bent his head, and the way he kissed her made Lou go hot all over. She'd never been in his arms, but she'd dreamed about it. The fever in that thin mouth, the way he twisted Nickie even closer, made her breath catch. She averted her eyes and flushed at the train of her own thoughts.

"Leave it to Coltrain to draw the prettiest girls." Ben chuckled. "The gossip mill will grind on that kiss for a month. He's not usually so uninhibited. He must be over his limit!"

She could have agreed. Her hand clenched around the piña colada she was nursing. "This computer system, is it reliable?" she asked through tight lips, forcing a smile.

"Yes, except in thunderstorms. Always unplug it, regardless of what they tell you about protective spikes. One good hit, and you could be down for days."

"I'll remember, if we get it."

"The system I have is expensive," Ben agreed, "but there are others available that would be just right for a small practice like yours and Copper's. In fact..."

His voice droned on and Lou tried valiantly to pay attention. She was aware at some level that Coltrain and Nickie were dancing and making the rounds of guests together. It was much later, and well into her second piña colada, when the lavish mistletoe began to get serious workouts.

Lou wasn't in the mood to dance. She refused Ben's offer, and several others. A couple of hours had passed and it felt safe to leave now, before her spirit was totally crushed by being consistently ignored by Coltrain. She put down her half-full glass. "I really do have to go," she told Ben. "I've been ill and I'm not quite back up to par yet." She shook his hand. "It was very nice to have met you."

"Same here. I wonder why Drew Morris didn't show up? I had hoped to see him again while I was here."

"I don't know," she said, realizing that she hadn't heard from Drew since she was released from the hospital. She had no idea where he was, and she hadn't asked.

"I'll check with Copper. He's certainly been elusive this evening. Not that I can blame him, considering his pretty companion over there." He raised his hand to catch the other man's eyes, to Lou's dismay.

Coltrain joined them with Nickie hanging on his arm. "Still here?" he asked Lou with a mocking smile. "I thought you'd be out the door and gone by now."

"I'm just about to leave. Do you know where Drew is?"

"He's in Florida at that pediatric seminar. Didn't Brenda tell you?"

"She was so busy she probably forgot," she said.

"So that's where the old devil has gone," Ben said ruefully. "I'm sorry I missed him."

"I'm sure he will be, too," Lou said. The sight of Nickie and Coltrain together was hurting her. "I'd better be off—"

"Oh, not yet," Copper said with glittery blue eyes. "Not before you've been kissed under the mistletoe, Doctor."

She flushed and laughed nervously. "I'll forgo that little ritual, I think."

"No, you won't." He sounded pleasant enough, but the expression on his face was dangerous. He moved away from Nickie and his lean arm shot around Lou's waist, maneuvering her under a low-hanging sprig of mistletoe tied with a red velvet bow. "You're not getting away this time," he said huskily.

Before she could think, react, protest, his head bent and his thin, cruel mouth fastened on hers with fierce intent. He didn't close his eyes when he kissed, she thought a bit wildly, he watched her all through it. His arm pressed her closer to the length of his muscular body, and his free hand came up so that his thumb could rub sensuously over her mouth while he kissed it, parting her lips, playing havoc with her nerves.

She gasped at the rough pleasure, and inadvertently gave him exactly what he wanted. His open mouth ground into hers, pressing her lips apart. She tasted him in an intimacy that she'd never shared with a man, in front of the amused hospital staff, while his cold eyes stared straight into hers.

She made a faint sound and he lifted his head, looking down at her swollen lips. His thumb traced over them with much greater tenderness than his mouth had given her, and he held her shocked eyes for a long moment before he reluctantly let her go.

"Merry Christmas, Dr. Blakely," he said in a mocking tone, although his voice was husky.

"And you, Dr. Coltrain," she said shakily, not quite meeting his eyes. "Good night, Ben...Nickie."

She slid away from them toward the door, on shaky legs, with a mouth that burned from his cold, fierce kiss. She barely remembered getting her coat and saying goodbye to the people she recognized on her way to the car park.

Coltrain watched her go with feelings he'd never encountered in his life. He was burning up with desire, and he'd had enough whiskey to threaten his control.

Nickie tugged on his sleeve. "You didn't kiss me like that," she protested, pouting prettily. "Why don't you take me home and we can..."

"I'll be back in a minute," he said, shaking her off.

She glared at him, coloring with embarrassment when she realized that two of the staff had overheard her. Rejection in private was one thing, but it hurt to have him make it so public. He hadn't called her since the night of the Rotary Club meeting. He'd just kissed her very nicely, but it looked different when he'd done it with his partner. She frowned. Something was going on. She followed at a distance. She was going to find out what.

Coltrain, unaware of her pursuit, headed after Lou with no real understanding of his own actions. He couldn't get the taste of her out of his head. He was pretty sure that she felt the same way. He couldn't let her leave until he knew...

Lou kept walking, but she heard footsteps behind her as she neared her car. She knew them, because she heard them every day on the slick tile of the office floor. She walked faster, but it did no good. Coltrain reached her car at the same time she reached it.

His hand came around her, grasping her car key and her fingers, pulling, turning her. She was pressed completely against the car by the warm weight of his body, and she looked up into a set, shadowy face while his mouth hovered just above her own in the starlit darkness.

"It wasn't enough," he said roughly. "Not nearly enough."

He bent and his mouth found hers expertly. His hands smoothed into hers and linked with her fingers. His hips slid sensuously over hers, seductive, refusing to entertain barriers or limits. His mouth began to open, brushing in soft strokes over her lips until they began to part, but she stiffened.

"Don't you know how to kiss?" he whispered, surprised. "Open your mouth, little one. Open it and fit it to mine... Yes, that's it."

She felt his tongue dance at the opening he'd made, felt it slowly ease into her mouth and penetrate, teasing, probing, tasting. Her fingers clutched helplessly at his and she shivered. It was so intimate, so...familiar! She moaned sharply as his hips began to caress hers. She felt him become aroused and her whole body vibrated.

His mouth grew more insistent then. He released one of her hands and his fingers played with her mouth, as they had inside, but now there was the heat and the magic they were generating, and it was no cold, clinical experiment. He groaned against her mouth and she felt his body go rigid all at once.

He bit her lower lip, hard, when her teeth clenched at the soft probing of his tongue. Suddenly she came to her senses and realized what was happening. He tasted blatantly of whiskey. He'd had too much to drink and he'd forgotten which woman he was with. Did he think she was Nickie? she wondered dizzily. Was that why he was making love to her? And that was what it was, she realized with a shock. Only a lover would take such intimacy for granted, be so blind to surroundings and restraint.

Chapter 5

Despite the pleasure she felt, the whiskey on his breath brought back unbearable memories of another man who drank; memories not of kisses, but of pain and fear. Her hands pressed against his warm shirtfront under the open dinner jacket and she pushed, only vaguely aware of thick hair under the silkiness of the fabric.

"No," she whispered into his insistent mouth.

He didn't seem to hear her. His mouth hardened and a sound rumbled out of the back of his throat. "For God's sake, stop fighting me," he whispered fiercely. "Open your mouth!"

The intimacy he was asking for frightened her. She twisted her face, breathing like a runner. "Jebediah...no!" she whispered frantically.

The fear in her voice got through the intoxication. His mouth stilled against her cheek, but his body didn't withdraw. She could feel it against every inch of her like a warm, steely brand. His breathing wasn't steady, and over her breasts, his heart was beating like a frenzied bass drum.

It suddenly dawned on him what he was doing, and with whom.

"My God!" he whispered fiercely. His hands tightened for an instant before they fell away from her. A faint shudder went through his powerful body as he slowly, so slowly, pushed himself away from her, balancing his weight on his hands against the car doorframe.

She felt his breath on her swollen mouth as he fought for control. He was still too close.

"You haven't used my given name before," he said as he levered farther away from her. "I didn't know you knew it."

"It's...on our contract," she said jerkily.

He removed his hands from the car and stood upright, dragging in air. "I've had two highballs," he said on an apologetic laugh. "I don't drink. It hit me harder than I realized."

He was apologizing, she thought dazedly. That was unexpected. He wasn't that kind of man. Or was he? She hadn't thought he was the type to get drunk and kiss women in that intimate, fierce way, either. Especially her.

She tried to catch her own breath. Her mouth hurt from the muted violence of his kisses and her legs felt weak. She leaned back against the car, only now noticing its coldness. She hadn't felt it while he was kissing her. She touched her tongue to her lips and she tasted him on them.

She eased away from the car a little, shy now that he was standing back from her.

She was so shaky that she wondered how she was going to drive home. Then she wondered, with even more concern, how *he* was going to drive home.

"You shouldn't drive," she began hesitantly.

In the faint light from the hospital, she saw him smile sardonically. "Worried about me?" he chided.

She shouldn't have slipped like that. "I'd worry about anyone who'd had too much to drink," she began.

"All right, I won't embarrass you. Nickie can drive. She doesn't drink at all."

Nickie. Nickie would take him home and she'd probably stay to nurse him, too, in his condition. God only knew what might happen, but she couldn't afford to interfere. He'd had too much to drink and he'd kissed her, and she'd let him. Now she was ashamed and embarrassed.

"I have to go," she said stiffly.

"Drive carefully," he replied.

"Sure."

She found her keys where they'd fallen to the ground when he kissed her and unlocked the car door. She closed it once she was inside and started it after a bad fumble. He stood back from it, his hands in his pockets, looking dazed and not quite sober.

She hesitated, but Nickie came out the door, calling him. When he turned and raised a hand in Nickie's direction and answered her, laughing, Lou came to her senses. She lifted a hand toward both of them and drove away as quickly as she could. When she glanced back in the rearview mirror, it was to see Nickie holding Coltrain's hand as they went toward the building again.

So much for the interlude, she thought miserably. He'd probably only just realized who he'd kissed and was in shock.

That was close to the truth. Coltrain's head was spinning. He'd never dreamed that a kiss could be so explosive or addictive. There was something about Lou Blakely that made his knees buckle. He had no idea why he'd reacted so violently to her that he couldn't even let her leave. God knew what would have happened if she hadn't pushed him away when she did.

Nickie held on to him as they went back inside. "You've got her lipstick all over you," she accused.

He paused, shaken out of his brooding. Nickie was pretty, he thought, and uncomplicated. She already knew that he wasn't going to get serious however long they dated, because he'd told her so. It made him relax. He smiled down at her. "Wipe it off."

She pulled his handkerchief out of his pocket and did as he asked, smiling pertly. "Want to sample mine again?"

He tapped her on the nose. "Not tonight," he said. "We'd better leave. It's getting late."

"I'm driving," she told him.

"Yes, you are," he agreed.

She felt better. At least she was the one going home with him, not Lou. She wasn't going to give him up without a struggle, not when he was the best thing that had ever happened to her. Wealthy bachelor surgeons didn't come along every day of the week.

Lou drove home in a similar daze, overcome by the fervor of Coltrain's hard kisses. She couldn't understand why a man who'd always seemed to hate her had suddenly become addicted to her mouth; so addicted, in fact, that he'd followed her to her car. It had been the sweetest night of her life, but she had to keep her head and realize that it was an isolated incident. If Coltrain hadn't been drinking, it would never have happened. Maybe by Monday, she thought, he'd have convinced himself that it hadn't. She wished she could. She was more in love with him than ever, and he was as far out of her reach as he had ever been. Except that now he'd probably go even farther out of reach, because he'd lost his head and he wouldn't like remembering it.

She did her usual housework and answered emergency calls. She got more than her share because Dr. Coltrain had left word with their answering service that he was going to be out of town until Monday and Dr. Blakely would be covering for him.

Nice of him to ask her first, she thought bitterly, and tell her that he was going to be out of town. But perhaps he'd been reluctant to talk to her after what had happened. If the truth were known, he was more than likely as embarrassed as she was and just wanted to forget the whole thing.

She did his rounds and hers at the hospital, noticing absently that she was getting more attention than usual. Probably, she reasoned, because people were remembering the way Coltrain had kissed her. Maybe they thought something was going on between them.

"How's it going?" Drew asked on Sunday afternoon, grinning at her. "I hear I missed a humdinger of a kiss at the Christmas party," he added wickedly.

She blushed to her hairline. "Lots of people got kissed."

"Not like you did. Not so that he followed you out to the parking lot and damn near made love to you on the hood of your car." He chuckled.

"Who...?"

"Nickie," he said, confirming her worst nightmare. "She was watching, apparently, and she's sweet on Copper. I guess she thought it might turn him off you if there was a lot of gossip about what happened. Rumors fly, especially when they're about two doctors who seem to hate each other."

"He'll walk right into it when he comes back," she said uneasily. "What can I do?"

"Nothing, I'm afraid."

Her eyes narrowed. "That's what you think."

She turned on her heel and went in search of Nickie. She found her in a patient's room and waited calmly while the girl, nervous and very insecure once she saw Lou waiting for her, finished the chore she was performing.

She went out into the hall with Lou, and she looked apprehensive.

Lou clutched a clipboard to her lab jacket. She didn't smile. "I understand you've been feeding the rumor mill. I'll give you some good advice. Stop it while you can."

By now, Nickie's face had gone puce. "I never meant...I was kidding!" she burst out. "That's all, just kidding!"

Lou studied her without emotion. "I'm not laughing. Dr. Coltrain won't be laughing, either, when he hears about it. And I'll make sure he knows where it came from."

"That's spiteful!" Nickie cried. "I'm crazy about him!"

"No, you aren't," Lou said shortly. "You'd never subject him to the embarrassment you have with all this gossip if you really cared."

Nickie's hands locked together. "I'm sorry," she said on a long sigh. "I really am. I was just jealous," she confessed, avoiding

Lou's eyes. "He wouldn't even kiss me good-night, but he'd kiss you that way, and he hates you."

"Try to remember that he'd had too much to drink," Lou said quietly. "Only a fool would read anything into a kiss under the mistletoe."

"I guess so," Nickie said, but she wasn't really convinced. "I'm sorry. You won't tell him it was me, will you?" she added worriedly. "He'll hate me. I care so much, Dr. Blakely!"

"I won't tell him," Lou said. "But no more gossip!"

"Yes, ma'am!" Nickie brightened, grinned and went off down the hall, irrepressibly young and optimistic. Watching her, Lou felt ancient.

The next morning was Monday, and Lou went into the office to come face-to-face with a furious partner, who blocked her doorway and glared at her with blue eyes like arctic ice.

"Now what have I done?" she asked before he could speak, and slammed her bag down on her desk, ready to do battle.

"You don't know?" he taunted.

She folded her arms over her breasts and leaned back against the edge of the desk. "There's a terrible rumor going around the hospital," she guessed.

His eyebrow jerked, but the ice didn't leave his eyes. "Did you start it?"

"Of course," she agreed furiously. "I couldn't wait to tell everybody on staff that you bent me back over the hood of my car and ravished me in the parking lot!"

Brenda, who'd started in the door, stood there with her mouth open, intercepted a furious glare from two pairs of eyes, turned on her heel and got out.

"Could you keep your voice down?" Coltrain snapped.

"Gladly, when you stop making stupid accusations!"

He glared at her and she glared back.

"I was drinking!"

"That's it, announce it to everyone in the waiting room, why don't you, and see how many patients run for their cars!'' she raged.

He closed her office door, hard, and leaned back against it. ''Who started the rumor?'' he asked.

''That's more like it,'' she replied. ''Don't accuse until you ask. I didn't start it. I have no wish to become the subject of gossip.''

''Not even to force me to do something about the rumors?'' he asked. ''Such as announce our engagement?''

Her eyes went saucer-wide. ''Please! I've just eaten!''

His jaw went taut. ''I beg your pardon?''

''And so you should!'' she said enthusiastically. ''Marry you? I'd rather chain myself to a tree in an alligator swamp!''

He didn't answer immediately. He stared at her instead while all sorts of impractical ideas sifted through his mind.

A buzzer sounded on her desk. She reached over and pressed a button. ''Yes?''

''What about the patients?'' Brenda prompted.

''He doesn't *have* any patience,'' Lou said without thinking.

''Excuse me?'' Brenda stammered.

''Oh. That sort of patients. Send my first one in, will you, Brenda? Dr. Coltrain was just leaving.''

''No, he wasn't,'' he returned when her finger left the intercom button. ''We'll finish this discussion after office hours.''

''After office hours?'' she asked blankly.

''Yes. But, don't get your hopes up about a repeat of Friday evening,'' he said with a mocking smile. ''After all, I'm not drunk today.''

Her eyes flashed murderously and her lips compressed. But he was already out the door.

Lou was never sure afterward how she'd managed to get through her patients without revealing her state of mind. She was furiously angry at Coltrain for his accusations and equally upset with Brenda for hearing what she'd said in retaliation. Now it would be all over the office as well as all over the hospital that

she and Coltrain had something going. And they didn't! Despite
Lou's helpless attraction to him, it didn't take much imagination
to see that Coltrain didn't feel the same. Well, maybe physically
he felt something for her, but emotionally he still hated her. A
few kisses wouldn't change that!

She checked Mr. Bailey's firm, steady heartbeat, listened to his
lungs and pronounced him over the pneumonia she'd been treating
him for.

As she started to go, leaving Brenda to help him with his shirt,
he called to her.

"What's this I hear about you and Doc Coltrain?" he teased.
"Been kissing up a storm at the hospital Christmas party, they
say. Any chance we'll be hearing wedding bells?"

He didn't understand, he told Brenda on his way out, why Dr.
Blakely had suddenly screamed like that. Maybe she'd seen a
mouse, Brenda replied helpfully.

When the office staff went home, Coltrain was waiting at the
front entrance for Lou. He'd stationed himself there after checking
with the hospital about a patient, and he hadn't moved, in case
Lou decided to try to sneak out.

He was wearing the navy blue suit that looked so good on him,
lounging against the front door with elegant carelessness, when
she went out of her office. His red hair caught the reflection of
the overhead light and seemed to burn like flames over his blue,
blue eyes. They swept down over her neat gray pantsuit to her
long legs encased in slacks with low-heeled shoes.

"That color looks good on you," he remarked.

"You don't need to flatter me. Just say what's on your mind,
please, and let me go home."

"All right." His eyes fell to her soft mouth and lingered there.
"Who started the rumors about us?"

She traced a pattern on her fanny pack. "I promised I wouldn't
tell."

"Nickie," he guessed, nodding at her shocked expression.

"She's young and infatuated," she began.

"Not that young," he said with quiet insinuation.

Her eyes flashed before she could avert them. Her hand dug into the fanny pack for her car keys. "It's a nine-days wonder," she continued. "People will find something else to talk about."

"Nothing quite this spicy has happened since Ted Regan went chasing off to Victoria after Coreen Tarleton and she came home wearing his engagement ring."

"There's hardly any comparison," she said, "considering that everyone knows how we feel about each other!"

"How *do* we feel about each other, Lou?" he replied quietly, and watched her expression change.

"We're enemies," she returned instantly.

"Are we?" He searched her eyes in a silence that grew oppressive. His arms fell to his sides. "Come here, Lou."

She felt her breathing go wild. That could have been an invitation to bypass him and leave the building. But the look in his eyes told her it wasn't. Those eyes blazed like flames in his lean, tanned face, beckoning, promising pleasures beyond imagination.

He lifted a hand. "Come on, coward," he chided softly, and his lips curled at the edges. "I won't hurt you."

"You're sober," she reminded him.

"Cold sober," he agreed. "Let's see how it feels when I know what I'm doing."

Her heart stopped, started, raced. She hesitated, and he laughed softly and started toward her, with that slow, deliberate walk that spoke volumes about his intent.

"You mustn't," she spoke quickly, holding up a hand.

He caught the hand and jerked her against him, imprisoning her there with a steely arm. "I must." He corrected her, letting his eyes fall to her mouth. "I *have* to know." He bit off the words against her lips.

She never found out what he had to know, because the instant she felt his lips probing her mouth, she went under in a blaze of desire unlike anything she'd felt before. She gasped, opened her lips, yielded to his enveloping arms without a single protest. If anything, she pushed closer into his arms, against that steely body that was instantly aroused by the feel of her.

She tried to speak, to protest, but he pushed his tongue into her mouth with a harsh groan, and his arms lifted her so that she fit perfectly against him from breast to thigh. She fought, frightened by the intimacy and the sensations kindled in her untried body.

Her frantic protest registered at once. He remembered she'd had the same reaction the night of the Christmas party. His mouth lifted, and his searching eyes met hers.

"You couldn't be a virgin," he said, making it sound more like an accusation than a statement of fact.

She bit her lip and dropped her eyes, shamed and embarrassed. "Rub it in," she growled.

"My God." He eased her back onto her feet and held her by the upper arms so that she wouldn't fall. "My God! How old are you, thirty?"

"Twenty-eight," she said unsteadily, gasping for breath. Her whole body felt swollen. Her dark eyes glowered up at him as she pushed back her disheveled hair. "And you needn't look so shocked, you of all people should know that some people still have a few principles! You're a doctor, after all!"

"I thought virgins were a fairy tale," he said flatly. "Damn it!"

Her chin lifted. "What's wrong, Doctor, did you see me as a pleasant interlude between patients?"

His lips compressed. He rammed his hands into his trouser pockets, all too aware of a throbbing arousal that wouldn't go away. He turned to the door and jerked it open. All weekend he'd dreamed of taking Louise Blakely home with him after work and seducing her in his big king-size bed. She was leaving anyway, and the hunger he felt for her was one he had to satisfy or go mad. It had seemed so simple. She wanted him; he knew she did. People were already talking about them, so what would a little more gossip matter? She'd be gone at the first of the year, anyway.

But now he had a new complication, one he'd never dreamed

of having. She was no young girl, but it didn't take an expert to know why she backed away from intimacy like a repressed adolescent. He'd been baiting her with that accusation of virginity, but she hadn't realized it. She'd taken it at face value and she'd given him a truth he didn't even want. She was innocent. How could he seduce her now? On the other hand, how was he going to get rid of this very inconvenient and noticeable desire for her?

Watching him, Lou was cursing her own headlong response. She hated having him know how much she wanted him.

"Any man could have made me react that way!" she flared defensively, red-faced. "Any experienced man!"

His head turned and he stared at her, seeing through the flustering words to the embarrassment.

"It's all right," he said gently. "We're both human. Don't beat your conscience to death over a kiss, Lou."

She went even redder and her hands clenched at her sides. "I'm still leaving!"

"I know."

"And I won't let you seduce me!"

He turned. "I won't try," he said solemnly. "I don't seduce virgins."

She bit her lip and tasted him on it. She winced.

"Why?" he asked quietly.

She glared at him.

"Why?" he persisted.

Her eyes fell under that piercing blue stare. "Because I don't want to end up like my mother," she said huskily.

Of all the answers he might have expected, that was the last. "Your mother? I don't understand."

She shook her head. "You don't need to. It's personal. You and I are business partners until the end of the month, and then nothing that happened to me will be any concern of yours."

He didn't move. She looked vulnerable, hurt. "Counseling might be of some benefit," he said gently.

"I don't need counseling."

"Tell me how your wrist got broken, Lou," he said matter-of-factly.

She stiffened.

"Oh, a layman wouldn't notice, it's healed nicely. But surgery is my business. I know a break when I see one. There are scars, too, despite the neat stitching job. How did it happen?"

She felt weak. She didn't want to talk to him, of all people, about her past. It would only reinforce what he already thought of her father, though God only knew why she should defend such a man.

She clasped her wrist defensively, as if to hide what had been done to it. "It's an old injury," she said finally.

"What sort of injury? How did it happen?"

She laughed nervously. "I'm not your patient."

He absently jingled the change in his pocket, watching her. It occurred to him that she was a stranger. Despite their heated arguments over the past year, they'd never come close to discussing personal matters. Away from the office, they were barely civil to each other. In it, they never discussed anything except business. But he was getting a new picture of her, and not a very reassuring one. This was a woman with a painful past, so painful that it had locked her up inside an antiseptic prison. He wondered if she'd ever had the incentive to fight her way out, or why it should matter to him that she hadn't.

"Can you talk to Drew about it?" he asked suddenly.

She hesitated and then shook her head. Her fingers tightened around her wrist. "It doesn't matter, I tell you."

His hand came out of his pocket and he caught the damaged wrist very gently in his long fingers, prepared for her instinctive jerk. He moved closer, drawing that hand to his chest. He pressed it gently into the thick fabric of his vest.

"There's nothing you can't tell me," he said solemnly. "I don't carry tales, or gossip. Anything you say to me will remain between the two of us. If you want to talk, ever, I'll listen."

She bit her bottom lip. She'd never been able to tell anyone.

Her mother knew, but she defended her husband, trying desperately to pretend that Lou had imagined it, that it had never happened. She excused her husband's affairs, his drinking bouts, his drug addiction, his brutality, his sarcasm...everything, in the name of love, while her marriage disintegrated around her and her daughter turned away from her. Obsessive love, one of her friends had called it—blind, obsessive love that refused to acknowledge the least personality flaw in the loved one.

"My mother was emotionally crippled," she said, thinking aloud. "She was so blindly in love with him that he could do no wrong, no wrong at all..." She remembered where she was and looked up at him with the pain still in her eyes.

"Who broke your wrist, Lou?" he asked gently.

She remembered aloud. "He was drinking and I tried to take the bottle away from him, because he'd hit my mother. He hit my wrist with the bottle, and it broke," she added, wincing at the memory of the pain. "And all the while, when they operated to repair the damage, he kept saying that I'd fallen through a glass door, that I'd tripped. Everyone believed him, even my mother. I told her that he did it, and she said that I was lying."

"He? Who did it, Lou?"

She searched his curious eyes. "Why...my father," she said simply.

Chapter 6

Coltrain searched her dark eyes, although the confession didn't really surprise him. He knew too much about her father to be surprised.

"So that was why the whiskey on my breath bothered you Friday night," he remarked quietly.

She averted her head and nodded. "He was a drunkard at the last, and a drug addict. He had to stop operating because he almost killed a patient. They let him retire and act in an advisory capacity because he'd been such a good surgeon. He was, you know," she added. "He might have been a terrible father, but he was a wonderful surgeon. I wanted to be a surgeon, to be like him." She shivered. "I was in my first year of medical school when it happened. I lost a semester and afterward, I knew I'd never be able to operate. I decided to become a general practitioner."

"What a pity," he said. He understood the fire for surgical work because he had it. He loved what he did for a living.

She smiled sadly. "I'm still practicing medicine. It isn't so bad. Family practice has its place in the scheme of things, and I've enjoyed the time I've spent in Jacobsville."

"So have I," he admitted reluctantly. He smiled at her expression. "Surprised? You've been here long enough to know how a good many people react to me. I'm the original bad boy of the community. If it hadn't been for the scholarship one of my teachers helped me get, I'd probably be in jail by now. I had a hard childhood and I hated authority in any form. I was in constant trouble with the law.''

"You?'' she asked, aghast.

He nodded. "People aren't always what they seem, are they?'' he continued. "I was a wild boy. But I loved medicine and I had an aptitude for it and there were people who were willing to help me. I'm the first of my family to escape poverty, did you know?''

She shook her head. "I don't know anything about your family,'' she said. "I wouldn't have presumed to ask anyone something so personal about you.''

"I've noticed that,'' he returned. "You avoid sharing your feelings. You'll fight back, but you don't let people close, do you?''

"When people get too close, they can hurt you,'' she said.

"A lesson your father taught you, no doubt.''

She wrapped her arms around her chest. "I'm cold,'' she said dully. "I want to go home.''

He searched her face. "Come home with me.''

She hesitated warily.

He made a face. "Shame on you for what you're thinking. You should know better. You're off the endangered list. I'll make chili and Mexican corn bread and strong coffee and we can watch a Christmas special. Do you like opera?''

Her eyes brightened. "Oh, I love it.''

His own eyes brightened. "Pavarotti?''

"And Domingo.'' She looked worried. "But people will talk…''

"They're already talking. Who cares?'' he asked. "We're both single adults. What we do together is nobody's business.''

"Yes, well, the general consensus of opinion is that we're public property, or didn't you hear what Mr. Bailey said?''

"I heard you scream,'' he mused.

She cleared her throat. "Well, it was the last straw.''

He caught her hand, the undamaged one, and locked her fingers into his, tugging her out the door.

"Dr. Coltrain," she began.

He locked the office door. "You know my name."

She looked wary. "Yes."

He glanced at her. "My friends call me Copper," he said softly, and smiled.

"We're not friends."

"I think we're going to be, though, a year too late." He tugged her toward his car.

"I can drive mine," she protested.

"Mine's more comfortable. I'll drive you home, and give you a lift to work in the morning. Is it locked?"

"Yes, but..."

"Don't argue, Lou. I'm tired. It's been a long day and we've still got to make rounds at the hospital later."

We. He couldn't know the anguish of hearing him link them together when she had less than two weeks left in Jacobsville. He'd said that he'd torn up her resignation, but she was level-headed enough to know that she had to go. It would be pure torment to be around him all the time and have him treat her as a friend and nothing more. She couldn't have an affair with him, either, so what was left?

He glanced down at her worried face and his fingers contracted. "Stop brooding. I promised not to seduce you."

"I know that!"

"Unless you want me to," he chided, chuckling at her expression. "I'm a doctor," he added in a conspiratorial whisper. "I know how to protect you from any consequences."

"Damn you!"

She jerked away from him, furiously. He laughed at her fighting stance.

"That was wicked," he acknowledged. "But I do love to watch you lose that hot temper. Are you Irish, by any chance?"

"My grandfather was," she muttered. She dashed a strand of

blond hair out of her eyes. "You stop saying things like that to me!"

He unlocked her door, still smiling. "All right. No more jokes."

She slid into the leather seat and inhaled the luxurious scent of the upholstery while he got in beside her and started the car. It was dark. She sat next to him in perfect peace and contentment as they drove out to his ranch, not breaking the silence as they passed by farms and ranches silhouetted against the flat horizon.

"You're very quiet," he remarked when he pulled up in front of the Spanish-style adobe house he called home.

"I'm happy," she said without thinking.

He was quiet, then. He helped her out and they walked a little apart on the flagstone walkway that led to the front porch. It was wide and spacious, with gliders and a porch swing.

"It must be heaven to sit out here in the spring," she remarked absently.

He glanced at her curiously. "I never pictured you as the sort to enjoy a porch swing."

"Or walks in the woods, or horseback riding, or baseball games?" she asked. "Because I like those things, too. Austin does have suburbs, and I had friends who owned ranches. I know how to ride and shoot, too."

He smiled. She'd seemed like such a city girl. He'd made sure that he never looked too closely at her, of course. Like father, like daughter, he'd always thought. But she was nothing like Fielding Blakely. She was unique.

He unlocked the door and opened it. The interior was full of Spanish pieces and dark furniture with creams and beiges and browns softened by off-white curtains. It had the look of professional decorating, which it probably was.

"I grew up sitting on orange crates and eating on cracked plates," he commented as she touched a bronze sculpture of a bronc rider. "This is much better."

She laughed. "I guess so. But orange crates and cracked plates wouldn't be so bad if the company was pleasant. I hate formal dining rooms and extravagant place settings.''

Now he was getting suspicious. They really couldn't have that much in common! His eyebrow jerked. ''Full of surprises, aren't you? Or did you just take a look at my curriculum vitae and tell me what I wanted to hear?'' he added in a crisp, suspicious tone.

Her surprise was genuine, and he recognized it immediately. She searched his face. ''This was a mistake,'' she said flatly. ''I think I'd like to go...''

He caught her arm. ''Lou, I'm constantly on the defensive with women,'' he said. ''I never know, you see...'' He hesitated.

''Yes, I understand,'' she replied. ''You don't have to say it.''

''All that, and you read minds, too,'' he said with cool sarcasm. ''Well, well.''

She drew away from him. She seemed to read his mind quite well, she thought, because she usually knew what he was going to say.

That occurred to him, too. ''It used to make me mad as hell when you handed me files before I asked for them,'' he told her.

''It wasn't deliberate,'' she said without thinking.

''I know.'' His jaw firmed as he looked at her. ''We know too much about each other, don't we, Lou? We know things we shouldn't, without ever saying them.''

She looked up, feeling the bite of his inspection all the way to her toes. ''We can't say them,'' she replied. ''Not ever.''

He only nodded. His eyes searched hers intently. ''I don't believe in happily ever after,'' he said. ''I did, once, until your father came along and shattered all my illusions. She wouldn't let me touch her, you see. But she slept with him. She got pregnant by him. The hell of it was that she was going to marry me without telling me anything.'' He sighed. ''I lost my faith in women on the spot, and I hated your father enough to beat him to his knees. When you came here, and I found out who you were...'' He shook his head. ''I almost decked Drew for not telling me.''

''I didn't know, either,'' she said.

"I realize that." He smiled. "You were an asset, after I got over the shock. You never complained about long hours or hard work, no matter how much I put on you. And I put a lot on you, at first. I thought I could make you quit. But the more I demanded, the more you gave. After a while, it occurred to me that I'd made a good bargain. Not that I liked you," he added sardonically.

"You made that perfectly clear."

"You fought back," he said. "Most people don't. They knuckle under and go home and fume about it, and think up things they wish they'd said. You just jump in with both feet and give it all you've got. You're a hell of an adversary, Lou. I couldn't beat you down."

"I always had to fight for things," she recalled. "My father was like you." Her face contorted and she turned away.

"I don't get drunk as a rule, and I've never hurt a woman!" he snapped.

"I didn't mean that," she said quickly. "It's just that you're forceful. You demand, you push. You don't ever give up or give in. Neither did he. If he thought he was right, he'd fight the whole world to prove it. But he fought the same when he was wrong. And in his later years, he drank to excess. He wouldn't admit he had a problem. Neither would my mother. She was his slave," she added bitterly. "Even her daughter was dispensable if the great man said so."

"Didn't she love you?"

"Who knows? She loved him more. Enough to lie for him. Even to die for him. And she did." She turned, her face hard. "She got into a plane with him, knowing that he was in no condition to fly. Maybe she had a premonition that he would go down and she wanted to go with him. I'm almost sure that she still would have gone with him if she'd known he was going to crash the plane. She loved him that much."

"You sound as if you can't imagine being loved that much."

"I can't," she said flatly, lifting her eyes. "I don't want that kind of obsessive love. I don't want to give it or receive it."

"What do you want?" he persisted. "A lifetime of loneliness?"

"That's what you're settling for, isn't it?" she countered.

He shrugged. "Maybe I am," he said after a minute. His blue eyes slid over her face and then averted. "Can you cook?" he asked on the way into the kitchen. Like the rest of the house, it was spacious and contained every modern device known to man.

"Of course," she said.

He glanced at her with a grin. "How well do you do chili?" he persisted.

"Well…"

"I've won contests with mine," he said smugly. He slid out of his jacket and vest and tie, opened the top buttons of his shirt and turned to the stove. "You can make the coffee."

"Trusting soul, aren't you?" she murmured as he acquainted her with the coffeemaker and the location of filters, coffee and measuring spoons.

"I always give a fellow cook the benefit of the doubt once," he replied. "Besides, you drink coffee all the time, just like I do. That means you must know how to make it."

She laughed. "I like mine strong," she warned.

"So do I. Do your worst."

Minutes later, the food was on the small kitchen table, steaming and delicious. Lou couldn't remember when she'd enjoyed a meal more.

"That's good chili," she had to admit.

He grinned. "It's the two-time winner of the Jacobsville Chili Cookoff."

"I'm not surprised. The corn bread was wonderful, too."

"The secret to good corn bread is to cook it in an iron skillet," he confessed. "That's where the crispness comes from."

"I don't own a single piece of iron cookware. I'll have to get a pan."

He leaned back, balancing his coffee mug in one hand as he studied her through narrow eyes. "It hasn't all been on my side," he remarked suddenly.

Her eyes lifted to his. "What hasn't?"

"All that antagonism," he said. "You've been as prickly as I have."

Her slender shoulders rose and fell. "It's instinctive to recoil from people when we know they don't like us. Isn't it?"

"Maybe so." He checked his watch and finished his coffee. "I'll get these things in the dishwasher, then we'd better get over to the hospital and do rounds before the Christmas concert comes on the educational channel."

"I don't have my car," she said worriedly.

"We'll go together."

"Oh, that will certainly keep gossip down," she said on a sigh.

He smiled at her. "Damn gossip."

"Was that an adjective or a verb?"

"A verb. I'll rinse, you stack."

They loaded the dishes and he started the dishwasher. He slid back into his jacket, buttoned his shirt and fixed his tie. "Come on. We'll get the chores out of the way."

The hospital was crowded, and plenty of people noticed that Drs. Coltrain and Blakely came in together to make rounds. Lou tried not to notice as she went from patient to patient, checking charts and making conversation.

But when she finished, Coltrain was nowhere in sight. She glanced out the window into the parking lot. His car was still there in his designated space. She went to the doctors' lounge looking for him, and turned the corner just in time to see him with a devastating blond woman in a dress that Lou would love to have been able to afford.

Coltrain saw Lou and he looked grim. He turned toward her with his hands in his pockets, and Lou noticed that the woman was clutching one of his arms tightly in both hands.

"This is my partner," he said, without giving her name. "Lou, this is Dana Lester, an old...friend."

"His ex-fiancée." The woman corrected him in a sweet tone.

"How nice to meet you! I've just accepted an appointment as nursing director here, so we'll be seeing a lot of each other!"

"You're a nurse?" Lou asked politely, while she caved in inside.

"A graduate nurse," she said, nodding. "I've been working in Houston, but this job came open and was advertised in a local paper. I applied for it, and here I am! How lovely it will be to come home. I was born here, you know."

"Oh, really?" Lou said.

"Darling," she told Copper, "you didn't tell me your partner's name."

"It's Blakely," he said evenly. "Dr. Louise Blakely."

"Blakely?" the woman queried, her blue eyes pensive. "Why does that name sound so familiar...." She suddenly went pale. "No," she said, shaking her head. "No, that would be too coincidental."

"My father," Lou said coolly, "was Dr. Fielding Blakely. I believe you...knew him?" she added pointedly.

Dana's face looked like rice paper. She drew away from Coltrain. "I...I must fly, darling," she said. "Things to do while I get settled! I'll have you over for supper one night soon!"

She didn't speak to Lou again, not that it was expected. Lou watched her go with cold, angry eyes.

"You didn't want to tell her my name," Lou accused softly.

His face gave away nothing. "The past is best left alone."

"Did you know about her job here?"

His jaw clenched. "I knew there was an opening. I didn't know she'd been hired. If Selby Wills hadn't just retired as hospital administrator, she wouldn't have gotten the job."

She probed into the pocket of her lab coat without really seeing it. "She's pretty."

"She's blond, too, isn't that what you're thinking?"

She raised her face. "So," she added, "is Jane Parker."

"Jane Burke, now." He corrected her darkly. "I like blondes."

His tone dared her to make another remark. She lifted a shoulder and turned. "Some men do. Just don't expect me to welcome her with open arms. I'm sure that my mother suffered because of her. At least my father was less careless with women in his later years."

"It was over a long time ago," Copper said quietly. "If I can overlook your father, you can overlook her."

"Do you think so?"

"What happened between them was nothing to do with you," he persisted.

"He betrayed my mother with her, and it's nothing to do with me?" she asked softly.

He rammed his hands into his pockets, his face set and cold. "Are you finished here?"

"Oh, yes, I'm finished here," she agreed fervently. "If you'll drop me off at my car, I'd like to go home now. We'll have to save the TV Special for another time."

He hesitated, but only for a minute. Her expression told him everything he needed to know, including the futility of having an argument with her right now.

"All right," he agreed, nodding toward the exit. "Let's go."

He stopped at her car in the office parking lot and let her out.

"Thanks for my supper," she said politely.

"You're welcome."

She closed the door and unlocked her own car. He didn't drive away until she was safely inside and heading out toward home.

Dana Lester's arrival in town was met with another spate of gossip, because there were people in Jacobsville who remembered the scandal very well. Lou tried to pay as little attention to it as possible as she weathered the first few days with the new nursing supervisor avoiding her and Coltrain barely speaking to her.

It was, she told herself, a very good thing that she was leaving after the first of January. The situation was strained and getting worse. She couldn't work out if Dana was afraid of her or jealous of her. Gossip about herself and Coltrain had been lost in the new rumors about his ex-fiancée's return, which did at least spare Lou somewhat. She couldn't help but see that Dana spent a fair amount of time following Coltrain around the hospital, and once or twice she phoned him at the office. Lou pretended not to notice and not to mind, but it was cutting her up inside.

The night she'd had supper with her taciturn partner had been something of a beginning. But Dana's arrival had nipped it all in the bud. He'd turned his back on Lou and now he only spoke to her when it was necessary and about business. If he'd withdrawn, so had she. Poor Brenda and the office receptionist worked in an armed camp, walking around like people on eggshells. Coltrain's temper strained at the bit, and every time he flared up, Lou flared right back.

"We hear that Nickie and Dana almost came to blows the other night about who got to take Dr. Coltrain a file," Brenda remarked a few days later.

"Too bad someone didn't have a hidden camera, isn't it?" Lou remarked. She sipped her coffee.

Brenda frowned. "I thought... Well, it did seem that you and the doctor were getting along better."

"A temporary truce, nothing more," she returned. "I'm still leaving after the first of the year, Brenda. Nothing's really changed except that Coltrain's old flame has returned."

"She was poison," Brenda said. "I heard all about her from some of the older nurses at the hospital. Did you know that at least two threatened to quit when they knew she was taking over as head nurse at the hospital? One of the nurses she worked with in Houston has family here. They said she was about to be fired when she grabbed this job. Her credentials look impressive, but she's not a good administrator, regardless of her college background, and she plays favorites. They'll learn that here, the hard way."

"It's not my problem."

"Isn't it?" Brenda muttered. "Well, they also say that her real purpose in applying for this job was to see if Copper was willing to take her back and try again. She's looking for a husband and he's number one on her list.''

''Lucky him,'' she said blithely. ''She's very pretty.''

''She's a blond tarantula,'' she said hotly. ''She'll suck him dry!''

''He's a big boy, Brenda,'' Lou returned imperturbably. ''He can take care of himself.''

''No man is immune to a beautiful face and figure and having a woman absolutely worship him. You take my word for it, there's going to be trouble.''

''I won't be here to see it,'' Lou reminded her. And for the first time, she was glad. Nickie and Dana could fight over Coltrain and may the best woman win, she thought miserably. At least she wouldn't have to watch the struggle. She'd always known that Coltrain wasn't for her. She might as well accept defeat with good grace and get out while she could.

She went back to work, all too aware of Coltrain's deep voice in one of the cubicles she passed. She wondered how her life was going to feel when this was all a bad memory, and she wouldn't hear his voice again.

Drew invited her out to eat and she went, gratefully, glad for the diversion. But the restaurant he chose, Jacobsville's best, had two unwelcome diners: Coltrain and his ex-fiancée.

''I'm sorry,'' Drew said with a smile and a grimace of apology. ''I didn't know they'd be here or I'd have chosen another place to take you for supper.''

''Oh, I don't mind,'' she assured him. ''I have to see them at the hospital every day, anyway.''

''Yes, *see* them being the key word here,'' he added knowingly. ''I understand that they both avoid you.''

''God knows why,'' she agreed. ''She's anywhere I'm not when I need to ask her a question, and he only talks to me about patients. I'm glad I'm leaving, Drew. And with all respect to you, I'm sorry I came.''

He smiled ruefully. "I'm sorry I got you into this," he said. "Nothing went as I planned."

"What exactly did you plan?" she asked probingly.

He lifted his water glass and took a sip. "Well, I had hoped that Copper would see something in you that he hadn't found anywhere else. You're unique, Lou. So is he, in some respects. You seemed like a match."

She glared at him. "We're chalk and cheese," she said, ignoring the things she and the redheaded doctor did have in common. "And we can't get along for more than five minutes."

"So I see." He looked around and made a face. "Oh, God, more complications!"

She followed his gaze. A determined Nickie, in a skintight dress cut almost to the navel, was dragging an embarrassed intern to a table right beside Coltrain and Dana's.

"That won't do," she remarked, watching Coltrain's blue eyes start to glitter. "He won't like that. And if she thinks he'll forgo a scene, she's very wrong. Any minute now he's going to get up and walk out."

When he did exactly that, leaving an astonished Dana at one table and a shocked Nickie at the other, Drew whistled through his teeth and gave Lou a pointed stare.

"You know him very well," was all he said, though.

"I know him," Lou said simply. "He says I read his mind. Maybe I do, on some level."

He frowned. "Do you realize how rare a rapport that is?"

She shrugged. "Not really. He seems to read my mind, too. I shouldn't feel sorry for him, but I do. Imagine shuffling two women in one restaurant."

He didn't add that it was really three, and that Copper had been watching Lou surreptitiously ever since she and Drew entered the restaurant. But of the three women, Lou was the only one who wasn't blatantly chasing him.

"He's paying the check," he remarked. "And, yes, there he

goes, motioning to Dana. Good thing they'd finished dessert, wasn't it? Poor Nickie. She won't forget this in a while.''

"I told her she was pushing too hard," Lou remarked. "Too bad. She's so young. I suppose she hasn't learned that you can chase a man too relentlessly and lose him.''

"Some women never chase a man at all," he said.

She looked up and saw the teasing expression on his face. She laughed. "Drew, you are a dear," she said genuinely.

He chuckled. "My wife always said that I was," he agreed. "What are you going to do?"

"Me? What do you mean? What am I going to do about what?"

"About Copper.''

"Nothing," she replied. "Right after the holidays, I leave for Austin."

He pursed his lips as he lifted his coffee cup. "You know," he said, "I have a feeling you'll never get out of town."

Chapter 7

Saturday morning, Lou woke to the sound of someone hammering on her front door. Half-asleep, with a pale pink satin robe whipped around her slender body and her hair disheveled, she made her way to open it.

The sight that met her eyes was shocking. Coltrain was standing there, dressed in jeans and boots and a faded cotton shirt under a fleece-lined jacket, with a weather-beaten gray Stetson in one lean hand.

She blinked. "Are we filming a new series called 'Cowboy Doctor'?"

"Cute," he remarked, but he wasn't smiling. "I have to talk to you."

She opened the door, still drowsy. "Come on in. I'll make coffee," she said, stifling a yawn as she shuffled toward the kitchen. She could have gone immediately to change, but she was more than adequately covered and he was a doctor. Besides, she reminded herself, he had two women chasing him relentlessly anyway.

"I'll make the coffee. How about some toast to go with it?"

"Plain or cinnamon?"

"Suit yourself."

She got out butter and cinnamon and, just as the coffee finished brewing, she had the toast ready—piping hot from the oven.

He watched her moving about the kitchen. He was sitting leaning back in one of her kitchen chairs with one booted foot on the floor and the chair propped against the wall. He looked out of humor and wickedly handsome all at the same time.

In the position he was occupying, his jeans clung closely to every powerful line of his long legs. He was muscular without being exaggerated, and with his faded shirt unbuttoned at the throat and his red hair disheveled from the hat, he looked more relaxed than she'd ever seen him.

It occurred to her that this was the way he usually was, except when he was working. It was like a private look into his secret life, and she was unexpectedly pleased to have been given it before she left town for good.

"Here." She put the toast on the table, handed him a plate, put condiments on the spotless white tablecloth and then poured coffee into two cups.

"The Christmas concert was nice," he remarked.

"Was it?" she replied. "I went to bed."

"I had nothing to do with getting Dana down here," he said flatly. "In case you wondered."

"It's none of my business."

"Yes, I know," he said heavily. He sipped coffee and munched toast, but he was preoccupied. "Nickie and Dana are becoming an embarrassment."

"Leave it to you to be irritated when two lovely women compete for your attention," she remarked dryly.

His eyes narrowed on her face. "Irritation doesn't quite cover it. I feel like the stud of the month," he said disgustedly.

She burst out laughing. "Oh, I'm sorry!" she said when he glared at her. "It was the way you said it."

He was ruffled, and looked it. He sipped more coffee. "I wasn't trying to make a joke."

"I know. It must be difficult, especially when you have to make rounds at the hospital, with both of them working there."

"I understand you're having some problems of your own in that regard."

"You might say that," she agreed. "I can't find Dana or Nickie when I need them. I seem to have the plague."

"You know that it can't continue?"

"Of course I do," she assured him. "And when I leave, things will settle down, I'm sure."

He scowled. "What do you mean, when you leave? How will that help? Anyway, we'd already agreed that you were staying."

"We agreed on nothing," she returned. "I gave you my resignation. If you tore it up, that's your problem. I consider it binding."

He stared down into his coffee cup, deep in thought. "I had no idea that you meant it."

"Amazing," she mused, watching him. "You have such a convenient memory, Dr. Coltrain. I can't forget a single word you said to Drew about me, and you can't remember?"

His face hardened. "I didn't know you were listening."

"That makes everything all right?" she asked with mock solemnity.

He ran a hand through his already disheveled hair. "Things came to a head," he replied. "I'd just had to diagnose leukemia in a child who should have had years of happiness to look forward to. I'd had a letter from my father asking for money..."

She shifted against the table. "I didn't know that your parents were still alive."

"My mother died ten years ago," he replied. "My father lives in Tucson. He wrangles horses, but he likes to gamble. When he gets in too deep, he always comes to me for a grubstake." He said it with utter contempt.

"Is that all you mean to him? Money?" she asked gently.

"It was all I ever meant to him." He lifted cold blue eyes to hers. He smiled unpleasantly. "Who do you think put me up to breaking and entering when I was a teenager? I was a juvenile, you know. Juveniles don't go to jail. Oh, we didn't do it here,'' he added. ''Not where he lived. We always went to Houston. He cased the houses and sent me in to do the actual work.''

Her gasp was audible. ''He should have been arrested!''

''He was,'' he replied. ''He served a year and got probation. We haven't spent any time together since I was placed with a foster family when I was thirteen, long before I started medical school. I put all that behind me. Apparently so did he. But now that I'm making a comfortable living, he doesn't really see any good reason not to ask me for help when he needs it.''

What sort of family life had *he* grown up in? she wondered. It was, in some ways, like her own upbringing. ''What a pity that we can't choose our parents,'' she remarked.

''Amen.'' His broad shoulders shifted against the wall. ''I was in a temper already, and Drew's phone call was the last straw. It irritated the hell out of me that you liked him, but you jerked away from my slightest touch as if I might contaminate you.''

She hadn't thought he'd noticed. He took her reaction as a sign of her distaste for him, when it was a fierce, painful attraction. It was ironic.

She lowered her eyes. ''You said when I first came to work with you that we would have a business relationship.''

''So I did. But that didn't mean you should treat me like a leper,'' he remarked. Oddly, he didn't seem to be concerned about it anymore. He smiled, in fact, his blue eyes sparkling. ''But I wouldn't have had you overhear what I told Drew for all the world, Lou. It shamed me when you asked to end our partnership.''

She toyed with a fingernail. ''I thought it would make you happy.''

Her choice of words delighted him. He knew exactly what she felt for him. He'd had suspicions for a while now, but he hadn't been certain until he kissed her. He couldn't let her leave until he was sure about what he felt for her. But how was he going to stop her? His blue eyes ran searchingly over her face and a crazy idea popped into his mind. "If you and I were engaged," he mused aloud, "Dana and Nickie would give up."

The words rambled around in her mind like marbles as she stared at him. The sun was out. It was a nice December day. Her Christmas decorations lined the windows and the tinsel on the Christmas tree in the living room caught the sun through the curtains and glittered.

"Did you hear me?" he asked when she didn't react.

Her cheeks burned. "I don't think that's very funny," she remarked, turning away.

He got to his feet with an audible thud and before she could move three feet, he had her by the waist from behind. Steely hands pulled her back against him and when she caught them, she felt their warm strength under her cool fingers. She felt his breath against her hair, felt it as his chest moved at her back.

"Shall we stop dancing around it?" he asked roughly. "You're in love with me. I've pretended not to see it, but we both know it's why you're leaving."

She gasped aloud. Frozen in his arms, she hadn't even a come-back, a face-saving reply. She felt his hands contract under hers, as if he thought she might pull away and run for it.

"Don't panic," he said quietly. "Dodging the issue won't solve it."

"I...didn't realize you could tell," she whispered, her pride in ashes at his feet.

His lean arms contracted, bringing her soft warmth closer to his taut body. "Take it easy. We'll deal with it."

"You don't have to deal with anything," she began huskily. "I'm going to..."

He turned her while she was speaking and his mouth was on hers before she could finish. She fought him for an instant, as he anticipated. But he was slow and very gentle, and she began to melt into him like ice against a flame.

He brought her closer, aware of her instant response when she felt his body harden. He made a rough sound against her mouth and deepened the kiss.

Her fingers caught in the cool flames of his hair, holding on for dear life as his ardor burned high and wild. He kissed her as he'd kissed Nickie at the party, not an inch of space between their bodies, no quarter in the thin lips devouring her open mouth. This time when his tongue penetrated, she didn't pull away. She accepted the intimate contact without a protest, shivering a little as it ignited new fires in her own taut body. The sensation was unlike anything she'd known. She held on tight, moaning, aware somewhere in the back of her mind that his hand was at the base of her spine, rubbing her against him, and that she should say something.

She was incapable of anything except blind response.

She didn't resist even when he eased her back onto her feet and, still kissing her hungrily, slid his hand under her robe against the soft, tight curve of her breast. He felt her heartbeat run away. With a groan, he fought his way under the gown, against the petal-soft warmth of her skin, and cupped her tenderly, dragging his thumb against the small hardness he found. She shivered again. Reeling, he traced the tight nub with his thumb and forefinger, testing its hardness. She sobbed against his mouth. Probably, he thought dizzily, she'd never had such a caress. And he could give her something more; another pleasure that she didn't know yet.

His mouth left hers and found its way down past her collarbone to the softness under his hand. It opened on her body, and he drank in the scented warmth of her while his tongue took the place of his thumb. She gasped and struggled, but he began to suckle her, his arms swallowing her, and she shuddered once and gave in. He felt her body go lax in his arms, so that if he hadn't supported her, she would have fallen. She caressed his nape with trembling hands, gasping a little as he increased the pressure, but clinging, not pushing.

When he thought he might explode from the pleasure it was

giving him, he forced his mouth to release her and he stood erect, pulling her up abruptly.

His face was ruddy with high color, his eyes blazing as they met her half-open, dazed ones. She was oblivious to everything except the taste of him. Her lips were swollen. Even her tongue felt swollen. She couldn't say a word.

He searched over her face and then dropped his eyes to her bodice. He moved it out of the way and looked at the small, firm breast he'd been tasting. She looked like a rosebud there, the nipple red from his mouth.

He traced around it lazily and then looked back up at the shocked pleasure in her dark, dark eyes.

"I could have you on the kitchen table, right now," he said in a deep, quiet tone. "And you think you're leaving in two weeks?"

She blinked. It was all so unreal. He'd all but seduced her. His hand was still on her breast and he'd pulled the robe and gown aside. He was looking at her...!

She gasped, horrified, jerking back from him. Her hands grappled with the unruly fabric before she finally got her body covered. She backed away, blushing, glaring at him accusingly.

He didn't move, except to lean back against the kitchen counter and cross his long legs. That action drew her eyes to something she'd felt earlier, and she blushed scarlet before she managed to look away. What had she done? What had she let him do?

"You look outraged," he mused. "I think I like having you blush when I look at you."

"Would you leave, please?" she asked tightly.

"No, I don't think so," he said pleasantly. "Get dressed. Wear jeans and boots. I'm taking you riding."

"I don't want to go anywhere with you!"

"You want to go to bed with me," he corrected, smiling gently. "I can't think of anything I'd enjoy more, but I saddled the horses and left them in the stable before I came over here."

She huddled in her robe, wincing as it rubbed against her body.

"Breast sore?" he asked softly. "I'm sorry. I lost my head a little."

She flushed more and the robe tightened. "Dr. Coltrain..."

"Copper," he reminded her. "Or you can call me Jeb, if you like." He pursed his lips and his eyes were hot and possessive. "You'd really better get dressed, Lou," he murmured. "I'm still pretty hot, and aroused men are devious."

She moved back. "I have things to do..."

"Horseback riding or...?" He moved toward her.

She turned and ran for the bedroom. She couldn't believe what had just happened, and he'd said something about them becoming engaged. She must be losing her mind. Yes, that was it, she'd worried over leaving so much that she was imagining things. The whole thing had probably been a hallucination.

He'd cleared away the breakfast things by the time she washed, dressed, pulled her hair back into a ponytail with a blue ribbon and came into the kitchen with a rawhide jacket on.

He smiled. "You look like a cowgirl."

She'd felt a bit uneasy about facing him after that torrid interlude, but apparently he wasn't embarrassed. She might as well follow his lead. She managed a smile in return. "Thanks. But I may not quite merit the title. I haven't ridden in a long time."

"You'll be all right. I'll look after you."

He opened the door and let her out, waiting for her to lock it. Then he helped her into the Jaguar and drove her to his ranch.

The woods were lovely, despite their lack of leaves. The slow, easy rhythm of the horses was relaxing, even if the company wasn't. She was all too aware of Coltrain beside her, tall and elegant even on horseback. With the Stetson pulled low over his eyes, he looked so handsome that he made her toes tingle.

"Enjoying yourself?" he asked companionably.

"Oh, yes," she admitted. "I haven't been riding in a long time."

"I do more of it than I like sometimes," he confessed. "This isn't a big ranch, but I run about fifty head of pedigree cattle. I have two married cowhands who help out."

"Why do you keep cattle?" she asked.

"I don't know. It was always a dream of mine, I guess, from the time I was a boy. My grandfather had one old milk cow and I'd try to ride her." He chuckled. "I fell off a lot."

She smiled. "And your grandmother?"

"Oh, she was a cook of excellent proportions," he replied. "She made cakes that were the talk of the county. When my dad went wrong, it broke her heart, and my grandfather's. I think they took it harder because he lured me into it with him." He shook his head. "When a kid goes bad, everyone blames it on the upbringing. But my grandparents were kind, good people. They were just poor. A lot of people were...still are."

She'd noticed that he had a soft spot for his needy patients. He made extra time for them, acting as counselor and even helping them get in touch with the proper government agencies when they needed help. At Christmas, he was the first to pledge a donation to local charities and contribute to parties for children who wouldn't otherwise have presents. He was a good man, and she adored him.

"Do you want children, eventually?" she asked.

"I'd like a family," he said noncommittally. He glanced at her. "How about you?"

She grimaced. "I don't know. It would be hard for me to juggle motherhood and medicine. I know plenty of people do, but it seems like begging from Peter to pay Paul, you know? Children need a lot of care. I think plenty of social problems are caused by parents who can't get enough time off from work to look after their children. And good day care is a terrible financial headache. Why isn't day care free?" she asked abruptly. "It should be. If women are going to have to work, companies should provide access to day care for them. I know of hospitals and some companies that do it for their employees. Why can't every big company?"

"Good question. It would certainly take a burden off working parents."

"All the same, if I had kids, I'd want to be with them while they were young. I don't know if I could give up practice for so long...."

He reined in his horse and caught her bridle, bringing her horse gently around so that they were facing each other at the side. "That's not the reason. Talk to me," he said quietly. "What is it?"

She huddled into her jacket. "I hated being a child," she muttered. "I hated my father and my mother and my life."

His eyebrows lifted. "Do you think a child would hate me?"

She laughed. "Are you kidding? Children love you. Except that you don't do stitches as nicely as I do," she added.

He smiled ruefully. "Thanks for small favors."

"The secret is the chewing gum I give them afterward."

"Ah, I see. Trade a few stitches for a few cavities."

"It's sugarless gum," she said smugly.

He searched her face with warm eyes. "Touché."

He wheeled his horse and led her off down a pasture path to where the big barn was situated several hundred yards away from the house. He explained the setup, and how he'd modernized his small operation.

"I'm not as up-to-date as a lot of ranchers are, and this is peanut scale," he added. "But I've put a lot of work and time into it, and I'm moderately proud of what I've accomplished. I have a herd sire who's mentioned in some of the bigger cattle magazines."

"I'm impressed. Do I get to see him?"

"Do you want to?"

"You sound surprised. I like animals. When I started out, it was a toss-up between being a doctor and being a vet."

"What swayed you?"

"I'm not really sure. But I've never regretted my choice."

He swung out of the saddle and waited for her to dismount. He tied the horses to the corral rail and led the way into the big barn.

It was surprisingly sanitary. The walkway was paved, the stalls were spacious with metal gates and fresh hay. The cows were sleek and well fed, and the bull he'd mentioned was beautiful even by bovine standards.

"Why, he's gorgeous," she enthused as they stood at the gate and looked at him. He was red-coated, huge, streamlined and apparently docile, because he came up to let Coltrain pet his muzzle.

"How are you, old man?" he murmured affectionately. "Had enough corn, have you?"

"He's a Santa Gertrudis, isn't he?" she asked curiously.

His hand stilled on the bull's nose. "How did you know that?" he asked.

"Ted Regan is one of my patients. He had a breeder's edition of some magazine with him one day, and he left it behind. I got a good idea of coat colors, at least. We have a lot of cattlemen around here," she added. "It never hurts to know a little bit about a good bull."

"Why, Lou," he mused. "I'm impressed."

"That's a first."

He chuckled. His blue eyes twinkled down at her as he propped one big boot on the low rail of the gate. "No, it's not. You impressed me the first week you were here. You've grown on me."

"Good heavens, am I a wart?"

He caught a strand of her hair and wound it around his finger. "You're a wonder," he corrected, searching her eyes. "I didn't realize we had so much in common. Funny, isn't it? We've worked together for a year, but I've found out more about you in the past two weeks than I ever knew."

"That goes for me, too."

She dropped her eyes to his chest, where the faded shirt clung to the hard muscles. She loved the way he stood, the way he walked, the way he looked with that hat tilted rakishly over one eye. She remembered the feel of his warm arms around her and she felt suddenly cold.

Her expressions fascinated him. He watched them change, saw the hunger filter into her face.

She drew a wistful breath and looked up at him with a wan smile.

He frowned. Without understanding why, he held out a lean arm.

She accepted the invitation without question. Her body went against his, pressing close. Her arms went under his and around him, so that her hands could flatten on the muscles of his long back. She closed her eyes and laid her cheek against his chest, and listened to his heart beat.

He was surprised, yet he wasn't. It felt natural to have Lou in his arms. He drew her closer, in a purely nonsexual way, and absently stroked her hair while he watched his bull eat corn out of the trough in his pen.

"Next week is Christmas," he said above her head.

"Yes, I know. What do you do for Christmas? Do you go to friends, or invite people over?"

He laughed gently. "I used to have it with Jane, before she married," he recalled, feeling her stiffen without really thinking much about it. "But last year, since she married, I cooked a TV dinner and watched old movies all day."

She didn't answer for a minute. Despite what she'd heard about Coltrain and Jane Parker in the past year, she hadn't thought that he and Jane had been quite so close. But it seemed that they were. It depressed her more than anything had in recent weeks.

He wasn't thinking about Christmases past. He was thinking about the upcoming one. His hand explored her hair strand by strand. "Where are we going to have Christmas dinner, and who's going to cook it?" he asked matter-of-factly.

That was encouraging, that he wanted to spend Christmas with her. She couldn't refuse, even out of hurt pride. "We could have it at my house," she offered.

"I'll help cook it."

She smiled. "It would be nice to have someone to eat it with," she confessed.

"I'll make sure we're on call Christmas Eve, not Christmas Day," he promised. His arm slid down her back and drew her closer. He was aware of a kind of contentment he'd never experienced before, a belonging that he hadn't known even with Jane. Funny, he thought, until Lou came along, it had never occurred to him that he and Jane couldn't have had a serious relationship even if Todd Burke hadn't married her.

It was a sobering thought. This woman in his arms had come to mean a lot to him, without his realizing it until he'd kissed her for the first time. He laid his cheek against her head with a long sigh. It was like coming home. He'd been searching all his life for something he'd never found. He was closer to it than he'd ever been right now.

Her arms tightened around his lean waist. She could feel the wall of his chest hard against her breasts, the buckle of his belt biting into her. But it still wasn't quite close enough. She moved just a little closer, so that her legs brushed his.

He moved to accommodate her, sliding one boot higher on the fence so that she could fit against him more comfortably. But the movement aroused him and he caught his breath sharply.

"Sorry," she murmured and started to step away.

But his hand stayed her hips. "I can't help that," he said at her temple, secretly delighted at his headlong physical response to her. "But it isn't a threat."

"I didn't want to make you uncomfortable."

He smiled lazily. "I wouldn't call it that." He brushed a kiss across her forehead. "Relax," he whispered. "It's pretty public here, and I'm sure you know as well as I do that making love in a hay barn is highly unsanitary."

She laughed at his humor. "Oh, but this barn is very clean."

"Not that clean," he murmured dryly. "Besides," he added,

"it's been a long, dry spell. When I'm not in the market for a companion, I don't walk around prepared for sweet interludes."

She lifted her face and searched his mocking eyes demurely. "A long, dry spell? With Nickie prancing around half-naked to get your attention?"

He didn't laugh, as she expected him to. He traced her pert nose. "I don't have affairs," he said. "And I'm the soul of discretion in my private life. There was a widow in a city I won't name. She and I were good friends, and we supplied each other with something neither of us was comfortable spreading around. She married year before last. Since then, I've concentrated on my work and my cattle. Period."

She was curious. "Can you...well, do it...without love?"

"I was fond of her," he explained. "She was fond of me. We didn't have to be in love."

She moved restlessly.

"It would have to be love, for you, wouldn't it, Lou?" he asked. "Even desperate desire wouldn't be enough." He traced her soft lips with deliberation. "But you and I are an explosive combination. And you do love me."

She laid her forehead at his collarbone. "Yes," she admitted. "I love you. But not enough to be your mistress."

"I know that."

"Then it's hopeless."

He laughed mirthlessly. "Is it? I thought I mentioned that we could get engaged."

"Engaged isn't married," she began.

He put a finger over her lips, and he looked solemn. "I know that. Will you let me finish? We can be engaged until the first of the year, when I can afford to take a little time off for a honeymoon. We could have a New Year's wedding."

Chapter 8

"You mean, get married? Us?" she echoed blankly.

He tilted up her chin and searched her dark, troubled eyes. "Sex doesn't trouble you half as much as marriage does, is that it? Marriage means commitment, and to you, that's like imprisonment."

She grimaced. "My parents' marriage was horrible. I don't want to become like my mother."

"So you said." He traced her cheek. "But I'm not like your father. I don't drink. Well," he murmured with a sheepish grin, "maybe just once, and I had justification for that. You were letting Drew hold your hand, when you always jerked back if I touched you at all."

She was surprised. She smiled. "Was *that* why?"

He chuckled. "Yes, that was why."

"Imagine that!"

"Take one day at a time, okay?" he asked. "Let's rock along for a couple of weeks, and spend Christmas together. Then we'll talk about this again."

"All right."

He bent and kissed her softly. She pressed up against him, but he stepped back.

"None of that," he said smartly. "We're going to get to know each other before we let our glands get in the way."

"*Glands!*"

"Don't you remember glands, Doctor?" He moved toward her threateningly. "Let me explain them to you."

"I think I've got the picture," she said on a laugh. "Keep away, you lecher!"

He laughed, too. He caught her hand and tangled her fingers with his as they walked back to where the horses were tied. He'd never been quite this interested in marriage, even if he'd once had it in the back of his mind when he'd dated Jane. But when he'd had Lou close in his arms, in the barn, he'd wanted it with a maddening desire. It wasn't purely physical, although she certainly attracted him that way. But despite the way she felt about him, he had a feeling that she'd have to be carefully coaxed down the aisle. She was afraid of everything marriage stood for because of her upbringing. Their marriage wouldn't be anything like her parents', but he was going to have to convince her of that first.

They made rounds together the next morning at the hospital, and as usual, Dana was lying in wait for Coltrain.

But this time, he deliberately linked Lou's hand in his as he smiled at her.

"Good morning," he said politely.

Dana was faintly startled. "Good morning, doctors," she said hesitantly, her eyes on their linked hands.

"Lou and I became engaged yesterday," he said.

Dana's face paled. She drew a stiff breath and managed the semblance of a smile. "Oh, did you? Well, I suppose I should offer my congratulations!" She laughed. "And I had such high hopes that you and I might regain something of the past."

"The past is dead," he said firmly, his blue eyes steady on her face. "I have no inclination whatsoever to revive it."

Dana laughed uncomfortably. "So I see." She glanced at Lou's left hand. "Quite a sudden engagement, was it?" she added slyly. "No ring yet?"

Lou's hand jerked in his, but he steadied it. "When Lou makes up her mind what sort she wants, I'll buy her one," he said lazily. "I'd better get started. Wait for me in the lounge when you finish, sweet," he told Lou and squeezed her fingers before he let them go.

"I will," she promised. She smiled at Dana carelessly and went down the hall to begin her own rounds.

Dana followed her. "Well, I hope you fare better than I did," she muttered. "He's had the hots for Jane Parker for years. He asked me to marry him because he wanted me and I wouldn't give in, but even so, I couldn't compete with dear Jane," she said bitterly. "Your father was willing, so I indulged in a stupid affair, hoping I might make him jealous. That was the lunatic act of the century!"

"So I heard," Lou said stiffly, glaring at the other woman.

"I guess you did," the older woman said with a grimace. "He hated me for it. There's one man who doesn't move with the times, and he never forgets a wrong you do him." Her eyes softened as she looked at Lou's frozen face. "Your poor mother must have hated me. I know your father did. He was livid that I'd been so careless, and of course, I ruined his chances of staying here. But he didn't do so bad in Austin."

Lou had different memories of that. She couldn't lay it all at Dana's door, however. She paused at her first patient's door. "What do you mean about Jane Parker?" she asked solemnly.

"You must have heard by now that she was his first love, his only love, for years. I gave up on him after my fling with your father. I thought it was surely over between them until I came back here. She's married, you know, but she still sees Copper socially." Her eyes glittered. "They say he sits and stares at her like an oil painting when they're anywhere together. You'll find that out for yourself. I should be jealous, but I don't think I am. I feel sorry for you, because you'll always be his second choice, even if he marries you. He may want you, but he'll never stop loving Jane."

She walked away, leaving a depressed, worried Lou behind. Dana's former engagement to Coltrain sounded so much like her own "engagement" with him that it was scary. She knew that he wanted her, but he didn't show any signs of loving her. Did he still love Jane? If he did, she couldn't possibly marry him.

Nickie came up the hall when Lou had finished her rounds and was ready to join Coltrain in the lounge.

"Congratulations," she told Lou with a resigned smile. "I guess I knew I was out of the running when I saw him kiss you in the car park. Good luck. From what I hear, you'll need it." She kept walking.

Lou was dejected. It was in her whole look when she went into the doctors' lounge, where Coltrain had just finished filling out a form at the table near the window. He looked up, frowning.

"What is it?" he asked curtly. "Have Dana and Nickie been giving you a hard time?"

"Not at all," she said. "I'm just a little tired." She touched her back and winced, to convince him. "Horseback riding takes some getting used to, doesn't it?"

He smiled, glad that he'd mistaken soreness for depression. "Yes, it does. We'll have to do more of it." He picked up the folder. "Ready to go?"

"Yes."

He left the form at the nurses' station, absorbing more congratulations from the nurses, and led Lou out to his Jaguar.

"We'll take some time off this afternoon for lunch and shop for a ring," he said.

"But I don't need..."

"Of course you do," he said. "We can't let people think I'm too miserly to buy you an engagement ring!"

"But what if...?"

"Lou, it's my money," he declared.

She grimaced. Well, if he wanted to be stuck with a diamond

ring when she left town, that was his business. The engagement, as far as she was concerned, was nothing more than an attempt to get his life back on an even keel and discourage Nickie and Dana from hounding him.

She couldn't forget what had been said about Jane Parker, Jane Burke now, and she was more worried than ever. She knew how entangled he'd been with Jane, all right, because she'd considered her a rival until the day Jane married Todd Burke. Coltrain's manner even when he spoke to the woman was tender, solicitous, almost reverent.

He'd proposed. But even though he knew Lou loved him, he'd never mentioned feeling anything similar for her. He was playing make-believe. But she wondered what would happen if Jane Burke suddenly became a free woman. It would be a nightmare to live with a man who was ever yearning for someone else, someone he'd loved most of his life. Jane was a habit he apparently couldn't break. She was married. But could that fact stop him from loving her?

"You're very quiet," he remarked.

"I was thinking about Mr. Bailey," she hedged. "He really needs to see a specialist about that asthma. What do you think of referring him to Dr. Jones up in Houston?"

He nodded, diverted. "A sound idea. I'll give you the number."

They worked in harmony until the lunch hour. Then, despite her arguments, they drove to a jewelry shop in downtown Jacobsville. As bad luck would have it, Jane Burke was in there, alone, making a purchase.

She was so beautiful, Lou thought miserably. Blond, blue-eyed, with a slender figure that any man would covet.

"Why hello!" Jane said enthusiastically, and hugged Copper as if he was family.

He held her close and kissed her cheek, his smile tender, his face animated. "You look terrific," he said huskily. "How's the back? Still doing those exercises?"

"Oh, yes," she agreed. She held him by the arms and searched his eyes. "You look terrific yourself." She seemed only then to notice that he wasn't alone. She glanced at Lou. "Dr. Blakely, isn't it?" she asked politely, and altered the smile a little. "Nice to see you again."

"What are you doing here?" Coltrain asked her.

"Buying a present for my stepdaughter for Christmas. I thought she might like a nice strand of pearls. Aren't these lovely?" she asked when the clerk had taken them out of the case to show them. "I'll take them," she added, handing him her credit card.

"Is she staying with you and Todd all the time now?"

She nodded. "Her mother and stepfather and the baby are off to Africa to research his next book," she said with a grin. "We're delighted to have her all to ourselves."

"How's Todd?"

Lou heard the strained note in his voice with miserable certainty that Dana had been telling the truth.

"He's as impossible as ever." Jane chuckled. "But we scratch along, me with my horses and my clothing line and he with his computer business. He's away so much these days that I feel deserted." She lifted her eyes to his and grinned. "I don't guess you'd like to come to supper tonight?"

"Sure I would," he said without thinking. Then he made a sound. "I can't. There's a hospital board meeting."

"Oh, well," she muttered. "Another time, then." She glanced at Lou hesitantly. "Are you two out Christmas shopping—together?" she added as if she didn't think that was the case.

Coltrain stuck his hands deep into his pockets. "We're shopping for an engagement ring," he said tersely.

Her eyes widened. "For whom?"

Lou wanted to sink through the floor. She flushed to the roots of her hair and clung to her shoulder bag as if it were a life jacket.

"For Lou," Coltrain said. "We're engaged."

He spoke reluctantly, which only made Lou feel worse.

Jane's shocked expression unfroze Lou's tongue. "It's just for appearances," she said, forcing a smile. "Dana and Nickie have been hounding him."

"Oh, I see!" Jane's face relaxed, but then she frowned. "Isn't that a little dishonest?"

"It was the only way, and it's just until my contract is up, the first of the year," Lou forced herself to say. "I'll be leaving then."

Coltrain glared at her. He wasn't certain what he'd expected, but she made the proposal sound like a hoax. He hadn't asked her to marry him to ward off the other women; he'd truly wanted her to be his wife. Had she misunderstood totally?

Jane was as startled as Coltrain was. She knew that Copper wasn't the sort of man to give an engagement ring lightly, although Lou seemed to think he was. Since Dana's horrible betrayal, Copper had been impervious to women. But even Jane had heard about the hospital Christmas party and the infamous kiss. She'd hoped that Copper had finally found someone to love, although it was surprising that it would be the partner with whom he fought with so enthusiastically. Now, looking at them together, she was confused. Lou looked as if she were being tortured. Copper was taciturn and frozen. And they said it was a sham. Lou didn't love him. She couldn't, and be so lighthearted about it. Copper looked worn.

Jane glared at Lou and put a gentle hand on Coltrain's arm. "This is a stupid idea, Copper. You'll be the butt of every joke in town when Lou leaves, don't you realize it? It could even damage your reputation, hurt your practice," she told Copper intently.

His jaw tautened. "I appreciate your concern," he said gently, even as it surprised him that Jane should turn on Lou, who was more an innocent bystander than Coltrain's worst enemy.

That got through to Lou, too. She moved restlessly, averting her gaze from the diamond rings in the display case. "She's right. It *is* stupid. I can't do this," she said suddenly, her eyes full of torment. "Please, excuse me, I have to go!"

She made it out the door before the tears were visible, cutting down an alley and ducking into a department store. She went straight to the women's rest room and burst into tears, shocking a store clerk into leaving.

In the jewelry store, Coltrain stood like a statue, unspeakably shocked at Lou's rash departure and furious at having her back out just when he'd got it all arranged.

"For God's sake, did you have to do that?" Coltrain asked harshly. He rammed his hands into his pockets. "It's taken me days just to get her to agree on any pretext...!"

Jane realized, too late, what she'd done. She winced. "I didn't know," she said miserably. "It's my fault that she's bolted," Jane said quickly. "Copper, I'm sorry!"

"Not your fault," he said stiffly. "I used Dana and Nickie to accomplish this engagement, but she was reluctant from the beginning." He sighed heavily. "I guess she'll go, now, in spite of everything."

"I don't understand what's going on."

He moved a shoulder impatiently. "She's in love with me," he said roughly, and rammed his hands deeper into his pockets.

"Oh, dear." Jane didn't know what to say. She'd lashed out at the poor woman, and probably given Lou a false picture of her relationship with Copper to boot. They were good friends, almost like brother and sister, but there had been rumors around Jacobsville for years that they were secret lovers. Until she married Todd, that was. Now, she wondered how much Lou had heard and if she'd believed it. And Jane had brazenly invited him to supper, ignoring Lou altogether.

She grimaced. "I've done it now, haven't I? I would have included her in my invitation if I'd had any idea. I thought she was just tagging along with you on her lunch hour!"

"I'd better go after her," he said reluctantly.

"It might be best if you didn't," she replied. "She's hurt. She'll want to be alone for a while, I should think."

"I can't strand her in town." He felt worse than he could ever remember feeling. "Maybe you're both right, and this whole thing was a stupid idea."

"If you don't love her, it certainly was," she snapped at him. "What are you up to? Is it really just to protect you from a couple of lovesick women? I'm shocked. A few years ago, you'd have cussed them both to a fare-thee-well and been done with it."

He didn't reply. His face closed up and his blue eyes glittered at her. "My reasons are none of your business," he said, shutting her out.

Obviously Lou had to mean something to him. Jane felt even worse. She made a face. "We were very close once. I thought you could talk to me about anything."

"Anything except Lou," he said shortly.

"Oh." Her eyes were first stunned and then amused.

"You can stop speculating, too," he added irritably, turning away.

"She sounds determined to leave."

"We'll see about that."

Despite Jane's suggestion, he went off toward the department store where Lou had vanished and strode back to the women's rest room. He knew instinctively that she was there. He caught the eye of a female clerk.

"Could you ask Dr. Blakely to come out of there, please?"

"Dr. Blakely?"

"She's so high—" he indicated her height with his hand up to his nose "—blond hair, dark eyes, wearing a beige suit."

"Oh, her! She's a doctor? Really? My goodness, I thought doctors never showed their emotions. She was crying as if her heart would break. Sure, I'll get her for you."

He felt like a dog. He'd made her cry. The thought of Lou, so brave and private a person, with tears in her eyes made him hurt inside. And it had been so unnecessary. If Jane had only kept her pretty mouth shut! She was like family, and she overstepped the bounds sometimes with her comments about how Coltrain should live his life. He'd been more than fond of her once, and he still had a soft spot for her, but it was Lou who was disrupting his whole life.

He leaned against the wall, his legs and arms crossed, and waited. The female clerk reappeared, smiled reassuringly, and went to wait on a customer.

A minute later, a subdued and dignified Lou came out of the small room, her chin up. Her eyes were slightly red, but she didn't look as if she needed anyone's pity.

"I'm ready to go if you are," she said politely.

He searched her face and decided that this wasn't the time for a row. They still had to get lunch and get back to the office.

He turned, leaving her to follow. "I'll stop by one of the hamburger joints and we can get a burger and fries."

"I'll eat mine at the office, if you don't mind," she said wearily. "I'm not in the mood for a crowd."

Neither was he. He didn't argue. He opened the car door and let her in, then he went by the drive-in window of the beef place and they carried lunch back.

Lou went directly into her office and closed the door. She hardly tasted what she was eating. Her heart felt as if it had been burned alive. She knew what Dana meant now. Jane Parker was as much a part of Coltrain's life as his cattle, his practice. No woman, no matter how much she loved him, could ever compete with his love for the former rodeo star.

She'd been living in a fool's paradise, but fortunately there was no harm done. They could say that the so-called "engagement" had been a big joke. Surely Coltrain could get Nickie and Dana out of his hair by simply telling them the truth, that he wasn't interested. God knew, once he got started, he wasn't shy about expressing his feelings any other time, regardless of who was listening. Which brought to mind the question of why he'd asked her to marry him. He wasn't in love with her. He wanted her. Had that been the reason? Was he getting even with Jane because she'd married and deserted him? She worried the question until she finished eating. Then her patients kept her occupied for the rest of the day, so that she had no time to think.

Jane had wondered if she could help undo the damage she'd already done to Copper's life, and at last she came up with a solution. She decided to give a farewell party for Lou. She called Coltrain a few days later to tell him the news.

"Christmas is next week," he said shortly. "And I doubt if she'd come. She only speaks to me when she has to. I can't get near her anymore."

That depressed Jane even more. "Suppose I phone her?" she asked.

"Oh, I know she won't talk to you." He laughed without humor. "We're both in her bad books."

Jane sighed. "Then who can we have talk to her?"

"Try Drew Morris," he said bitterly. "She likes him."

That note in his voice was disturbing. Surely he knew that Drew was still mourning his late wife. If he and Lou were friends, it was nothing more than that, despite any social outings together.

"You think she'd listen to Drew?" she asked.

"Why not?"

"I'll try, then."

"Don't send out any invitations until she gives you an answer," he added. "She's been hurt enough, one way or the other."

"Yes, I know," Jane said gently. "I had no idea, Copper. I really meant well."

"I know that. She doesn't."

"I guess she's heard all the old gossip, too."

He hadn't considered that. "What old gossip?"

"About us," she persisted. "That we had something going until I married Todd."

He smoothed his fingers absently over the receiver. "She might have, at that," he said slowly. "But she must know that—" He stopped dead. She'd have heard plenty from Dana, who had always considered Jane, not her affair with Fielding Blakely, the real reason for their broken engagement. Others in the hospital knew those old rumors, too, and Jane had given Lou the wrong impression of their relationship in the jewelry store.

"I'm right, aren't I?" Jane asked.

"You might be."

"What are you going to do?"

"What can I do?" he asked shortly. "She doesn't really want to marry anyone."

"You said she loves you," she reminded him.

"Yes, and she does. It's the only thing I'm sure of. But she doesn't want to marry me. She's so afraid that she'll become like her mother, blindly accepting faults and abuse without question, all in the name of love."

"Poor girl," she said genuinely. "What a life she must have had."

"I expect it was worse than we'll ever know," he agreed. "Well, call Drew and see if he can get through to her."

"If he can, will you come, too?"

"It would look pretty bad if I didn't, wouldn't it?" he asked dryly. "They'd say we were so antagonistic toward each other that we couldn't even get along for a farewell party. And coming on the heels of our 'engagement,' they'd really have food for thought."

"I'd be painted as the scarlet woman who broke it up, wouldn't I?" Jane groaned. "Todd would love that! He's still not used to small-town life."

"Maybe Drew can reach her. If he can't, you'll have to cancel it. We can't embarrass her."

"I wouldn't dream of it."

"I know that. Jane, thanks."

"For what?" she asked. "I'm the idiot who got you into this mess in the first place. The least I owe is to try to make amends for what I said to her. I'll let you know what happens."

"Do that."

He went back to work, uncomfortably aware of Lou's calm

demeanor. She didn't even look ruffled after all the turmoil. Of course, he remembered that she'd been crying like a lost child in the department store after Jane's faux pas. But that could have been so much more than a broken heart.

She hadn't denied loving him, but could love survive a year of indifference alternating with vicious antagonism, such as he'd given her? Perhaps loving him was a sort of habit that she'd finally been cured of. After all, he'd given her no reason to love him, even to like him. He'd missed most of his chances there. But if Drew could convince her to come to a farewell party, on neutral ground, Coltrain had one last chance to change her mind about him. That was his one hope; the only one he had.

Chapter 9

Drew invited Lou to lunch the next day. It was Friday, the week before the office closed for Christmas holidays. Christmas Eve would be on a week from Saturday night, and Jane had changed her mind about dates. She wanted to give the farewell party the following Friday, the day before New Year's Eve. That would, if Lou didn't reconsider her decision, be Lou's last day as Coltrain's partner.

"I'm surprised," Lou told him as they ate quiche at a local restaurant. "You haven't invited me to lunch in a long time. What's on your mind?"

"It could be just on food."

She laughed. "Pull the other one."

"Okay. I'm a delegation of one."

She held her fork poised over the last morsel of quiche on her plate. "From whom?"

"Jane Burke."

She put the fork down, remembering. Her expression hardened. "I have nothing to say to her."

"She knows that. It's why she asked me to talk to you. She got the wrong end of the stick and she's sorry. I'm to make her apologies to you," he added. "But she also wants to do something to make up for what she said to you. She wants to give you a farewell party on the day before New Year's Eve.''

She glared at Drew. "I don't want anything to do with any parties given by that woman. I won't go!''

His eyebrows lifted. "Well! You are miffed, aren't you?''

"Accusing me of trying to ruin Jebediah's reputation and destroy his privacy...how dare she! I'm not the one who's being gossiped about in connection with him! And she's married!''

He smiled wickedly. "Lou, you're as red as a beet.''

"I'm mad,'' she said shortly. "That...woman! How dare she!''

"She and Copper are friends. Period. That's all they've ever been. Are you listening?''

"Sure, I'm listening. Now,'' she added, leaning forward, "tell me he wasn't ever in love with her. Tell me he isn't still in love with her.''

He wanted to, but he had no idea of Coltrain's feelings for Jane. He knew that Coltrain had taken her marriage hard, and that he seemed sometimes to talk about her to the exclusion of everyone else. But things had changed in the past few weeks, since the hospital Christmas dance the first week of December.

"You see?'' she muttered. "You can't deny it. He may have proposed to me, but it was...''

"Proposed?"

"Didn't you know?'' She lifted her coffee cup to her lips and took a sip. "He wanted me to pretend to be engaged to him, just to get Nickie and Dana off his back. Then he decided that we might as well get married for real. He caught me at a weak moment,'' she added, without details, "and we went to buy an engagement ring. But Jane was there. She was rude to me,'' she said miserably, "and Jebediah didn't say a word to stop her. In fact, he acted as if I wasn't even there.''

"And that was what hurt most, wasn't it?'' he queried gently.

"I guess it was. I have no illusions about him, you know,'' she added with a rueful smile. "He likes kissing me, but he's not in love with me.''

"Does he know how you feel?"

She nodded. "I don't hide things well. It would be hard to miss."

He caught her hand and held it gently. "Lou, isn't he worth taking a chance on?" he asked. "You could let Jane throw this party for you, because she badly wants to make amends. Then you could talk to Copper and get him to tell you exactly why he wants to marry you. You might be surprised."

"No, I wouldn't. I know why he wants to marry me," she replied. "But I don't want to get married. I'm crazy about him, that's the truth, but I've seen marriage. I don't want it."

"You haven't seen a good marriage," he emphasized. "Lou, I had one. I had twelve years of almost ethereal happiness. Marriage is what you make of it."

"My mother excused every brutal thing my father did," she said shortly.

"That sort of love isn't love," he said quietly. "It's a form of domination. Don't you know the difference? If she'd loved your father, she'd have stood up to him and tried to help him stop drinking, stop using drugs."

She felt as if her eyes had suddenly been opened. She'd never seen her parents' relationship like that. "But he was terrible to her..."

"Codependence," he said to her. "You must have studied basic psychology in college. Don't you remember any of it?"

"Yes, but they were my parents!"

"Your parents, anybody, can be part of a dysfunctional family." He smiled at her surprise. "Didn't you know? You grew up in a dysfunctional family, not a normal one. That's why you have such a hard time accepting the idea of marriage." He smoothed her hand with his fingers and smiled. "Lou, I had a normal upbringing. I had a mother and father who doted on me, who supported me and encouraged me. I was loved. When I married, it was a good, solid, happy marriage. They are possible, if you love someone and have things in common, and are willing to compromise.''

She studied the wedding ring on Drew's left hand. He still wore it even after being widowed.

"It's possible to be happily married?" she asked, entertaining that possibility for the first time.

"Of course."

"Coltrain doesn't love me," she said.

"Make him."

She laughed. "That's a joke. He hated me from the beginning. I never knew it was because of my father, until I overheard him talking to you. I was surprised later when he was so cool to Dana, because he'd been bitter about her betrayal. But when I found out how close he was to Jane Burke, I guess I gave up entirely. You can't fight a ghost, Drew." She looked up. "And you know it, because no woman will ever be able to come between you and your memories. How would you feel if you found out some woman was crazily in love with you right now?"

He was stunned by the question. "Well, I don't know. I guess I'd feel sorry for her," he admitted.

"Which is probably how Coltrain feels about me, and might even explain why he offered to be engaged to me," she added. "It makes sense, doesn't it?"

"Lou, you don't propose to people out of pity."

"Coltrain might. Or out of revenge, to get back at Jane for marrying someone else. Or to get even with Dana."

"Coltrain isn't that scatty."

"Men are unpredictable when they're in love, aren't they?" she mused. "I wish he loved me, Drew. I'd marry him, with all my doubts and misgivings, in a minute if I thought there was half a chance that he did. But he doesn't. I'd know if he did feel that way. Somehow, I'd know."

He dropped his gaze to their clasped hands. "I'm sorry."

"Me, too. I've been invited to join a practice in Houston. I'm going Monday to speak with them, but they've tentatively accepted me.'' She lifted her sad face. ''I understand that Coltrain is meeting some prospects too. So I suppose he's finally taken me at my word that I want to leave.''

''Don't you know?''

She shrugged. ''We don't speak.''

''I see.'' So it was that bad, he thought. Coltrain and Lou had both withdrawn, afraid to take that final step to commitment. She had good reasons, but what were Copper's? he wondered. Did he really feel pity for Lou and now he was sorry he'd proposed? Or was Lou right, and he was still carrying a torch for Jane?

''Jane is a nice woman,'' he said. ''You don't know her, but she isn't the kind of person who enjoys hurting other people. She feels very unhappy about what she said. She wants to make it up to you. Let her. It will be a nice gesture on your part and on hers.''

''Dr. Coltrain will come,'' she muttered.

''He'd better,'' he said, ''or the gossips will say he's glad to be rid of you.''

She shook her head. ''You can't win for losing.''

''That's what I've been trying to tell you. Let Jane give the party. Lou, you'd like her if you got to know her. She's had a hard time of it since the wreck that took her father's life. Just being able to walk again at all is a major milestone for her.''

''I remember,'' she said. And she did, because Coltrain had been out at the ranch every waking minute looking after the woman.

''Will you do it?''

She took a long breath and let it out. ''All right.''

''Great! I'll call Jane the minute I get home and tell her. You won't regret it. Lou, I wish you'd hold off about that spot in Houston.''

She shook her head. ''No, I won't do that. I have to get away. A fresh start is what I need most. I'm sure I won't be missed. After all, Dr. Coltrain didn't want me in the first place.''

He grimaced, because they both knew her present circumstances were Drew's fault. Saying again that he meant well wouldn't do a bit of good.

"Thanks for lunch," she said, remembering her manners.

"That was my pleasure. You know I'll be going to Maryland to have Christmas with my in-laws, as usual. So Merry Christmas, if I don't see you before I leave."

"You, too, Drew," she said with genuine affection.

It wasn't until the next Thursday afternoon that the office closed early for Christmas holidays—if Friday and Monday, added to the weekend, qualified as holidays—that Coltrain came into Lou's office. Lou had been to Houston and formally applied for a position in the family practitioner group. She'd also been accepted, but she hadn't been able to tell Coltrain until today, because he'd been so tied up with preholiday surgeries and emergencies.

He looked worn-out, she thought. There were new lines in his lean face, and his eyes were bloodshot from lack of sleep. He looked every year of his age.

"You couldn't just tell me, you had to put it in writing?" he asked, holding up the letter she'd written him.

"It's legal this way," she said politely. "I'm very grateful for the start you gave me."

He didn't say anything. He looked at the letter from the Houston medical group. It was written on decal-edge bond, very expensive, and the lettering on the letterhead was embossed.

"I know this group," he said. "They're high-powered city physicians, and they practice supermarket medicine. Do you realize what that means? You'll be expected to spend five minutes or less with every patient. A buzzer will sound to alert you when that time is up. As the most junior partner, you'll get all the dirty jobs, all the odd jobs, and you'll be expected to stay on call on weekends and holidays for the first year. Or until they can get another partner, more junior than you are."

"I know. They told me that." They had. It had depressed her no end.

He folded his arms across his chest and leaned back against the wall, his stethoscope draped around his neck. "We haven't talked."

"There's nothing to say," she replied, and she smiled kindly. "I notice that Nickie and Dana have become very businesslike, even to me. I'd say you were over the hump."

"I asked you to marry me," he said. "I was under the impression that you'd agreed and that was why we were picking out a ring."

The memory of that afternoon hurt. She lowered her eyes to the clipboard she held against her breasts. "You said it was to get Nickie and Dana off your back."

"You didn't want to get married at all," he reminded her.

"I still don't."

He smiled coldly. "And you're not in love with me?"

She met his gaze levelly. This was no time to back down. "I was infatuated with you," she said bluntly. "Perhaps it was because you were out of reach."

"You wanted me. Explain that."

"I'm human," she told him, blushing a little. "You wanted me, too, so don't look so superior."

"I hear you're coming to Jane's party."

"Drew talked me into it." She smoothed her fingers over the cold clipboard. "You and Jane can't help it," she said. "I understand."

"Damn it! You sound just like her husband!"

She was shocked at the violent whip of his deep voice. He was furious, and it showed.

"Everyone knows you were in love with her," she faltered.

"Yes, I was," he admitted angrily, and for the first time. "But she's married now, Lou."

"I know. I'm sorry," she said gently. "I really am. It must be terrible for you...."

He threw up his hands. "My God!"

"It's not as if you could help it, either of you," she continued sadly.

He just shook his head. "I can't get through to you, can I?" he asked with a bite in his deep voice. "You won't listen."

"There's really nothing to say," she told him. "I hope you've found someone to replace me when I go."

"Yes, I have. He's a recent graduate of Johns Hopkins. He wanted to do some rural practice before he made up his mind where he wanted to settle." He gazed at her wan face. "He starts January 2."

She nodded. "That's when I start, in Houston." She tugged the clipboard closer.

"We could spend Christmas together," he suggested.

She shook her head. She didn't speak. She knew words would choke her.

His shoulders rose and fell. "As you wish," he said quietly. "Have a good Christmas, then."

"Thanks. You, too."

She knew that she sounded choked. She couldn't help herself. She'd burned her bridges. She hadn't meant to. Perhaps she had a death wish. She'd read and studied about people who were basically self-destructive, who destroyed relationships before they could begin, who found ways to sabotage their own success and turn it to failure. Perhaps she'd become such a person, due to her upbringing. Either way, it didn't matter now. She'd given up Coltrain and was leaving Jacobsville. Now all she had to do was survive Jane's little going-away party and get out of town.

Coltrain paused in the doorway, turning his head back toward her. His eyes were narrow, curious, assessing. She didn't look as if the decision she'd made had lifted her spirits any. And the expression on her face wasn't one of triumph or pleasure.

"If Jane hadn't turned up in the jewelry store, would you have gone through with it?" he asked abruptly.

Her hands tightened on the clipboard. "I'll never know."

He leaned against the doorjamb. "You don't want to hear this, but I'm going to say it. Jane and I were briefly more than friends. It was mostly on my side. She loves her husband and wants nothing to do with anyone else. Whatever I felt for her is in the past now.''

"I'm glad, for your sake," she said politely.

"Not for yours?" he asked.

She bit her lower lip, worriedly.

He let his blue gaze fall to her mouth. It lingered there so long that her heart began to race, and she couldn't quite breathe properly. His gaze lifted then, to catch hers, and she couldn't break it. Her toes curled inside her sensible shoes, her heart ran wild. She had to fight the urge to go to him, to press close to his lean, fit body and beg him to kiss her blind.

"You think you're over me?" he drawled softly, so that his voice didn't carry. "In a pig's eye, Doctor!"

He pushed away from the door and went on his way, whistling to himself as he went down the corridor to his next patient.

Lou, having given herself away, muttered under her breath and went to read the file on her next patient. But she waited until her hands stopped shaking before she opened the examining room door and went in.

They closed up the office. Coltrain had been called away at the last minute to an emergency at the hospital, which made things easier for Lou. She'd be bound to run into him while she was making her rounds, but that was an occupational hazard, and there would be plenty of other people around. She wouldn't have to worry about being alone with him. Or so she thought.

When she finished her rounds late in the afternoon, she stopped by the nurses' station to make sure they'd been able to contact a new patient's husband, who had been out of town when she was admitted.

"Yes, we found him," the senior nurse said with a smile. "In fact, he's on his way over here right now."

"Thanks," she said.

"No need. It goes with the job," she was assured.

She started back down the hall to find Coltrain coming from the emergency room. He looked like a thundercloud, all bristling bad temper. His red hair flamed under the corridor lights, and his blue eyes were sparking.

He caught Lou's arm, turned and drew her along with him without saying a word. People along the corridor noticed and grinned amusedly.

"What in the world are you doing?" she asked breathlessly.

"I want you to tell a—" he bit off the word he wanted to say "—*gentleman* in the emergency room that I was in the office all morning."

She gaped at him, but he didn't stop or even slow down. He dragged her into a cubicle where a big, angry-looking blond man was sitting on the couch having his hand bandaged.

Coltrain let Lou go and nodded curtly toward the other man. "Well, tell him!" He shot the words at Lou.

She gave him a stunned glance, but after a minute, she turned back to the tall man and said, "Dr. Coltrain was in the office all morning. He couldn't have escaped if he'd wanted to, because we had twice our usual number of patients, anticipating that we'd be out of the office over the holidays."

The blond man relaxed a little, but he was still glaring at Coltrain when there was a small commotion in the corridor and Jane Burke came in the door, harassed and frightened.

"Todd! Cherry said that you'd had an accident and she had to call an ambulance…!" She grabbed the blond man's hand and fought tears. "I thought you were killed!"

"Not hardly," he murmured. He drew her head to his shoulder and held her gently. "Silly woman." He chuckled. "I'm all right. I slammed the car door on my hand. It isn't even broken, just cut and bruised."

Jane looked at Coltrain. "Is that true?"

He nodded, still irritated at Burke.

Jane looked from him to Lou and back to her husband. "Now what's wrong?" she asked heavily.

Todd just glowered. He didn't say anything.

"You and I had been meeting secretly this morning at your house, while he and Cherry were away," Coltrain informed her. "Because the mailman saw a gray Jaguar sitting in your driveway."

"Yes, he did," Jane said shortly. "It belongs to the new divisional manager of the company that makes my signature line of leisure wear. *She* has a gray Jaguar exactly like Copper's."

Burke's hard cheekbones flushed a little.

"That's why you slammed the door on your hand, right?" she muttered. "Because the mailman is our wrangler's sister and he couldn't wait to tell you what your wife was doing behind your back! He'll be lucky if I don't have him for lunch!"

The flush got worse. "Well, I didn't know!" Todd snapped.

Coltrain slammed his clipboard down hard on the examination couch at Burke's hip. "That does it, by God," he began hotly.

He looked threatening and Burke stood up, equally angry.

"Now, Copper," Jane interrupted. "This isn't the place."

Burke didn't agree, but he'd already made a fool of himself once. He wasn't going to try for twice. He glanced at Lou, who looked as miserable as he felt. "They broke up your engagement, I understand," he added. "Pity they didn't just marry each other to begin with!"

Lou studied his glittery eyes for a moment, oblivious to the other two occupants of the cubicle. It was amazing how quickly things fell into place in her mind, and at once. She leaned against the examination couch. "Dr. Coltrain is the most decent man I know," she told Todd Burke. "He isn't the sort to do things in an underhanded way, and he doesn't sneak around. If you trusted your wife, Mr. Burke, you wouldn't listen to old gossip or invented tales. Small towns are hotbeds of rumor, that's normal. But only an idiot believes everything he hears."

Coltrain's eyebrows had arched at the unexpected defense.

"Thanks, Lou," Jane said quietly. "That's more than I deserve from you, but thank you." She turned back to her husband. "She's absolutely right," Jane told her husband. She was mad, too, and it showed. "I married you because I loved you. I still love you, God knows why! You won't even listen when I tell you the truth. You'd rather cling to old gossip about Copper and me."

Lou blushed scarlet, because she could have been accused of the same thing.

She wouldn't look at Coltrain at all.

"Well, here's something to take your mind off your foul suspicions," Jane continued furiously. "I was going to wait to tell you, but you can hear it now. I'm pregnant! And, no, it isn't Copper's!"

Burke gasped. "Jane!" He exploded, his injured hand forgotten as he moved forward to pull her hungrily into his arms. "Jane, is it true?"

"Yes, it's true," she muttered. "Oh, you idiot! You idiot…!"

He was kissing her, so she had to stop talking. Lou, a little embarrassed, edged out of the cubicle and moved away, only to find Coltrain right beside her as she left the emergency room.

"Maybe that will satisfy him," he said impatiently. "Thank you for the fierce defense," he added. "Hell of a pity that you didn't believe a word you were saying!"

She stuck her hands into her slacks pockets. "I believe she loves her husband," she said quietly. "And I believe that there's nothing going on between the two of you."

"Thanks for nothing."

"Your private life is your own business, Dr. Coltrain, none of mine," she said carelessly. "I'm already a memory."

"By your own damn choice."

The sarcasm cut deep. They walked through the parking lot to the area reserved for physicians and surgeons, and she stopped beside her little Ford.

"Drew loved his wife very much," she said. "He never got over losing her. He still spends holidays with his in-laws because he feels close to her that way, even though she's dead. I asked him how he'd feel if he knew that a woman was in love with him. Know what he said? He said that he'd pity her."

"Do you have a point?" he asked.

"Yes." She turned and looked up at him. "You haven't really gotten over Jane Burke yet. You have nothing to offer anyone else until you do. That's why I wouldn't marry you."

His brows drew together while he searched her face. He didn't say a word. He couldn't.

"She's part of your life," she continued. "A big part of it. You can't let go of the past, even if she can. I understand. Maybe someday you'll come to terms with it. Until you do, it's no good trying to be serious about anyone else."

He jiggled the change in his pockets absently. His broad shoulders rose and fell. "She was just starting into rodeo when I came back here as an intern in the hospital. She fell and they brought her to me. We had an instant rapport. I started going to watch her ride, she went out with me when I was free. She was special. Her father and I became friends as well, and when I bought my ranch, he helped me learn the ropes and start my herd. Jane and I have known each other a long, long time."

"I know that." She studied a button on his dark jacket. "She's very pretty, and Drew says she has a kind nature."

"Yes."

Her shoulders rose and fell. "I have to go."

He put out a lean hand and caught her shoulder, preventing her from turning away. "I never told her about my father."

She was surprised. She didn't think he had any secrets from Jane. She lifted her eyes and found him staring at her intently, as if he were trying to work out a puzzle.

"Curious, isn't it?" he mused aloud. "There's another curious thing, but I'm not ready to share that just yet."

He moved closer and she wanted to move away, to stop him... No, she didn't. His head bent and his mouth closed on hers, brushing, lightly probing. She yielded without a protest, her arms sliding naturally around his waist, her mouth opening to the insistence of his lips. He kissed her, leaning his body heavily on hers, so that she could feel the metal of the car at her back and his instant, explosive response to her soft warmth.

She made a sound, and he smiled against her lips.

"What?" He bit off the words against her lips.

"It's…very…public," she breathed.

He lifted his head and looked around. The parking lot was dotted with curious onlookers. So was the emergency room ramp.

"Hell," he said irritably, drawing away from her. "Come home with me," he suggested, still breathing roughly.

She shook her head before her willpower gave out. "I can't."

"Coward," he drawled.

She flushed. "All right, I want to," she said fiercely. "But I won't, so there. Damn you! It isn't fair to play on people's weaknesses!"

"Sure it is," he said, correcting her. He grinned at her maddeningly. "Come on, be daring. Take a chance! Risk everything on a draw of the cards. You live like a scientist, every move debated, planned. For once in your life, be reckless!"

"I'm not the reckless sort," she said as she fought to get her breath back. "And you shouldn't be, either." She glanced ruefully toward the emergency room exit, where a tall blond man and a pretty blond woman were standing, watching. "Was it for her benefit?" she added, nodding toward them.

He glanced over her shoulder. "I didn't know they were there," he said genuinely.

She laughed. "Sure." She pulled away from him, unlocked her car, got in and drove off. Her legs were wobbly, but they'd stop shaking eventually. Maybe the rest of her would, too. Coltrain was driving her crazy. She was very glad that she'd be leaving town soon.

Chapter 10

It didn't help that the telephone rang a few minutes after Lou got home.

"Still shaky, are we?" Coltrain drawled.

She fumbled to keep from dropping the receiver. "What do you want?" she faltered.

"An invitation to Christmas dinner, of course," he said. "I don't want to sit in front of the TV all day eating TV dinners."

She was still angry at him for making a public spectacle of them for the second time. The hospital would buzz with the latest bit of gossip for weeks. At least she wouldn't have long to put up with it.

"TV dinners are good for you," she said pointedly.

"Home cooking is better. I'll make the dressing and a fruit salad if you'll do turkey and rolls."

She hesitated. She wanted badly to spend that day with him, but in the long run, it would make things harder.

"Come on," he coaxed in a silky tone. "You know you want to. If you're leaving town after the first, it will be one of the last times we spend together. What have you got to lose?"

My self-respect, my honor, my virtue, my pride, she thought. But aloud, she said, "I suppose it wouldn't hurt."

He chuckled. "No, it wouldn't. I'll see you at eleven on Christmas morning."

He hung up before she could change her mind. "I don't want to," she told the telephone. "This is a terrible mistake, and I'm sure that I'll regret it for the rest of my life."

After a minute, she realized that she was talking to a piece of equipment. She shook her head sadly. Coltrain was driving her out of her mind.

She went to the store early on Christmas Eve and bought a turkey. The girl at the check-out stand was one of her patients. She grinned as she totaled the price of the turkey, the bottle of wine and the other groceries Lou had bought to cook Christmas dinner.

"Expecting company, Doctor?" she teased.

Lou flushed, aware that the woman behind her was one of Coltrain's patients. "No. No. I'm going to cook the turkey and freeze what I don't eat."

"Oh." The girl sounded disappointed.

"Going to drink all that wine alone, too?" the woman behind her asked wickedly. "And you a doctor!"

Lou handed over the amount the cashier asked for. "I'm not on duty on Christmas Day," she said irritably. "Besides, I cook with wine!"

"You won't cook with that," the cashier noted. She held up the bottle and pointed to the bottom of the label. It stated, quite clearly, Nonalcoholic Wine.

Lou had grabbed the bottle from the wrong aisle. But it worked to her advantage. She grinned at the woman behind her, who looked embarrassed.

The clerk packaged up her purchases and Lou pushed them out to her car. At least she'd gotten around that ticky little episode.

Back home, she put the turkey on to bake and made rolls from scratch. Nonalcoholic wine wasn't necessarily a bad thing, she told herself. She could serve it at dinner without having to worry about losing her wits with Coltrain.

The weather was sunny and nice, and the same was predicted for the following day. A white Christmas was out of the question, of course, but she wondered what it would be like to have snow on the ground.

She turned on the television that night, when the cooking was done and everything was put into the refrigerator for the next day. Curled up in her favorite armchair in old jeans, a sweatshirt and in her sock feet, she was relaxing after her housecleaning and cooking when she heard a car drive up.

It was eight o'clock and she wasn't on call. She frowned as she went to the front door. A gray Jaguar was sitting in the driveway and as she looked, a tall, redheaded man in jeans and a sweatshirt and boots got out of the car carrying a big box.

"Open the door," he called as he mounted the steps.

"What's that?" she asked curiously.

"Food and presents."

She was surprised. She hadn't expected him tonight and she fumbled and faltered as she let him in and closed the door again.

He unloaded the box in the kitchen. "Salad." He indicated a covered plastic bowl. "Dressing." He indicated a foil-covered pan. "And a chocolate pound cake. No, I didn't make it," he added when she opened her mouth. "I bought it. I can't bake a cake. Is there room in the fridge for this?"

"You could have called to ask before you brought it," she reminded him.

He grinned. "If I'd phoned, you'd have listened to the answering machine and when you knew it was me, you'd have pretended not to be home."

She flushed. He was right. It was disconcerting to have someone so perceptive second-guessing her every move. "Yes, there's room."

She opened the refrigerator door and helped him fit his food in.

He went back to the big box and pulled out two packages. "One for me to give you—" he held up one "—and one for you to give me."

She glared at him. "I got you a present," she muttered.

His eyebrows shot up. "You did?"

Her lower lip pulled down. "Just because I didn't plan to spend Christmas with you didn't mean I was low enough not to get you something."

"You didn't give it to me at the office party," he recalled.

She flushed. "You didn't give me anything at the office party, either."

He smiled. "I was saving it for tomorrow."

"So was I," she returned.

"Can I put these under the tree?"

She shrugged. "Sure."

Curious, she followed him into the living room. The tree was live and huge; it covered the whole corner and reached almost to the nine-foot ceiling. It was full of lights and decorations and under it a big metal electric train sat on its wide tracks waiting for power to move it.

"I didn't notice that when I was here before," he said, delighted by the train. He stooped to look at it more closely. "This is an American Flyer by Lionel!" he exclaimed. "You've had this for a while, haven't you?"

"It's an antique," she recalled. "My mother got it for me." She smiled. "I love trains. I have two more sets and about a mile of track in a box in the closet, but it seemed sort of pointless to set all those trains up with just me to run them."

He looked up at her with sparkling eyes. "Which closet are they in?" he asked in a conspiratorial tone.

"The hall closet." Her eyes brightened. "You like trains?"

"Do I like trains? I have HO scale, N scale, G scale and three sets of new Lionel O scale trains at home."

She gasped. "Oh, my goodness!"

"That's what I say. Come on!"

He led her to the hall closet, opened it, found the boxes and started handing them out to her.

Like two children, they sat on the floor putting track together with switches and accessories for the next two hours. Lou made coffee and they had it on the floor while they made connections and set up the low wooden scale buildings that Lou had bought to go with the sets.

When they finished, she turned on the power. The wooden buildings were lit. So were the engines and the cabooses and several passenger cars.

"I love to sit and watch them run in the dark," she said breathlessly as he turned on the switch box and the trains began to move. "It's like watching over a small village with the people all snug in their houses."

"I know what you mean." He sprawled, chest down, on the floor beside her to watch the trains chug and whistle and run around the various tracks. "God, this is great! I had no idea you liked trains!"

"Same here," she said, chuckling. "I always felt guilty about having them, in a way. Somewhere out there, there must be dozens of little kids who would do anything for just one train and a small track to run it on. And here I've got all this and I never play with it."

"I know how it is. I don't even have a niece or nephew to share mine with."

"When did you get your first train?"

"When I was eight. My granddad bought it for me so he could play with it," he added with a grin. "He couldn't afford a big set, of course, but I didn't care. I never had so much fun." His face hardened at the memories. "When Dad took me to Houston, I missed the train almost as much as I missed my granddad and grandmother. It was a long time before I got back there." He shrugged. "The train still worked by then, though, and it was more fun when the threat of my father was gone."

She rolled onto her side, peering at him in the dim light from the tree and the small village. "You said that you never told Jane about your father."

"I didn't," he replied. "It was something I was deeply ashamed of for a long time."

"Children do what they're told, whether it's right or wrong," she reminded him. "You can't be held responsible for everything."

"I knew it was wrong," he agreed. "But my father was a brutal man, and when I was a young boy, I was afraid of him." His head turned. He smiled at her. "You'd understand that."

"Yes."

He rested his chin on his hands and watched the trains wistfully. "I took my medicine—juvenile hall and years of probation. But people helped me to change. I wanted to pass that on, to give back some of the care that had been given to me. That's why I went into medicine. I saw it as an opportunity to help people."

"And you have," she said. Her eyes traced the length of his fit, hard-muscled body lovingly. He was so different away from the office. She'd never known him like this, and so soon, it would all be over. She'd go away. She wouldn't see him again. Her sad eyes went back to the trains. The sound of them was like a lullaby, comforting, delightful to the ears.

"We need railroad caps and those wooden whistles that sound like old steam engines," he remarked.

She smiled. "And railroad gloves and crossing guards and flashing guard lights."

"If there was a hobby shop nearby, we could go and get them. But everything would be closed up on Christmas Eve, anyway."

"I guess so."

He pursed his lips, without looking at her. "If you stayed, after the New Year, we could pool our layouts and have one big one. We could custom-design our own buildings and bridges, and we could go in together and buy one of those big transformer outfits that runs dozens of accessories."

She was thinking more of spending that kind of time with Coltrain than running model engines, but it sounded delightful all the same. She sighed wistfully. "I would have enjoyed that," she murmured. "But I've signed a new contract. I have to go."

"Contracts can be broken," he said. "There's always an escape clause if you look hard enough."

Her hips shifted on the rug they were lying on. "Too many people are gossiping about us already," she said. "Even at the grocery store, the clerk noticed that I bought a turkey and wine and the lady behind me said I couldn't possibly be going to drink it alone."

"You bought wine?" he mused.

"Nonalcoholic wine," she said, correcting him.

He chuckled. "On purpose?"

"Not really. I picked up the wrong bottle. But it was just as well. The lady behind me was making snide comments about it." She sighed. "It rubbed me the wrong way. She wouldn't have known that my father was an alcoholic."

"How did he manage to keep his job?"

"He had willing young assistants who covered for him. And finally, the hospital board forced him into early retirement. He *had* been a brilliant surgeon," she reminded him. "It isn't easy to destroy a career like that."

"It would have been better than letting him risk other people's lives."

"But he didn't," she replied. "Someone was always there to bail him out."

"Lucky, wasn't he, not to have been hit with a multimillion-dollar malpractice suit."

He reached out and threw the automatic switches to change the trains to another set of tracks. "Nice," he commented.

"Yes, isn't it? I love trains. If I had more leisure time, I'd do this every day. I'm glad we're not on call this weekend. How did you manage it?"

"Threats and bribery," he drawled. "We both worked last Christmas holidays, remember?"

"I guess we did. At each other's throats," she recalled demurely.

"Oh, that was necessary," he returned, rolling lazily onto his side and propping on an elbow. "If I hadn't snapped at you constantly, I'd have been laying you down on examination couches every other day."

"Wh...what?" she stammered.

He reached out and brushed back a long strand of blond hair from her face. "You backed away every time I came close to you," he said quietly. "It was all that saved you. I've wanted you for a long, long time, Dr. Blakely, and I've fought it like a madman."

"You were in love with Jane Parker," she said.

"Not for a long time," he said. He traced her cheek lightly. "The way I felt about her was a habit. It was one I broke when she married Todd Burke. Although, like you, he seems to think Jane and I were an item even after they married. He's taken a lot of convincing. So have you."

She moved uncomfortably. "Everyone talked about you and Jane, not just me."

"I know. Small communities have their good points and their bad points." His finger had reached her mouth. He was exploring it blatantly.

"Could you...not do that, please?" she asked unsteadily.

"Why? You like it. So do I." He moved closer, easing one long, hard-muscled leg over hers to stay her as he shifted so that she lay on her back, looking up at him in the dim light.

"I can feel your heart beating right through your rib cage," he remarked with his mouth poised just above hers. "I can hear your breath fluttering." His hand slid blatantly right down over her breast, pausing there to tease its tip into a hard rise. "Feel that?" he murmured, bending. "Your body likes me."

She opened her mouth, but no words escaped the sudden hard, warm pressure of his lips. She stiffened, but only for a few seconds. It was Christmas Eve and she loved him. There was no defense; none at all.

He seemed to know that, because he wasn't insistent or demanding. He lay, just kissing her, his lips tender as they moved against hers, his hand still gently caressing her body.

"We both know," he whispered, "why your body makes every response it does to the stimuli of my touch. But what no one really understands is why we both enjoy it so much."

"Cause...and effect?" she suggested, gasping when his hand found its way under the sweatshirt and the lacy bra she was wearing to her soft flesh.

He shook his head. "I don't think so. Reach behind you and unfasten this," he added gently, tugging on the elastic band.

She did as he asked, feeling brazen.

"That's better." He traced over her slowly, his eyes on her face while he explored every inch of her above the waist. "Can you give this up?" he asked seriously.

"Wh...what?"

"Can you give it up?" he replied. "You aren't responsive to other men, or you wouldn't still be in your present pristine state. You allow me liberties that I'm certain you've never permitted any other man." He cupped her blatantly and caressed her. She arched, shivering. "You see?" he asked quietly. "You love my touch. I can give you something that you've apparently never experienced. Do you think you can find it with someone else, Lou?"

She felt his mouth cover hers. She didn't have enough breath to answer him, although the answer was certainly in the negative. She couldn't bear the thought of letting someone else be this intimate with her. She looped her arms around his neck and only sighed jerkily when he moved, easing his length against her, his legs between both of hers, so that when his hips pressed down again, she could feel every hardening line of his body.

"Jebediah," she moaned, and she wasn't certain if she was protesting or pleading.

His mouth found her closed eyelids and tasted the helpless tears of pleasure that rained from them. His hips shifted and she jerked at the surge of pleasure.

He felt it, too, like a throbbing ache. "We're good together," he whispered. "Even like this. Can you imagine how it would feel to lie naked under me like this?"

She cried out, burying her face in his neck.

His lips traced her eyelashes, his tongue tasted them. But his body lay very still over hers, not moving, not insisting. Her nails dug into his shoulders as she felt her control slipping away.

But he still had his own control. He soothed her, every soft kiss undemanding and tender. But he didn't move away.

"A year," he whispered. "And we knew nothing about each other, nothing at all." He nibbled her lips, smiling when they trembled. "Trains and old movies, opera and cooking and horseback riding. We have more in common than I ever dreamed."

She had to force her body to lie still. She wanted to wrap her legs tight around him and kiss him until she stopped aching.

He seemed to know it, because his hips moved in a sensual caress that made her hands clench at his shoulders. "No fear of the unknown?" he whispered wickedly. "No virginal terror?"

"I'm a doctor." She choked out the words.

"So am I."

"I mean, I know…what to expect."

He chuckled. "No, you don't. You only know the mechanics of it. You don't know that you're going to crave almost more than I can give you, or that at the last minute you're going to sob like a hurt child."

She was too far gone to be embarrassed. "I don't have anything," she said miserably.

"Anything…?" He probed gently.

"To use."

"Oh. That." He chuckled and kissed her again, so tenderly that she felt cherished. "You won't need it tonight. I don't think babies should be born out of wedlock. Do you?"

She wasn't thinking. "Well, no. What does that have to do... with this?"

"Lou!"

She felt her cheeks burn. "Oh! You mean...!"

He laughed outrageously. "You've really gone off the deep end, haven't you?" he teased. "When people make love, the woman might get pregnant," he explained in a whisper. "Didn't you listen to the biology lectures?"

She hit him. "Of course I did! I wasn't thinking...Jeb!"

He was closer than he'd ever been and she was shivering, lost, helpless as she felt him in a burning, aching intimacy that only made it all worse.

He pressed her close and then rolled away, while he could. "God, we're explosive!" he said huskily, lying very still on his belly. "You're going to have to marry me soon, Lou. Very soon."

She was sitting up, holding her knees to her chest, trying to breathe. It had never been that bad. She said so, without realizing that she'd spoken aloud.

"It will get worse, too," he said heavily. "I want you. I've never wanted you so much."

"But, Jane..."

He was laughing, very softly. He wasn't angry anymore. He rolled over and sat up beside her. He turned her face up to his. "I broke it off with Jane," he said gently. "Do you want to know why, now?"

"You...you did?"

He nodded.

"You never said that you ended it."

"There was no reason to. You wouldn't let me close enough to find out if we had anything going for us, and it didn't seem to matter what I said, you wanted to believe that I was out of my mind over Jane."

"Everyone said you were," she muttered.

He lifted an eyebrow. "I'm not everyone."

"I know." She reached out hesitantly and touched him. It was earthshaking, that simple act. She touched his hair and his face and then his lean, hard mouth. A funny smile drew up her lips.

"Don't stop there," he murmured, drawing her free hand down to his sweatshirt.

Her heart jumped. She looked at him uncertainly.

"I won't let you seduce me," he mused. "Does that make you feel more confident?"

"It was pretty bad a few minutes ago," she said seriously. "I don't want... Well, to hurt you."

"This won't," he said. "Trust me."

"I suppose I must," she admitted. "Or I'd have left months ago for another job."

"That makes sense."

He guided her hand under the thick, white fabric and drew it up until her fingers settled in the thick, curling hair that covered his chest. But it wasn't enough. She wanted to look...

There was just enough light so that he could see what she wanted in her expression. With a faint smile, he pulled the sweatshirt off and tossed it to one side.

She stared. He was beautiful like that, she thought dizzily, with broad shoulders and muscular arms. His chest was covered by a thick, wide wedge of reddish-gold hair that ran down to the buckle of his belt.

He reached for her, lifting her over him so that they were sitting face-to-face, joined where their bodies forked. She shivered at the stark intimacy, because she could feel every muscle, almost every cell of him.

"It gets better," he said softly. He reached down and found the hem of her own sweatshirt. Seconds later, that and her bra joined his sweatshirt on the floor. He looked down at her, savoring the hard peaks that rose like rubies from the whiteness of her breasts. Then he drew her to him and enveloped her against him, so that they were skin against skin. And he shivered, too, this time.

Her hands smoothed over his back, savoring his warm muscles. She searched for his mouth and for the first time, she kissed him.

But even though it was sensual, and she could feel him wanting her, there was tenderness between them, not lust.

He groaned as his body surged against her, and then he laughed at the sudden heat of it.

"Jeb?" she whispered at his lips.

"It's all right," he said. "We won't go all the way. Kiss me again."

She did, clinging, and the world rocked around them.

"I love you," she murmured brokenly. "So much!"

His mouth bit into hers hungrily, his arms contracted. For a few seconds, it was as if electricity fused them together. Finally he was able to lift his lips, and his hands caught her hips to keep them still.

"Sorry," she said demurely.

"Oh, I like it," he replied ruefully. "But we're getting in a bit over our heads."

He lifted her away and stood up, pulling her with him. They looked at each other for a long moment before he handed her things to her and pulled his sweatshirt back on.

He watched the trains go around while she replaced her disheveled clothing. Then, with his hands in his pockets, he glanced down at her.

"That's why I broke up with Jane," he said matter-of-factly.

She was jealous, angry. "Because she wouldn't go all the way with you?"

He chuckled. "No. Because I didn't want her sexually."

She watched the trains and counted the times they crossed the joined tracks. Her mind must not be working. "What did you say?" she asked politely, turning to him.

"I said I was never able to want Jane sexually," he said simply. "To put it simply, she couldn't arouse me."

Chapter 11

"A woman can arouse any man if she tries hard enough," she said pointedly.

"Maybe so," he said, smiling, "but Jane just never interested me like that. It was too big a part of marriage to take a chance on, so I gradually stopped seeing her. Burke came along, and before any of us knew it, she was married. But I was her security blanket after the accident, and it was hard for her to let go. You remember how she depended on me."

She nodded. Even at the time, it had hurt.

"But apparently she and her husband have more than a platonic relationship, if their forthcoming happy event is any indication," he said, chuckling. "And I'm delighted for them."

"I never dreamed that it was like that for you, with her," she said, dazed. "I mean, you and I...!"

"Yes, indeed, you and I," he agreed, nodding. "I touch you and it's like a shot of lightning in my veins. I get drunk on you."

"So do I, on you," she confessed. "But there's a difference, isn't there? I mean, you just want me."

"Do I?" he asked gently. "Do I really just want you? Could lust be as tender as this? Could simple desire explain the way we are together?"

"I love you," she said slowly.

"Yes," he said, his eyes glittering at her. "And I love you, Lou," he added quietly.

Dreams came true. She hadn't known. Her eyes were full of wonder as she looked at him and saw them in his own eyes. It was Christmas, a time of miracles, and here was one.

He didn't speak. He just looked at her. After a minute, he picked up the two parcels he'd put under the tree and handed them to her.

"But it's not Christmas," she protested.

"Yes, it is. Open them."

She only hesitated for a minute, because the curiosity was too great. She opened the smallest one and inside was a gray jeweler's box. With a quick glance at him, she opened it, to find half a key chain inside. She felt her heart race like a watch. It was half of a heart, in pure gold.

"Now the other one," he said, taking the key chain while she fumbled the paper off the second present.

Inside that box was the other half of the heart.

"Now put them together," he instructed.

She did, her eyes magnetized to the inscription. It was in French: *plus que hier, moins que demain.*

"Can you read it?" he asked softly.

"It says—" she had to stop and clear her throat "—more than yesterday, less than tomorrow."

"Which is how much I love you," he said. "I meant to ask you again tomorrow morning to marry me," he said. "But this is as good a time as any for you to say yes. I know you're afraid of marriage. But I love you and you love me. We've got enough in common to keep us together even after all the passion burns out, if it ever does. We'll work out something about your job and children. I'm not your father and you're not your mother. Take a chance, Lou. Believe me, there's very little risk that we won't make it together."

She hadn't spoken. She had both halves of the key chain in her hands and she was looking at them, amazed that he would have picked something so sentimental and romantic for a Christmas gift. He hadn't known if he could get her to stay or not, but he would have shown her his heart all the same. It touched her as a more expensive present wouldn't have.

"When did you get them?" she asked through a dry throat.

"After you left the jeweler's," he said surprisingly. "I believe in miracles," he added gently. "I see incredible things every day. I'm hoping for another one, right now."

She raised her eyes. Even in the dim light, he could see the sparkle of tears, the hope, the pleasure, the disbelief in her face.

"Yes?" he asked softly.

She couldn't manage the word. She nodded, and the next instant, she was in his arms, against him, close and safe and warm while his mouth ravished her lips.

It was a long time before he had enough to satisfy him, even momentarily. He wrapped her up tightly and rocked her in his arms, barely aware of the train chugging along at their feet. His arms were faintly unsteady and his voice, when he laughed, was husky and deep.

"My God, I thought I was going to lose you." He ground out the words. "I didn't know what to do, what to say, to keep you here."

"All you ever had to say was that you loved me," she whispered. "I would have taken any risk for it."

His arms tightened. "Didn't you know, you blind bat?"

"No, I didn't! I don't read minds, and you never said—!"

His mouth covered hers again, stopping the words. He laughed against her breath, anticipating arguments over the years that would be dealt with in exactly this way, as she gave in to him generously, headlong in her response, clinging as if she might die without his mouth on hers.

"No long engagement," he groaned against her mouth. "I can't stand it!"

"Neither can I," she admitted. "Next week?"

"Next week!" He kissed her again. "And I'm not going home tonight."

She laid her cheek against his chest, worried.

He smoothed her hair. "We won't make love," he assured her. "But you'll sleep in my arms. I can't bear to be parted from you again."

"Oh, Jeb," she whispered huskily. "That's the sweetest thing to say!"

"Don't you feel it, too?" he asked knowingly.

"Yes. I don't want to leave you, either."

He chuckled with the newness of belonging to someone. It was going to be, he decided, the best marriage of all time. He looked down into her eyes and saw years and years of happiness ahead of them. He said so. She didn't answer him. She reached up, and her lips said it for her.

The going-away party that Jane Burke threw for Lou became a congratulatory party, because it fell on the day after Coltrain and Lou were married.

They almost stayed at home, so wrapped up in the ecstasy of their first lovemaking that they wouldn't even get out of bed the next morning.

That morning, he lay looking at his new bride with wonder and unbounded delight. There were tears in her eyes, because it had been painful for her at first. But the love in them made him smile.

"It won't be like that again," he assured her.

"I know." She looked at him blatantly, with pride in his fit, muscular body, in his manhood. She lifted her eyes back up. "I was afraid..."

He traced her mouth, his eyes solemn. "It will be easier the next time," he said tenderly. "It will get better every time we love each other."

"I know. I'm not afraid anymore." She touched his hard mouth and smiled. "You were apprehensive, too, weren't you?"

"At first," he had to admit.

"I thought you were never going to start," she said on a sigh. "I know why you took so long, so that I'd be ready when it happened, but I wondered if you were planning on a night of torture."

He chuckled. "You weren't the only one who suffered." He kissed her tenderly. "It hurt me, to have to hurt you, did you know? I wanted to stop, but it was too late. I was in over my head before I knew it. I couldn't even slow down."

"Oh, I never noticed," she told him, delighted. "You made me crazy."

"That goes double for me."

"I thought I knew everything," she mused. "I'm a doctor, after all. But theory and practice are very different."

"Yes. Later, when you're in fine form again, I'll show you some more ways to put theory into practice," he drawled.

She laughed and pummeled him.

They were early for Jane's get-together, and the way they clung to each other would have been more than enough to prove that they were in love, without the matching Victorian wedding bands they'd chosen.

"You look like two halves of a whole," Jane said, looking from Lou's radiant face to Copper's.

"We know," he said ruefully. "They rode us high at the hospital when we made rounds earlier."

"Rounds!" Todd exclaimed. "On your honeymoon?"

"We're doctors," Lou reminded him, grinning. "It goes with the job description. I'll probably be trying to examine patients on the way into the delivery room eventually."

Jane clung to her husband's hand and sighed. "I can't wait for that to happen. Cherry's over the moon, too. She'll be such a good older sister. She works so hard at school. She's studying to be a surgeon, you know," she added.

"I wouldn't know," Copper muttered, "having already had four letters from her begging for an hour of my time to go over what she needs to study most during her last few years in school."

Jane chuckled. "That's my fault. I encouraged her to talk to you."

"It's all right," he said, cuddling Lou closer. "I'll make time for her."

"I see that everything finally worked out for you two," Todd said a little sheepishly. "Sorry about the last time we met."

"Oh, you weren't the only wild-eyed lunatic around, Mr. Burke," Lou said reminiscently. "I did my share of conclusion jumping and very nearly ruined my life because of it." She looked up at Coltrain adoringly. "I'm glad doctors are persistent."

"Yes." Coltrain chuckled. "So am I. There were times when I despaired. But Lionel saved us."

They frowned. "What?"

"Electric trains," Coltrain replied. "Don't you people know anything?"

"Not about trains. Those are kids toys, for God's sake," Burke said.

"No, they are not," Lou said. "They're adult toys. People buy them for their children so they'll have an excuse to play with them. Not having children, we have no excuses."

"That's why we want to start a family right away," Coltrain said with a wicked glance at Lou. "So that we have excuses. You should see her layout," he added admiringly. "My God, it's bigger than mine!"

Todd and Jane tried not to look at each other, failed and burst into outrageous laughter.

Coltrain glared at them. "Obviously," he told his new wife, "some people have no class, no breeding and no respect for the institution of marriage."

"What are you two laughing at?" Drew asked curiously, having returned to town just in time for the party, if not the wedding.

Jane bit her lower lip before she spoke. "Hers is bigger than his." She choked.

"Oh, for God's sake, come and dance!" Coltrain told Lou,

shaking his head as he dragged her away. The others, behind them, were still howling.

Coltrain pulled Lou close and smiled against her hair as they moved to the slow beat of the music. There was a live band. Jane had pulled out all the stops, even if it wasn't going to be a good-bye party.

"Nice band," Dana remarked from beside them. "Congratulations, by the way," she added.

"Thanks," they echoed.

"Nickie didn't come," she added, tongue-in-cheek. "I believe she's just accepted a job in a Victoria hospital as a nurse trainee."

"Good for her," Coltrain said.

Dana chuckled. "Sure. See you."

She wandered away toward one of the hospital staff.

"She's a good loser, at least," Lou said drowsily.

"I wouldn't have been," he mused.

"You've got a new partner coming," she remembered suddenly, having overlooked it in the frantic pace of the past few days.

"Actually," he replied, "I don't know any doctors from Johns Hopkins who would want to come to Jacobsville to practice in a small partnership. The minute I do, of course, I'll hire him on the…oof!"

She'd stepped on his toe, hard.

"Well, I had to say something," he replied, wincing as he stood on his foot. "You were holding all the aces. A man has his pride."

"You could have said you loved me," she said pointedly.

"I did. I do." He smiled slowly. "In a few hours, I'll take you home and prove it and prove it and prove it."

She flushed and pressed closer into his arms. "What a delicious idea."

"I thought so, too. Dance. At least while we're dancing I can hold you in public."

"So you can!"

Drew waltzed by with a partner. "Why don't you two go home?" he asked.

They laughed. "Time enough for private celebrations."

"I hope you have enough champagne," Drew said dryly, and danced on.

As it happened, they had a magnum of champagne between them before Coltrain coaxed his wife back into bed and made up for her first time in ways that left her gasping and trembling in the aftermath.

"That," she gasped, "wasn't in any medical book I ever read!"

"Darlin', you've been reading the wrong books," he whispered, biting her lower lip softly. "And don't go to sleep. I haven't finished yet."

"What?"

He laughed at her expression. "Did you think that was *all?*"

Her eyes widened as he moved over her and slid between her long legs. "But, it hasn't been five minutes, you can't, you *can't...!"*

He not only could. He did.

Two months later, on Valentine Day, Copper Coltrain gave his bride of six weeks a ruby necklace in the shape of a heart. She gave him the results of the test she'd had the day before. He told her later that the "valentine" she'd given him was the best one he'd ever had.

Nine months later, Lou's little valentine was delivered in Jacobsville's hospital; and he was christened Joshua Jebediah Coltrain.

*   *   *   *   *

BELOVED

To Debbie and the staff at Books Galore,
in Watkinsville, GA
and to all my wonderful readers there and in Athens.

Prologue

Simon Hart sat alone in the second row of the seats reserved for family. He wasn't really kin to John Beck, but the two had been best friends since college. John had been his only real friend. Now he was dead, and there *she* sat like a dark angel, her titian hair veiled in black, pretending to mourn the husband she'd cast off like a worn coat after only a month of marriage.

He crossed his long legs, shifting uncomfortably against the pew. He had an ache where his left arm ended just at the elbow. The sleeve was pinned, because he hated the prosthesis that disguised his handicap. He was handsome enough even with only one arm—he had thick, wavy black hair on a leonine head, with dark eyebrows and pale gray eyes. He was tall and well built, a dynamo of a man; former state attorney general of Texas and a nationally known trial lawyer, in addition to being one of the owners of the Hart ranch properties, which were worth millions. He and his brothers were as famous in cattle circles as Simon was in legal circles. He was filthy rich and looked it. But the money didn't make up for the loneliness. His wife had died in the accident that took his arm. It had happened just after Tira's marriage to John Beck.

Tira had nursed him in the hospital, and gossip had run rampant.

Simon was alluded to as the cause of the divorce. Stupid idea, he thought angrily, because he wouldn't have had Tira on a bun with catsup. Only a week after the divorce, she was seen everywhere with playboy Charles Percy, who was still her closest companion. He was probably her lover, as well, Simon thought with suppressed fury. He liked Percy no better than he liked Tira. Strange that Percy hadn't come to the funeral, but perhaps he did have some sense of decency, however small.

Simon wondered if Tira realized how he really felt about her. He had to be pleasant to her; anything else would have invited comment. But secretly, he despised her for what she'd done to John. Tira was cold inside—selfish and cold and unfeeling. Otherwise, how could she have turned John out after a month of marriage, and then let him go to work on a dangerous oil rig in the North Atlantic in an attempt to forget her? John had died there this week, in a tragic accident, having drowned in the freezing, churning waters before he could be rescued. Simon couldn't help thinking that John wanted to die. The letters he'd had from his friend were full of his misery, his loneliness, his isolation from love and happiness.

He glared in her direction, wondering how John's father could bear to sit beside her like that, holding her slender hand as if he felt as sorry for her as he felt for himself at the loss of his son, his only child. Putting on a show for the public, he concluded irritably. He was pretending, to keep people from gossiping.

Simon stared at the closed casket and winced. It was like the end of an era for him. First he'd lost Melia, his wife, and his arm; now he'd lost John, too. He had wealth and success, but no one to share it with. He wondered if Tira felt any guilt for what she'd done to John. He couldn't imagine that she did. She was always flamboyant, vivacious, outgoing and mercurial. Simon had watched her without her knowing it, hating himself for what he felt when he looked at her. She was tall, beautiful, with long, glorious red-gold hair that went to her waist, pale green eyes and a figure right out of a fashion magazine. She could have been a model, but she was surprisingly shy for a pretty woman.

Simon had already been married when they met, and it had been at his prompting that John had taken Tira out for the first time. He'd thought they were compatible, both rich and pleasant people. It had seemed a marriage made in heaven; until the quick divorce. Simon would never have admitted that he threw Tira together with John to get her out of his own circle and out of the reach of temptation. He told himself that she was everything he despised in a woman, the sort of person he could never care for. It worked, sometimes. Except for the ache he felt every time he saw her; an ache that wasn't completely physical....

When the funeral service was over, Tira went out with John's father holding her elbow. The older man smiled sympathetically at Simon. Tira didn't look at him. She was really crying; he could see it even through the veil

Good, Simon thought with cold vengeance. *Good, I'm glad it's hurt you. You killed him, after all!*

He didn't look her way as he got into his black limousine and drove himself back to the office. He wasn't going to the graveside service. He'd had all of Tira's pathetic charade that he could stand. He wouldn't think about those tears in her tragic eyes, or the genuine sadness in her white face. He wouldn't think about her guilt or his own anger. It was better to put it all in the past and let it lie, forgotten. If he could. If he *could....*

Chapter 1

The numbered lot of Hereford cattle at this San Antonio auction had been a real steal at the price, but Tira Beck had let it go without a murmur to the man beside her. She wouldn't ever have admitted that she didn't need to add to her substantial Montana cattle herd, which was managed by her foreman, since she lived in Texas. She'd only wanted to attend the auction because she knew Simon Hart was going to be there. Usually his four brothers in Jacobsville, Texas, handled cattle sales. But Simon, like Tira, lived in San Antonio where the auction was being held, so it seemed natural to let him make the bids.

He wasn't a rancher anymore. He was still tall and well built, with broad shoulders and a leonine head topped by thick black wavy hair. But the empty sleeve on his left side attested to the fact that his days of working cattle were pretty much over. It didn't affect his ability to make a living, at least. He was a former state attorney general and a nationally famous trial attorney who could pick and choose high-profile cases. He made a substantial wage. His voice was still his best asset, a deep velvety one that projected well in a courtroom. In addition to that was a dangerously deceptive manner that lulled witnesses into a false sense of security before he cut them to pieces on the stand. He had a verbal killer instinct, and he used it to good effect.

Tira, on the other hand, lived a hectic life doing charity work and was independently wealthy. She was a divorcée who had very little to do with men except on a platonic basis. There weren't many friends, either. Simon Hart and Charles Percy were the lot, and Charles was hopelessly in love with his brother's wife. She was the only person who knew that. Many people thought that she and Charles were lovers, which amused them both. She had her own secrets to keep. It suited her purposes to keep Simon in the dark about her emotional state.

"That was a hell of an anemic bid you made," Simon remarked as the next lot of cattle were led into the sale ring. "What's wrong with you today?"

"My heart's not in it," she replied. "I haven't had a lot to do with the Montana ranch since Dad died. I've given some thought to selling the property. I'll never live there again."

"You'll never sell. You have too many attachments to the ranch. Besides, you've got a good manager in place up there," he said pointedly.

She shrugged, pushing away a wisp of glorious hair that had escaped from the elegant French twist at her nape. "So I have."

"But you'd rather swan around San Antonio with Charles Percy," he murmured, his chiseled mouth twisting into a mocking smile.

She glanced at him with lovely green eyes and hid a carefully concealed hope that he might be jealous. But his expression gave no hint of his feelings. Neither did those pale gray eyes under thick black eyebrows. It was the same old story. The wreck eight years ago that had cost him his arm had also cost him his beloved wife, Melia. Despite their differences, no one had doubted his love for her. He hadn't been serious about a woman since her death, although he escorted his share of sophisticated women to local social events.

"What's the matter?" he asked when his sharp eyes caught her disappointment.

She shrugged in her elegant black pantsuit. "Oh, nothing. I just thought that you might like to stand up and threaten to kill Charles if he came near me again." She glanced at his shocked face and chuckled. "I'm kidding!" she chided.

His gaze cut into hers for a second and then they moved back to the sale ring. "You're in an odd mood today."

She sighed, returning her attention to the program in her beautifully manicured hands. "I've been in an odd mood for years. Not that I ever expect you to notice."

He closed his own program with a snap and glared down at her. "That's another thing that annoys me, those throwaway remarks you make. If you want to say something to me, just come out and say it."

Typically blunt, she thought. She looked straight at him and she made a gesture of utter futility with one hand. "Why bother?" she asked. Her eyes searched his and for the first time, a hint of the pain she felt was visible. She averted her gaze and stood up. "I've done all the bidding I came to do. I'll see you around, Simon."

She picked up her long black leather coat and folded it over her arm as she made her way out of the row and up the aisle to the exit. Eyes followed her, and not only because she was one of only a handful of women present. Tira was beautiful, although she never paid the least attention to her appearance except with a critical scrutiny. She wasn't vain.

Behind her, Simon sat scowling silently as she walked away. Her behavior piqued his curiousity. She was even more remote lately and hardly the same flamboyant, cheerful, friendly woman who'd been his secret solace since the accident that had cost Melia her life. His wife had been his whole heart, until that last night when she betrayed a secret that destroyed his pride and his love for her.

Fool that he was, he'd believed that Melia married him for love.

In fact, she'd married him for money and kept a lover in the background. Her stark confession about her long-standing affair and the abortion of his child had shocked and wounded him. She'd even laughed at his consternation. Surely he didn't think she wanted a child? It would have ruined her figure and her social life. Besides, she'd added with calculating cruelty, she hadn't even been certain that it was Simon's, since she'd been with her lover during the same period of time.

The truth had cut like a knife into his pride. He'd taken his eyes off the road as they argued, and hit a patch of black ice on that winter evening. The car had gone off the road into a gulley and Melia, who had always refused to wear a seat belt because they were uncomfortable to her, had been thrown into the windshield headfirst. She'd died instantly. Simon had been luckier, but the airbag on his side of the car hadn't deployed, and the impact of the crash had driven the metal of the door right into his left arm. Amputation had been necessary to save his life.

He remembered that Tira had come to him in the hospital as soon as she'd heard about the wreck. She'd been in the process of divorcing John Beck, her husband, and her presence at Simon's side had started some malicious rumors about infidelity.

Tira never spoke of her brief marriage. She never spoke of John. Simon had already been married when they'd met for the first time, and it had been Simon who played matchmaker with John for her. John was his best friend and very wealthy, like Tira herself, and they seemed to have much in common. But the marriage had been over in less than a month.

He'd never questioned why, except that it seemed unlike Tira to throw in the towel so soon. Her lack of commitment to her marriage and her cavalier attitude about the divorce had made him uneasy. In fact, it had kept him from letting her come closer after he was widowed. She'd turned out to be shallow, and he wasn't risking his heart on a woman like that, even if she was a knockout to look at. As he knew firsthand, there was more to a marriage than having a beautiful wife.

John Beck, like Tira, had never said anything about the marriage. But John had avoided Simon ever since the divorce, and once when he'd had too much to drink at a party they'd both attended, he'd blurted out that Simon had destroyed his life, without explaining how.

The two men had been friends for several years until John had married Tira. Not too long after the divorce, John had moved out of Texas entirely and a year later that tragic oil rig accident had claimed his life. Tira had seemed devastated by John's death and for a time, she went into seclusion. When she came back into society, she was a changed woman. The vivacious, happy Tira of earlier days had become a dignified, elegant matron who seemed to have lost her fighting spirit. She went back to college and finished her degree in art. But three years after graduation, she seemed to have done little with her degree. Not that she skimped on charity work or political fund-raising. She was a tireless worker. Simon wondered sometimes if she didn't work to keep from thinking.

Perhaps she blamed herself for John's death and couldn't admit it. The loss of his former friend had hurt Simon, too. He and Tira had become casual friends, but nothing more, he made sure of it. Despite her attractions, he wasn't getting caught by such a shallow woman. But if their lukewarm friendship had been satisfying once, in the past year, she'd become restless. She was forever mentioning Charles Percy to him and watching his reactions with strange, curious eyes. It made him uncomfortable, like that crack she'd made about kindling jealousy in him.

That remark hit him on the raw. Did she really think he could ever want a woman of her sort, who could discard a man she professed to love after only one month of marriage and then parade around openly with a philanderer like Charles Percy? He laughed coldly to himself. That really would be the day. His heart was safely encased in ice. Everyone thought he mourned Melia—no one knew how badly she'd hurt him, or that her memory disgusted him. It served as some protection against women like Tira. It kept him safe from any emotional involvement.

Unaware of Simon's hostile thoughts, Tira went to her silver Jaguar and climbed in behind the wheel. She paused there for a few minutes, with her head against the cold steering wheel. When was she ever going to learn that Simon didn't want her? It was like throwing herself at a stone wall, and it had to stop. Finally she admitted that nothing was going to change their shallow relationship. It was time she made a move to put herself out of Simon's orbit for good. Tearing her emotions to pieces wasn't going to help, and every time she saw him, she died a little more. All these years she'd waited and hoped and suffered, just to be around him occasionally. She'd lived too long on crumbs; she had to find some sort of life for herself without Simon, no matter how badly it hurt.

Her first step was to sell the Montana property. She put it on the market without a qualm, and her manager pooled his resources with a friend to buy it. With the ranch gone, she had no more reason to go to cattle auctions.

She moved out of her apartment that was only a couple of blocks from Simon's, too, and bought an elegant house on the outskirts of town on the Floresville Road. It was very Spanish, with graceful arches and black wrought-iron scrollwork on the fences that enclosed it. There was a cobblestone patio complete with a fountain and a nearby sitting area with a large goldfish pond and a waterfall cascading into it. The place was sheer magic. She thought she'd never seen anything quite so beautiful.

"It's the sort of house that needs a family," the real estate agent had remarked.

Tira hadn't said a word.

She remembered the conversation as she looked around the empty living room that had yet to be furnished. There would never be a family now. There would only be Tira, putting one foot in front of the other and living like a zombie in a world that no longer contained Simon, or hope.

It took her several weeks to have the house decorated and furnished. She chose every fabric, every color, every design herself. And when the house was finished, it echoed her own personality. Her real personality, that was, not the face she showed to the world.

No one who was acquainted with her would recognize her from the decor. The living room was done in soft white with a pastel blue, patterned wallpaper. The carpet was gray. The furniture was Victorian, rosewood chairs and a velvet-covered sofa. The other rooms were equally antique. The master bedroom boasted a four-poster bed in cherry wood, with huge ball legs and a headboard and footboard resplendent with hand-carved floral motifs. The curtains were Priscillas, the center panels of rose patterns with faint pink and blue coloring. The rest of the house followed the same subdued elegance of style and color. It denoted a person who was introverted, sensitive and old-fashioned. Which, under the flamboyant camouflage, Tira really was.

If there was a flaw, and it was a small one, it was the mouse who lived in the kitchen. Once the house was finished, and she'd moved in, she noticed him her first night in residence, sitting brazenly on a cabinet clutching a piece of cracker that she'd missed when she was cleaning up.

She bought traps and set them, hoping that the evil things would do their horrible work correctly and that she wouldn't be left nursing a wounded mouse. But the wily creature avoided the traps. She tried a cage and bait. That didn't work, either. Either the mouse was like those in that cartoon she'd loved, altered by some secret lab and made intelligent, or he was a figment of her imagination and she was going mad.

She laughed almost hysterically at the thought that Simon had finally, after all those years, driven her crazy.

Despite the mouse, she loved her new home. But even though

she led a hectic life, there were still the lonely nights to get through. The walls began to close around her, despite the fact that she involved herself in charity work committees and was a tireless worker for political action fund-raisers. She worked long hours, and pushed herself unnecessarily hard. But she had no outside interests and too much money to work a daily job. What she needed was something interesting to do at home, to keep her mind occupied at night, when she was alone. But what?

It was a rainy Monday morning. She'd gone to the market for fresh vegetables and wasn't really watching where she was walking when she turned a corner and went right into the path of Corrigan Hart and his new wife, Dorothy.

"Good Lord," she gasped, catching her breath. "What are you two doing in San Antonio?"

Corrigan grinned. "Buying cattle," he said, drawing a radiant Dorothy closer. "Which reminds me, I didn't see you at the auction this time. I was standing in for Simon," he added. "For some reason, he's gone off sales lately."

"So have I, coincidentally," Tira remarked with a cool smile. It stung to think that Simon had given up those auctions that he loved so much to avoid her, but that was most certainly the reason. "I sold the Montana property."

Corrigan scowled. "But you loved the ranch. It was your last link with your father."

That was true, and it had made her sad for a time. She twisted the shopping basket in her hands. "I'd gotten into a rut," she said. "I wanted to change my life."

"So I noticed," Corrigan said quietly. "We went by your apartment to say hello. You weren't there."

"I moved." She colored a little at his probing glance. "I've bought a house across town."

Corrigan's eyes narrowed. "Someplace where you won't see Simon occasionally," he said gently.

The color in her cheeks intensified. "Where I won't see Simon at all, if you want the truth,'' she said bluntly. "I've given up all my connections with the past. There won't be any more accidental meetings with him. I've decided that I'm tired of eating my heart out for a man who doesn't want me. So I've stopped.''

Corrigan looked surprised. Dorie eyed the other woman with quiet sympathy.

"In the long run, that's probably the best thing you could have done," Dorie said quietly. "You're still young and very pretty," she added with a smile. "And the world is full of men.''

"Of course it is,'' Tira replied. She returned Dorie's smile. "I'm glad things worked out for you two, and I'm very sorry I almost split you up," she added sincerely. "Believe me, it was unintentional.''

"Tira, I know that,'' Dorie replied, remembering how a chance remark of Tira's in a local boutique had sent Dorie running scared from Corrigan. That was all in the past, now. "Corrigan explained everything to me. I was uncertain of him then, that's all it really was. I'm not anymore.'' She hesitated. "I'm sorry about you and Simon.''

Tira's face tautened. "You can't make people love you," she said with a poignant sadness in her eyes. She shrugged fatalistically. "He has a life that suits him. I'm trying to find one for myself.''

"Why don't you do a collection of sculptures and have a show?'' Corrigan suggested.

She chuckled. "I haven't done sculpture in three years. Anyway, I'm not good enough for that.''

"You certainly are, and you've got an art degree. Use it.''

She considered that. After a minute, she smiled. "Well, I do enjoy sculpting. I used to sell some of it occasionally.''

"See?'' Corrigan said. "An idea presents itself.'' He paused. "Of course, there's always a course in biscuit-making…?''

Knowing his other three brothers' absolute mania for that particular bread, she held up both hands. "You can tell Leo and Cag and Rey that I have no plans to become a biscuit chef.''

"I'll pass the message along. But Dorie's dying for a replacement," he added with a grin at his wife. "They'd chain her to the stove if I didn't intervene." He eyed Tira. "They like you."

"God forbid," she said with a mock shudder. "For years, people will be talking about how they arranged your marriage."

"They meant well," Dorie defended them.

"Baloney," Tira returned. "They had to have their biscuits. Fatal error, Dorie, telling them you could bake."

"It worked out well, though, don't you think?" she asked with a radiant smile at her husband.

"It did, indeed."

Tira fielded a few more comments about her withdrawal from the social scene, and then they were on their way to the checkout stand. She deliberately held back until they left, to avoid any more conversation. They were a lovely couple, and she was fond of Corrigan, but he reminded her too much of Simon.

In the following weeks, she signed up for a refresher sculpting course at her local community college, a course for no credit since she already had a degree. In no time, she was sculpting recognizable busts.

"You've got a gift for this," her instructor murmured as he walked around a fired head of her favorite movie star. "There's money in this sort of thing, you know. Big money."

She almost groaned aloud. How could she tell this dear man that she had too much money already? She only smiled and thanked him for the compliment.

But he put her sculpture in a showing of his students' work. It was seen by a local art gallery owner, who tracked Tira down and offered her an exclusive showing. She tried to dissuade him, but the offer was all too flattering to turn down. She agreed, with the priviso that the proceeds would go to an outreach program from the local hospital that worked in indigent neighborhoods.

After that, there was no stopping her. She spent hours at the task, building the strength in her hands and attuning her focus to more detailed pieces.

It wasn't until she finished one of Simon that she even realized she'd been sculpting him. She stared at it with contained fury and was just about to bring both fists down on top of it when the doorbell rang.

Irritated at the interruption, she tossed a cloth over the work in progress and went to answer it, wiping the clay from her hands on the way. Her hair was in a neat bun, to keep it from becoming clotted with clay, but her pink smock was liberally smeared with it. She looked a total mess, without makeup, even without shoes, wearing faded jeans and a knit top.

She opened the door without questioning who her visitor might be, and froze in place when Simon came into view on the porch. She noticed that he was wearing the prosthesis he hated so much, and she noted with interest that the hand at the end of it looked amazingly real.

She lifted her eyes to his, but her face wasn't welcoming. She didn't open the door to admit him. She didn't even smile.

"What do you want?" she asked.

He scowled. That was new. He'd visited Tira's apartment infrequently in the past, and he'd always been greeted with warmth and even delight. This was a cold reception indeed.

"I came to see how you were," he replied quietly. "You've been conspicuous by your absence around town lately."

"I sold the ranch," she said flatly.

He nodded. "Corrigan told me." He looked around at the front yard and the porch of the house. "This is nice. Did you really need a whole house?"

She ignored the question. "What do you want?" she asked again.

He noted her clay-smeared hands, and the smock she was wearing. "Laying bricks, are you?" he mused.

She didn't smile, as she might have once. "I'm sculpting."

"Yes, I remember that you took courses in college. You were quite good."

"I'm also quite busy," she said pointedly.

His eyebrow arched. "No invitation to have coffee?"

She hardened her resolve, despite the frantic beat of her heart. "I don't have time to entertain. I'm getting ready for an exhibit."

"At Bob Henderson's gallery," he said knowledgeably. "Yes, I know. I have part ownership in it." He held up his hand when she started to speak angrily. "I had no idea that he'd seen any of your work. I didn't suggest the showing. But I'd like to see what you've done. I do have a vested interest."

That put a new complexion on things. But she still didn't want him in her house. She'd never rid herself of the memory of him in it. Her reluctant expression told him that whatever she was feeling, it wasn't pleasure.

He sighed. "Tira, what's wrong?" he asked.

She stared at the cloth in her hands instead of at him. "Why does anything have to be wrong?"

"Are you kidding?" He drew in a heavy breath and wondered why he should suddenly feel guilty. "You've sold the ranch, moved house and given up any committees that would bring you into contact with me...."

She looked up in carefully arranged surprise. "Oh, heavens, it wasn't because of you," she lied convincingly. "I was in a rut, that's all. I decided that I needed to turn my life around. And I have."

His eyes glittered down at her. "Did turning it around include keeping me out of it?"

Her expression was unreadable. "I suppose it did. I was never able to get past my marriage. The memories were killing me, and you were a constant reminder."

His heavy eyebrows lifted. "Why should the memories bother you?" he asked with visible sarcasm. "You didn't give a damn about John. You divorced him a month after the wedding and never seemed to care if you saw him again or not. Barely a week later, you were keeping company with Charles Percy.''

The bitterness in his voice opened her eyes to something she'd never seen. Why, he blamed her for John's death. She didn't seem to breathe as she looked up into those narrow, cold, accusing eyes. It had been three years since John's death and she'd never known that Simon felt this way.

Her hands on the cloth stilled. It was the last straw. She'd loved this big, formidable man since the first time she'd seen him. There had never been anyone else in her heart, despite the fact that she'd let him push her into marrying John. And now, years too late, she discovered the reason that Simon had never let her come close to him. It was the last reason she'd ever have guessed.

She let out a harsh breath. ''Well,'' she said with forced lightness, ''the things we learn about people we thought we knew!'' She tucked the smeared cloth into a front pocket of her equally smeared smock. ''So I killed John. Is that what you think, Simon?''

The frontal assault was unexpected. His guard was down and he didn't think before he spoke. ''You played at marriage,'' he accused quietly. ''He loved you, but you had nothing to give him. A month of marriage and you were having divorce papers served to him. You let him go without a word when he decided to work on oil rigs, despite the danger of it. You didn't even try to stop him. Funny, but I never realized what a shallow, cold woman you were until then. Everything you are is on the outside,'' he continued, blind to her white, drawn face. ''Glorious hair, a pretty face, sparkling eyes, pretty figure...and nothing under it all. Not even a spark of compassion or love for anyone except yourself.''

She wasn't breathing normally. Dear God, she thought, don't let me faint at his feet! She swallowed once, then twice, trying to absorb the horror of what he was saying to her.

''You never said a word,'' she said in a haunted tone. ''In all these years.''

''I didn't think it needed saying,'' he said simply. ''We've been friends, of a sort. I hope we still are.'' He smiled, but it didn't reach his eyes. "As long as you realize that you'll never be allowed within striking distance of my heart. I'm not a masochist, even if John was.''

Later, when she was alone, she was going to die. She knew it. But right now, pride spared her any further hurt.

She went past him, very calmly, and opened the front door, letting in a scent of dead leaves and cool October breeze. She didn't speak. She didn't look at him. She just stood there.

He walked past her, hesitating on the doorstep. His narrow eyes scanned what he could see of her face, and its whiteness shocked him. He wondered why she looked so torn up, when he was only speaking the truth.

Before he could say a thing, she closed the door, threw the dead bolt and put on the chain latch. She walked back toward her studio, vaguely aware that he was trying to call her back.

The next morning, the housekeeper she'd hired, Mrs. Lester, found her sprawled across her bed with a loaded pistol in her hands and an empty whiskey bottle lying on its side on the stained gray carpet. Mrs. Lester quickly looked in the bathroom and found an empty bottle that had contained tranquilizers. She jerked up the telephone and dialed the emergency services number with trembling hands. When the ambulance came screaming up to the front of the house, Tira still hadn't moved at all.

Chapter 2

It took all of that day for Tira to come out of the stupor and discover where she was. It was a very nice hospital room, but she didn't remember how she'd gotten there. She was foggy and disoriented and very sick to her stomach.

Dr. Ron Gaines, an old family friend, came in the door ahead of a nurse in neat white slacks and a multicolored blouse with many pockets.

"Get her vitals," the doctor directed.

"Yes, sir."

While her temperature and blood pressure and pulse rate were taken, Dr. Gaines leaned against the wall quietly making notations on her chart. The nurse reported her findings, he charted them and he motioned her out of the room.

He moved to the bed and sat down in the chair beside Tira. "If anyone had asked me two weeks ago, I'd have said that you were the most levelheaded woman I knew. You've worked tirelessly for charities here, you've spearheaded fund drives... Good God, what's the matter with you?"

"I had a bad blow," she confessed in a subdued tone. "It was unexpected and I did something stupid. I got drunk."

"Don't hand me that! Your housekeeper found a loaded pistol in your hand."

"Oh, that." She started to tell him about the mouse, the one she'd tried unsuccessfully to catch for weeks. Last night, with half a bottle of whiskey in her, shooting the varmint had seemed perfectly logical. But her dizzy mind was slow to focus. "Well, you see—" she began.

He sighed heavily and cut her off. "Tira, if it wasn't a suicide attempt, I'm not a doctor. Tell me the truth."

She blinked. "I wouldn't try to kill myself!" she said, outraged. She took a slow breath. "I was just a little depressed, that's all. I found out yesterday that Simon holds me responsible for John's death."

There was a long, shocked pause. "He doesn't know why the marriage broke up?"

She shook her head.

"Why didn't you tell him, for God's sake?" he exclaimed.

"It isn't the sort of thing you tell a man about his best friend. I never dreamed that he blamed me. We've been friends. He never wanted it to be anything except friendship, and I assumed it was because of the way he felt about Melia. Apparently I've been five kinds of an idiot." She looked up at him. "Six, if you count last night," she added, flushing.

"I'm glad you agree that it was stupid."

She frowned. "Did you pump my stomach?"

"Yes."

"No wonder I feel so empty," she said. "Why did you do that?" she asked. "I only had whiskey on an empty stomach!"

"Your housekeeper found an empty tranquilizer bottle in the bathroom," he said sternly.

"Oh, that," she murmured. "The bottle was empty. I never throw anything away. That prescription was years old. It's one Dr. James gave me to get me through final exams in college three years ago. I was a nervous wreck!" She gave him another unblinking stare. "But you listen here, I'm not suicidal. I'm the least suicidal person I know. But everybody has a breaking point and I reached mine. So I got drunk. I never touch alcohol. Maybe that's why it hit me so hard.''

He took her hand in his and held it gently. While he was trying to find the words, the door suddenly swung open and a wild-eyed Simon Hart entered the room. He looked as if he'd been in an accident, his face was so white. He stared at Tira without speaking.

It wasn't his fault, really, but she hated him for what she'd done to herself. Her eyes told him so. There was no welcome in them, no affection, no coquettishness. She looked at him as if she wished she had a weapon in her hands.

"You get out of my room!" she raged at him, sitting straight up in bed.

The doctor's eyebrows shot straight up. Tira had never raised her voice to Simon before. Her face was flaming red, like her wealth of hair, and her green eyes were shooting bolts of lightning in Simon's direction.

"Tira," Simon began uncertainly.

"Get out!" she repeated, ashamed of being accused of a suicide attempt in the first place. It was bad enough that she'd lost control of herself enough to get drunk. She glared at Simon as if he was the cause of it all—which he was. "Out!" she repeated, when he didn't move, gesturing wildly with her arm.

He wouldn't go, and she burst into tears of frustrated fury. Dr. Gaines got between Simon and Tira and hit the Call button. "Get in here, stat," he said into the intercom, following the order with instructions for a narcotic. He glanced toward Simon, standing frozen in the doorway. "Out," he said without preamble. "I'll speak to you in a few minutes."

Simon moved aside to let the skurrying nurse into the room with a hypodermic. He could hear Tira's sobs even through the door. He moved a little way down the hall, to where his brother Corrigan was standing.

It had been Corrigan whom the housekeeper called when she

discovered Tira. And he'd called Simon and told him only that Tira had been taken to the hospital in a bad way. He had no knowledge of what had pushed Tira over the edge or he might have thought twice about telling his older brother at all.

"I heard her. What happened?" Corrigan asked, jerking his head toward the room.

"I don't know," Simon said huskily. He leaned back against the wall beside his brother. His empty sleeve drew curious glances from a passerby, but he ignored it. "She saw me and started yelling." He broke off. His eyes were filled with torment. "I've never seen her like this."

"Nobody has," Corrigan said flatly. "I never figured a woman like Tira for a suicide."

Simon gaped at him. "A *what?*"

"What would you call combining alcohol and tranquilizers?" Corrigan demanded. "Good God, Mrs. Lester said she had a loaded pistol in her hands!"

"A *pistol...?*" Simon closed his eyes on a shudder and ran a hand over his drawn face. He couldn't bear to think about what might have happened. He was certain that he'd prompted her actions. He couldn't forget, even now, the look on her face when he'd almost flatly accused her of killing John. She hadn't said a word to defend herself. She'd gone quiet; dangerously quiet. He should never have left her alone. Worse, he should never have said anything to her. He'd thought her a strong, self-centered woman who wouldn't feel criticism. Now, almost too late, he knew better.

"I went to see her yesterday," Simon confessed in a haunted tone. "She'd made some crazy remark at the last cattle auction about trying to make me jealous. She said she was only teasing, but it hit me the wrong way. I told her that she wasn't the sort of woman I could be jealous about. Then, yesterday, I told her how I felt about her careless attitude toward the divorce only a month after she married John, and letting him go off to get himself killed on an oil rig." His broad shoulders rose and fell defeatedly. "I shouldn't have said it, but I was angry that she'd tried to make me jealous, as if she thought I might actually feel attracted to her." He sighed. "I thought she was so hard that nothing I said would faze her."

"And I thought I used to be blind," Corrigan said.

Simon glanced at him, scowling. "What do you mean?"

Corrigan looked at his brother and tried to speak. Finally he just smiled faintly and turned away. "Forget it."

The door to Tira's room opened a minute later and Dr. Gaines came out. He spotted the two men down the hall and joined them.

"Don't go back in there," he told Simon flatly. "She's too close to the edge already. She doesn't need you to push her the rest of the way."

"I didn't do a damned thing," Simon shot back, and now he looked dangerous, "except walk in the door!"

Dr. Gaines' lips thinned. He glanced at Corrigan, who only shrugged and shook his head.

"I'm going to try to get her to go to a friend of mine, a therapist. She could use some counseling," Gaines added.

"She's not a nut case," Simon said, affronted.

Dr. Gaines looked into that cold, unaware face and frowned. "You were state attorney general for four years," he said. "You're still a well-known trial lawyer, an intelligent man. How can you be this stupid?"

"Will someone just tell me what's going on?" Simon demanded.

Dr. Gaines looked at Corrigan, who held out a hand, palm-up, inviting the doctor to do the dirty work.

"She'll kill us both if she finds out we told him," Gaines remarked to Corrigan.

"It's better than letting her die."

"Amen." He looked at Simon, who was torn between puzzlement and fury. "Simon, she's been in love with you for years," Dr. Gaines said in a hushed, reluctant tone. "I tried to get her to give up the ranch and all that fund-raising mania years ago, because they were only a way for her to keep near you. She wore herself out at it, hoping against hope that if you were in close contact, you might begin to feel something for her, but I knew that wasn't going to happen. All I had to do was see you together to realize she didn't have a chance. Am I right?'' he asked Corrigan, who nodded.

Simon leaned back against the wall. He felt as if someone had put a knife right through him. He couldn't even speak.

''What you said to her was a kindness, although I don't imagine you see it that way now,'' Dr. Gaines continued doggedly. ''She had to be made to see that she couldn't go on living a lie, and the changes in her life recently are proof that she's realized how you feel about her. She'll accept it, in time, and get on with her life. It will be the very best thing for her. She's trying to be all things to all people, until she was worn to a nub. She's been headed for a nervous breakdown for weeks, the way she's pushed herself, with this one-woman art show added to the load she was already carrying. But she'll be all right.'' He put a sympathetic hand on Simon's good arm. ''It's not your fault. She's levelheaded about everything except you. But if you want to help her, for old time's sake, stay away from her. She's got enough on her plate right now.''

He nodded politely to Corrigan and went on down the hall.

Simon still hadn't moved, or spoken. He was pale and drawn, half crazy from the doctor's revelation.

Corrigan got on the other side of him and took his arm, drawing him along. ''We'll get a cup of coffee somewhere on the way back to your office,'' he told his older brother.

Simon allowed himself to be pulled out the door. He wasn't sure he remembered how to walk. He felt shattered.

Minutes later, he was sitting in a small café with his brother, drinking strong coffee.

''She tried to kill herself over me,'' Simon said finally.

''She missed. She won't try again. They'll make sure of it.''

He leaned forward. "Simon, she's been overextending for years, you know that. No one woman could have done as much as she has without risking her health, if not her sanity. If it hadn't been what you said to her, it would have been something else...maybe even this showing at the gallery that she was working night and day to get ready for."

Simon forced himself to breathe normally. He still couldn't quite believe it all. He sipped his coffee and stared into space.

"Did you know how she felt?" he asked Corrigan.

"She didn't tell me, if that's what you mean," his brother said. "But it was fairly obvious, the way she talked about you. I felt sorry for her. We all knew how much you loved Melia, that you've never let yourself get close to another woman since the wreck. Tira had to know that there was no hope in that direction."

The coffee in Simon's cup sloshed a little as he put it down. "It seems so clear now," he remarked absently. "She was always around, even when there didn't seem a reason for it. She worked on committees for organizations I belonged to, she did charity work for businesses where I was a trustee." He shook his head. "But I never noticed."

"I know."

He looked up. "John knew," he said suddenly.

Corrigan hesitated. Then he nodded.

Simon sucked in a harsh breath. "Good God, I broke up their marriage!"

"Maybe. I don't know. Tira never talks about John." His eyes narrowed thoughtfully. "But haven't you ever noticed that she and John's father are still friends? He doesn't blame her for his son's death. Shouldn't he, if it was all Tira's fault?"

Simon didn't want to think about it. He was sick to his stomach. "I pushed her at John," he recalled.

"I remember. They seemed to have a lot in common."

"They had me in common." Simon laughed bitterly. "She loved *me*..." He took a long sip of coffee and burned his mouth. The pain was welcome; it took his mind off his conscience.

"She can't ever know that we told you that," Corrigan said firmly, looking as formidable as his brother. "She's entitled to salvage a little of her pride. The newspapers got hold of the story, Simon. It's in the morning edition. The headline's really something—local socialite in suicide attempt. She's going to have hell living it down. I don't imagine they'll let her see a newspaper, but someone will tell her, just the same." His voice was harsh. "Some people love rubbing salt in wounds."

Simon rested his forehead against his one hand. He was so drained that he could barely function. It had been the worst day of his life; in some ways, worse than the wreck that had cost him everything.

For years, Tira's eyes had warmed at his approach, her mouth had smiled her welcome. She'd become radiant just because he was near her, and he hadn't known how she felt, with all those blatant signs.

Now, this morning, she'd looked at him with such hatred that he still felt sick from the violence of it. Her eyes had flashed fire, her face had burned with rage. He'd never seen her like that.

Corrigan searched his brother's worn face. "Don't take it so hard, Simon. None of this is your fault. She put too much pressure on herself and now she's paying the consequences. She'll be all right."

"She loved me," he said again, speaking the words harshly, as if he still couldn't believe them.

"You can't make people love you back," his brother replied. "Funny, Dorie and I saw her in the grocery store a few weeks ago, and she said that same thing. She had no illusions about the way you felt, regardless of how it looks."

Simon's eyes burned with anguish. "You don't know what I said to her, though. I accused her of killing John, of being so unconcerned about his happiness that she let him go into a dangerous job that he didn't have the experience to handle." His face twisted. "I said that she was shallow and cold and selfish, that I had nothing but contempt for her and that I'd never let a woman like her get close to me…" His eyes closed. "Dear God, how it must have hurt her to hear that from me."

Corrigan let out a savage breath. "Why didn't you just load the gun for her?"

"Didn't I?" the older man asked with tortured eyes.

Corrigan backed off. "Well, it's water under the bridge now. She's safely out of your life and she'll learn to get along on her own, with a little help. You can go back to your law practice and consider yourself off the endangered species list."

Simon didn't say another word. He stared into his coffee with sightless eyes until it grew cold.

Tira slept for the rest of the day. When she opened her eyes, the room was empty. There was a faint light from the wall and she felt pleasantly drowsy.

The night nurse came in, smiling, to check her vital signs. She was given another dose of medicine. Minutes later, without having dared remember the state she was in that morning, she went back to sleep.

When she woke up, a tall, blond, handsome man with dark eyes was sitting by the bed, looking quite devastating in white slacks and a red pullover knit shirt.

"Charles," she mumbled, and smiled. "How nice of you to come!"

"Who'll I talk to if you kill yourself, you idiot?" he muttered, glowering at her. "What a stupid thing to do."

She pushed herself up on an elbow, and pushed the mass of red-gold hair out of her eyes. She made a rough sound in her throat. "I wasn't trying to commit suicide!" she grumbled. "I got drunk and Mrs. Lester found an old empty prescription bottle and went ballistic." She shifted sleepily and yawned. "Well, I can't blame her, I guess. I still had the pistol in my hand and there was a hole in the wall…"

"Pistol!?"

"Calm down," she said, grimacing. "My head hurts. Yes, a

pistol." She grinned at him a little sheepishly. "I was going to shoot the mouse."

His eyes widened. "Excuse me?"

"There's a mouse," she said. "I've set traps and put out bait, and he just keeps coming back into my kitchen. After a couple of drinks, I remembered a scene in *True Grit,* where John Wayne shot a rat, and when I got halfway through the whiskey bottle, it seemed perfectly logical that I should do that to my mouse." She chuckled a little weakly. "You had to be there," she added helplessly.

"I suppose so." He searched her bloodshot eyes. "All those charity events, anybody calls and asks you to help, and you work day and night to organize things. You're everybody's helper. Now you're working on a collection of sculpture and still trying to keep up with your social obligations. I'm surprised you didn't fall out weeks ago. I tried to tell you. You know I did."

She nodded and sighed. "I know. I just didn't realize how hard I was working."

"You never do. You need to get married and have kids. That would keep you busy."

She lifted both eyebrows. "Are you offering to sacrifice yourself?"

He chuckled. "Maybe it would be the best thing for both of us," he said wistfully. "We're in love with people who don't want us. At least we like each other."

"Yes. But marriage should be more than that."

He shrugged. "Just a thought." He leaned over and patted her hand. "Get well. There's a society ball next week and you have to go with me. She's going to be there."

Tira knew who *she* was—his sister-in-law, the woman that Percy would have died to marry. She'd never noticed him, despite his blazing good looks, before she married his half brother. In fact, she seemed to actually dislike him, and Charles's half brother was twenty years her senior, a stiff-necked stuffed-shirt whom nobody in their circle had any use for. The marriage was a complete mystery.

"I don't have a dress."

"Buy one," he instructed.

She hesitated.

"I'll protect you from him," he said after a minute, having realized that Simon would most likely be in attendance. "I swear on my glorious red Mark VIII that I won't leave your side for an instant all evening."

She gave him a wary glance. His mania about that car was well-known. He wouldn't even entrust it to a car wash. He washed and waxed it lovingly, inch by inch, and called it "Big Red."

"Well, if you're willing to swear on your car," she agreed.

He grinned. "You can ride in it."

"I'm honored!"

"I brought you some flowers," he added. "One of the nurses volunteered to put them in a vase for you."

She gave him a cursory appraisal and smiled. "The way you look, I'm not surprised. Women fall over each other to get to you."

"Not the one I wanted," he said sadly. "And now it's too late."

She slid her hand into his and pressed it gently. "I'm sorry."

"So am I." He shrugged. "Isn't it a damned shame? I mean, look what they're missing!"

She knew he was talking about Simon and the woman Charles wanted, and she grinned in spite of herself. "It's their loss. I'd love to go to the ball with you. He'll let me out of here today. Like to take me home?"

"Sure!"

But when the doctor came into the room, he was reluctant to let her leave.

She was sitting on the side of the bed. She gave him a long, wise look. "I wasn't lying," she said. "Suicide was the very last thing from my mind."

"With a loaded pistol, which had been fired."

She pursed her lips. "Didn't anyone notice where the shot landed? At a round hole in the baseboard?"

He frowned.

"The mouse!" she said. "I've been after him for weeks! Don't you watch old John Wayne movies? It was in *True Grit!*"

All at once, realization dawned in his eyes. "The rat writ."

"Exactly!"

He burst out laughing. "You were going to shoot the mouse?"

"I'm a good shot," she protested. "Well, when I'm sober. I won't miss him next time!"

"Get a trap."

"He's too wily," she protested. "I've tried traps and baits."

"Buy a cat."

"I'm allergic to fur," she confessed miserably.

"How about those electronic things you plug into the wall?"

She shook her head. "Tried it. He bit the electrical cord in half."

"Didn't it kill him?"

Her eyebrows arched. "No. Actually he seemed even healthier afterward. I'll bet he'd enjoy arsenic. Nope, I have to shoot him."

The doctor and Charles looked at each other. Then they both chuckled.

The doctor did see her alone later, for a few minutes while Charles was bringing the car around to the hospital entrance. "Just one more thing," he said gently. "Regardless of what Simon said, you didn't kill John. Nobody, no woman, could have stopped what happened. He should never have married you in the first place."

"Simon kept throwing us together," she said. "He thought we made the perfect couple," she added bitterly.

"Simon never knew," he said. "I'm sure John didn't tell him, and you kept your own silence."

She averted her eyes. "John was the best friend Simon had in the world. If he'd wanted Simon to know, he'd have told him. That being the case, I never felt that I had the right." She looked at him. "I still don't. And you're not to tell him, either. He deserves to have a few unshattered illusions. His life hasn't been a bed of roses so far. He's missing an arm, and he's still mourning Melia."

"God knows why," Dr. Gaines added, because he'd known all about the elegant Mrs. Hart, things that even Tira didn't know.

"He loved her," she said simply. "There's no accounting for taste, is there?"

He smiled gently. "I guess not."

"You know, you really are a nice man, Dr. Gaines," she added.

He chuckled. "That's what my wife says all the time."

"She's right," she agreed.

"Don't you have family?"

She shook her head. "My father died of a heart attack, and my mother died even before he did. She had cancer. It was hard to watch, especially for Dad. He loved her too much."

"You can't love people too much."

She looked up at him with such sadness that her face seemed to radiate it. "Yes, you can," she said solemnly. "But I'm going to learn how to stop."

Charles pulled up at the curb and Dr. Gaines waved them off.

"Look at him," Charles said with a grin. "He's drooling! He wants my car." He stepped down on the accelerator. "Everybody wants my car. But it's mine. Mine!"

"Charles, you're getting obsessed with this automobile," she cautioned.

"I am not!" He glanced at her. "Careful, you'll get fingerprints on the window. And I do hope you wiped your shoes before you got in."

She didn't know whether to laugh or cry.

"I'm kidding!" he exclaimed.

She let out a sigh of relief. "And Dr. Gaines wanted *me* to have therapy," she murmured.

He threw her a glare. "I do not need therapy. Men love their cars. One guy even wrote a song about how much he loved his truck.''

She glanced around the luxurious interior of the pretty car, leather coated with a wood-grained dash, and nodded. ''Well, I could love Big Red,'' she had to confess. She leaned back against the padded headrest and closed her eyes.

He patted the dash. ''Hear that, guy? You're getting to her!''

She opened one eye. ''I'm calling the therapist the minute we get to my house.''

He lifted both blond eyebrows. ''Does he like cars?''

''I give up!''

When she arrived home, she was met at the door by a hovering, worried Mrs. Lester.

''It was an old, empty prescription bottle!'' Tira told the kindly older woman. ''And the pistol wasn't for me, it was for that mouse we can't catch in the kitchen!''

''The mouse?''

''Well, we can't trap him or drive him out, can we?'' she queried.

The housekeeper blushed all the way to her white hairline and wrung her hands in the apron. ''It was the way it looked...''

Tira went forward and hugged her. ''You're a doll and I love you. But I was only drunk.''

''You never drink,'' Mrs. Lester stated.

''I was driven to it,'' she replied.

Mrs. Lester looked at Charles. ''By him?'' she asked with a twinkle in her dark eyes. ''You shouldn't let him hang around here so much, if he's driving you to drink.''

''See?'' he murmured, leaning down. ''She wants my car, that's why she wants me to leave. She can't stand having to look at it day after day. She's obsessed with jealousy, eaten up with envy...''

''What's he talking about?'' Mrs. Lester asked curiously.

''He thinks you want his car.''

Mrs. Lester scoffed. "That long red fast flashy thing?" She sniffed. "Imagine me, riding around in something like that!"

Charles grinned. "Want to?" he asked, raising and lowering his eyebrows.

She chuckled. "You bet I do! But I'm much too old for sports cars, dear. Tira's just right."

"Yes, she is. And she needs coddling."

"I'll fatten her up and see that she gets her rest. I knew I should never have let her talk me into that vacation. The first time I leave her in a month, and look what happens! And the newspapers…!" She stopped so suddenly that she almost bit her tongue through.

Tira froze in place. "What newspapers?"

Mrs. Lester made a face and exchanged a helpless glance with Charles.

"You, uh, made the headlines," he said reluctantly.

She groaned. "Oh, for heaven's sake, there goes my one-woman show!"

"No, it doesn't," Charles replied. "I spoke to Bob this morning before I came after you. He said that the phone's rung off the hook all morning with queries about the show. He figures you'll make a fortune from the publicity."

"I don't need…"

"Yes, but the outreach program does," he reminded her. He grinned. "They'll be able to buy a new van!"

She smiled, but her heart wasn't in it. She didn't want to be notorious, whether or not she deserved to.

"Cheer up," he said. "It'll be old news tomorrow. Just don't answer the phone for a day or two. It will blow over as soon as some new tragedy catches the editorial eye."

"I guess you're right."

"Next Saturday," he reminded her. "I'll pick you up at six."

"Where will you be until then?" she asked, surprised, because he often came by for coffee in the afternoon.

"Memphis," he said with a sigh. "A business deal that I have to conduct personally. I'll be out of town for a week. Bad timing, too.''

"I'll be fine," she assured him. "Mrs. Lester's right here."

"I guess so. I do worry about you." He smiled sheepishly. "I don't have any family, either. You're sort of the only relative I have, even though you aren't."

"Same here."

He searched her eyes. "Two of a kind, aren't we? We loved not wisely, and too well."

"As you said, it's their loss," she said stubbornly. "Have a safe trip. Are you taking Big Red?"

He shook his head. "They won't let me take him on the plane," he said. "Walters is going to stand guard over him in the garage with a shotgun while I'm gone, though. Maybe he won't pine."

She burst out laughing. "I'm glad I have you for a friend," she said sincerely.

He took her hand and held it gently. "That works both ways. Take care. I'll phone you sometime during the week, just to make sure you're okay. If you need me…"

"I have your mobile number," she assured him. "But I'll be fine."

"See you next week, then."

"Thanks for the ride home," she said.

He shrugged and flashed her a white smile. "My pleasure."

She watched him drive away with sad eyes. She was going to have to live down the bad publicity without telling her side of the story. Well, what did it matter, she reasoned. It could, after all, have been worse.

Chapter 3

The week passed slowly until the charity ball on Saturday evening. It was to be a lavish one, hosted by the Carlisles, a founding family in the area and large supporters of the local hospital's charity work. Their huge brick mansion was just south of the perimeter of San Antonio, set in a grove of mesquite and pecan trees with its own duck pond and a huge formal garden. Tira had always loved coming to the house in the past for these gatherings, but she knew that Simon would be on the guest list. It was going to be hard facing him again after what had happened. It was going to be difficult appearing in public at all.

She did plan to go down with all flags flying, however, having poured her exquisite figure into a sleeveless, long black velvet evening gown with lace appliqués in entrancing places and a lace-up bodice that left little gaps from her diaphragm to her breasts. Her hair was in an elegant French twist with a diamond clip that matched her dangling earrings and delicate waterfall diamond necklace. She looked wealthy and sophisticated and Charles gave her a wicked grin when she came through to the living room with a black velvet and jewel wrap over one bare shoulder. It was November and the weather was unseasonably warm, so the wrap was just right.

Charles dressed up nicely, she thought, studying him. His tuxedo played up his extreme good looks and his fairness.

"Don't we make a pair?" he mused, glancing in the hall mirror at them. "Pity it isn't the right one."

"We'll both survive the evening," she assured him.

"Only if we drink hard enough," he said with graveyard humor. Then he noticed her expression and grimaced. "Sorry," he said genuinely.

"No need to apologize," she replied with a wry smile. "I did something stupid and had the misfortune to be found doing it. I'll survive all the gossip. But whatever you do, don't leave me alone with Simon, okay?"

"Count on it. What are friends for?"

She smiled at him. "To get us through rough times," she said, and was suddenly very grateful that she had a friend as good as Charles.

Charles chided her gently for her growing and obvious nervousness as he drove rapidly down the road that led to the Carlisle estate. "Don't worry so. You're old news," he reminded her. "There's the local political scandal to latch onto now."

"What political scandal?" she asked. "And how do you know about it when you've been out of town?"

"Because our lieutenant governor has been participating in a conference on the problems of inner cities in Memphis. I sat next to him on the flight home," he said smugly. Keeping his eyes on the road, he leaned toward her. "It seems that the attorney general intervened in a criminal case for a friend. The criminal he got paroled was serving time for armed robbery, but when he got out, he went right home and killed his ex-wife for testifying against him and is now back in prison. But the wheels of political change are going to roll over the governor's fair-haired boy."

"Oh, my goodness," she burst out. "But he was only doing a kindness. How could he know...?"

"He couldn't, and he isn't really to blame, but the opposition party is going to use it to crucify him. I understand his resignation is forthcoming momentarily.''

"What a shame," Tira said honestly. "He's done a wonderful job. I met him at one of the charity benefits earlier this year and thought how lucky we were to have elected someone so capable to the position! Now, if he resigns, I guess the governor will have to temporarily appoint someone to finish his term."

"No doubt he will."

"Maybe he'll slide out of it. Lots of politicians do."

"Not this time, I'm afraid," Charles said. "He's made some bitter enemies since he took office. They'll love the opportunity to settle the score."

She recalled that Simon had antagonized plenty of people when he held the office of state attorney general. But it would have taken more than a scandal to unseat him. He had a clever habit of turning weapons against their wielders.

She closed her eyes and ground her teeth as she realized how pitiful she was about him, still. Everything reminded her of Simon. She hadn't wanted to come tonight, either, but the alternative was to stay home and let the whole city know what a coward she was. She had to hold her head up high and pretend that everything was fine, when her whole world was lying in shards around her feet.

She hadn't tried to kill herself, but one particularly lurid newspaper account said she had, and added that it had been over former attorney general Simon Hart, who'd rejected her. It was in a newspaper published by a relative of Jill Sinclair, a woman who'd been a rival of Tira's for Simon during the past few years. Tira had been even more humiliated at that particular story, but when she'd phoned the reporter who wrote it, he denied any knowledge of Jill Sinclair. Still, she was certain dear Jill had a hand in it.

Tira shuddered, realizing that Simon must have seen the story, too. He'd know what a fool she'd been over him, which was just one more humiliation. Living that down wasn't going to be easy. But she did have Charles beside her. And he had his own ordeal to face, because his sister-in-law would certainly be present.

A valet came to park the car for Charles, who was torn between escorting Tira inside or accompanying the elegantly dressed young man assigned to the car placement to make sure he didn't put a scratch on "Big Red."

"Go ahead," Tira said with amused resignation. "I'll wait on the steps for you."

"You're such a doll," he murmured and made a kissing motion toward her. "How many women in the world would understand a man's passion for his car? Here, son, I'll just ride down with you to the parking lot."

The valet seemed torn between shock and indignation.

"He's in love with it!" Tira called to the young man. "He can't help himself. Just humor him!"

The valet broke into a wide grin and climbed under the steering wheel.

It was unfortunate that while she was waiting on the wide porch for Charles to return, Simon and his date got out of his elegant Town Car at the steps and let the valet drive it off. He looked devastating, as usual. He was wearing the prosthesis, she noticed, and wondered at how much he seemed to use it these days. Just after the wreck, he wouldn't be caught dead wearing an artificial arm.

The woman with him was Jill Sinclair herself, a socialite, twice divorced and wealthy, with short black hair and dark eyes and a figure that drew plenty of interest. It would, Tira thought wickedly, considering that her red sequined dress must have been sprayed on and the paint ran out at midthigh. Advertising must pay, she mused, because Simon certainly seemed pleased as he smiled down at the small woman and held her elbow as they climbed up the steps.

He didn't see Tira until they were almost at the top. When he did, he seemed to jerk, as if the sight of her was unexpected.

She didn't let anything of her feelings show, despite the pain of seeing him now when her whole life had been laid bare in the press. She did her best not to let her embarrassment show, either.

She smiled carelessly and nodded politely at the couple and deliberately turned away in the direction where Charles and the valet were just coming into view.

"Why, how brave she is," Jill Sinclair purred to Simon, just loud enough for Tira to hear her. "I'd never have had the nerve to face all these people after that humiliating story in the— Simon!"

Her voice died completely. Tira didn't look toward them. Her face was flaming and she knew her accelerated heartbeat was making her shake visibly. She and Jill had never liked each other, but the woman seemed to be looking for a way to hurt her. She was obviously exuding her power since she'd finally managed to get Simon to notice her and take her out. God knew, she'd been after him for years. Tira's fall from grace had obviously benefitted her.

Charles bounded up the steps and took Tira's arm. "Sorry about that," he said sheepishly.

"You love your car," she replied with a warm smile. "I understand."

"You're one in a million," he mused. His hand fell to grasp hers, and when she looked inside the open doors she knew why. His half brother was there, and so was his sister-in-law, looking unhappy.

"Gene," he called to his older half brother. "Nice to see you." He shook the other man's hand. Gene was tall and severe-looking with thinning gray hair. The woman beside him was tiny and blond and lovely, but she had the most tragic brown eyes Tira had ever seen.

"Hello, Nessa," Charles said to the woman, his face guarded, a polite smile on his lips.

"Hello, Charles, Tira," Nessa replied in her soft, sweet voice. "You both look very nice. Isn't this a good turnout?" she added nervously. "They'll make a lot of money at five hundred dollars a couple."

"Yes," Tira agreed with a broad smile. "The hospital outreach program will probably be able to afford two vans and the services of another nurse!''

"For indigents," Gene Marlowe said huffily, "who won't pay a penny of their own health care."

The other three people looked at him as if he'd gone mad. He glared at them, reddening. "I have to see Todd Groves about a contract we're pursuing. If you'll excuse me? Nessa, don't just stand there! Come along."

Nessa ground her teeth together as Gene took her arm roughly. Charles looked as if he might attack his own brother right there. Tira caught his hand and tugged.

"I'm starving," she told him quickly, exchanging speaking glances with a suddenly relieved Nessa. "Feed me!"

Charles hesitated for an instant, during which Gene dragged Nessa away toward a group of men.

"Damn him!" Charles bit off, his normally pleasant face contorted and threatening.

Tira shook his hand gently. "You're broadcasting," she murmured, bumping deliberately against his side to distract him. "Come on, before you cause her any more trouble than she's already got."

He let out a weary sigh. "Why did she marry him?" he groaned. *"Why?"*

"Whatever the reason doesn't matter much now. Let's go."

She pulled until he let her lead him to the long buffet table, where expensive nibbles and champagne were elegantly arranged.

"This is going to eat up all the profits," Tira murmured worriedly, noting the crystal flutes that were provided for the champagne, and the fact that caviar was furnished as well.

Charles leaned toward her. "It's grocery store caviar, and the champagne is the sort they deliver in big round metal tractor trucks..."

"Charles!" She couldn't repress a giggle at the insinuation, and just as she felt her face going red from glee, she looked up and saw Simon's pale eyes glittering at her from across the room. She averted her eyes to the table and didn't look in that direction again. His expression had been far different from the one he'd worn when he'd seen her in the hospital. Now it was indignant and outraged, as if he blamed her for the publicity that made him look guilty, too.

Charles did waltz divinely. Tira found herself on the floor with him time after time. People noticed her, and there were some obvious whispers, which probably concerned her "suicide attempt." She was uncomfortable at first, but then she realized that the opinion of most of these people didn't matter to her. She knew the truth about what had happened and so did Charles. If the others wanted to believe her to be so weak and helpless that she'd die rather than face up to her failures, let them.

"Doesn't it worry you, being seen with such a notorious woman?" she chided when they were standing again at the buffet table with more champagne.

"Notorious women are fascinating," he returned, and smiled. His eyes lifted to his half brother and Nessa and his jaw clenched. The two of them were going out the door and Nessa looked as if she were crying.

"You can't," she said, catching his arm when he looked as if he might follow them.

"She should leave him."

"She'll have to make that decision for herself."

He glanced down at her with worried eyes. "She isn't like you. She isn't independent and spirited. She's shy and gentle and people take advantage of her."

"And you want to protect her. I understand. But you can't, not tonight."

He made a rough sound in his throat. "Damn it!"

She leaned against him affectionately for an instant. "I'm sorry. I really am."

His arm slipped around her shoulders. "One day," he promised himself.

She nodded. "One day."

"Why, Charles, how handsome you look!" Jill Sinclair's high-pitched, grating voice turned them around. "Are you enjoying yourself?"

"I'm having a great time," Charles said through his teeth. "How about you?"

"Oh, Simon is just the most wonderful escort," she sighed and glanced at Tira with half-closed eyes. "We've been everywhere together lately. There are *so* many charity dos this time of year. And how are you, Tira? I was so sorry to hear about your near tragedy!" She was almost purring, enjoying Tira's stiff posture and cold face. She raised her voice, drawing attention from the couples hovering near the buffet table. "Isn't it a pity that the newspapers made such a big thing of your suicide attempt? I mean, the humiliation of having your feelings made public must be awful. And for the gossips to say that you wanted to die just because Simon couldn't love you back...why he was just shattered that you made him look like a coldhearted villain in the eyes of his friends. God knows, it isn't his fault that he doesn't love you!"

Tira was too shaken by the unexpected attack to reply. Charles wasn't.

"Why, you prissy little cat," Charles said with cold venom, making Jill actually catch her breath in surprise at the unexpected verbal jab. "Why don't you go sharpen your claws on the curtains?"

He took Tira's arm and led her away. She was so shocked and outraged that she couldn't even manage words. She wanted to empty the punch bowl over the woman, but that was hardly the sort of thing to do at a benefit ball. Her proud spirit had all but been broken by recent events. She was still licking her wounds.

Simon was talking to a man near the door that Charles was urging her toward. He paused in midsentence and looked at Tira's white face with curious concern.

Before he could speak, Charles did. "Never mind adding your two cents worth. Your girlfriend said it all for you."

Charles prodded her forward and Tira didn't look Simon's way. She was barely able to see where she was going at all. Until Jill's piece of mischief, she'd actually thought she could get through the evening unscathed.

"That cat!" Charles muttered as they made their way to the bottom of the steps.

"The world is full of them," she breathed. "And how they love to claw you when you're down!"

None of the valets were anywhere in sight. Charles grumbled. "I'll have to go fetch the car. Stay right here. Will you be all right?"

"I'm fine, now that we're outside," she said.

He gave her a last, worried glance, and went around the house to the parking area.

She drew her wrap closer, because the air was chilly. Once, she'd have made Jill pay dearly for her nasty comments, but not anymore. Now, her proud spirit was dulled and she'd actually walked away from a fight. It wasn't like her. Charles obviously knew that, or he wouldn't have rushed her out the door so quickly.

She heard footsteps behind her and her heart jumped, because she knew the very sound of Simon's feet. Her eyes closed as she wished him in China—anywhere but here!

"What did she say to you?" he asked shortly.

She wouldn't turn; she wouldn't look at him. She couldn't bear to look at him. The humiliation of having him know how she felt about him was so horrible that it suffocated her. All those years of hiding it from him, cocooning her love in secrecy. And now he knew, the whole world knew. And worst of all, she loved him still. Just being near him was agony.

"I said, what did she say to you?" he repeated, moving directly in front of her so that she had to look at him.

She lifted her eyes to his black tie and no further. Her voice was choked, and stiff with wounded pride. "Go and ask her."

There was a rough sigh and she saw his good hand go irritably into the pocket of his trousers. "This isn't like you," he said after a minute. "You don't run and you don't cry, regardless of what people say to you. You fight back. Why are you leaving?"

She lifted tired eyes to his and hated the sudden jolt of her heart at the sight of his beloved face. She clenched every muscle in her body to keep from sobbing out her rage and hurt. "I don't care what anyone thinks of me," she said huskily, "least of all your malicious girlfriend. Yes, I've spent most of my life fighting, one way or another, but I'm tired. I'm tired of everything."

Her lack of animation disturbed him, along with the defeat in her voice, the cool poise. "You can't be worried about what the newspapers said," he said, his voice deep and slow and oddly tender.

"Can't I? Why not? They believed every word." She inclined her head toward the ballroom.

His features were unusually solemn. "I know you better than they do."

She searched his pale eyes in the dim light from the house. Her heart clenched. "You don't know me at all, Simon," she said with painful realization. "You never did."

He seemed to stiffen. "I thought I did. Until you divorced John."

Her heart stilled at the reference. "And until he died." Defeat was in every line of her elegant body. "Yes, I know, I'm a murderess."

His face went taut. "I didn't say that!"

"You might as well have!" she shot back, raising her voice, not caring if the whole world heard her. "If Melia had died in a similar manner, I'd never have believed you guilty of her death! I'd have known you well enough to be certain that you had no part in anything that would cause another human being harm. But then, I had a mad infatuation for you that I couldn't cure." She saw his sudden stillness. "Don't pretend that you didn't read all about it in the paper, Simon. Yes, it's true, why shouldn't I admit it? I was obsessed with you, desperate to be with you, in any way that I could. It didn't even matter that you only tolerated me. I could have lived on crumbs for the rest of my life—'' Her voice broke. She shifted on trembling legs and laughed with pure self-contempt. "What a fool I was! What a silly fool. I'm twenty-eight years old and I've only just realized how stupid I am!''

He frowned. "Tira…''

She moved back a step, her green eyes blazing with ruptured pride. "Jill told me what you said, that you blame me for making you look like a villain in public with my so-called suicide attempt, as well as for John's death. Well, go ahead, hate me! I don't give a damn anymore!'' she spat, out of control and not caring. "I'm not even surprised to see you with Jill, Simon. She's as opinionated and narrow-minded as you are, and she knows how to put the knife in, too. I daresay you're a match made in heaven!''

His face clenched visibly. "And you don't care that I'm with another woman tonight, instead of with you?'' he chided, hitting back as hard as he could, with a mocking smile on his lips.

Her face went absolutely white. But if it killed her, he'd never hear from her how she did care. She smiled deliberately. "No,'' she agreed softly. "Actually I don't. All this notoriety accomplished one good thing. It made me see how I'd wasted the past few miserable years mooning over you! You did me a favor when you told me what you really thought of me. I'm free of you at last, Simon,'' she lied with deliberation. "And I've never been quite so happy in all my life!''

And with that parting shot, she turned and walked slowly to the driveway where Charles was pulling up in front of the house, leaving Simon rigidly in place with an expression of shock that delighted her wounded pride.

After what she'd said, she didn't expect Simon to follow her, and he didn't. When Charles had installed her in the passenger seat, she caught just a glimpse of Simon's straight back rapidly returning to the house. She even knew the posture. He was furious. Good! Let him be furious. She was not going to care. She wasn't!

"Take it easy,'' Charles said softly. "You'll burst something.''

"I know how you felt earlier,'' she returned, leaning her hot forehead against the glass of the window. "Damn him! And damn her, too!"

"What did he say to you?"

"He wanted to know what she said, and then he gave me his opinion of my character again. But this time, he didn't know he'd hit me where it hurt. I made sure of it."

Charles let out a long breath. "Why can't we love to order?" he asked philosophically.

"I don't know. If you ever find out, you can tell me." She stared out the dark window at the flat landscape passing by. Her heart felt as if it might break all over again.

"He's an idiot."

"So is Jill. So is Gene. We're all idiots. Maybe we're certifiable and we can become a circus act."

They drove in silence until they reached her house. He turned off the engine and stared at her worriedly. She was pale and she looked so miserable that he hurt for her.

"Go inside and change your clothes and pack a suitcase," he said suddenly.

"What?"

"We'll fly down to Nassau for a long weekend. It's just Saturday. We'll take a three-day vacation. I have a friend who owns a villa there. He and his wife love company. We'll eat conch chowder and play at the casino and lay on the beach. How about it?"

She brightened. "Could we?"

"We could. You need a break and so do I. Be a gambler."

It sounded like fun. She hadn't been happy in such a long time. "Okay," she said.

"Okay." He grinned. "Maybe we'll cheer up in foreign parts. Don't take too long. I'll run home and change and make a few phone calls. I should be back within an hour."

"Great!"

It was great. The brief holiday made Tira feel as if she had a new lease on life. Charles was wonderful, undemanding company,

much more like a beloved brother than a boyfriend. They padded
all over Nassau, down West Bay Street to the docks and out on
the pier to look at the ships in port, and all the way to the shopping
district and the vast straw markets. Nassau was the most exciting,
cosmopolitan city in the world to Tira. She never tired of going
there. Just now, it was a godsend. She hated the memory of Jill's
taunting words and Simon's angry accusations. It was good to
have a breathing space from them, and the publicity.

They stretched their stay to five days instead of three and returned to San Antonio refreshed and rested, although Charles had
confessed that he did miss his car. He proved it by rushing home
as soon as the limousine he'd hired to meet them at the airport
delivered Tira at her house.

"I'll phone you in the morning. We might have a game of
tennis Saturday, if you're up to it," he said.

"I will be. Thanks, Charles. Thanks so much!"

He chuckled. "I enjoyed it. So long."

She watched the limousine pull away and walked slowly up to
her front door. She hated homecomings. She had nothing here but
Mrs. Lester and an otherwise empty house, and her work. It was
cold compensation.

Mrs. Lester greeted her with enthusiasm. "I'm so glad you're
home!" she said. "The phone rang off the hook the day after you
left and didn't stop until three days ago." She shook her head. "I
can't imagine why those newspaper people wanted to drag the
whole subject up again, but I guess the shooting downtown Tues-
day afternoon gave them something new to go after."

"What shooting?"

"Well, that man the attorney general had paroled—you remember?—was in court to be arraigned and he went right over the
table toward the judge and almost killed him. They managed to
pull him away and he grabbed the bailiff's gun. They had to shoot
him! It's been on all the television stations. They had the most
awful photographs of it!"

Tira actually gasped. "For heaven's sake!"

"Mr. Hart was right in the middle of it, too. He had a case and was waiting for it to be called when the prisoner got loose."

"Simon? Was he...hurt?" Tira had to ask.

"No. He was the one who pulled the man off the judge. The man had that bailiff's gun leveled right at him, they said, when a deputy sheriff shot the man. It was a close call for Mr. Hart. A real close call. But you'd never think it worried him to hear him talk on television. He was as cold as ice."

She sat down on the edge of the sofa and thanked God for Simon's life. She wished that they were still friends, even distant ones, so that she could phone him and tell him so. But there was a wall between them now.

"Mr. Hart wondered why you hadn't gotten in touch with him, afterward," Mrs. Lester said, hesitating.

Tira glanced at her breathlessly. "He called?"

She nodded and then grimaced. "He wanted to know if you heard about the shooting and if you'd been concerned. I had to tell him that you were away, and didn't know a thing, and when he asked where, he got that out of me, too. I hope it was all right that I told him."

Simon would think she went on a lover's holiday with Charles. Well, why shouldn't he? He believed she was a murderess and a flighty, shallow flirt and suicidal. Let him think whatever else he liked. She couldn't be any worse in his eyes than she already was.

"Give a dog a bad name," she murmured.

"What?" Mrs. Lester asked.

She dragged her mind back to the subject at hand. "Yes, of course, it's perfectly all right that you told him, Mrs. Lester," Tira said quietly. "I had a wonderful time in Nassau."

"Did you good, I expect, and Mr. Percy is a nice man."

"A very nice man," Tira agreed. She got to her feet. "I'm tired. I think I'll lie down for a while, so don't fix anything to eat for another hour or so, will you?"

"Certainly, dear. You just rest. I'll have some coffee and sandwiches ready when you want them."

Would she ever want them? Tira wondered as she went slowly toward her bedroom. She was empty and cold and sick at heart. But that seemed to be her normal condition. At least for now.

Chapter 4

It was raining the day Tira began taking her sculptures to Bob Henderson's "Illuminations" art gallery for her showing. She was so gloomy she hardly felt the mist on her face. Christmas was only two weeks away and she was miserable and lonely. Only months before, she'd have phoned Simon and asked him to meet her for lunch in town, or she'd have shown up at some committee meeting or benefit conference at which he was present, just to feed her hungry heart on the sight of him. Now, she had nothing. Only Charles and his infrequent, undemanding company. Charles was a sweetheart, but it was like having a brother over for coffee.

She carried the last box carefully in the back door, which Lillian Day, the gallery's manager was holding open for her.

"That's the last of them, Lillian," Tira told her, smiling as she surveyed the cluttered storage room. She shook her head. "I can't believe I did all those myself."

"It's a lot of work," Lillian agreed, smiling back. She bent to open one of the boxes and frowned slightly at what was inside. "Did you mean to include this?" she asked, indicating a bust of Simon that was painfully lifelike.

Tira's face closed up. "Yes, I meant to," she said curtly. "I don't want it."

Lillian wisely didn't say another word. "I'll place it with the others, then. The catalogs have been printed and they're perfect, I checked them myself. Everything's ready, including the caterer for the snack buffet and the media coverage. We're doing a Christmas motif for the buffet."

Media coverage. Tira ground her teeth. The last thing in the world she wanted to see now was a reporter.

Lillian, sensitive to moods, glanced at her reassuringly. "Don't worry. These were handpicked, by me," she added. "They won't ask any embarrassing questions, and anything they write for print will be about the show. Period."

Tira relaxed. "What would I do without you?" she asked, and meant it.

Lillian grinned. "Don't even think about trying. We're very glad to have your exhibit here."

Tira had worried about Simon's reaction to the showing, since he was a partner in Bob Henderson's gallery. They hadn't spoken since before his close call in the courtroom and she half expected him to cancel her exhibit. But he hadn't. Perhaps Mrs. Lester had been mistaken and he hadn't been angry that Tira hadn't phoned to check on him. Just because she hadn't called, it didn't mean that she hadn't worried. She'd had a few sleepless nights thinking about what could have happened to him. Despite her best efforts, her feelings for him hadn't changed. She was just as much in love with him now as she had been. She was only better at concealing it.

The night of the exhibit arrived. She was all nerves, and she was secretly glad that Charles would be by her side. Not that she expected Simon to show up, with the media present. He wouldn't want to give them any more ammunition to embarrass him with. But Charles would be a comfort to her.

Fate stepped in, however, to rob her of his presence. Charles phoned at the last minute, audibly upset, to tell her he couldn't go with her to the show.

"I'm more sorry than I can tell you, but Gene's had a heart attack," he said curtly.

"Oh, Charles, I'm so sorry!"

"No need to be. You know there's no love lost between us. But he's my half brother, just the same, and there's no one else to look after him. Nessa is in shock herself. I can't let her cope alone."

"How is he?"

"Stabilized, for the moment. I'm on my way to the hospital. Nessa's with him and he's giving her hell, as usual, even flat on his back," he said curtly.

"If there's anything I can do…"

"Thanks for your support. I'm sorry you have to go on your own. But it's unlikely that Simon will be there, you know," he added gently. "Just stick close to Lillian. She'll look out for you."

She smiled to herself. "I know she will. Let me know how it goes."

"Of course I will. See you."

He hung up. She stared at the phone blankly as she replaced the receiver. She looked good, she reasoned. Her black dress was a straight sheath, ankle-length, with spaghetti straps and a diamond necklace and earrings to set it off. It was a perfect foil for her pale, flawless complexion and her red-gold hair, done in a complicated topknot with tendrils just brushing her neck. From her austere get up, she looked more like a widow in mourning than a woman looking forward to Christmas, and she felt insecure and nervous. It would be the first time she'd appeared alone in public since the scandal and she was still uncomfortable around most people.

Well, she comforted herself as she went outside and climbed into her Jaguar, at least she didn't have to add Simon to her other complications tonight.

The gallery was packed full of interested customers, some of whom had probably only come for curiosity's sake. It wasn't hard to discern people who could afford the four-figure price tags on the sculptures from those who couldn't. Tira pretended not to notice. She took a flute of expensive champagne and downed half of it before she went with Lillian to mingle with the guests.

It didn't help that the first two people she saw were Simon and Jill.

"Oh, God," she ground out through her teeth, only too aware of the reporters and their sudden interest in him. "Why did he have to come?!"

Lillian took her arm gently. "Don't let him know that it bothers you. Smile, girl! We'll get through this."

"Do you think so?"

She plastered a cool smile to her lips as Simon pulled Jill along with him and came to a halt just in front of the two women.

"Nice crowd," he told Tira, his eyes slowly going over her exquisite figure in the close-fitting dress with unusual interest.

"A few art fans and a lot of rubberneckers, hadn't you noticed?" Tira said, sipping more champagne. Her fingers trembled a little and she held the flute with both hands, something Simon's keen eyes picked up on at once.

"Nice of you to come by," Lillian said quietly.

He glanced at her. "It would have been noticeable if I hadn't, considering that I own half the gallery." His attention turned back to Tira and his silvery eyes narrowed. "All alone? Where's your fair-haired shadow?"

She knew he meant Charles. She smiled lazily. "He couldn't make it."

"On the first night of your first exhibition?" he chided.

She drew in a sharp breath. "His half brother had a heart attack, if you must know," she said through her teeth. "He's at the hospital."

Simon's eyes flickered strangely. "And you have to be here, instead of at his side. Pity."

"He doesn't need comforting. Nessa does."

Jill, dressed in red again with a sprig of holly secured with a diamond clip in her black hair, moved closer to Simon. "We just stopped in for a peek at your work," she said, almost purring as she looked up at the tall man beside her. "We're on our way to the opera."

Tira averted her eyes. She loved opera. Many times in the past, Simon had escorted her during the season. It hurt to remember how she'd looked forward to those chaste evenings with him.

"I don't suppose you go anymore?" Simon asked coldly.

She shrugged. "Don't have time," she said tightly.

"I noticed. You couldn't even be bothered to phone and check on me when that lunatic went wild in the courtroom."

Tira wouldn't look at him. "You can't hurt someone who's steel right through," she said.

"And you were out of the country when it happened."

She lifted her eyes to his hard face. "Yes. I was in Nassau with Charles, having a lovely time!"

His eyes seemed to blaze up at her.

Before the confrontation could escalate, Lillian diplomatically got between them. "Have you had time to look around?" she asked Simon.

"Oh, we've seen most everything," Jill answered for him. "Even the bust of Simon that Tira did. I was surprised that she was willing to sell it," she added in an innocent tone. "I wouldn't part with something so personal, Simon being such an old friend and all. But I guess under the circumstances, it was too painful a reminder of...things, wasn't it, dear?" she asked Tira.

Tira's hand automatically drew back, with the remainder of the champagne, but before she could toss it, Simon caught her wrist with his good hand.

"No catfights," he said through his teeth. "Jill, wait for me at the door, will you?"

"If you say so. My, she does look violent, doesn't she?" Jill chided, but she walked away quickly just the same.

"Get a grip on yourself!" Simon shot at Tira under his breath. "Don't you see the reporters staring at you?"

"I don't give a damn about the reporters," she flashed at him. "If she comes near me again, I swear I'll empty the punch bowl over her vicious little head!"

He let go of her wrist and something kindled in his pale eyes as he looked at her animated face. "That's more like you," he said in a deep, soft tone.

Tira flushed, aware that Lillian was quietly deserting her, stranding her with Simon.

"Why did you come?" she asked furiously.

"So the gossips wouldn't have a field day speculating about why I didn't," he explained. "It wouldn't have done either of us much good, considering what's been in print already."

She lifted her face, staring at him with cold eyes at the reference to things she only wanted to forget. "You've done your duty," she said. "You might as well go. And take the Wicked Witch of the West with you," she added spitefully.

"Jealous?" he asked in a sensuous tone.

Her face hardened. "I once asked you the same question. You can give yourself the same answer that you gave me. Like hell I'm jealous!"

He was watching her curiously, his eyes acutely alive in a strangely taciturn face. "You've lost weight," he remarked. "And you look more like a widow than a celebrity tonight. Why wear black?"

"I've decided that you were right. I should have mourned my husband. So now I'm in mourning," she said icily and with an arctic smile. "I expect to be in mourning for him until I die, and I'll never look at a man again. Doesn't that make you happy?"

He frowned slightly. "Tira…"

"Tira!"

The sound of a familiar voice turned them both around. Harry Beck, Tira's father-in-law, came forward, smiling, to embrace Tira. He turned to shake Simon's hand. "Great to see you both!" he said enthusiastically. "Dollface, you've outdone yourself," he told Tira, nodding toward two nearby sculptures. "I always knew you were talented, but this is sheer genius!"

Simon looked puzzled by Harry's honest enthusiasm for Tira's work, by his lack of hostility. She'd killed his only son, didn't he care?

"I'm glad to see you, Simon," Harry added with a smile. "It's been a long time."

"Simon was just leaving. Weren't you?" Tira added meaningfully.

"Someone's motioning to you," Harry noted, indicating Lillian frantically waving from across the room.

"It's Lillian. Will you excuse me?" Tira asked, smiling at Harry. "I won't be a minute." Simon, she ignored entirely.

The two men watched her go.

"I'm glad to see her looking so much better," Harry said on a sigh, shoving his hands into his pockets. "I've been worried since she went to the hospital."

"Do you really care what happens to her?" Simon asked curiously.

Harry was surprised. "Why wouldn't I be? She was my daughter-in-law. I've always been fond of her."

"She divorced John a month after they married and let him go off to work on a drill rig in the ocean," Simon returned. "He died there."

Harry stared at him blankly. "But that wasn't her fault."

"Wasn't it?"

"Why are you so bitter?" Harry wanted to know. "For God's sake, you can't think she didn't try to change him? He should have told her the truth before he married her, not let her find it out that way!"

Simon was puzzled. "Find what out?"

Jill glared at Simon, but he made a motion for her to wait another minute and turned back to Harry. "Find what out?" he repeated curtly.

"That John was homosexual, of course," Harry said, puzzled.

The blood drained out of Simon's face. He stared down at the older man with dawning comprehension.

"She didn't tell you?" Harry asked gently. He sighed and shook his head. "That's like her, though. She wanted to preserve your illusions about John, even if it meant sacrificing your respect for her. She couldn't tell you, I guess. I can't blame her. If he'd only been able to accept what he was...but he couldn't. He tried so hard to be what he thought I wanted. And he never seemed to understand that I'd have loved him regardless of how he saw his place in the world."

Simon turned away, his eyes finding Tira across the room. She wouldn't meet his gaze. She turned her back. He felt the pain right through his body.

"Dear God!" he growled when he realized what he'd done.

"Don't look like that," Harry said gently. "John made his own choice. It was nobody's fault. Maybe it was mine. I should have seen that he was distraught and done something."

Simon let out a breath. He was sick right to his soul. What a fool he'd been.

"She should have told you," Harry was saying. "You're a grown man. You don't need to be protected from the truth. She was always like that, even with John, trying to protect him. She'd have gone on with the marriage if he hadn't insisted on a divorce."

"I thought...she got the divorce."

"He got it, in her name, and cited mental cruelty." He shrugged. "I don't think he considered how it might look to an outsider. It made things worse for him. He only did it to save her reputation. He thought it would hurt her publicly if he made it look like she was at fault." He glanced at Simon. "That was right after your wreck and she was trying to take care of you. He thought it might appear as if she was having an affair with you and he found out. It might have damaged both of you in the public eye."

His teeth clenched. "I never touched her."

"Neither did John," Harry murmured heavily. "He couldn't. He cried in my arms about it, just before he saw an attorney. He wanted to love her. He did, in his way. But it wasn't in a conventional way at all."

Simon pushed back a strand of dark, wavy hair that had fallen on his brow. He was sweating because the gallery was overheated.

"Are you all right?" Harry asked with concern.

"I'm fine." He wasn't. He'd never be all right again. He glanced toward Tira with anguish in every line of his face. But she wouldn't even look at him.

Jill, sensing some problem, came back to join him, sliding her hand into his arm. "Aren't you ready? We'll miss the curtain."

"I'm ready," he said. He looked down at her and realized that here was one more strike against him. He was giving aid and comfort to Tira's worst enemy in the city. He'd done it deliberately, of course, to make her even more uncomfortable. But that was before he knew the whole truth. Now he felt guilty.

"Hello. I'm Jill Sinclair. Have we met?" she asked Harry, smiling.

"No, we haven't. I'm—"

"We have to go," Simon said abruptly. He didn't want to add any more weapons to Jill's already full arsenal by letting Harry tell her about John, too. "See you, Harry."

"Sure. Good night."

"Who was that?" Jill asked Simon as they went toward the door.

"An old friend. Just a minute. There's something I have to do."

"Simon...!"

"I won't be a minute," he promised, and caught one of the gallery's sales-people alone long enough to make a request. She seemed puzzled, but she agreed. He went back to Jill and escorted her out of the gallery, casting one last regretful look toward Tira, who was speaking to a group of socialites at the back of the gallery.

"Half the works are sold already," Jill murmured. "I guess she'll make a fortune."

"She's donating it all to charity," he replied absently.

"She can afford to. It will certainly help her image and, God knows, she needs that right now."

He glanced at her. "That isn't why."

She shrugged. "Whatever you say, darling. *Brrrr,* I'm cold! Christmas is week after next, too." She peered up at him. "I hope you got me something pretty."

"I wouldn't count on it. I probably won't be in town for Christmas," he said not quite truthfully.

She sighed. "Oh, well, I might go and spend the holidays with my aunt in Connecticut. I do love snow!"

She was welcome to all she could find of it, he thought. His heart already felt as if he were buried in snow and ice. He knew that Harry's revelation would keep him awake all night.

Tira watched Simon leave with Jill. She was glad he'd gone. Perhaps now she could enjoy her show.

Lillian was giving her strange looks and when Harry came to say goodbye, he looked rather odd, too.

"What's wrong?" she asked Harry.

He started to speak and thought better of it. Let Simon tell her what he wanted her to know. He was tired of talking about the past; it was too painful.

He smiled. "It's a great show, kiddo, you'll make a mint."

"Thanks, Harry. I had fun doing it. Keep in touch, won't you?"

He leaned forward and kissed her cheek. "You know I will. How's Charlie?"

"His brother-in-law had a heart attack. He's not doing well."

"I'm really sorry. Always liked Charlie. Still do."

"I'll tell him you asked about him," she promised.

He smiled at her. "You do that. Keep well."

"You, too."

* * *

By the end of the evening, Tira was calmer, despite the painful memory of her argument with Simon's and Jill's catty remarks. She could just picture the two of them in Simon's lavish apartment, sprawled all over each other in an ardent tangle. It made her sick. Simon had never kissed her, never touched her in anything but an impersonal way. She'd lived like a religious recluse for part of her life and she had nothing to show for her reticence except a broken heart and shattered pride.

"What a great haul," Lillian enthused, breaking into her thoughts. "You sold three-forths of them. The rest we'll keep on display for a few weeks and see how they do."

"I'm delighted," Tira said, and meant it. "It's all going to benefit the outreach program at St. Mark's."

"They'll be very happy with it, I'm sure."

Tira was walking around the gallery with the manager. Most of the crowd had left and a few stragglers were making their way to the door. She noticed the bust of Simon had a Sold sign on it, and her heart jumped.

"Who bought it?" Tira asked curtly. "It wasn't Jill Sinclair, was it?"

"No," Lillian assured her. "I'm not sure who bought it, but I can check, if you like."

"No, that's not necessary," Tira said, clamping down hard on her curiosity. "I don't care who bought it. I only wanted it out of my sight. I don't care if I never see Simon Hart again!"

Lillian sighed worriedly, but she smiled when Tira glanced toward her and offered coffee.

Simon watched the late-night news broadcast from his easy chair, nursing a whiskey sour, his second in half an hour. He'd taken Jill home and adroitly avoided her coquettish invitation to stay the night. After what he'd learned from Harry Beck, he had to be by himself to think things out.

There was a brief mention of Tira's showing at the gallery and how much money had been raised for charity. He held his breath, but nothing was said about her suicide attempt. He only hoped the newspapers would be equally willing to put the matter aside.

He sipped his drink and remembered unwillingly all the horrible things he'd thought about and said to Tira over John. How she must have suffered through that mockery of a marriage, and how horrible if she'd loved John. She must have had her illusions shattered. She was the injured party. But Simon had taken John's side and punished her as if she was guilty for John's death. He'd deliberately put her out of his life, forbidding her to come close, even to touch him.

He closed his eyes in anguish. She would never let him near her again, no matter how he apologized. He'd said too much, done too much. She'd loved him, and he'd savaged her. And it had all been for nothing. She'd been innocent.

He finished his drink with dead eyes. Regrets seemed to pile up in the loneliness of the night. He glanced toward the Christmas tree his enthusiastic housekeeper had set up by the window, and dreaded the whole holiday season. He'd spend Christmas alone. Tira, at least, would have the despised Charles Percy for company.

He wondered why she didn't marry the damned man. They seemed to live in each others' pockets. He remembered that Charles had always been her champion, bolstering her up, protecting her. Charles had been her friend when Simon had turned his back on her, so how could he blame her for preferring the younger man?

He put his glass down and got to his feet. He felt every year of his age. He was almost forty and he had nothing to show for his own life. The child he might have had was gone, along with Melia, who'd never loved him. He'd lived on illusions of love for a long time, when the reality of love had ached for him and he'd turned his back.

If he'd let Tira love him…

He groaned aloud. He might as well put that hope to rest right now. She'd hate him forever and he had only himself to blame. Perhaps he deserved her hatred. God knew, he'd hurt her enough.

He went to bed, to lie awake all night with the memory of Tira's wounded eyes and drawn face to haunt him.

Chapter 5

Simon was not in a good mood the next morning when he went into work. Mrs. Mackey, his middle-aged secretary, stopped him at the door of his office with an urgent message to call the governor's office as soon as he came in. He knew what it was about and he groaned inwardly. He didn't want to be attorney general, but he knew for a fact that Wally was going to offer it to him. Wallace Bingley was a hard man to refuse, and he was a very popular governor as well as a friend. Both Simon and Tira had been actively involved in his gubernatorial campaign.

"All right, Mrs. Mack," he murmured, smiling as he used her nickname, "get him for me."

She grinned, because she knew, too, what was going on.

Minutes later, the call was put through to his office.

"Hi, Wally," Simon said. "What can I do for you?"

"You know the answer to that already," came the wry response. "Will you or won't you?"

"I'd like a week or so to think about it," Simon said seriously. "It's a part of my life I hadn't planned to take up again. I don't like living in a goldfish bowl and I hear it's open season on attorneys general in Texas."

Wallace chuckled. "You don't have as many political enemies

as he does, and you're craftier, too. All right, think about it. Take
the rest of the month. But two weeks is all you've got. After the
holidays, his resignation takes effect, and I have to appoint someone.''

"I promise to let you know by then," Simon assured him.

"Now, to better things. Are you coming to the Starks's Christmas party?"

"I'd have liked to, but my brothers are throwing a party down
in Jacobsville and I more or less promised to show up."

"Speaking of the 'fearsome four,' how are they?"

"Desperate." Simon chuckled. "Corrigan phoned day before
yesterday and announced that Dorie thinks she's pregnant. If she
is, the boys are going to have to find a new victim to make biscuits
for them."

"Why don't they hire a cook?"

"They can't keep one. You know why," Simon replied dryly.

"I guess I do. He hasn't changed."

"He never will," Simon agreed, referring to his brother Leopold, who was mischievous and sometimes outrageous in his treatment of housekeepers. Unlike the other two of the three remaining
Hart bachelor brothers, Callaghan and Reynard, Leopold was a
live wire.

"How's Tira?" Wallace asked unexpectedly. "I hear her showing was a huge success."

The mention of it was uncomfortable. It reminded him all too
vividly of the mistakes he'd made with Tira. "I suppose she's
fine," Simon said through his teeth.

"Er, well, sorry, I forgot. The publicity must have been hard
on both of you. Not that anybody takes it seriously. It certainly
won't hurt your political chances, if that's why you're hesitating
to accept the position."

"It wasn't. I'll talk to you soon, Wally, and thanks for the
offer."

"I hope you'll accept. I could use you."

"I'll let you know."

He said goodbye and hung up, glaring out the window as he recalled what he'd learned about Tira so unexpectedly. It hurt him to talk about her now. It would take a long time for her to forgive him, if she ever did.

If only there was some way that he could talk to her, persuade her to listen to him. He'd tried phoning from home early this very morning. As soon as she'd heard his voice, she'd hung up, and the answering machine had been turned on when he tried again. There was no point in leaving a message. She was determined to wipe him right out of her life, apparently. He felt so disheartened he didn't know what to try next.

And then he remembered Sherry Walker, a mutual friend of his and Tira's in the past who loved opera and had season tickets in the aisle right next to his, in the dress circle. He knew that Sherry had broken a leg skiing just recently and had said that she wasn't leaving the house until it healed completely. Perhaps, he told himself, there was a way to get Tira to talk to him after all.

The letdown after the showing made Tira miserable. She had nothing to do just now, with the holiday season in full swing, and she had no one to buy a present for except Mrs. Lester and Charles. She went from store to colorfully decorated store and watched mothers and fathers with their children and choked on her own pain. She wouldn't have children or the big family she'd always craved. She'd live and die alone.

As she stood at a toy store window, watching the electric train sets flashing around a display of papier mache mountains and small buildings, she wondered what it would be like to have children to buy those trains for.

A lone, salty tear ran down her cold-flushed cheek and even as she caught it on her knuckles, she felt a sudden pervasive warmth at her back.

Her heart jumped even before she looked up. She always knew when Simon was anywhere nearby. It was a sort of unwanted radar and just lately it was more painful than ever.

"Nice, aren't they?" he asked quietly. "When I was a boy, my father bought my brothers and me a set of 'O' scale Lionel trains. We used to sit and run them by the hour in the dark, with all the little buildings lighted, and imagine little people living there." He turned, resplendent in a charcoal gray cashmere overcoat over his navy blue suit. His white shirt was spotless, like the patterned navy-and-white tie he wore with it. He looked devastating. And he was still wearing the hated prosthesis.

"Isn't this a little out of your way?" she asked tautly.

"I like toy stores. Apparently so do you." He searched what he could see of her averted face. Her glorious hair was in a long braid today and she was wearing a green silk pantsuit several shades darker than her eyes under her long black leather coat.

"Toys are for children," she said coldly.

He frowned slightly. "Don't you like children?"

She clenched her teeth and stared at the train. "What would be the point?" she asked. "I won't have any. If you'll excuse me..."

He moved in front of her, blocking the way. "Doesn't Charles want a family?"

It was a pointed question, and probably taunting. Charles's brother was still in the hospital and no better, and from what Charles had been told, he might not get better. There was a lot of damage to Gene's heart. Charles would be taking care of Nessa, whom he loved, but Simon knew nothing about that.

"I've never asked Charles how he feels about children," she said carelessly.

"Shouldn't you? It's an issue that needs to be resolved before two people make a firm commitment to each other."

Was he deliberately trying to lacerate her feelings? She wouldn't put it past him now. "Simon, none of this is any of your business," she said in a choked tone. "Now will you please let me go?" she asked on a nervous laugh. "I have shopping to do."

His good hand reached out to lightly touch her shoulder, but she jerked back from him as if he had a communicable disease.

"Don't!" she said sharply. "Don't ever do that!"

He withdrew his hand, scowling down at her. She was white in the face and barely able to breathe from the look of her.

"Just...leave me alone, okay?" She choked, and darted past him and into the thick of the holiday crowd on the sidewalk. She couldn't bear to let her weakness for him show. Every time he touched her, she felt vibrations all the way to her toes and she couldn't hide it. Fortunately she was away before he noticed that it wasn't revulsion that had torn her from his side. She was spared a little of her pride.

Simon watched her go with welling sadness. It could have been so different, he thought, if he'd been less judgmental, if he'd ever bothered to ask her side of her brief marriage. But he hadn't. He'd condemned her on the spot, and kept pushing her away for years. How could he expect to get back on any sort of friendly footing with her easily? It was going to take a long time, and from what he'd just seen, his was an uphill climb all the way. He went back to his office so dejected that Mrs. Mack asked if he needed some aspirin.

Tira brushed off the chance meeting with Simon as a coincidence and was cheered by an unexpected call from an old friend, who offered her a ticket to *Turandot,* her favorite opera, the next evening.

She accepted with pure pleasure. It would do her good to get out of the house and do something she enjoyed.

She put on a pretty black designer dress with diamanté straps and covered it with her flashy velvet wrap. She didn't look half bad for an old girl, she told her reflection in the mirror. But then, she had nobody to dress up for, so what did it matter?

She hired a cab to take her downtown because finding a parking space for the visiting opera performance would be a nightmare. She stepped out of the cab into a crowd of other music lovers and some of her painful loneliness drifted away in the excitement of the performance.

The seat she'd been given was in the dress circle. She remembered so many nights being here with Simon, but his reserved seat, thank God, was empty. If she'd thought there was a chance of his being here, she'd never have come. But she knew that Simon had taken Jill to see this performance already. It was unlikely that he'd want to sit through it again.

There was a drumroll. The theater went dark. The curtain started to rise. The orchestra began to play the overture. She relaxed with her small evening bag in her lap and smiled as she anticipated a joyful experience.

And then everything went suddenly wrong. There was a movement to her left and when she turned her head, there was Simon, dashing in dark evening clothes, sitting down right beside her.

He gave her a deliberately careless glance and a curt nod and then turned his attention back to the stage.

Tira's hands clenched on the evening bag. Simon's shoulder brushed against hers as he shifted in his seat and she felt the touch as if it were fire all the way down her body. It had never been so bad before. She'd walked with him, talked with him, shared seats at benefits and auctions and operas and plays with him, and even though his presence had been a bittersweet delight, it had never been so physically painful to her in the past. She wanted to turn and find his mouth with her lips, she wanted to press her body to his and feel his cheek against her own. The longing so was poignant that she shivered with it.

"Cold?" he whispered.

She clenched her jaw. "Not at all," she muttered, sliding further into her velvet wrap.

His good arm went, unobtrusively, over the back of her seat and rested there. She froze in place, barely daring to move, to breathe. It was just like the afternoon in front of the toy store. Did he know that it was torture for her to be close to him? Probably he did. He'd found a new way to get to her, to make her pay for all the terrible things he thought she'd done. She closed her eyes and groaned silently.

The opera, beautiful as it was, was forgotten. She was so miserable that she sat stiffly and heard none of it. All she could think about was how to escape.

She started to get up and Simon's big hand caught her shoulder a little too firmly.

"Stay where you are," he said gruffly.

She hesitated, but only for an instant. She was desperate to escape now. "I have to go to the necessary room, if you don't mind," she bit off near his ear.

"Oh."

He sighed heavily and moved his arm, turning to allow her to get past him. She apologized all the way down the row. Once she made it to the aisle, she felt safe. She didn't look back as she made her way gracefully and quickly to the back of the theater and into the lobby.

It was easy to dart out the door and hail a cab. This time of night, they were always a few of them cruising nearby. She climbed into the first one that stopped, gave him her address, and sat back with a relieved sigh. She'd done it. She was safe.

She went home more miserable than ever, changed into her nightgown and a silky white robe and let her hair down with a long sigh. She couldn't blame her friend, Sherry, for the fiasco. How could anyone have known that Simon would decide to see the opera a second time on this particular night? But it was a cruel blow of fate. Tira had looked forward to a performance that Simon's presence had ruined for her.

She made coffee, despite the late hour, and was sitting down in the living room to drink it when the doorbell rang.

It might be Charles, she decided. She hadn't heard from him today, and he could have stopped by to tell her about Gene. She went to the front door and opened it without thinking.

Simon was standing there with a furious expression on his face.

She tried to close the door, but one big well-shod foot was inside it before she could even move. He let himself in and closed the door behind him.

"Well, come in, then," she said curtly, her green eyes sparkling with bad temper as she pulled her robe closer around her.

He stared at her with open curiosity. He'd never seen her in night clothing before. The white robe emphasized her creamy skin, and the lace of her gown came barely high enough to cover the soft mounds of her breasts. With her red-gold hair loose in a glorious tangle around her shoulders, she was a picture to take a man's breath away.

"Why did you run?" he asked softly.

Her face colored gently. "I wasn't expecting you to be there," she said, and it came out almost as an accusation. "You've already seen the performance once."

"Yes, with Jill," he added deliberately, watching her face closely.

She averted her eyes. He looked so good in an evening jacket, she thought miserably. His dark, wavy hair was faintly damp, as if the threatening clouds had let some rain fall. His pale gray eyes were watchful, disturbing. He'd never looked at her this way before, like a predator with its prey. It made her nervous.

"Do you want some coffee?" she asked to break the tense silence.

"If you don't put arsenic in it."

She glanced at him. "Don't tempt me."

She led him into the kitchen, got down a cup and poured a cup of coffee for him. She didn't offer cream and sugar, because she knew he took neither.

He turned a chair around and straddled it before he picked up the cup and sipped the hot coffee, staring at her disconcertingly over the rim.

With open curiosity, she glanced at the prosthesis hand, which was resting on the back of the chair.

"Something wrong?" he asked.

She shrugged and picked up her own cup. "You used to hate that." She indicated the artificial arm.

"I hate pity even more," he said flatly. "It looks real enough to keep people from staring."

"Yes," she said. "It does look real."

He sipped coffee. "Even if it doesn't feel it," he murmured dryly. He glanced up at her face and saw it color from the faint insinuation in his deep voice. "Amazing, that you can still blush, at your age," he remarked.

It wouldn't have been if he knew how totally innocent she still was at her advanced age, but she wasn't sharing her most closely guarded secret with the enemy. He thought she and Charles were lovers, and she was content to let him. But that insinuation about why he used the prosthesis was embarrassing and infuriating. She hated being jealous. She had to conceal it from him.

"I don't care how it feels, or to whom," she said stiffly. "In fact, I have no interest whatsoever in your personal life. Not anymore."

He drew in a long breath and let it out. "Yes, I know." He finished his coffee in two swallows. "I miss you," he said simply. "Nothing is the same."

Her heart jumped but she kept her eyes down so that he wouldn't see how much pleasure the statement gave her. "We were friends. I'm sure you have plenty of others. Including Jill."

His intake of breath was audible. "I didn't realize how much you and Jill disliked each other."

"What difference does it make?" She glanced at him with a mocking smile. "I'm not part of your life."

"You were," he returned solemnly. "I didn't realize how much a part of it you were, until it was too late."

"Some things are better left alone," she said evasively. "More coffee?"

He shook his head. "It keeps me awake. Wally called and offered me the attorney general's post," he said. "I've got two weeks to think about it."

"You were a good attorney general," she recalled. "You got a lot of excellent legislation through the general assembly."

He smiled faintly, studying his coffee cup. "I lived in a goldfish bowl. I didn't like it."

"You have to take the bad with the good."

He looked at her closely. "Tell me what happened the night they took you to the hospital."

She shrugged. "I got drunk and passed out."

"And the pistol?"

"The mouse." She nodded toward the refrigerator. "He's under there, I can hear him. He can't be trapped and he's brazen. I got drunk and decided to take him out like John Wayne, with a six-shooter. I missed."

He chuckled softly. "I thought it was something like that. You're not suicidal."

"You're the only person who thinks so. Even Dr. Gaines didn't believe me. He wanted me to have therapy," she scoffed.

"The newspapers had a field day. I guess Jill helped feed the fire."

She glanced up, surprised. "You knew?"

"Not until she commented on it, when it was too late to do anything. For what it's worth," he added quietly, "I don't know many people who believed the accounts in her cousin's paper."

She leaned back in her chair and stared at him levelly. "That I did it for love of you?" she drawled with a poisonous smile. "You hurt my feelings when you accused me of killing my husband," she said flatly. "I was already overworked and depressed and I did something stupid. But I hope you don't believe that I sit around nights crying in my beer because of unrequited passion for you!"

Her tone hit him on the raw. He got slowly to his feet and his eyes narrowed as he stared down at her.

She felt at a distinct disadvantage. She'd only seen Simon lose his temper once. She'd never forgotten and she didn't want to repeat the experience.

"It's late," she said quickly. "I'd like to go to bed."

"Would you really?" His pale gaze slid over her body as he

said it, his voice so sensuous that it made her bare toes curl up on the spotless linoleum floor.

She didn't trust that look. She started past him and found one of her hands suddenly trapped by his big one. He moved in, easing her hand up onto the silky fabric of his vest, inside it against the silky warmth of his body under the thin cotton shirt. She could feel the springy hair under it as well, and the hard beat of his heart as his breath whispered out at her temple, stirring her hair. She'd never been so close to him. It was as if her senses, numb for years, all came to life at once and exploded in a shattering rush of physical sensation. It frightened her and she pushed at his chest.

"Simon, let go!" she said huskily, all in a rush.

He didn't. He couldn't. The feel of her in his arms exceeded his wildest imaginings. She was soft and warm and she smelled of flowers. He drank in the scent and felt her begin to tremble. It went right to his head. His hand left hers and slid into her hair at her nape, clenching, so that she was helpless against him. He fought for control. He mustn't do this. It was too soon. Far too soon.

His breath came quickly. She could hear it, feel it. His cheek brushed against hers roughly, as if he wanted to feel the very texture of her skin there. He had a faint growth of beard and it rasped a little, but it was more sensual than uncomfortable.

Her heart raced as wildly as his. She wanted to draw back, to run, but that merciless hand wasn't unclenching. If anything, it had an even tighter grip on her long hair.

She wasn't protesting anymore. He felt her yield and his body clenched. His cheek drew slowly against hers. She felt his mouth at the corner of her own, felt his breath as his lips parted.

"Don't..." The little cry was all but inaudible.

"It's too late," he said roughly. "Years too late. God, Tira, turn your mouth against mine!"

She heard the soft, gruff command with a sense of total unreality. Her cold hands pressed against his shirtfront, but it was, as he said, already too late.

He moved his head just a fraction of an inch, and his hard, hot mouth moved completely onto hers, parting her lips as it explored, settled, demanded. There was a faint hesitation, almost of shock, as sensual electricity flashed between them. He felt her mouth tremble, tasted it, savored it, devoured it.

He groaned as his mouth began to part her lips insistently. Then his arm was around her, the one with the prosthesis holding her waist firmly while the good one lifted and traced patterns from her cheek down to her soft, pulsing throat. He could hear the tortured sound of his own breath echoed by her own.

She whimpered as she felt the full force of his mouth, felt the kiss she'd dreamed of for so many years suddenly becoming reality. He tasted of coffee. His lips were hard and demanding on her mouth, sensual, insistent. She didn't protest. She clung to him, savoring the most ecstatic few seconds of her life as if she never expected to feel anything so powerful again.

Her response puzzled him, because it wasn't that of an experienced woman. She permitted him to kiss her, clung to him closely, even seemed to enjoy his rough ardor; but she gave nothing back. It was almost as if she didn't know how...

He drew back slowly. His pale, fierce eyes looked down into hers with pure sensual arrogance and more than a little curiosity.

This was a Simon she'd never seen, never known, a sensual man with expert knowledge of women that was evident even in such a relatively chaste encounter. She was afraid of him because she had no defense against that kind of ardor, and fear made her push at his chest.

He put her away from him abruptly and his arms fell to his sides. She moved back, her eyes like saucers in a flushed, feverish face, until she was leaning against the counter.

Simon watched her hungrily, his eyes on the noticeable signs of her arousal in her body under the thin silk gown, in her swollen mouth and the faint redness on her cheek where his own had rubbed against it with his faint growth of beard. He'd never dreamed that he and Tira would kindle such fires together. In all their years of careless friendship, he'd never really approached her physically until tonight. He felt as if he were drowning in uncharted waters.

Tira went slowly to the back door and opened it, unnaturally calm. She still looked gloriously beautiful, even more so because she was emotionally aroused.

He took the hint, but he paused at the open door to stare down at her averted face. She was very flustered for a woman who had a lover. He found himself bristling with sudden and unexpected jealousy of the most important man in her life.

"Lucky Charles," he said gruffly. "Is that what he gets?"

Her eyes flashed at him. "You get out of here!" she managed to say through her tight throat. She pulled her robe tight against her throat. "Go. Just, please, go!"

He walked past her, hesitating on the doorstep, but she closed the door after him and locked it. She went back through the kitchen and down the hall to her bedroom before she dared let the tears flow. She was too shaken to try to delve into his motives for that hungry kiss. But she knew it had to be some new sort of revenge for his friend John. Well, it wouldn't work! He was never going to hurt her again, she vowed. She only wished she hadn't been stupid enough to let him touch her in the first place.

Simon stood outside by his car in the misting rain, letting the coolness push away the flaring heat of his body. He shuddered as he leaned his forehead against the cold roof of the car and thanked God he'd managed to get out of there before he did something even more stupid than he already had.

Tira had submitted. He could have had her. He was barely able to draw back at all. What a revelation that had been, that a woman he'd known for years should be able to arouse such instant, sweeping passion in him. Even Melia hadn't had such a profound effect on him, in the days when he'd thought he loved her.

He hadn't meant to touch her. But her body, her exquisite body, in that thin robe and gown had driven him right over the edge. He still had the taste of her soft, sweet lips on his mouth, he could still feel her pressed completely to him. It was killing him!

He clenched his hand and forced himself to breathe slowly until he began to relax. At least she hadn't seen him helpless like this. If she knew how vulnerable he was, she might feel like a little revenge. He couldn't blame her, but his pride wouldn't stand it. She might decide to seduce him and then keep him dangling. That would be the cruelest blow of all, when he knew she was Charles Percy's lover. He had sick visions of Tira telling him everything Simon had done to her and laughing about how easily she'd knocked him off balance. Charles was Tira's lover. Her lover. God, the thought of it made him sick!

He could see why Charles couldn't keep away from her. It made him bitter to realize that he could probably have cut Charles out years ago if he hadn't been so blind and prejudiced. Tira could have been his. But instead, she was Charles's, and she could only hate Simon now for the treatment he'd dealt out to her. He couldn't imagine her still loving him, even if he had taunted her with it to salvage what was left of his pride.

He got into his car finally and drove away in a roar of fury. Damn her for making him lose his head, he thought, refusing to remember that he'd started the whole damned thing. And damn him for letting her do it!

Chapter 6

After consuming far more whiskey than he should have the night before, Simon awoke with vivid memories of Tira in his arms and groaned heavily. He'd blown it, all over again. He didn't know how he was going to smooth things over this time. Jill called and invited herself to lunch with him, fishing for clues to his unusual bad humor. He mumbled something about going to the opera and having an argument with Tira, but offered no details at all. She asked him if he'd expected Tira to be there, and he brushed off further questions, pleading work.

Jill was livid at the thought that Tira was cutting in on her territory, just when things were going so well. She phoned the house and was told by Mrs. Lester that Tira had gone shopping. The rest was easy....

Tira, still smoldering from the betrayal of her weak body the night before, treated herself to lunch at a small sandwich shop downtown. Fate seemed to be against her, she thought with cold resignation, when Jill Sinclair walked into the shop and made a beeline for her just as she was working on dessert and a second cup of coffee.

"Well, how are you doing?" Jill asked with an innocent smile.

"Just sandwiches? Poor you! Simon's taking me to Chez Paul for crepes and cherries jubilee."

"Then why are you here?" Tira asked, not disposed to be friendly toward her worst enemy.

Jill's perfect eyebrows arched. "Why, I was shopping next door for a new diamond tennis bracelet and I spotted you in here," she lied. "I thought a word to the wise, you know," she added, glancing around with the wariness of a veteran intelligence agent before she leaned down to whisper, "Simon was very vexed to have found you sitting next to him at the opera last night. You really should be more careful about engineering these little 'accidental' meetings and chasing after him, dear. He's in a vicious mood today!"

"Good!" Tira said with barely controlled rage. She glared at the other woman. "Would you like to have coffee with me, Jill?" She asked, and drew back the hand that was holding the cup of lukewarm coffee. "Let me introduce you to Miss Cup!"

Jill barely stepped back in time as the coffee cup flew through the air and hit the floor inches in front of her. Her eyes were wide open, and her mouth joined it. She hadn't expected her worst enemy to fight back.

"My, my, aren't I the clumsy one!" Tira said sweetly. "I dropped Miss Cup and spilled my coffee!"

Jill swallowed, hard. "I'll just be off," she said quickly.

"Oh, look," Tira added, lifting the plastic coffeepot the waitress had left on her table with a whimsical smile. "Mr. Coffeepot's coming after Miss Cup!"

Jill actually ran. If Tira hadn't been so miserable, she might have laughed at the sight. As it was, she apologized profusely to the waitress about the spilled coffee and left a tip big enough to excuse the extra work she'd made for the woman.

But it didn't really cheer her up. She went back home and started sculpting a new piece for the gallery. It wasn't necessary work, but it gave her something to do so that she wouldn't spend the day remembering Simon's hard kisses or thinking about how good Jill would look buried up to her armpits in stinging nettles.

The next day she was asked to serve on a committee to oversee Christmas festivities for a local children's shelter. It was a committee that Simon chaired, and she refused politely, only to have him call her right back and ask why.

She was furious. "Don't you know?" she demanded. "You had Jill rub my nose in it for—how did she put this?—chasing you to the opera!"

There was a long pause. "I asked Sherry to give you the ticket to the opera, since she couldn't use it," he confessed, to her surprise. "If anyone was chasing, it was me."

She felt her heart stop. "What?"

"You heard me," he said curtly. There was another pause. "Work with me on the committee. You'll enjoy it."

She would. But she was reluctant to get closer to him than a telephone receiver. "I don't know that I would," she said finally. "You're not yourself lately."

"I know that." He was feeling his way. "Can't we start again?"

She hesitated. "As what?" she asked bluntly.

"Co-workers. Friends. Whatever you like."

That was capitulation, of a sort, at least. Perhaps he was through trying to make her pay for John's untimely death. Whatever his reason, her life was empty without him, wasn't it? Surely friendship was better than nothing at all? She refused to think about how his kisses had felt.

"Is Jill on the committee?" she asked suddenly, wary of plots. "No!"

That was definite enough. "All right, then," she said heavily. "I'll do it."

"Good! I'll pick you up for the meeting tomorrow night."

"No, you won't," she returned shortly. "I'll drive myself. Where is it?"

He told her. There was nothing in his voice to betray whether
or not he was irritated by her stubborn refusal to ride with him.
He was even more irritated by Jill's interference. He'd made a
bad mistake there, taking out Tira's worst enemy. He'd been depressed and Jill was good company, but it would have to stop.
Tira wasn't going to take kindly to having Jill antagonize her out
of sheer rivalry.

Tira went to the meeting, finding several old friends serving on
the committee. They worked for three hours on preparations for a
party, complete with an elderly local man who had agreed to play
Santa Claus for the children. Tira was to help serve and bring two
cakes, having volunteered because she had no plans for Christmas
Eve other than to lay a trap for that mouse in the kitchen. Another
woman, a widow, also volunteered to help, and two of the men,
including Simon.

He stopped her by her car after the meeting. "The boys are
having a Christmas party Saturday night in Jacobsville. They'd
like you to come."

"I don't…"

He put a big forefinger across her soft mouth, startling her. The
intimacy was unfamiliar and worrisome.

"Charles can do without you for one Saturday night, can't he?"
he asked curtly.

"I haven't seen Charles lately. His brother, Gene, is in the
hospital," she said, having forgotten whether or not she'd mentioned it to him. "Nessa isn't coping well at all, and Charles can't
leave her alone."

"Nessa?"

"Gene's wife." She wanted to tell him about Nessa and
Charles, but it wasn't her secret and letting him think she and
Charles were close was the only shield she had at the moment.
She couldn't let her guard down. She still didn't quite trust him.
His new attitude toward her was puzzling and she didn't under-
stand why he'd changed.

"I see."

"You don't, but it doesn't matter. I want to go home. I'm cold."

He searched her quiet face. "I could offer an alternative," he said in a soft, velvety tone.

She looked up at him with cool disdain. "I don't do casual affairs, Simon," she said bluntly. "Just in case the thought had crossed your mind lately."

He looked as if he'd been slapped. His jaw tautened. "Don't you? Then if your affair with Charles Percy isn't casual, why hasn't he married you?"

"I don't want to marry again," she said in a husky voice, averting her eyes. "Not ever."

He hesitated. He knew why she felt that way, that she'd been betrayed in the worst way. Her father-in-law had told him everything, but he was uncertain about whether or not to tell her that he knew.

She glanced at him warily. "Does Jill know that you're still grieving for your wife?" she asked, taking the fight right into the enemy camp. "Or is she just an occasional midnight snack?"

His eyebrows arched. "That's a hell of a comparison."

"Isn't it?" She smiled sweetly. "I'm going home."

"Come to Jacobsville with me."

"And into the jaws of death or kitchen slavery?" she taunted. "I know all about the biscuit mania. I'm not about to be captured by your loopy brothers."

"They won't come near you," he promised. "Corrigan's hired a new cook. She's redheaded and she can bake anything."

"She won't last two weeks before Leopold has her running for the border," she assured him.

It pleased him that she knew his brothers so well, that she took an interest in his family. She and Corrigan had been friends and occasionally had dated in the past, but there had been no spark between them. In fact, Charles Percy had always been in the way of any other man and Tira. Why hadn't he noticed that before?

"You've been going around with Charles ever since you left John," he recalled absently.

"Charles is my friend," she said.

"Friend," he scoffed, his eyes insulting. "Is that what it's called these days?"

"You should know," she returned. "What does Jill call it?"

His eyes narrowed angrily. "At least she's honest about what she wants from me," he replied. "And it isn't my money."

She shrugged. "To each his own."

He searched her face quietly. "You kissed me back the other night."

Her cheeks went ruddy and she looked away, clutching her purse. "I have to go."

He was right behind her. He didn't touch her, but she could feel the warm threat of him all down her spine, oddly comforting in the chilly December air.

"Stop running!"

Her eyes closed for an instant before she reached for the door handle. "We seemed to be friends once," she said in a husky tone. "But we weren't, not really. You only tolerated me. I'm amazed that I went through all those years so blind that I never saw the contempt you felt when you looked at me."

"Tira…"

She turned, holding up a hand. "I'm not accusing you. I just want you to know that I'm not carrying a torch for you or breaking my heart because you go around with Jill." Her eyes were lackluster and he realized with a start that she'd lost a lot of weight in the past few months. She looked fragile, breakable.

"What are you saying?" he asked.

"That I don't need you to pity me, Simon," she said with visible pride. "I don't really want a closer association with you, whatever Jill says or you think. I'm rearranging my life. I've started over. I don't want to go back to the way we were."

He felt those words like a knife. She meant them. It was in her whole expression.

"I see," he said quietly.

"No, you don't," she replied heavily. "You're sort of like a drug," she mused. "I was addicted to you and I've been cured, but even small doses are dangerous to my recovery."

His heart leaped. He caught her gaze and held it relentlessly. "What did you say?"

"You know what I mean," she returned. "I'm not going to let myself become addicted again. I have Charles and you have Jill. Let's go our separate ways and get on with our lives. I was serious about the pistol and the mouse, you know, it wasn't some face-saving excuse. I never meant to kill myself over you."

"Oh, hell, I knew that."

"Then why…"

"Yes?"

She turned her purse in her hands. "Why do you keep engineering situations where we'll be thrown together?" she asked. "It serves no purpose."

His hand came out of his pocket and lifted to touch, lightly, her upswept hair. She flinched and he dropped his hand with a long sigh.

"You can't forget, can you?" he asked slowly.

"I'm trying," she assured him. "But every time we're together, people speculate. The newspaper stories were pretty hard to live down, even for me. I don't really want to rekindle speculation."

"You never cared about gossip before."

"I was never publicly savaged before," she countered. "I've been made to look like some clinging, simpering nymph crying for a man who doesn't want her. My pride is in shreds!"

He was watching her narrowly. "How do you know that I don't want you, Tira?" he asked deliberately.

She stared at him without speaking, floored by the question.

"I'll pick you up at six on Saturday and drive you to Jacobsville," he said. "Wear something elegant. It's formal."

"I won't go," she said through her teeth.

"You'll go," he replied with chilling certainty.

He turned and walked to his own car with her glaring after him. Well, they'd just see about that! she told herself.

It was barely a week until Christmas. Tira had the party for the children to look forward to on Christmas Eve, to help her feel some Christmas spirit. She had an artificial tree that she set up in her living room every year. She'd have loved a real one, with its own dirt ball so that it could be set out in the yard after the holidays, but she was violently allergic to fir trees of any kind. The expensive artificial tree was very authentic-looking and once she decorated it, it could have fooled an expert at a distance.

She had a collection of faux gold-plated cherubs and elegant gold foil ribbons to use for decorations, along with gold and silver bead strands and fairy lights. For whimsy, there were a few mechanical ornaments scattered deep within the limbs, which could be activated by the touch of a finger. She had a red-and-white latch-hook rug that went around the base of the tree, and around that was a Lionel "O" scale train set—the one she'd seen in the window of the department store that day she'd come across Simon on the sidewalk. She'd gone back and bought the train, and now she enjoyed watching it run. It only lacked one or two little lighted buildings to go beside it. Those, she reasoned, she could add later.

She stood back and admired her handiwork. She was wearing a gold-and-white caftan that echoed the color scheme of the tree, especially with her hair loose. It was Saturday, but she wasn't going to the Hart party. In fact, when Simon rang the doorbell, he wasn't going to get into the house. She felt very smug about the ease with which she'd avoided him.

"Very nice," came a deep, amused voice from behind her.

She whirled and found Simon, in evening clothing, watching her from the doorway.

"How…how did you get in?" she gasped.

"Mrs. Lester kindly left the back door unlocked for me," he mused. "I told her that we were going out and that you'd probably forget. She's very obliging. A real romantic, Mrs. Lester."

"I'll fire her Monday the minute she gets back from her sister's!" she snarled.

"No, you won't. She's a treasure."

She swept back her hair. "I'm not going to Jacobsville!"

"You are," he said. "Either you get dressed, or I dress you."

"Ha!" She folded her arms across her chest and dared him to do his worst.

The prospect seemed to amuse him. He took her by the arm with his good hand and led her down the hall to her bedroom, opened the door, put her in and closed it behind them. He'd already been here, she could tell, because a white strapless evening gown was laid out on the bed, along with filmy underthings that matched it.

"You...you invaded my bedroom!" she raged.

"Yes, I did. It was very educational. You don't dress like a siren at all. Most of your wardrobe seems to consist of cotton underthings and jeans and tank tops." He glanced at her. "I like that caftan you're wearing, but it's not quite appropriate for tonight's festivities."

"I'm not putting on that dress."

He chuckled softly. "You are. Sooner or later."

She started toward the door and found herself swept up against him, held firmly by that damned prosthesis that seemed to work every bit as well as the arm it had replaced.

"I'm not going to hurt you," he promised softly. "But you're going."

"I will...what are you...doing?"

She'd forgotten the front zip that kept the caftan on her. He released it with a minimum of fuss and the whole thing dropped to the floor, leaving her in her bare feet and nude except for her serviceable white briefs.

She gaped at him. He looked at her body with the appreciation of an artist, noting the creamy soft rise of her breasts with their tight rosy nipples and the supple curve of her waist that flared to rounded hips and long, elegant legs.

"Don't you…look at me!" she gasped, trying to cover herself.

His eyes met hers quizzically. "Don't you want me to?" he asked softly.

The question surprised her. She only stared at him, watching his gaze fall again to her nudity and sweep over it with pure delight. She shivered at the feel of his gaze.

"It's all right," he said gently, surprised by the way she was reacting. "I'm not even going to touch you. I promise."

She drew in a shaky breath, held close by one arm while his other hand traced along her flushed cheek and down to the corner of her tremulous mouth.

What an unexpected creature she was, he thought with some confusion. She was embarrassed, shy, even a little ashamed to stand here this way. She blushed like a girl. He knew that she couldn't be totally innocent, but her reaction was nothing like that of an experienced woman.

His fingers traced over her mouth and down the curve of her pulsating throat to her collarbone. They hesitated there and his gaze fell to her mouth.

The silence in the bedroom was like the silence in the eye of a hurricane. If she breathed the wrong way, it would break the spell, and he'd draw away. His fingers, even now, were hesitating at her collarbone and his mouth hovered above hers as if he couldn't quite decide what to do next.

She shivered, her own eyes lingering helplessly on the long, wide curve of his mouth.

He moved, just slightly, so that her body was completely against his, and he let her feel the slow burgeoning of his arousal. It shocked her. He saw the flush spread all over her high cheekbones.

"Tira," he said roughly, "tell me what you want."

"I don't…know," she whispered brokenly, searching his pale, glittering eyes. "I don't know!"

He felt her hips move, just a fraction, felt her body shift so that she was faintly arched toward him. "Don't you?" he whispered back. "Your body does. Shall I show you what it's asking me to do?"

She couldn't manage words, but he didn't seem to need them. With a faint smile, he lifted his hand and spread it against her rib cage, slowly, torturously sliding it up until it was resting just at the underside of her taut breast. She shivered and caught her breath, her eyes wide and hungry and still frightened.

"It won't hurt," he whispered, and his hand moved up and over her nipple, softly caressing.

She clutched his shoulders and hid her face against him in a torment of shattered sensations, moaning sharply at the intimate touch.

He hesitated. "What's wrong?" he asked gently. His face nuzzled against her cheek, forcing her head back so that he could see her shocked, helpless submission. He touched her again, easing his fingers together over the hard nipple as he tugged at it gently. The look on her face made his whole body go rigid.

Her head went back. Her eyes closed. She shivered, biting her lip to keep from weeping, the pleasure was so overwhelming.

If she was shaken, so was he. It was relatively chaste love play, but she was already reacting as if his body was intimately moving on hers. Her response was as unexpected as it was flattering.

"Come here," he said with rough urgency, tugging her to the bed. He pulled her down with him on the coverlet beside her gown and shifted so that she was beneath him. His rapid heartbeat was causing him to shake even before he found her mouth with his and began to caress her intimately.

"Simon," she sobbed. But she was pulling, not pushing. Her mouth opened for him, her body rose as he caressed it with his hand and then with his open mouth. He suckled her, groaning when she shivered and cried out from the pleasure. He was in so deep that he couldn't have pulled back to save his own life. He'd never known an exchange so heated, so erotic. He wanted to do things to and with her that he'd never dreamed of doing to a woman in his life.

His mouth eased back onto hers and gentled her as his hand moved under the elastic at her hips and descended slowly. Her legs parted for him. She gasped as he began to touch her, sobbed, wept, clutched him. She was ready for him, and he'd barely begun.

Even while his head spun with delight, he knew that it was wrong. It was all wrong. He'd been too long without a woman and this was too fiery, too consuming, for a first time with her. He was going in headfirst and she wouldn't enjoy it. But he couldn't stop himself.

"Tira," he groaned at her ear. "Sweetheart, not now. Not like this. For God's sake, help me…!"

His hand stilled, his mouth lay hot and hard against her throat while he lay against her, his big body faintly tremulous as he tried to overcome his urgent, aching need for her.

Chapter 7

Tira barely heard him. Her body was shivering with new sensations, with exquisite glimpses of the pleasure he could offer her. She felt him go heavy in her arms and slowly, breath by breath, she began to realize where they were and what they were doing.

She caught her breath sharply, aware that her hands were still tangled in the thick, cool darkness of his wavy hair. She was almost completely nude and he'd touched her....

"Simon!" she exclaimed, aghast.

"Shhh." His mouth turned against her throat. His hand withdrew to her waist and his head lifted. He was breathing as raggedly as she was. The turbulence of his eyes surprised her, because his usual impeccable control was completely gone. He saw her expression and managed a smile. "Are you shocked that we could be like this, together?" he asked gently.

"Yes."

"So am I. But I don't want you like this, not in a fever so high that I can't think past relief," he said quietly. He moved away from her with obvious reluctance and took one last, sweeping glance at her yielded body before he sat up with his back to her and leaned forward to breathe.

She tugged the coverlet over her heated flesh and bit her swollen lips in an agony of shame and embarrassment. How in the world had *that* happened? If he hadn't stopped…!

He got to his feet, stretched hugely and then turned toward her. She lay with her glorious hair in a tangle around her white face, looking up at him almost fearfully.

"There's no need to look like that, Tira," he said softly, with eyes so tender that they confused her. He reached down and tugged the coverlet away, pulling her slowly to her feet. "The world won't end."

He reached for the strapless bra he'd taken from her bureau and using the prosthesis to anchor it, he looped it around her and held it in place.

"You'll have to fasten it," he said with a complete lack of self-consciousness. "I can't do operations that complex."

She obeyed him as if she were a puppet and he was pulling strings.

He held the half-slip and coaxed her to lean against him while she stepped into it. He pulled it up. He reached for the exquisite gown and deftly slid it over her head, watching while she tugged it into place. He turned her around and while she held up her hair, he zipped it into place.

He led her to the vanity and handed her a brush. She sat down obediently and put her unruly hair back into some sort of order, belatedly using a faint pink lipstick and a little powder. He stood behind her the whole while, watching.

When she finished, he drew her up again and held her in front of him.

"How long have we known each other?" he asked solemnly.

"A long time. Years." She couldn't meet his probing gaze. She felt as if she had absolutely no will of her own. The sheer vulnerability was new and frightening. She took a deep breath. "We should go."

He tilted her remorseful eyes up to his. "Don't be ashamed of what we did together," he said quietly.

She winced. "You don't even like me…!"

He drew her close and rocked her against his tall body, his cheek pressed to her hair as he stroked the silken length of it. "Shhh." He kissed her hair and then her cheek, working his way up to her wet eyes. He kissed the tears away gently and then lifted his head and looked down into the drowned green depths. He couldn't remember ever feeling so tender with a woman. He remembered how her soft skin felt against his mouth and his breathing became labored. He stepped back a little, so that she wouldn't notice how easily she aroused him now.

She sniffed inelegantly and reached on the vanity for a tissue. "My nose will be as red as my eyes," she commented, trying to break the tension.

"As red as the highlights in your glorious hair," he murmured, touching it. He sighed. "I want you with me tonight," he said softly. "But if you really don't want to go, I won't force you."

She looked up, puzzled by his phrasing. "You said you would."

He frowned slightly. "I don't like making you cry," he said bluntly. "Until now, I didn't know that I could. It's uncomfortable."

"I've had a long week," she said evasively.

"We both have. Come with me. No strings. You'll have fun."

She hesitated, but only for a minute. "All right."

He reached down and curled her small hand into his big one. The contact was thrilling, exciting. She looked up into eyes that confused her.

"Don't think," he said. "Come along."

He pulled her along with him, out of the bedroom, out the door. It was new to have Simon act possessively about her, to be tender with her. It hurt terribly, in a way, because now she knew exactly what she'd missed in her life. Simon would be all she'd ever need, but she cared too much to settle for a casual affair. Regardless of what he thought of her marriage to John, and she had no reason to believe that he'd changed his mind about it, she did believe in marriage. She didn't want to be anyone's one-night stand; not even Simon's.

The long drive down to Jacobsville wasn't as harrowing as she'd expected it to be. Simon talked about politics and began asking pointed questions about an upcoming fund-raiser.

She wasn't comfortable with the new relationship between them, so when he asked if she might like to help with some projects for the governor if he took on the attorney general's job, she immediately suspected that he was using her helpless attraction to him to win her support.

She looked down at the small white beaded evening bag in her lap. "If I have time," she said, stalling.

He glanced at her as they passed through the gaily decorated downtown section of Jacobsville, dressed like a Christmas tree for the holidays with bright colored lights and tinsel.

"What else have you got to do lately?" he asked pointedly.

She stared at her bag. "I might do another exhibit."

He didn't ask again, but he looked thoughtful.

The Hart ranch was impressive, sprawling for miles, with the white fence that surrounded the house and immediate grounds draped with green garlands and artificial poinsettias.

"They haven't done that before," she commented as they went down the long paved driveway to the house.

"Oh, they've made a number of improvements since Dorie married Corrigan last Christmas and moved into their new house next door to this one," he explained.

"Reluctant improvements, if I know Callaghan."

He chuckled. "Cag doesn't go in much for frills."

"Is he still not eating pork?"

He gave her a wry glance. "Not yet."

It was a family joke that the eldest bachelor brother wouldn't touch any part of a pig since he'd seen the movie about the one that talked, a box office smash.

"I can't say that I blame him," she murmured. "I saw the movie three times myself."

He chuckled. It was a rare sound these days and she glanced at him with a longing that she quickly concealed when his eyes darted toward her.

He pulled up in front of the sprawling ranch house and got out, noting that Tira did the same without waiting for him to open her door. Her independent spirit irritated him at times, but he respected her for it.

When she started up the steps ahead of him, he caught her hand and kept it in his as they reached the porch, where Corrigan and Dorie greeted them with warm hugs and smiles. Tira smiled automatically, so aware of Simon's big hand in hers that she was almost floating.

"You're just in time," Corrigan said. "Leopold spiked the punch and didn't tell Tess, and she got the wrong side of Evan Tremayne's tongue. She's in the kitchen giving Leo hell and swearing that he'll never get another biscuit."

"He must be in tears by now," Simon mused.

"He's on his knees, in fact, groveling." Corrigan grinned. "It suits him."

They went inside, where they met Evan and his wife, Anna, who was obviously and joyfully pregnant with their first child, and the Ballenger brothers, Calhoun and Justin, with their wives Abby and Shelby, all headed toward the front door together. They were all founding families in the area, with tremendous wealth and power locally. Tira knew of them, but it was the first time she'd met them face-to-face. It didn't surprise her that the brothers had such contacts. They made friends despite their sometimes reclusive tendencies. All the same, the party looked as if it had only just started, and it puzzled her that these people were leaving so soon. They didn't seem angry, but with those bland expressions, it was sometimes hard to tell if they were.

Tira looked around for Cag and Rey and just spotted them going through the swinging door of the kitchen. In the open doorway she caught a glimpse of Leopold on his knees in a prayerful stance with a thin young redhead standing over him looking outraged.

Tira chuckled. Simon, having seen the same thing, laughed out loud.

"This is too good to miss. Come on." He nodded at other people he knew as they wove their way through the crowd and reached the kitchen.

Stealthily Simon pushed open the door. The sight that met their eyes was pitiful. Leopold was still on his knees, with Cag verbally flaying him while Rey looked on approvingly.

They glanced toward the door when Simon and Tira entered. Leopold actually blushed as he scrambled to his feet.

Tess grimaced as she spotted Simon, one of the only two brothers who actively intimidated her. "I don't care what they say, I'm quitting!" she told him despite her nervousness. "He—" she pointed at Leopold "—poured two bottles of vodka in my special tropical punch, and Evan Tremayne didn't realize it was spiked until he'd had his second glass and fell over a chair." She blushed. "He said terrible things to me! And he—" she pointed at Leopold again "—thought it was funny!"

"Evan Tremayne falling over a chair would make most people in Jacobsville giggle," Tira stated, "knowing how he hates alcohol."

"It gets worse," Tess continued, brushing back a short strand of red hair, her blue eyes flashing. "Evan thought the punch was so good that he gave a glass of it to Justin Ballenger."

"Oh, God," Simon groaned. "Two of the most fanatical teetotalers in the county."

"Justin got a guitar and started singing some Spanish song. Shelby dragged the guitar out of his hands just in time," Tess explained. She put her face in her hands. "That was when Evan realized the punch was spiked and he said I should be strung up over the barn by my apron strings for doing such a nasty thing to your guests."

"I'll speak to Evan."

"Not now, you won't," Tira mentioned. "We just met the Tremaynes going out the front door, along with both Ballenger brothers and their wives."

"Oh, God!" Leo groaned again.

"I'll phone him and apologize," Rey promised. "I'll call them all and apologize. You can't leave!"

"Yes, I can. I quit." Tess had taken off her apron and thrown it at Leopold. "You'd better learn how to bake biscuits, is all I can say. They—" she pointed toward Cag and Rey "—will probably kill you when I leave, and I'm glad! I hope they throw you out in the corral and let the crows eat you! That would get rid of two evils, because the crows will die of food poisoning for sure!"

She stormed through the door and Leopold groaned out loud. Cag's quiet eyes followed her and his face tautened curiously.

"Leo, how could you?" Rey asked, aghast.

"It wasn't two bottles of vodka," he protested. "It was one. And I meant to give it to Tess, just to irritate her, but I got sidetracked and Evan and Justin...well, you know." He brightened. "At least Calhoun didn't get a taste of it!" he added, as if that made things all right. Calhoun, once a playboy, was as bad as his brother about liquor since his marriage.

"He left, just the same. But you've got problems closer to home. You'd better go after her," Simon pointed out.

"And fast!" Rey said through his teeth, black eyes flashing.

"Like a twister," Cag added with narrowed eyes. "If she leaves, you're going to get branded along with that stock I had shipped in today."

"I'm going, I'm going!" Leopold rushed out the back door after their housekeeper.

"Isn't she a little young for a housekeeper?" Simon asked his brothers. "She barely looks nineteen."

"She's twenty-two," Cag said. "Her dad was working for us when he dropped dead of a heart attack. There's no family and she can cook." His powerful shoulders lifted and fell. "It seemed an ideal solution. If we could just keep Leo away from her, things would be fine.''

"Why does he have to torment the housekeepers all the time?'' Rey asked miserably.

"He'll settle down one day,'' Cag murmured. He looked distracted, and he was glaring toward the back door. "He'd better not upset her again. In fact, I think I'll make sure he doesn't.''

He nodded to the others and went after Leo and Tess.

"He's sweet on her,'' Rey said when the door closed behind him. "Not that he'll admit it. He thinks she's too young, and she's scared to death of him. She finds every sort of excuse to get out of the kitchen if he's the first one down in the mornings. It's sort of comical, in a way. I don't guess she knows that she could bring him to his knees with a smile.''

"She's very young,'' Tira commented.

Rey glanced at her. "Yes, she is. Just what Cag needs, too, something to nurture. He's always bringing home stray kittens and puppies...just like her.'' He pointed to a small kitten curled up in a little bed in the corner of the kitchen. "She rescued the kitten from the highway. Cag bought the bed for it. They're a match made in heaven, but Leo's going to ruin everything. I think he's sweet on her, too, and trying to cut Cag out before she notices how much time he spends watching her.''

"This is not our problem,'' Simon assured his brother. "But I'd send Leo off to cooking school if I were you. No woman is ever going to be stupid enough to marry him and if he learns to make biscuits, you can do without housekeepers.''

"He made scrambled eggs one morning when Tess had to go to the eye doctor early to pick up her contacts,'' Rey said. "The dogs wouldn't even touch them!'' He glared at Tira and Simon and shrugged. "Come on. We've still got a few guests who haven't gone home. I'll introduce you to them.''

He led them into the other room and stopped suddenly, turning to look at them. "Wait a minute. Corrigan said you weren't speaking to each other after that newspaper stupidity.''

Simon still had Tira's slender hand tight in his. "A slight misunderstanding. We made up. Didn't we?" he asked, looking down at Tira with an expression that made her face turn red.

Rey made a sound under his breath and quickly changed the subject.

Corrigan and Dorie joined them at the punch bowl, which had been refilled and dealcoholized. Dorie looked almost as pregnant as Anna Tremayne had, and she was radiant. Not even the thin scar on her delicate cheek could detract from her beauty.

"We'd almost given up hope," she murmured, laughing up at her adoring husband. "And then, wham!"

"We're over the moon," Corrigan said. The limp left over from his accident of years ago was much less noticeable now, he didn't even require a cane.

"I'm going to be an uncle," Simon murmured. "I might like that. I saw a terrific set of "O" scale electric trains in a San Antonio toy store a few days ago. Kids love trains."

"That's right, boys and girls alike," Tira murmured, not mentioning that she'd bought that train set for herself.

"Did you know that two of our local doctors, who are married to each other, have several layouts of them?" Corrigan murmured. "The doctors Coltrain. They invited kids from the local orphanage over for Christmas this year and have them set up and running. It's something of a local legend."

"I like trains," Simon said. "Remember that set Dad bought us?" he asked Corrigan.

"Yeah." The brothers shared a memory, not altogether a good one judging from their expression.

"This isn't spiked, anymore?" Tira asked, changing the subject as she stared at the punch bowl.

"I swear," Corrigan said, smiling affectionately at her. "Help yourself."

She did, filling one for Simon as well, and talk went to general subjects rather than personal ones.

*   *   *

The local live cowboy band played a slow, lazy tune and Simon pulled Tira onto the dance floor, wrapping her up tight in his arms.

The one with the prosthesis was a little uncomfortable and she moved imperceptibly.

"Too tight?" Simon asked softly, and let up on the pressure. "Sorry. I'm used to the damned thing, but I still can't quite judge how much pressure to use."

"It's all right. It didn't hurt."

He lifted his head and looked down into her eyes. "You're the only woman who's ever seen me without it," he mused. "In the hospital, when it was a stump—"

"You may have lost part of your arm, but you're alive," she interrupted. "If you hadn't been found for another hour, nothing would have saved you. As it was, you'd lost almost too much blood."

"You stayed with me," he recalled. "You made me fight. You made me live. I didn't want to."

She averted her eyes. "I know how much Melia meant to you, Simon. You don't have to remind me."

Secrets, he thought. There were so many secrets that he kept, that she didn't know about. Perhaps it kept the distance between them. It was time to shorten it.

"Melia had an abortion."

She didn't grasp what he was saying at first, and the lovely green eyes she lifted to his were curious. "What?"

"I made her pregnant and she ended it, and never told me," he said shortly. "She didn't want to ruin her figure. Of course, she wasn't positive that the baby was mine. It could have been by one of her other lovers."

She'd stopped dancing to stare up at him uncomprehendingly.

"She told me, the night of the accident," he continued. "That's why I lost control of the car in a curve, in the rain, and I remember thinking in the split second before it crashed that I didn't care to live with all my illusions dead."

"Illusions?" she echoed.

"That my marriage was perfect," he said. "That my beloved wife loved me equally, that she wanted my children and a lifetime with only me." He laughed coldly. "I married a cheap, selfish woman whose only concern was living in luxury and notching her bedpost. It excited her that she had men and I didn't know. She had them in my bed." His voice choked with anger, and he looked over her head. His arm had unconsciously tightened around Tira, and this time she didn't protest. She was shocked by what he was telling her. She'd thought, everyone had thought, that he'd buried his heart in Melia's grave and had mourned her for years.

"The child was what hurt the most," he said stiffly. "I believed her when she said she thought she was sterile. It was a lie. Everything she said was a lie, and I was too besotted to realize it. She made a fool of me."

"I'm so sorry for all the pain you've been through." Her eyes filled with tears. "It must have been awful."

He looked down at her, his eyes narrow and probing. "You were married to John when it happened. You came to the hospital every day. You held my hand, my good hand, and talked to me, forced me to get up, to try. I always felt that you left John because of me, and it made me feel guilty. I thought I'd broken up your marriage."

She dropped her gaze to his strong neck. "No," she said tersely. "You didn't break it up."

He curled her fingers into his and brought them to his chest, holding them there warmly. "Were you in love with him, at first?"

"I was attracted to him, very fond of him," she confessed softly. "And I wanted, badly, to make our marriage work." She shivered a little and he drew her closer. Her eyes closed. "I thought…I wasn't woman enough."

His indrawn breath was audible. He knew the truth about her marriage now, but he hesitated to bring up a painful subject again when things were going so well for them. His lips moved down to her eyes and kissed the eyelids with breathless tenderness.

"Don't cry," he said curtly. "You're more than woman enough. Come closer, and I'll prove it to you, right here."

"Simon..."

His arm slid down, unobtrusively, and drew her hips firmly against his. He shuddered as the touch of her body produced an immediate, violent effect.

She gasped, but he wouldn't let her step back.

"Do you feel how much I want you?" he whispered in her ear. "I've barely touched you and I'm capable."

"You're a man..."

"It doesn't, it never has, happened that fast with anyone else," he said through his teeth. "I want you so badly that it hurts like hell. Yes, Tira, you're woman enough for any man. I'm sorry that your husband didn't... No, that's a lie." He lifted his head and looked into her shocked eyes. "I'm glad he couldn't have you."

The words went right over her head because she was so shocked at what he was saying. She stared at him in evident confusion and embarrassment, her eyes darting around to see if anyone was watching. Nobody was.

"It doesn't show. There's no reason to be so tense." His arm moved back up to her waist and loosened a little.

She drew in steadying breaths, but she felt weak. Her head went to his chest and she made a plaintive little sound against it.

His fingers contracted around hers. "We opened Pandora's box together in your bedroom, on your bed," he whispered at her ear. "We want each other, Tira."

She swallowed. "I can't."

"Why not?"

She hesitated, but only for an instant. "I don't have affairs, Simon."

"Of course you do, darling," he drawled with barely concealed jealousy. "What else do you have with Charles Percy?"

Chapter 8

Tira stopped dancing. She wasn't sure why she was upset, because Simon had made no bones about thinking she was sleeping with Charles. Apparently when he'd made light love to her earlier, he'd thought her responses were those of an experienced woman. She wondered what he'd think if he knew the truth, that she'd waited for him all these years, that she wanted no other man.

"Go ahead," he invited, a strange light in his eyes. "Deny it."

She let her gaze fall to his wide, firm mouth. "Think what you like," she invited. "You will anyway. And I'll remind you, Simon, that you have no right to question me about Charles."

"No right? After what you let me do to you?"

She flushed and her teeth clenched. "One weak moment..."

"Weak, the devil," he muttered quietly. "You were starving to death. Doesn't he make love to you anymore?"

"Simon, please don't," she pleaded. "Not tonight."

The hand holding hers contracted. "Were you thinking of him, then?"

"Heavens, no!" she burst out, aghast.

He searched her eyes for a long moment, until he saw her cheeks flush. His hand relaxed.

"I wasn't the only one who was starving," she murmured, a little embarrassed.

He coaxed her cheek onto his chest. "No, you weren't," he agreed. He closed his eyes as they moved to the music.

She was surprised that he could admit his own hunger. They were moving into a totally new relationship. She didn't know what to make of it, and she didn't quite trust him, either. But what she was feeling was so delicious that she couldn't fight it. She let her body go lax against him and breathed in the spicy scent of his cologne. Her hand moved gently against his shirt, feeling hair and hard, warm muscle under it. He stiffened and it delighted her that he could react so strongly to such an innocent caress.

"You'd better not," he whispered at her ear.

Her hand stilled. "Are you...hairy all over?" she whispered back.

He stiffened even more. "In places."

Her cheek moved against his chest and she sighed. "I'm sleepy," she murmured, closing her eyes as they moved lazily to the music.

"Want to go home?"

"We haven't been here very long."

"It doesn't matter. I've had a hard week, too." He let her move away. "Come on. We'll make our excuses and leave."

They found Corrigan and asked him to tell the others Merry Christmas for them.

"They're still trying to talk Tess out of leaving," he murmured dryly. "I hope they can. The smell of baking biscuits makes Dorie sick right now," he said, glancing down at his wife lovingly. "So they'll have to go without if they can't change her mind."

"I wish them luck," Simon said. "We enjoyed the party. Next year, maybe I'll throw one and you can all come up to San Antonio for it."

"I'll hold you to that," Corrigan replied. He glanced from one of them to the other. "Have you two given up combat?"

"For the moment," Tira agreed with a wan smile.

"For good," Simon added.

"We'll see about that," Tira returned, her eyes flashing at him even through her fatigue.

They said their goodbyes and Simon drove them back to San Antonio. But instead of taking her home, he took her to his apartment.

She wondered why she didn't protest, which she certainly should have. She was too curious about why he'd come here.

"No questions?" he asked when they stepped out of the elevator on the penthouse floor.

"I suppose you'll tell me when you're ready," she replied, but with a faintly wary gaze.

"No need to worry," he said as he unlocked his door. "You won't get seduced unless you want to."

She blushed again and hated her own naivete. She followed him inside.

She'd never seen his apartment before. This was one invitation she'd always hoped for and never got. Simon's private life was so private that even his brothers knew little of it.

The apartment was huge and furnished in browns and creams and oranges. He had large oil paintings, mostly of landscapes, on the walls, and the furniture had a vaguely Mediterranean look to it. It was heavy and old, and beautifully polished.

She ran her hand over the rosewood back of the green velvet-covered sofa that graced the living room. "This is beautiful," she commented.

"I hoped you might think so."

There was a long pause, during which she became more and more uncomfortable. She glanced at Simon and found him watching her with quiet, unblinking silvery eyes.

"You're making me nervous," she laughed unsteadily.

"Why?"

She shrugged in the folds of her velvet wrap. "I'm not sure."

He moved toward her with a walk that was as blatant as if he'd been whispering seductive comments to her. He took the cloak from her shoulders and the evening bag from her hands, tossing both onto the sofa. His jacket followed it. He took her hands and lifted them to his tie.

She hesitated. His fingers pressed her hands closer.

With breath that was coming hard and fast into her throat, she unfastened the silk tie and tossed it onto the sofa. He guided her fingers back to the top buttons of his shirt.

The silence in the apartment was tense, like the set of Simon's handsome, lean face. He stood quietly before her, letting her unfasten the shirt. But when she started to push it away, he shook his head.

"Looking at the prosthesis doesn't bother me," she said huskily.

"Humor me."

He drew her close and, pressing her fingers into the thick hair that covered his broad, muscular chest, he bent to her mouth.

His lips were tender and slow. He kissed her with something akin to reverence, brushing her nose with his as he made light contacts that provoked a new and sweeping longing for more.

Her fingers contracted in the hair on his chest and she went on tiptoe to coax his mouth harder against her own.

She felt his good hand on the zipper that held up her gown. She didn't protest as he slid it down and let the dress fall to the floor. She didn't protest, either, when he undid the catches to her longline bra with just the fingers of one hand. That, too, fell away and his gaze dropped hungrily to her pretty, taut breasts.

She stepped out of her shoes and he took her hand, pulling her along with him to his bedroom. It was decorated in the same earth tones as the living room. The bed was king-size, overlaid with a cream-and-brown striped quilted bedspread and a matching dust ruffle.

He reached behind him and closed the door, locking it as well.

She looked into his eyes with mingled hunger and apprehension. She knew exactly what he was going to do. She wanted to tell him how inexperienced she was, but she couldn't quite get the words out.

He led her to the bed and eased her down onto it. His hand went to his belt. He let his slacks fall to the floor and, clad only in black silk boxer shorts, he sat down on the bed and removed his shoes and socks.

"Your shirt," she whispered.

He eased down beside her, levering himself just above her at an angle. "I don't think I can do this without the prosthesis," he said quietly. "But I'd rather you didn't see it. Do you mind?"

She shook her head. He was devastating at close range. She loved the look of him, the feel of his hand on her face, her throat, then suddenly whispering over her taut breasts.

She arched under even that light pressure and her hands clenched as she looked up at him.

"Are you going to let me take you?" he asked in a soft, blunt tone.

She bit her lower lip worriedly. "Simon, I'm not sure—"

"Yes, you are," he interrupted. "You want me every bit as badly as I want you."

She still hesitated, but then she spoke. "Yes, I do." that was all she said—she couldn't tell him her secret yet.

He touched the hard tip of her breast and watched her shiver. "You beautiful creature," he said half under his breath. "I only hope I can do you justice."

While she was searching for the right words to make her confession, his head bent and his mouth suddenly opened right on her breast.

She caught his head, her nails biting into his scalp.

He lifted himself just enough to see her worried eyes. "I'm only going to suckle you," he said with soft surprise, wondering what sort of lover Charles Percy must have been to make her so afraid. "I won't hurt you."

He bent again, and this time she didn't protest. She couldn't. It was so sweet that it made her head spin to feel his hot, hard, moist mouth closing over the tight nipple. She moaned under her breath and writhed with pleasure. He nibbled her for a long time, moving slowly from one breast to the other while his hand traced erotic patterns on her belly and the insides of her thighs.

She barely noticed when he removed her briefs and then his own. His practiced caresses overwhelmed her. She was so enthralled by them that she ached to know him completely.

A long, feverish few minutes later, he moved between her long legs and his mouth pushed hard against her lips as his hips eased down against hers and he penetrated her.

The sensation was shocking, frightening. She drifted from a euphoric tension to harsh pain. Her nails bit into his broad shoulders and she called his name. But he was in over his head, all too quickly. He groaned harshly and pushed harder, crying out as he felt her envelope him.

"Oh…!" she sobbed, pushing against his chest.

He stilled for an instant, shuddering, and lifted tortured eyes to hers. "I'm hurting you?" he whispered shakenly. "Dear God… no, sweetheart!…don't move like that…!"

She shifted her hips in an effort to avoid the pain, and her sharp movements took him right over the edge.

His face tautened. He pushed, hard, his body totally out of control. "Oh, God, Tira, I'm so sorry…!" he said through his teeth, his eyes closed, his body suddenly urgent on hers.

He whispered it constantly until he completed his possession of her, and seconds later, he arched and shuddered and cried out in a hoarse groan as completion left him exhausted and shivering on her damp body.

She felt him relax heavily onto her damp skin, so that she could barely breathe for the weight. She wept silently at the reality of intimacy. It wasn't glorious fireworks of ecstasy at all. It was just a painful way to give a man pleasure. She hated him. She hated herself more for giving in.

"Please," she choked. "Let me go."

There was a pause. He drew in a long breath. "Not on your life," he said huskily.

He lifted his head and stared into her eyes with an expression on his lean face that she couldn't begin to understand.

"Charles Percy," he said deliberately, "is definitely not your lover."

She swallowed and her face flamed. "I...I never said he was, not really," she stammered.

He supported himself on the prosthesis and looked down at what he could see of her damp, shivering body. He touched her delicately on her stomach and then trailed his hand down to her thighs. There was a smear of blood on them that seemed to capture his attention for a moment.

"Simon, it hurts," she whispered, embarrassed.

His eyes went back to hers. "I know," he replied gently. His hand moved gently between her long legs to where their bodies were still completely joined, and she caught his wrist, gasping.

"Shhh," he whispered. Ignoring her protests, he began to touch her.

Shocked at the sudden burst of unexpected pleasure, her wide eyes went homing to his. Her mouth opened as the breath came careening out of her. She caught his shoulders again, digging her nails in. This was...it was... Her eyes closed and she moaned harshly and shivered.

"That's it," he whispered, easing his mouth down onto hers as she shivered and shivered again. "This isn't going to hurt. Open your mouth. I want you to know me completely, in every way there is." His hips moved slowly, and he felt her whole body jump as his sensual caresses began to kindle a frightening sweet tension in her. "I'm going to teach you to feel pleasure."

She gripped his shoulders and held on, her eyes closed as his mouth worked its way even deeper into her own. She moved her legs around his muscular thighs to help him, to bring him into even closer contact, and gasped when she felt his invasion of her grow even more powerful, more insistent. The pain was still there, but it didn't matter anymore, because there was such pleasure overlaying it. She wanted him!

She heard her own voice sobbing, pleading with him, as the frenzy of pleasure grew to unbearable proportions. She was beyond pride, beyond protest. He was giving her pleasure of a sort she'd never dreamed existed. She belonged to him, was part of him, owned by him.

His movements grew urgent, deep. He whispered something into her open mouth but she couldn't hear him anymore. She was focused on some dark, sweet goal, every muscle straining toward it, her heartbeat pulsing in time with it, her tense body lifting to meet his as she pleaded for it.

His hips shifted all at once in a violent, hard rhythm that brought the ecstasy rushing over her like a wave of white-hot sensation. She cried out endlessly as it swept her away, her body pressing to his in a convulsive arch as the pleasure went on and on and on and she couldn't get close enough...!

This time, she didn't feel the weight of him as he collapsed onto her exhausted body. She held him tightly, pulsing in the soft aftermath, her legs trembling as they curled around his. She could hear his ragged breathing as she heard her own.

A long time later, he lifted his head and looked down into her wide eyes. He smiled at the faint shock in them. "Yes," he whispered. "It was good, wasn't it?"

She made an embarrassed sound and hid her face against him.

He smiled against her hair. "I thought it would never stop," he whispered huskily, brushing damp strands of hair away from her lips, her eyes as he turned her toward him. "I've never been fulfilled so completely in all my life."

She searched his eyes, seeing such tenderness in them that she felt warm all over. She reached up and touched his damp face with pure wonder, from his thick eyebrows to his wide, firm mouth and his stubborn chin. She couldn't even speak.

"You must be the only twenty-eight-year-old virgin in Texas," he murmured, and he wasn't joking. His eyes were solemn. "Did you save it for me, all these years?"

She didn't want to admit that. He probably guessed that she had, but only a little pride remained in her arsenal.

She sighed quietly. "I never knew a man that I wanted enough," she confessed, averting a direct answer. She dropped her gaze to his broad, bare chest where the thick hair was damp with sweat. "I suppose you've lost count of all the women you've had in the past few years."

His finger traced her soft mouth. "I haven't had a woman since Melia died. I dated Jill, but we were never intimate."

Her surprise was all too evident as she met his rueful gaze. "What?"

His powerful shoulders rose and fell. "A one-armed man isn't a lover many women would choose. I've been sensitive about it, and perhaps a little standoffish when it came to invitations." He searched her eyes. "I've always been comfortable with you. I knew that if I fumbled, you wouldn't laugh at me."

"Never that," she agreed quietly. She looked at the way they were laying and flushed.

"Now you know," he murmured with a warm smile.

"Yes. Now I know."

"I'm sorry I had to hurt you." Regret was in his eyes as well as his tone. He traced her eyebrows. "It had been too long and I lost control. I couldn't pull away."

"I understood."

"You were tight," he said bluntly. "And very much a virgin. I apologize wholeheartedly for every nasty insinuation I've ever made about you."

She was uncomfortable. Was he apologizing for making love to her?

He tilted her face back up to his and kissed her tenderly. "I won't say I'm sorry," he whispered into her mouth. "You can't imagine how it felt, to know I was the first with you."

She frowned worriedly.

He lifted his head and saw her expression. "What's wrong?" he asked.

"You didn't use anything," she said.

"No. I assumed that you were on the pill," he replied. "That went along with the assumption that you were sleeping with Charles and you'd never gotten pregnant."

The very word made her flush even more. "Well, I'm not," she faltered.

An expression crossed his face that she couldn't understand. He looked down at her body pressed so closely, so intimately to his, and curiously, his big hand smoothed over her flat belly in a strangely protective caress.

"If I made you pregnant..."

He didn't have to finish the sentence. She always seemed to know what he was thinking. She reached up and put her cool fingers against his wide mouth.

"You know me," she whispered, anticipating the question he was afraid to ask.

He sighed and let the worry flow out of him. He bent to her mouth and traced it with his lips. "It would complicate things."

She only smiled. "Yes."

His mouth pressed down hard on hers all at once and his hips moved suggestively.

She cried out.

He stilled instantly, because it wasn't a cry of pleasure. "This is uncomfortable for you now," he said speculatively.

"It is," she confessed reluctantly. "I'm sorry."

"No, I'm sorry that I hurt you." He lifted his weight away and met her eyes. "It may be uncomfortable when I withdraw. I'll be as slow as I can."

The blunt remark made her cheeks go hot, but she watched him lift away from her with frank curiosity and a little awe.

"Oh, my," she whispered when he rolled over onto his back.

"Yes, isn't it shocking?" he whispered and pulled her gently against his side. "And now you know why it was so uncomfortable, don't you?" he teased softly.

She laid her cheek on his broad shoulder. "I have seen the occasional centerfold," she murmured, embarrassed. "Although I have to admit that they weren't in your class!"

He chuckled and took a deep, slow breath. "Your body will adjust to me."

That sounded as if he didn't mean tonight to be an isolated incident, and she frowned, because it worried her. She didn't want to be his mistress. Did he think that she'd agreed to some casual sexual relationship because she'd given in to his ardor?

His hand smoothed over her long, graceful fingers. "When you heal a little, I'll teach you how to give it back," he murmured sleepily. "That was the first thing I noticed when I kissed you," he added. "You didn't fight me, but you didn't respond, either."

She sighed. "I didn't know how," she said honestly. Her wide eyes stared across his chest to the big, dark bureau against the wall. Her nails scraped through the thick hair on his chest and she felt him move sinuously, as if he enjoyed it.

His hand pressed hers closer and he stretched, shivering a little in the aftermath. "I'd forgotten how good it could be," he murmured. He tugged on a damp strand of red-gold hair. "I'm not taking you home."

She stiffened. "But I..."

"But, nothing. You're mine. I'm not letting you go."

That sounded possessive. Perhaps it was a sexual thing that men felt afterward. She knew so little about intimacy and how men reacted to it.

As if he sensed her concern, he eased her over onto her side so that he could see her face. It disturbed him to see her expression.

"This was a mistake," he said at once when he saw her eyes. "Probably my biggest in a long line of them." His big hand pressed hard against her stomach. "But we're going to make it right. If you've got my baby in here, there's no way you're raising it alone. We'll get married as soon as I can get a license."

She was even more shocked by that statement than if he'd asked her to live in sin with him.

She took a breath and hesitated.

His eyes held hers firmly. "Do you want my baby?"

The way he said it made delicious chills run down her spine. There was all the tenderness in the world in the soft question, and tears stung her eyes.

"Oh, yes," she whispered.

He looked at her until her breathing changed, his eyes solemn and possessive as they trailed down to her submissive body and her soft, pretty breasts. He touched them delicately.

"Then we won't use anything," he murmured, lifting his eyes back to hers.

Her lips parted. There were so many questions spinning around in her mind that she couldn't grasp one to single out.

His fingers went up to her lips and traced them very slowly. "Why did you give yourself to me?" he asked.

She stared at him worriedly. "I thought you knew."

"I hope I do." He looked worried now. "I really didn't have any intention of seducing you, in case you wondered. I was going to kiss you. Maybe a little more than just that," he added with a rueful smile. "But you came in here with me like a lamb," he said, as if it awed him that she'd yielded so easily. "You never protested once, until I hurt you." He grimaced and brought her hand to his mouth, kissing the palm hungrily. "I never thought it would hurt you so much!" he said, as if the memory itself was painful. "You cried and started moving, and I lost my head completely. I couldn't even stop…"

"But, it's…it's normal for it to be a little uncomfortable the first time," she said quickly, putting her fingers against his hard mouth. "Simon, some girls are just a little unlucky. I suppose I was one of them. It's all right."

He met her eyes. His were still turbulent. "I wouldn't have hurt you for the world," he whispered huskily. "I wanted you to feel what I was feeling. I wanted you to feel as if the sun had exploded inside you.'' His fingers tangled softly in her hair. ''It was...never like that,'' he added in quiet wonder as he searched her eyes. ''I never knew it could be.'' He bent and touched his mouth to hers with breathless tenderness. ''Dear God, I wanted to cherish you, and I couldn't keep my head long enough! It should have been tender between us, as tender as I feel inside when I touch you. But it had been years, and I was like an animal. I thought you were experienced...!''

She drew his face down to hers and kissed his eyelids closed. Her lips touched softly all over his face, his cheeks, his nose, his hard mouth. She kissed him as if he needed comforting.

''You wanted me,'' she whispered against his ear as she held him to her. ''I wanted you, too. It didn't hurt the second time.''

His arms slid under her and he shivered. ''It won't ever hurt again. I swear it.''

Her legs curled into his and she smiled dreamily. He might not love her, but he felt something much more than physical desire for her. That long, stumbling speech had convinced her of one thing, at least. She would marry him. There was enough to build on.

''Simon?'' she whispered.

''Hmmm?''

''I'll marry you.''

His mouth turned against her warm throat. ''Of course you will,'' he whispered tenderly.

She closed her eyes and linked her arms around him, her fingers encountering the leather strap of the prosthesis. ''Why don't you take it off?'' she murmured sleepily.

He lifted his head and frowned. ''Tira...''

She sat up, proudly nude, and drew him up with her so that she could push the shirt away. She watched his teeth clench as she undid the straps and eased the artificial appliance away, along with the sleeve that covered the rest of his missing arm.

She drew it softly to her breasts and held it there, watching the expression that bloomed on his lean, hard face at the gesture.

"Yes, you still have feeling in it, don't you?" she murmured with the first glint of humor she'd felt in a long time as she saw the desire kindle in his pale eyes.

"There, and other places," he said tautly. "And you're walking wounded. Don't torture me."

"Okay." She pushed him back down and curled up against him with absolute trust.

She looked like a fairy lying there next to him, as natural as rain or sun with his torn body. He looked at her with open curiosity.

"Doesn't it bother you, really?" he asked.

She nuzzled closer. "Simon, would it bother you if I was missing an arm?" she asked unexpectedly.

He thought about that for a minute. "No."

"Then that answers your question." She smiled. "I'm sleepy."

He laughed softly. "So am I."

He reached up and turned off the lamp, drowsily pulling the covers over them.

She stiffened and he held her closer.

"What is it?" he asked quickly.

"Simon, do you have a housekeeper?"

"Sure. She comes in on Tuesdays and Thursdays." His mouth brushed her forehead. "It's Saturday night," he reminded her. "And we're engaged."

"Okay."

His arm gathered her even closer. "We'll get the license first thing Monday morning and we'll be married Thursday. Who do you want to stand up with us?"

"I suppose it will have to be your brothers," she groaned.

He grinned. "Just thank your lucky stars you didn't refuse to marry me. Remember what happened to Dorie?"

She did. She closed her eyes. "I'm thankful." She drank in the spicy scent of him. "Simon, are you sure?"

"I'm sure." He drew her closer. "And so are you. Go to sleep."

Chapter 9

They got up and showered and then made breakfast together. Tira was still shy with him, after what they'd done, and he seemed to find it enchanting. He watched her fry bacon and scramble eggs while he made coffee. She was wearing one of his shirts and he was wearing only a pair of slacks.

"We'll make an economical couple," he mused. "I like the way you look in my shirts. We'll have to try a few more on you."

"I like the way you look without your shirt," she murmured, casting soft glances at him.

He wasn't wearing the prosthesis and he frowned, as if he wasn't certain whether she was teasing.

She took up the eggs, slid them onto the plate with the bacon, turned the burner off and went to him.

"You're still Simon," she said simply. "It never mattered to me. It never will, except that I'm sorry it had to happen to you." She touched his chest with soft, tender hands. "I like looking at you," she told him honestly. "I wasn't teasing."

He looked at her in the morning light with eyes that puzzled her. He touched the glory of her long hair tenderly. "This is all wrong," he said quietly. "I should have taken you out, bought you roses and candy, called you at two in the morning just to talk.

Then I should have bought a ring and asked you, very correctly, to marry me. I spoiled everything because I couldn't wait to get you into bed with me.''

She was surprised that it worried him so much. She studied his hard face. "It's all right."

He drew in a harsh breath and bent to kiss her forehead tenderly. "I'm sorry, just the same."

She smiled and snuggled close to him. "I love you."

The words hit him right in the stomach. He drew in his breath as if he felt them. His hand tightened on her shoulder until it bruised. Inevitably he thought of all the wasted years when he'd kept her at a distance, treated her with contempt, ignored her.

"Hey." She laughed, wiggling.

He let go belatedly. His expression disturbed her. He didn't look like a happy prospective bridegroom. The eyes that met hers were oddly tortured.

He put her away from him with a forced smile that wouldn't have fooled a total stranger, much less Tira.

"Let's have breakfast."

"Of course."

They ate in silence, hardly speaking. He had a second cup of coffee and then excused himself while she put the breakfast things into the dishwasher.

She assumed that he was dressing and wanted her to do the same. She went back into the bedroom and quickly donned the clothing he'd removed the night before, having retrieved half of it from the living room. She didn't understand what was wrong with him, unless he really had lost his head and was now regretting everything including the marriage proposal. She knew from gossip that men often said things they didn't mean to make a woman go to bed with them. She must have been an easy mark, at that, so obviously in love with him that he knew she wouldn't resist him.

Last night it had seemed right and beautiful. This morning it seemed sordid and she felt cheap. Looking at herself in his mirror, she saw the new maturity in her face and eyes and mourned the hopeful young woman who'd come home with him.

He paused in the doorway, watching her. He was fully dressed, right down to the prosthesis.

"I'll take you home," he said quietly.

She turned, without looking at him. "That would be best."

He drove her there in a silence as profound as the one they'd shared over breakfast. When he pulled into her driveway, she held up a hand when he started to cut off the engine.

"You don't need to walk me to the door," she said formally. "I'll...see you."

She scrambled out of the car and slammed the door behind her, all but running for her front door.

The key wouldn't go in the first time, and she could hardly see the lock anyway for the tears.

She didn't realize that Simon had followed her until she felt his hand at her back, easing her inside the house.

"No, please..." she sobbed.

He pulled her into his arms and held her, rocked her, his lips in her hair.

"Sweetheart, don't," he whispered, his deep voice anguished. "It's all right! Don't cry!"

Which only made the tears fall faster. She cried until she was almost sick from crying, and when she finally lifted her head from his chest and saw his grim expression, it was all she could manage not to start again.

"I wish I could carry you," he murmured angrily, catching her by the hand to pull her toward the living room. "It used to give me a distinct advantage at times like these to have two good arms."

He sat down on the sofa and pulled her down into his lap, easing her into the elbow that was part prosthesis so that he could mop up her tears with his handkerchief.

"I don't even have to ask what you're thinking," he muttered irritably as he dried her eyes and nose. "I saw it all in my mirror. Good God, don't you think I'm sorry, too?"

"I know you are," she choked. "It's all right. You don't have to feel guilty. I could have said no."

He stilled. "Guilty about what?"

"Seducing me!"

"I didn't."

Her eyes opened wide and she gaped at him. "You did!"

"You never once said you didn't want to," he reminded her. "In fact, I distinctly remember asking if you did."

She flushed. "Well?"

"I don't feel guilty about *that*," he said curtly.

Her eyebrows lifted. "Then what are you sorry about?"

"That you had to come home in your evening gown feeling like a woman I bought for the night," he replied irritably. He touched her disheveled hair. "You didn't even have a brush or makeup with you."

She searched his face curiously. He was constantly surprising her these days.

He touched her unvarnished lips with a wry finger. "Now you're home," he said. "Go put on some jeans and a shirt and we'll go to Jacobsville and ride horses and have a picnic."

She lost her train of thought somewhere. "You want to take me riding?"

He let his gaze slide down her body and back up and his lips drew up into a sardonic smile. "On second thought, I guess that isn't a very good idea."

She realized belatedly what he was saying and flushed. "Simon!"

"Well, why dance around it? You're sore, aren't you?" he asked bluntly.

She averted her eyes. "Yes."

"We'll have the picnic, but we'll go in a truck when we get to the ranch."

She lifted her face back to his and searched his pale eyes. He looked older today, but more relaxed and approachable than she'd ever seen him. There were faint streaks of silver at his temples now, and silver threads mixed in with the jet black of his hair. She reached up and touched them.

"I'm almost forty," he said.

She bit her lower lip, thinking how many years had passed when they could have been like this, younger and looking forward to children, to a life together.

He drew her face to his chest and smoothed over her hair. She was so very fragile, so breakable now. He'd seen her as a flamboyant, independent, spirited woman who was stubborn and hot-tempered. And here she lay in his arms as if she were a child, trusting and gentle and so sweet that she made his heart ache.

He nuzzled his cheek against hers so that he could find her soft mouth, and he kissed it until a groan of anguish forced its way out of his throat. Oh, God, he thought, the years he'd wasted!

She heard the groan and drew back to look at him.

He was breathing roughly. His eyes, turbulent and fierce, lanced down into hers. He started to speak, just as the doorbell rang.

They both jumped at the unexpected loudness of it.

"That's probably Mrs. Lester," she said worriedly.

"On a Sunday? I thought she spent weekends with her sister?"

She did. Tira climbed out of his arms with warning bells going off in her head. She had a sick feeling that when she opened that door, her whole life was going to change.

And it did.

Charles Percy stood there with both hands in his pockets, looking ten years older and sick at heart.

"Charles!" she exclaimed, speechless.

His eyes ran over her clothing and his eyebrows arched. "Isn't it early for evening gowns?" He scowled. "Surely you aren't just getting home?"

"As a matter of fact, she is," Simon said from the doorway of the living room, and he looked more dangerous than Tira had ever seen him.

He approached Charles with unblinking irritation. "Isn't it early for you to be calling?" he asked pointedly.

"I have to talk to Tira," Charles said, obviously not understanding the situation at all. "It's urgent."

Simon leaned against the doorjamb and waved a hand in invitation.

Charles glared at him. "Alone," he emphasized. His scowl deepened. "And what are you doing here, anyway?" he added, having been so occupied with Gene and Nessa that he still thought Simon and Tira were feuding. "After what you and your vicious girlfriend said to her at the charity ball, I'm amazed she'll even speak to you."

Jill had gone right out of Tira's mind in the past twenty-four hours. Now she looked at Simon and remembered the other woman vividly, and a look of horror overtook her features.

Simon saw his life coming apart in those wide green eyes. Tira hadn't remembered Jill until now, thank God, but she was going to remember a lot more, thanks to Charles here. He glared at the man as if he'd have liked to punch him.

"Jill is part of the past," he said emphatically.

"Is she, really?" Charles asked haughtily. "That's funny. She's been hinting to all and sundry that you're about to pop the question."

Tira's face drained of color. She couldn't even look at Simon.

Simon called him a name that made her flush and caused Charles to stiffen his spine.

Charles opened the door wide. "I think this would be a good time to let Tira collect herself. Don't you?"

Simon didn't budge. "Tira, do you want me to leave?" he asked bluntly.

She still couldn't lift her eyes. "It might be best."

What a ghostly, thin little voice. The old Tira would have laid about him with a baseball bat. But he'd weakened her, and now she thought he'd betrayed her. Jill had lied. If Tira loved him, why couldn't she see that? Why was she so ready to believe Charles?

Unless... He glared at the other man. Did she love Charles? Had she given in to a purely physical desire the night before and now she was ashamed and using Jill as an excuse?

"Please go, Simon," Tira said when he hesitated. She couldn't bear the thought that he'd seduced her on a whim and everything he'd said since was a lie. But how could Jill make up something as serious as an engagement? She put a hand to her head. She couldn't think straight!

Simon shot a cold glare at Tira and another one at Charles. He didn't say a single word as he stalked out the door to his car.

Tira served coffee in the living room, having changed into jeans and a sweater. She didn't dare think about what had happened or she'd go mad. Simon and Jill. Simon and Jill...

"What happened?" Charles asked curtly.

"One minute we were engaged and the next minute he was gone," she said, trying to make light of it.

"Engaged?"

She nodded, refusing to meet his eyes.

He put the evening gown and Simon's fury together and groaned. "Oh, no. Please tell me I didn't put my foot in it again?"

She shrugged. "If Jill says he's proposed to her, I don't know what to think. I guess I've been an idiot."

"I shouldn't have come. I shouldn't have opened my mouth." He put his face in his hands. "I'm so sorry."

"Why did you come?" she asked suddenly.

He drew his hands over his face, down to his chin. "Gene died this morning," he said gruffly. "I've just left Nessa with a nurse and made the arrangements at the funeral home. I came by to ask if you could stay with her tonight. She doesn't want to be alone, and for obvious reasons, I can't stay in my own house with her right now."

"You want me to stay with her in your house?" she asked.

He nodded. "Can you?"

"Charles, of course I can," she said, putting aside her own broken relationship for the moment. Charles's need was far greater. "I'll just pack a few things."

"I'll drive you over," he said. "You won't need your car until tomorrow. I'll bring you home then."

"Nessa can come with me," she said. "Mrs. Lester and I will take good care of her."

"That would be nice. But tonight, she doesn't need to be moved. She's sedated, and sleeping right now."

"Okay."

"Tira, do you want me to call Simon and explain, before we go?" he asked worriedly.

"No," she said. "It can wait."

Charles was the one in trouble right now. She refused to think about her own situation. She packed a bag, left a note for Mrs. Lester and locked the door behind them.

The next morning Mrs. Lester found only a hastily scribbled note saying that Tira had gone home with Charles—and not why. So when Simon called the next morning, she told him with obvious reluctance that apparently Tira had gone to spend the night at Charles's house and hadn't returned.

"I suppose it was his turn," he said with bridled fury, thanked her and hung up. He packed a bag without taking time to think things through and caught the next flight to Austin to see the governor about the job he'd been offered.

Gene's funeral was held on the Wednesday, and from the way Nessa clung to Charles, Tira knew that at least somebody's life was eventually going to work out. Having heard from Mrs. Lester that Simon had phoned and gone away furious having thought she spent the night with Charles, she had no hope at all for her own future.

She spent the next few days helping Nessa clear away Gene's things and get her life in some sort of order. Charles was more than willing to do what he could. By the time Christmas Eve rolled around, Tira was all by herself and so miserable that she felt like doing nothing but cry.

Nevertheless, she perked herself up, dressed in a neat red pant-suit and went to the orphans' Christmas party that she'd promised to attend.

She carried two cakes that she and Mrs. Lester had baked, along with all the paraphernalia that went with festive eats. Other people on the committee brought punch and cookies and candy, and there were plenty of gaily wrapped presents.

Tira hadn't expected to see Simon, and she didn't. But Jill, of all people, showed up with an armload of presents.

"Why, how lovely to see you, Tira," Jill exclaimed. She didn't get too close—she probably remembered the cup of coffee.

"Lovely to see you, too, Jill," Tira said with a noxious smile. "Do join the fun."

"Oh, I can't stay," she said quickly. "I'm filling in for Simon. Poor dear, he's got a raging headache and he couldn't make it."

"Simon doesn't have headaches," Tira said curtly, averting her eyes. "He gives them."

"I thought you knew he frequently gets them when he flies," Jill murmured condescendingly. "I've nursed him through several. Anyway, he just got back from Austin. He's accepted the appointment as attorney general, by the way." She sighed dramatically. "I'm to go with him to the governor's New Year's Ball! And I've got just the dress to wear, too!"

Tira wanted to go off and be sick. Her life had become a nightmare.

"Must run, dear," Jill said quickly. "I have to get home to Simon. Hope the party's a great success. See you!"

She was gone in the flash of an eye. Tira put on the best act she'd ever given for the orphans, handing out cake and presents with a smile that felt glued-on. The media showed up to film the event for the eleven o'clock news, as a human interest story, and

Tira managed to keep her back to the cameras. She didn't want Simon to gloat if he saw how she really looked.

After the party, she wrapped herself in her leather coat, went home and threw up for half an hour. The nausea was new. She never got sick. There could only be one reason for it, and it wasn't anything she'd eaten. Two weeks into her only pregnancy with Tira, her mother had said, the nausea had been immediately apparent long before the doctors could tell she was pregnant.

Tira went to bed and cried herself to sleep. She did want the child, that was no lie, but she was so mad at Simon that she could have shot him. Poor little baby, to have such a lying pig for a father!

Just as she opened her eyes, there was a scratching sound and she looked up in time to see the unwelcome mouse, who'd been delightfully absent for two weeks, return like a bad penny. He scurried down the hall and she cursed under her breath. Well, now she had a mission again. She was going to get that mouse. Then she was going to get Simon!

She fixed herself a small milk shake for Christmas dinner and carried it to her studio. She wasn't even dressed festively. She was wearing jeans and a sweater and socks, with her hair brushed but not styled and no makeup on. She felt lousy and the milk shake was the only thing she could look at without throwing up.

Charles and Nessa had offered to let her spend Christmas with them, but she declined. The last thing she felt like was company.

She wandered through the studio looking at her latest creations. She sat down at her sculpting table and stared at the lump of clay under the wet cloth that she'd only started that morning. She wasn't really in the mood to work, least of all on Christmas Day, but she didn't feel like doing anything else, either.

Why, oh, why, had she gone to Simon's apartment? Why hadn't she insisted that he take her home? In fact, why hadn't she left him strictly alone after John died? She couldn't blame anyone for the mess her life was in. She'd brought it on herself by chasing after a man who didn't want her. Well, he did now—but only in one way. And after he married Jill...

She placed a protective hand over her stomach and sighed. She had the baby. She knew that she was pregnant. She'd have the tests, but they really weren't necessary. Already she could feel the life inside her instinctively, and she wondered if the baby would look like her or like Simon.

There was a loud tap at the back door. She frowned. Most people rang the doorbell. It wasn't likely to be Charles and Nessa, and it was completely out of the question that it could be Simon. Perhaps a lost traveler?

She got up, milk shake in hand, and went to the back door, slipping the chain before she opened it.

Simon stared down at her with quiet, unreadable eyes. He had dark circles under his eyes and new lines in his face. "It's Christmas," he said. "Do I get to come in?"

He was wearing a suit and tie. He looked elegant, hardly a match for her today.

She shrugged. "Suit yourself," she said tautly. She looked pointedly past him to see if he was alone.

His jaw tautened. "Did you expect me to bring someone?"

"I thought Jill might be with you," she said.

He actually flinched.

She let out a long breath. "Sorry. Your private life is none of my business," she said as she closed the door.

When she turned around, it was to find his hand clenched hard at his side.

"Speaking of private lives, where's Charles?" he asked icily.

She stared at him blankly. "With Nessa, of course."

He scowled. "What's he still doing with her?"

"Gene died and Nessa needs Charles now more than ever." She frowned when he looked stunned. "Charles has been in love with Nessa for years. Gene tricked her into marrying him, hoping to inherit her father's real estate company. It went broke and he made Nessa his scapegoat. She wouldn't leave him because she knew he had a bad heart, and Charles almost went mad. Now that Gene's gone, they'll marry as soon as they can.''

He looked puzzled. ''You went home with him...''

''I went to his house to stay with Nessa, the night after Gene had died,'' she said flatly. ''Charles said that it wouldn't look right for her to be there alone, and she wouldn't stay at her own house.''

He averted his eyes. He couldn't look at her. Once again, it seemed, he'd gotten the whole thing upside down and made a mess of it.

''Why are you here?'' she asked with some of her old hauteur. ''In case you were wondering, I'm not going to shoot myself,'' she added sarcastically. ''I'm through pining for you.''

He shoved his hand into his pocket and glanced toward her, noticing her sock-clad feet and the milk shake in her hand. ''What's that?'' he asked suddenly.

''Lunch,'' she returned curtly.

His face changed. His eyes lifted to hers and he didn't miss her paleness or the way she quickly avoided meeting his searching gaze.

''No turkey and dressing?''

She shifted. ''No appetite,'' she returned.

He lifted an eyebrow and his eyes began to twinkle as they dropped eloquently to her stomach. ''Really?''

She threw the milk shake at him. He ducked, but it hit the kitchen cabinet in its plastic container and she groaned at the mess she was going to have to clean up later. Right now, though, it didn't matter.

''I hate you!'' she raged. ''You seduced me and then you ran like the yellow dog you are! You let Jill nurse you through headaches and spend Christmas Eve with you, and I hope you do marry her, you deserve each other, you...you...!''

She was sobbing by now, totally out of control, with tears streaming down her red face.

He drew her close to him and rocked her warmly, his hand smoothing her wild hair while she cried. ''There, there,'' he whispered at her ear. "The first few months are hard, but it will get better. I'll buy you dill pickles and feed you ice cream and make dry toast and tea for you when you wake up in the morning feeling queasy."

She stilled against him. "W...what?"

"My baby, you're almost certainly pregnant," he whispered huskily, holding her closer. "From the look of things, very, very pregnant, and I feel like dancing on the lawn!"

Chapter 10

She looked up at him with confusion, torn between breaking his neck and kissing him.

"Wh…what makes you think I'm pregnant?" she asked haughtily.

He smiled lazily. "The milk shake."

She shifted. "It's barely been two weeks."

"Two long, lonely weeks," he said heavily. He touched her hair, her face, as if he'd ached for her as badly as she had for him. "I can't seem to stop putting my foot in my mouth."

She lowered her eyes to his tie. It was a nice tie, she thought absently, touching its silky red surface. "You had company."

He tilted her face up to his eyes. "Jill likes to hurt you, doesn't she?" he asked quietly. "Why are you so willing to believe everything she says? I've never had any inclination to marry her, in the past or now. And as for her nursing me through a headache, you, of all people, should know I don't get them, ever."

"She said…!"

"I came home from Austin miserable and alone and I got drunk for the first time since the wreck," he said flatly. "She got in past the doorman at the hotel and announced that she'd come to nurse me. I had her shown to the front door."

Her eyebrows arched. That wasn't what Jill had said.

His eyes searched over her wan face. "And you don't believe me, do you?" he asked with resignation. "I can't blame you. I've done nothing but make mistakes with you, from the very beginning. I've lived my whole life keeping to myself, keeping people at bay. I loved Melia, in my way, but even she was never allowed as close as you got. Especially," he added huskily, "in bed."

"I don't understand."

His fingers traced her full lower lip. "I never completely lost control with her," he said softly. "The first time with you, I went right over the edge. I hurt you because I couldn't hold anything back." He smiled gently. "You didn't realize, did you?"

"I don't know much about...that."

"So I discovered." His jaw tautened as he looked at her. "Married but untouched."

Something niggled at the back of her mind, something he'd said about John. She couldn't remember it.

He bent and brushed his mouth gently over her forehead. "We have to get married," he whispered. "I want to bring our baby into the world under my name."

"Simon..."

He drew her close and his lips slid gently over her half-open mouth. She could feel his heartbeat go wild the minute he touched her. His big body actually trembled.

She looked up at him with quiet curiosity, seeing the raging desire he wasn't bothering to conceal blazing in his eyes, and her whole body stilled.

"That's right," he murmured. "Take a good look. I've managed to hide it from you for years, but there's no need now."

"You wanted me, before?" she asked.

"I wanted you the first time I saw you," he said huskily. His lean hand moved from her neck down to the hard peak of her breast visible under the sweater, and he brushed over it with his fingers, watching her shiver. "You were the most gloriously beautiful creature I'd ever seen. But I was married and I imagined that it was nothing more than the sort of lust a man occasionally feels for a totally inappropriate sort of woman.''

"You thought I was cheap.''

"No. I thought you were experienced,'' he said, and there was regret in his eyes. "I threw you at John to save myself, without having the first idea what I was about to subject you to. I'm sorry, if it matters. I never used to think of myself as the sort of man to run from trouble, but I spent years running from you.''

She lowered her gaze to his tie again. Her heart was racing. He'd never spoken to her this way in the past. She felt his hand in her hair, tangling in it as if he loved its very feel, and her eyes closed at the tenderness in the caress.

"I don't want to be vulnerable,'' he said through his teeth. "Not like this.''

She let out a long sigh. She understood what he meant. "Neither did I, all those years ago,'' she said heavily. "Charles was kind to me. He knew how I felt about you, and he provided me with the same sort of camouflage I gave him for Nessa's sake. Everyone thought we were lovers.''

"I suppose you know I thought you were experienced when I took you to bed?''

She nodded.

"Even when you cried out, the first time, I thought it was pleasure, not pain. I'll never forget how I felt when I realized how wrong I'd been about you.'' His hand tightened on her soft body unconsciously. "I know how bad it was. Are you...all right?''

"Yes.''

He drew her forehead against him and held it there while he fought for the right words to heal some of the damage he'd done. His eyes closed as he bent over her. It was like coming home. He'd never known a feeling like it.

She sighed and slid her arms under his and around him, giving him her weight.

He actually shivered.

She lifted her head and looked up, curious. His face was tight, his eyes brilliant with feeling. She didn't need a crystal ball to understand why. His very vulnerability knocked down all the barriers. She knew how proud he was, how he hated having her see him this way. But it was part of loving, a part he had yet to learn.

She took his hand in hers. "Come on," she said softly. "I can fix what's wrong with you."

"How do you know what's wrong with me?" he taunted.

She tugged at his hand. "Don't be silly."

She pulled him along with her out of the kitchen to her bedroom and closed the door behind her. She was a little apprehensive. Despite the pleasure he'd given her, the memory of the pain was still very vivid.

He took a slow breath. "I'll always have to be careful with you," he said, as if he read the thoughts in her eyes. "I'm over-endowed and you're pretty innocent, in spite of what we did together."

She blinked. "You...are?"

He scowled. "You said you'd seen centerfolds."

She colored wildly. "Not...of men...like that!"

"Well, well." He chuckled softly and moved closer to her. "I feel like a walking anatomy lab."

"Do you, really?" She drew his hand under her sweater and up to soft, warm skin, and shivered when he touched her. Her heart was in the eyes she lifted to his. "It won't hurt...?"

He drew her close and kissed her worried eyes shut. "No," he whispered tenderly. "I promise it won't!"

She let him undress her, still hesitant and shy with him, but obviously willing.

When she was down to her briefs, she began undressing him, to his amusement.

"This is new," he mused. "I've had to do it myself for a number of years."

She looked up, hesitating. "All that time," she said. "Didn't you want anyone?"

"I wanted you," he replied solemnly. "Sometimes, I wanted you desperately."

"You never even hinted...!"

"You know why," he said, as if it shamed him to remember. "I should have been shot."

She lowered her eyes to the bare, broad chest she'd uncovered. "That would have been a waste," she said with a husky note in her voice. Her fingers spread over the thick hair that covered him, and he groaned softly. She put her mouth against his breastbone. "I've missed you," she whispered, and her voice broke.

"I've missed you!"

He bent to her mouth and kissed her slowly, tenderly, while between them, they got the rest of the obstacles out of the way.

When she reached for the strap of the prosthesis, his fingers stayed her.

"We'll have to find out sometime if you can do without it," she said gently. Her eyes searched his. "You can always put it back on, if you have to."

He sighed heavily. "All right."

He let her take it off, the uncertainty plain in his dark face. It made him vulnerable somehow, and he felt vulnerable enough with his hunger for her blatantly clear.

She stretched out on the pale pink sheets and watched him come down to her with wide, curious eyes.

Amazingly he was able to balance, if a little heavily at first. But she helped him, her body stabilizing his as they kissed and touched in the most tender exchange of caresses they'd ever shared for long, achingly sweet minutes until the urgency began to break through.

It was tender even as he eased down against her and she felt him probing at her most secret place. She tensed, expecting pain, but it was easy now, if a little uncomfortable just at first.

He turned her face to his and made her watch his eyes as they moved together slowly. He pressed soft, quiet kisses against her mouth as the lazy tempo of his hips brought them into stark intimacy.

She gasped and pushed upward as the pleasure shot through her, but he shook his head, calming her.

"Wh...why?" she gasped.

"Because I want it to be intense," he whispered unsteadily, nuzzling her face with his as he fought for enough breath to speak. His teeth clenched as he felt the first deep bites of pleasure rippling through him. "I want it to take a long time. I want to...touch you...as deeply inside...as it's humanly possible!"

She felt him in every pore, every cell. Her fingers clenched behind his strong neck because he was even more potent now than he'd been their first time together. Her teeth worried her lower lip as she looked up at him, torn between pleasure and apprehension.

"Don't be afraid," he whispered brokenly. "Don't be afraid of me."

"It wasn't like this...before," she sobbed. Her eyes closed on a wave of pleasure so sharp that it stiffened her from head to toe. "Dear...God...Simon!"

"Baby," he choked at her ear. His body moved tenderly, even in its great urgency, from side to side, intensifying the pleasure, bringing her to the brink of some unbelievably deep chasm. She was going to fall...to fall...

She barely heard her own voice shattering into a thousand pieces as she reached up to him in an arc, sobbing, wanting more of him, more, ever more!

"Oh, God, don't...I'll hurt you!" he bit off as she pulled him down sharply to her.

"Never," she breathed. "Never! Oh, Simon...!"

She sobbed as the convulsions took her. It had never been this sweeping. Her eyes opened in the middle of the spasms and met his, and she saw in them the same helpless loss of control, the ecstasy that made a tight, agonized caricature of his face. It faded into a black oblivion as the pleasure became unbearable and she lost consciousness for a space of seconds.

"Tira? *Tira!*"

His hand was trembling as it touched her face, her neck where the pulse hammered.

"Oh, God, honey, open your eyes and look at me! Are you all right?"

She felt her eyelids part slowly. His face was above hers, worried, tormented, his eyes glittering with fear.

She smiled lazily. "Hello," she whispered, so exhausted that she could barely manage words. She moved and felt him deep in her body and moaned with pleasure.

"Good God, I thought I'd killed you!" he breathed, relaxing on her. He was heavy, and she loved his weight. She held him close, nuzzling her face into his cool, damp throat. "You fainted!"

"I couldn't help it," she murmured. "Oh, it was so good. So good, so good!"

He rolled over onto his back, carrying her with him. He shivered, too, as the movements kindled little skirls of pleasure.

She curled her legs into his and closed her eyes. "I love you," she whispered sleepily.

He drew in a shaky breath. "I noticed."

She kissed his neck lazily and sighed. "Simon, I think I really am pregnant."

"So do I."

She moved against him sinuously. "Are you sorry?"

"I'm overjoyed."

That sounded genuine, and reassuring.

"I'm sleepy."

He stretched under her. He'd used more muscles than he realized he had. "So am I."

It was the last thing she heard for a long time. When she woke again, she was under the sheet with her hair spread over the pillow. Simon was wearing everything but his jacket, and he was sitting on the edge of the bed just looking at her.

She opened her eyes and stared up at him. She'd never seen

that expression on his face before. It wasn't one she could understand.

"Is something wrong?" she asked.

His hand went to her flat stomach over the sheet. "You don't think we hurt the baby?"

She smiled sleepily. "No. We didn't hurt the baby."

He wasn't quite convinced. "The way we loved this time..."

"Oh, that sounds nice," she murmured, smiling up at him with quiet, dreamy eyes.

His hand moved to hers and entangled with it. "What? That we loved?"

She nodded.

He drew their clasped hands to his broad thigh and studied them. "I've been thinking."

"What about?"

"It shouldn't be a quick ceremony in a justice of the peace's office," he said. He shrugged. "It should be in a church, with you in white satin."

"White? But..."

He lifted his eyes. They glittered at her. "White."

She swallowed. "Okay."

He relaxed a little. "I don't want people talking about you, as if we'd done something to be ashamed of—even though we have."

Her eyes opened wide. "What?"

"I used to go to church. I haven't forgotten how things are supposed to be done. We jumped the gun, twice, and I'm not very proud of it. But considering the circumstances, and this," he added gently, touching her belly with a curious little smile, "I think we're not quite beyond redemption."

"Of course we're not," she said softly. "God is a lot more understanding than most people are."

"And it isn't as if we aren't going to get married and give our baby a settled home and parents who love him," he continued. "So with all that in mind, I've put the wheels in motion."

"Wheels?"

He cleared his throat. "I phoned my brothers."

She sat straight up in bed with eyes like an owl's. "*Them?* You didn't! Simon, you couldn't!"

"There, there," he soothed her, "it won't be so bad. They're old hands at weddings. Look what a wonderful one they arranged for Corrigan. You went. So did I. It was great."

"They arranged Corrigan's wedding without any encouragement from Dorie at all! They kidnapped her and wrapped her in ribbons and carried her home to Corrigan for Christmas, for heaven's sake! I know all about those hooligans, and I can arrange my own wedding!" she burst out.

Just as she said that, the back door—the one they'd forgotten to lock—opened and they heard footsteps along with voices in the corridor.

The bedroom door flew open, and there they were, all of them except Corrigan. They stopped dead at the sight that met their eyes.

Cag glared at Simon. "You cad!" he snarled. "No wonder you needed us to arrange a wedding! How could you do that to a nice girl like her?"

"Disgraceful," Leopold added, with a rakish grin. "Doesn't she look pretty like that?"

"Don't leer at your future sister-in-law," Rey muttered, hitting him with his Stetson. He put half a hand over his eyes. "Simon, we'd better do this quick."

"All we need is a dress size," Leopold said.

"I am not giving you my dress size, you hooligans!" Tira raged, embarrassed.

"Better get it one size larger, she's pregnant," Simon offered.

"Oh, thank you very much!" Tira exclaimed, horrified.

"You're welcome." He grinned, unrepentant.

"*Pregnant?*" three voices echoed.

The insults were even worse now, and Leopold began flogging Simon with that huge white Stetson.

"Oh, Lord!" Tira groaned, hiding her head in the hands propped on her upbent knees.

"It's a size ten," Rey called from the closet, where he'd been inspecting Tira's dresses. "We'd better make it a twelve. Lots of lace, too. We can get the same minister that married Corrigan and Dorie. And it had better be no later than three weeks," he added with a black glare at Simon. "Considering her condition!"

"It isn't a condition," Simon informed him curtly, "it's a baby!"

"And we thought they weren't speaking." Leopold grinned.

"We don't know yet that it's a baby," Tira said with a glare.

"She was having a milk shake for Christmas dinner," Simon told them.

"We saw it. Goes well with the cabinets, I thought," Rey commented.

"Don't worry, the mouse will eat it," Tira muttered.

"Mouse?" Cag asked.

"He can't be trapped or run out or baited," she sighed. "I've had three exterminators in. They've all given up. The mouse is still here."

"I'll bring Herman over," Cag said.

The others looked at him wide-eyed. "No!" they chorused.

"About the service," Simon diverted them, "we need to invite the governor and his staff—Wally said he'd give her away," he added, glancing at Tira.

"The governor is going to give me away? Our governor? The governor of our state?" Tira asked, aghast.

"Well, we've only got one." He grimaced. "Forgot to tell you, didn't I? I've accepted the attorney general slot. I hope you won't mind living in Austin."

"Austin."

She looked confused. Simon glanced at his brothers and waved his hand toward them. "Get busy, we haven't got a lot of time," he said. "And don't forget the media. It never hurts any political party to have coverage of a sentimental event."

"There he goes again, being a politician," Cag muttered.

"Well, he is, isn't he?" Rey chuckled. "Okay, boys, let's go. We've got a busy day ahead of us tomorrow. See you."

Cag hesitated as they went out the door. "This wasn't done properly," he told his brother. "Shame on you."

Simon actually blushed. "One day," he told the other man, "you'll understand."

"Don't count on it."

Cag closed the door, leaving two quiet people behind.

"He's never been in love," Simon murmured, staring at his feet. "He doesn't have a clue what it's like to want someone so bad that it makes you sick."

She stared at him curiously. "Is that how it was for you, today?"

"Today, and the first time," he said, turning his face to her. He searched her eyes quietly. "But in case you've been wondering, I'm not marrying you for sex."

"Oh."

He glowered. "Or for the baby. I want him very much, but I would have married you if there wasn't going to be one."

She was really confused now. Did this mean what it sounded like? No, it had to have something to do with politics. It certainly wouldn't hurt his standing in the political arena to have a pregnant, pretty, capable wife beside him, especially when there was controversy.

That was when the reality of their situation hit her. She was going to marry a public official, not a local attorney. He was going to be appointed attorney general to fill the present unexpired term, but he'd have to run for the office the following year. They'd live in a goldfish bowl.

She stared at him with horror in every single line of her face as the implications hit her like a ton of bricks. She sat straight up in bed, with the sheet clutched to her breasts, and stared at Simon horrified. He didn't know about John. Despite the enlightened times, some revelations could be extremely damaging, and not only to her and, consequently, Simon. There was John's father, a successful businessman. How in the world would it affect him to have the whole state know that John had been gay?

The fear was a living, breathing thing. Simon had no idea about all this. He hadn't spoken of John or what he thought now that he knew Tira wasn't a murderess, but the truth could hurt him badly. It might hurt the governor as well; the whole political party, in fact.

She bit her lip almost through and lowered her eyes to the bed. "Simon, I can't marry you," she whispered in a ghostly tone.

"You what?"

"You heard me. I can't marry you. I'm sorry."

He moved closer, and tilted her face up to his quiet eyes. "Why not?"

"Because..." She hesitated. She didn't want to ever have to tell him the truth about his best friend. "Because I don't want to live in a goldfish bowl," she lied.

He knew her now. He knew her right down to her soul. He sighed and smiled at her warmly. "You mean, you don't want to marry me because you're afraid the truth about John will come to light and hurt me when I run for office next year."

Chapter 11

She was so astonished that she couldn't even speak. "You... know?" she whispered.

He nodded. "I've known since that night at the gallery, when I spoke to your ex-father-in-law," he replied quietly. "He told me everything." His face hardened. "That was when I knew what I'd done to you, and to myself. That was when I hit rock bottom."

"But you never said a word..." Things came flying back into her mind. "Yes, you did," she contradicted herself. "You said that you were glad John couldn't have me...you knew then!"

He nodded. "It must have been sheer hell for you."

"I was fond of him," she said. "I would have tried to be a good wife. But I married him because I couldn't have you and it didn't really matter anymore." Her eyes were sad as they met his. "You loved Melia."

"I thought I did," he replied. "I loved an illusion, a woman who only existed in my imagination. The reality was horrible." He reached out and touched her belly lightly, and she knew he was remembering.

Her fingers covered his. "You don't even have to ask how I feel about the baby, do you?"

He chuckled. "I never would have. You love kids." He grimaced. "I hated missing the Christmas Eve party. I watched you on television. I even knew why you kept your back to the camera. It was eloquent."

"Jill has been a pain," she muttered.

"Not only for you," he agreed. He sighed softly. "Tira, I hope you know that there hasn't been anyone else."

"It would have been hard to miss today," she said, and flushed a little.

He drew her across him and into the crook of his arm, studying her pretty face. "It doesn't bother you at all that I'm crippled, does it?"

"Crippled?" she asked, as if the thought had never occurred to her.

That surprise was genuine. He leaned closer. "Sweetheart, I'm missing half my left arm," he said pointedly.

"Are you, really?" She drew his head down to hers and kissed him warmly on his hard mouth. "You didn't need the prosthesis, either, did you?"

He chuckled against her lips. "Apparently not." His eyes shone warmly into hers. "How can you still love me after all I've put you through?" he asked solemnly.

She let the sheet fall away from her high, pretty breasts and laid back against his arm to let him look. "Because you make love so nicely?"

He shook his head. "No, that's not it." He touched her breasts, enjoying their immediate reaction. "Habit, perhaps. God knows, I don't deserve you."

She searched his face quietly. "I never knew you were vulnerable at all," she said, "that you could be tender, that you could laugh without being cynical. I never knew you at all."

"I didn't know you, either." He bent and kissed her softly. "What a lot of secrets we kept from each other."

She snuggled close. "What about John?" she asked worriedly. "If it comes out, it can hurt you and the party, it could even hurt John's father."

"You worry entirely too much," he said. "So what if it does? It's ancient history. I expect to be an exemplary attorney general—again—and what sort of pond scum would attack a beautiful pregnant woman?"

"I won't always be pregnant."

He lifted his head and gave her a wicked look. "No?"

She hit his chest. "I don't want to be the mother of a football team!"

"You'd love it," he returned, smiling at the radiance of her face. He chuckled. "I can see you already, letting them tackle you in mud puddles."

"They can tackle you. I'll carry the ball."

He glanced ruefully at the arm that was supporting her. "You might have to."

She touched his shoulder gently. "Does it really worry you so much?"

"It used to," he said honestly. "Until the first time you let me make love to you." He drew in a long breath. "You can't imagine how afraid I was to let you see the prosthesis. Then I was afraid to take it off, because I thought I might not be able to function as a man without using it for balance."

"We'd have found a way," she said simply. "People do."

He frowned slightly. "You make everything so easy."

She lifted her fingers and smoothed away the frown. "Not everything. You don't feel trapped?"

He caught her hand and pulled the soft palm to his lips, kissing it with breathless tenderness. "I feel as if I've got the world in my arms," he returned huskily.

She smiled. "So do I."

He looked as if he wanted to say something more, but he brought her close and wrapped her up against him instead.

The arrangements were complicated. Instead of a wedding, they seemed to be planning a political coup as well. The governor sent his private secretary and the brothers ended up in a furious fight with her over control of the event. It almost came to blows before Simon stepped in and reminded them that they couldn't plan the wedding without assistance. They informed him haughtily that they'd done it before. He threw up his hand and left them to it.

Tira had coffee with him in her living room in the midst of wedding invitations that she was hand signing. There must have been five hundred.

"I'm being buried," she said pointedly, gesturing toward the overflowing coffee table. "And that mouse is getting to me," she added. "I found *him* under one of the envelopes earlier!"

"Cag will take care of him while we're on our honeymoon. We can stay here until we find a house in Austin in a neighborhood you like."

"One you like, too," she said.

"If you like it, so will I."

It bothered her that he was letting her make all these decisions. She knew she was being cosseted, but she wasn't sure why.

"The brothers haven't been by today."

"They're in a meeting with Miss Chase, slugging it out," he replied. "When I left, she was reaching for a vase."

"Oh, dear."

"She's a tough little bird. She's not going to let them turn our wedding into a circus."

"They have fairly good taste," she admitted.

"They called Nashville to see how many country music stars they could hire to appear at the reception."

"Oh, good Lord!" she burst out.

"That isn't what Miss Chase said. She really needs to watch her language," he murmured. "Rey was turning red in the face when I ran for my life."

"You don't run."

"Only on occasion. Rey has the worst temper of the lot."

"I'd put five dollars on Miss Chase," she giggled.

He watched her lift the cup to her lips. "Should you be drinking coffee?"

"It's decaf, darling," she teased.

The endearment caught him off guard. His breath caught in his throat.

The reaction surprised her, because he usually seemed so unassailable. She wasn't quite sure of herself even now. "If you don't like it, I won't..." she began.

"Oh, I like it," he said huskily. "I'm not used to endearments, that's all."

"Yes, I know. You don't use them often."

"Only when I make love to you," he returned.

She lowered her eyes. He hadn't done that since the day they got engaged, when the brothers had burst into their lives again. She'd wondered why, but she was too shy to ask him.

"Hey," he said softly, coaxing her eyes up. "It isn't lack of interest. It's a lack of privacy."

She smiled wanly. "I wondered." She shrugged. "You haven't been around much."

"I've been trying to put together an office staff before I'm sworn in the first of January," he reminded her. "It's been a rush job."

"Of course. I know how much pressure you're under. If you'd like, we could postpone the wedding," she offered.

"Do you really want to be married in a maternity dress?" he teased.

Her reply was unexpected. She started crying.

He got up and pulled her up, wrapping her close. "It's nerves," he whispered. "They'll pass."

She didn't stop. The tears were worse.

"Tira?"

"I started," she sobbed.

"What?"

She looked up at him. Her eyes were swimming and red. "I'm not pregnant." She sounded as if the world had ended.

He pulled out a handkerchief and dried the tears. "I'm sorry," he whispered, and looked it. "I really am."

She took the handkerchief and made a better job of her face, pressing her cheek against his chest. "I didn't know how to tell you. But now you know. So if you don't want to go through with it..."

He stiffened. His head lifted and he looked at her as if he thought she was possessed. "Why wouldn't I want to go through with it?" he burst out.

"Well, I'm not pregnant, Simon," she repeated.

He let out the breath he was holding. "I told you I wasn't marrying you because of the baby. But you weren't completely convinced, were you?"

She looked sheepish. "I had my doubts."

He searched her wet eyes slowly. He held her cheek in his big, warm hand and traced her mouth with his thumb. "I'm sorry that you aren't pregnant. I want a baby very much with you. But I'm marrying you because I love you. I thought you knew."

Her heart jumped into her throat. "You never said."

"Some words come harder than others for me," he replied. He drew in a long breath. "I thought, I hoped, you'd know by the way we were in bed together. I couldn't have been so out of control the first time or so tender the next if I hadn't loved you to distraction."

"I don't know much about intimacy."

"You'll learn a lot more pretty soon," he murmured dryly. He frowned quizzically. "You were going to marry me, thinking I only wanted you for the baby?"

"I love you," she said simply. "I thought, when the baby came, you might learn to love me." Her face dissolved again into tears. "And then...then I knew there wasn't going to be a baby."

He kissed her tenderly, sipping the tears from her wet eyes, smiling. "There will be," he whispered. "One day, I promise you, there will be. Right now, I only want to marry you and live with you and love you. The rest will fall into place all by itself."

She looked into his eyes and felt the glory of it all the way to her soul. "I love you," she sobbed. "More than my life."

"That," he whispered as he bent to her mouth, "is exactly the way I feel about you!"

The wedding, despite the warring camps of its organizers, came off perfectly. It was a media event, at the ranch in Jacobsville, with all the leading families of the town in attendance and Tira glorious in a trailing white gown as she walked down the red carpet to the rose arbor where Simon and all his brothers and the minister waited. Dorie Hart was her matron of honor and the other Hart boys were best men.

The service was brief but eloquent, and when Simon placed the ring on her finger and then lifted her veil and kissed her, it was with such tenderness that she couldn't even manage to speak afterward. They went back down the aisle in a shower of rice and rose petals, laughing all the way.

The reception didn't have singers from Nashville. Instead the whole Jacobsville Symphony Orchestra turned out to play, and the food was flown in from San Antonio. It was a gala event and there were plenty of people present to enjoy it.

Tira hid a yawn and smiled apologetically at her new husband. "Sorry! I'm so tired and sleepy I can hardly stand up. I don't know what's wrong with me!"

"A nice Jamaican honeymoon is going to cure you of wanting sleep at all," he promised in a slow, deep drawl. "You are the most beautiful bride who ever walked down an aisle, and I'm the luckiest man alive."

She reached a hand up to his cheek and smiled lovingly at him. "I'm the luckiest woman."

He kissed her palm. "I wish we were ten years younger, Tira," he said with genuine regret. "I've wasted all that time."

"It wasn't wasted. It only made what we have so much better," she assured him.

"I hope we have fifty years," he said, and meant it.

They flew out late that night for their Caribbean destination. Cag, who hadn't forgotten the mouse, asked for the key to Tira's house and assured her that the mouse would be a memory when they returned. She had a prick of conscience, because in a way the mouse had brought her and Simon together. But it was for the best, she told herself. They couldn't go on living with a mouse! Although she did wonder what plan Cag had in mind that hadn't already been tried.

The Jamaican hotel where they stayed was right on the beach at Montego Bay, but they spent little time on the sand. Simon was ardent and inexhaustible, having kept his distance until the wedding.

He lay beside her, barely breathing after a marathon of passion that had left them both drenched in sweat and too tired to move.

"You need to take more vitamins," he teased, watching her yawn yet again. "You aren't keeping up with me."

She chuckled and rolled against him with a loving sigh. "It's the wedding and all the preparations," she whispered. "I'm just worn-out. Not that worn-out, though," she added, kissing his bare shoulder softly. "I love you, Simon."

He pulled her close. "I love you, Mrs. Hart. Very, very much."

She trailed her fingers across his broad, hair-roughened chest and wanted to say something else, but she fell asleep in the middle of it.

A short, blissful week later, they arrived back at her house with colorful T-shirts and wonderful memories.

"I could use some coffee," Simon said. "Want me to make it?"

"I'll do it, if you'll take the cases into the bedroom," she replied, heading for the kitchen.

She opened the cupboard to get out the coffee and came face-to-face with the biggest snake she'd ever seen in her life.

Simon heard a noise in the kitchen, put down the suitcases and went to see what had happened.

His heart jumped into his throat when he immediately connected the open cupboard, the huge snake and his new wife lying unconscious on the floor.

He bent, lifting her against his chest. "Tira, sweetheart, are you all right?" he asked softly, smoothing back her hair. "Can you hear me?"

She moved. Her eyelids fluttered and she opened her eyes, saw Simon, and immediately remembered why she was on the floor.

"Simon, there's a...a...*ssssssnake!*"

"Herman."

She stared at him. "There's a snake in the cupboard," she repeated.

"Herman," he repeated. "It's Cag's albino python."

"It's in *our* cupboard," she stated.

"Yes, I know. He brought it over to catch the mouse. Herman's a great mouser," he added. "Hell of a barrier to Cag's social life, but a really good mousetrap. We won't have a mouse now. Looks healthy, doesn't he?" he added, nodding toward the cupboard.

While they were staring at the huge snake, the back door suddenly opened and Cag came in with a gunnysack. He saw Tira and Simon on the floor and groaned.

"Oh, God, I'm too late!" he said heartily. "I'm sorry, Tira, I let the time slip away from me. I forgot all about Herman until I remembered the date, and you'd already left the airport when I tried to catch you." He sighed worriedly. "I haven't killed you, have I?"

"Not at all," Tira assured him with grim humor. "I've been tired a lot lately, too. I guess I'm getting fragile in my old age."

Simon helped her to her feet, but he was watching her with a curious intensity. She made coffee while Cag got his scaly friend into a bag and assured her that she'd have no more mouse problems. Tira offered him coffee, but he declined, saying that he had to get Herman home before the big python got irritable. He was shedding, which was always a bad time to handle him.

"Any time would be a bad time for me," Tira told her husband when their guest had gone.

"You fainted," he said.

"Yes, I know. I was frightened."

"You've been overly tired and sleeping a lot, and I notice that you don't eat breakfast anymore." He caught her hand and pulled her down onto his lap. "You were sure you weren't pregnant. I'm sure you are. I want you to see a doctor."

"But I started," she tried to explain.

"I want you to see a doctor."

She nuzzled her face into his throat. "Okay," she said, and kissed him. "But I'm not getting my hopes up. It's probably just some female dysfunction."

The telephone rang in Simon's office, where he was winding up his partnership before getting ready to move into the state government office that had been provided for him.

"Hello," he murmured, only half listening.

"Mr. Hart, your wife's here," his secretary murmured with unusual dryness.

"Okay, Mrs. Mack, send her in."

"I, uh, think you should come out, sir."

"What? Oh. Very well."

His mind was still on the brief he'd been preparing, so when he opened the door he wasn't expecting the surprise he got.

Tira was standing there in a very becoming maternity dress, and had an ear-to-ear smile on her face.

"It's weeks too early, but I don't care. The doctor says I'm pregnant and I'm wearing it," she told him.

He went forward in a daze and scooped her close, bending over her with eyes that were suspiciously bright. "I knew it," he whispered huskily. "I knew!"

"I wish I had!" she exclaimed, hugging him hard. "All that wailing and gnashing of teeth, and for nothing!"

He chuckled. "What a nice surprise!"

"I thought so. Will you take me to lunch?" she added. "I want dill pickles and strawberry ice cream."

"Yuuuck!" Mrs. Mack said theatrically.

"Never you mind, Mrs. Mack, I'll take her home and feed her," Simon said placatingly. He glanced at his wife with a beaming smile. "We'll have Mrs. Lester fix us something. I want to enjoy looking at you in that outfit while we eat."

She held his hand out the door and felt as if she had the world.

Later, after they arrived home, Mrs. Lester seated them at the dining-room table and brought in a nice lunch of cold cuts and omelets with decaffeinated coffee for Tira. She was smiling, too, because she was going with them to Austin.

"A baby and a husband who loves me, a terrific cook and housekeeper, and a mouseless house to leave behind," Tira said. "What more could a woman ask?"

"Mouseless?" Mrs. Lester asked.

"Yes, don't you remember?" Tira asked gleefully. "Cag got rid of the mouse while we were on our honeymoon and you were at your sister's."

Mrs. Lester nodded. "Got rid of the mouse. Mmm-hmm." She went and opened the kitchen door and invited them to look at the cabinet. They peered in the door and there he was, the mouse, sitting on the counter with a cracker in his paws, blatantly nibbling away.

"I don't believe it!" Tira burst out.

It got worse. Mrs. Lester went into the kitchen, held out her hand, and the mouse climbed into it.

"He's domesticated," she said proudly. "I came in here the other morning and he was sitting on the cabinet. He didn't even try to run, so I held out my hand and he climbed into it. I had a suspicion, so I put him in a box and took him to the vet. The vet says that he isn't a wild mouse at all, he's somebody's pet mouse that got left behind and had to fend for himself. Obviously he belonged to the previous owners of this house. So I thought, if you don't mind, of course," she added kindly, "I'd keep him. He can come with us to Austin."

Tira looked at Simon and burst out laughing. The mouse, who had no interest whatsoever in human conversation, continued to nibble his cracker contentedly, safe in the hands of his new owner.

*　*　*　*　*

PAPER HUSBAND

Chapter 1

The summer sun was rising. Judging by its place in the sky, Dana Mobry figured that it was about eleven o'clock in the morning. That meant she'd been in her present predicament for over two hours, and the day was growing hotter.

She sighed with resigned misery as she glanced at her elevated right leg where her jeans were hopelessly tangled in two loose strands of barbed wire. Her booted foot was enmeshed in the strands of barbed wire that made up the fence, and her left leg was wrapped in it because she'd twisted when she fell. She'd been trying to mend the barbed-wire fence to keep cattle from getting out. She was using her father's tools to do it, but sadly, she didn't have his strength. At times like this, she missed him unbearably, and it was only a week since his funeral.

She tugged at the neck of her short-sleeved cotton shirt and brushed strands of her damp blond hair back into its neat French braid. Not so neat now, she thought, disheveled and unkempt from the fall that had landed her in this mess. Nearby, oblivious to her mistress's dilemma, her chestnut mare, Bess, grazed. Overhead, a hawk made graceful patterns against the cloudless sky. Far away could be heard the sound of traffic on the distant highway that led around Jacobsville to the small Texas ranch where Dana was tangled in the fence wire.

Nobody knew where she was. She lived alone in the little ramshackle house that she'd shared with her father. They'd lost everything after her mother deserted them seven years ago. After that terrible blow, her father, who was raised on a ranch, decided to come back and settle on the old family homeplace. There were no other relatives unless you counted a cousin in Montana.

Dana's father had stocked this place with a small herd of beef cattle and raised a truck garden. It was a meager living, compared to the mansion near Dallas that her mother's wealth had maintained. When Carla Mobry had unexpectedly divorced her husband, he'd had to find a way of making a living for himself, quickly. Dana had chosen to go with him to his boyhood home in Jacobsville, rather than endure her mother's indifferent presence. Now her father was dead and she had no one.

She'd loved her father, and he'd loved her. They'd been happy together, even without a huge income. But the strain of hard physical labor on a heart that she had not even known was bad had been too much. He'd had a heart attack a few days ago, and died in his sleep. Dana had found him the next morning when she went in to his room to call him to breakfast.

Hank had come immediately at Dana's frantic phone call. It didn't occur to her that she should have called the ambulance first instead of their nearest, and very antisocial, neighbor. It was just that Hank was so capable. He always knew what to do. That day he had, too. After a quick look at her father, he'd phoned an ambulance and herded Dana out of the room. Later he'd said that he knew immediately that it was hours too late to save her father. He'd done a stint overseas in the military, where he'd seen death too often to mistake it.

Most people avoided Hayden Grant as much as possible. He owned the feed and mill store locally, and he ran cattle on his huge tracts of land around Jacobsville. He'd found oil on the same land, so lack of money wasn't one of his problems. But a short temper, a legendary dislike of women and a reputation for out-spokenness made him unpopular in most places.

He liked Dana, though. That had been fascinating from the very beginning, because he was a misogynist and made no secret of the fact. Perhaps he considered her safe because of the age difference. Hank was thirty-six and Dana was barely twenty-two. She was slender and of medium height, with dark blond hair and a plain little face made interesting by the huge dark blue eyes that dominated it. She had a firm, rounded chin and a straight nose and a perfect bow of a mouth that was a natural light pink, without makeup. She wasn't pretty, but her figure was exquisite, even in blue jeans and a faded checked cotton shirt with the two buttons missing, torn off when she'd fallen. She grimaced. She hadn't taken time to search for a bra in the clean wash this morning because she'd been in a hurry to fix the fence before her only bull got out into the road. She looked like a juvenile stripper, with the firm, creamy curves of her breasts very noticeable where the buttons were missing.

She shaded her eyes with her hand and glanced around. There was nothing for miles but Texas and more Texas. She should have been paying better attention to what she was doing, but her father's death had devastated her. She'd cried for three days, especially after the family attorney had told her about that humiliating clause in the will he'd left. She couldn't bear the shame of divulging it to Hank. But how could she avoid it, when it concerned him as much as it concerned her? Papa, she thought miserably, how could you do this to me? Couldn't you have spared me a little pride!

She wiped stray tears away. Crying wouldn't help. Her father was dead and the will would have to be dealt with.

A sound caught her attention. In the stillness of the field, it was very loud. There was a rhythm to it. After a minute, she knew why it sounded familiar. It was the gait of a thoroughbred stallion. And she knew exactly to whom that horse belonged.

Sure enough, a minute later a tall rider came into view. With his broad-brimmed hat pulled low over his lean, dark face and the elegant way he rode, Hank Grant was pretty easy to spot from a distance. If he hadn't been so noticeable, the horse, Cappy, was. Cappy was a palomino with impeccable bloodlines, and he brought handsome fees at stud. He was remarkably gentle for an ungelded horse, although he could become nervous at times. Still, he wouldn't allow anyone except Hank on his back.

As Hank reined in beside her prone body, she could see the amused indulgence in his face before she heard it in his deep voice.

"Again?" he asked with resignation, obviously recalling the other times he'd had to rescue her.

"The fence was down," she said belligerently, blowing a strand of blond hair out of her mouth. "And that stupid fence tool needs hands like a wrestler's to work it!"

"Sure it does, honey," he drawled, crossing his forearms over the pommel. "Fences don't know beans about the women's liberation movement."

"Don't you start that again," she muttered.

His mouth tugged up. "Aren't you in a peachy position to be throwing out challenges?" he murmured dryly, and his dark eyes saw far too much as they swept over her body. For just an instant, something flashed in them when they came to rest briefly on the revealed curves of her breasts.

She moved uncomfortably. "Come on, Hank, get me loose," she pleaded, wriggling. "I've been stuck here since nine o'clock and I'm dying for something to drink. It's so hot."

"Okay, kid." He swung out of the saddle and threw Cappy's reins over his head, leaving him to graze nearby. He squatted by her trapped legs. His worn jeans pulled tight against the long, powerful muscles of his legs and she had to grit her teeth against the pleasure it gave her just to look at him. Hank was handsome. He had that sort of masculine beauty about him that made even older women sigh when they saw him. He had a rider's lean and graceful look, and a face that an advertising agency would have loved. But he was utterly unaware of his own attractions. His wife had run out on him ten years before, and he'd never wanted to marry anyone else since the divorce. It was well-known in the community that Hank had no use for a woman except in one way. He was discreet and tight-lipped about his liaisons, and only Dana seemed to know that he had them. He was remarkably outspoken with her. In fact, he talked to her about private things that he shared with nobody else.

He was surveying the damage, his lips pursed thoughtfully, before he began to try to untangle her from the barbed wire with gloved hands. Hank was methodical in everything he did, single-minded and deliberate. He never acted rashly. It was another trait that didn't go unnoticed.

"Nope, that won't do," he murmured and reached into his pocket. "I'm going to have to cut this denim to get you loose, honey. I'm sorry. I'll replace the jeans."

She blushed. "I'm not destitute yet!"

He looked down into her dark blue eyes and saw the color in her cheeks. "You're so proud, Dana. You'd never ask for help, not if it meant you starved to death." He flipped open his pocketknife. "I guess that's why we get along so well. We're alike in a lot of ways."

"You're taller than I am, and you have black hair. Mine's blond," she said pointedly.

He grinned, as she knew he would. He didn't smile much, especially around other people. She loved the way his eyes twinkled when he smiled.

"I wasn't talking about physical differences," he explained unnecessarily. He cut the denim loose from the wire. It was a good thing he was wearing gloves, because the barbed-wire was sharp and treacherous. "Why don't you use electrified fence like modern ranchers?"

"Because I can't afford it, Hank," she said simply.

He grimaced. He freed the last strand and pulled her into a sitting position, which was unexpectedly intimate. Her blouse fell open when she leaned forward and, like any male, he filled his eyes with the sight of her firm, creamy breasts, their tips hard and mauve against the soft pink mounds. He caught his breath audibly.

Embarrassed, she grasped the edges of her shirt and pulled them together, flushing. She couldn't meet his eyes. But she was aware of his intent stare, of the smell of leather and faint cologne that clung to his skin, of the clean smell of his long-sleeve chambray shirt. Her eyes fell to the opening at his throat, where thick black hair was visible. She'd never seen Hank without his shirt. She'd always wanted to.

His lean hand smoothed against her cheek and his thumb pressed her rounded chin up. His eyes searched her shy ones. "And that's what I like best about you," he said huskily. "You don't play. Every move you make is honest." He held her gaze. "I wouldn't be much of a man if I'd turned my eyes away. Your breasts are beautiful, like pink marble with hard little tips that make me feel very masculine. You shouldn't be ashamed of a natural reaction like that."

She wasn't quite sure what he meant. "Natural...reaction?" she faltered, wide-eyed.

He frowned. "Don't you understand?"

She didn't. Her life had been a remarkably sheltered one. She'd first discovered her feelings for Hank when she was just seventeen, and she'd never looked at anyone else. She'd only dated two boys. Both of them had been shy and a little nervous with her, and when one of them had kissed her, she'd found it distasteful.

She did watch movies, some of which were very explicit. But they didn't explain what happened to people physically, they just showed it.

"No," she said finally, grimacing. "Well, I'm hopeless, I guess. I don't date, I haven't got time to read racy novels...!"

He was watching her very closely. "Some lessons carry a high price. But it's safe enough with me. Here."

He took her own hand and, shockingly, eased the fabric away from her breast and put her fingers on the hard tip. He watched her body as he did it, which made the experience even more sensual.

"Desire causes it," he explained quietly. "A man's body swells where he's most a man. A woman's breasts swell and the tips go hard. It's a reaction that comes from excitement, and nothing at all to be ashamed of."

She was barely breathing. She knew her face was flushed, and her heart was beating her to death. She was sitting in the middle of an open field, letting Hank look at her breasts and explain desire to her. The whole thing had a fantasy quality that made her wide-eyed.

He knew it. He smiled. "You're pretty," he said gently, removing her hand and tugging the edges of the blouse back together. "Don't make heavy weather of it. It's natural, isn't it, with us? It always has been. That's why I can talk to you so easily about the most intimate things." He frowned slightly. "I wanted my wife all the time, did I ever tell you? She taunted me and made me crazy to have her, so that I'd do anything for it. But I wasn't rich enough to suit her. My best friend hit it big in real estate and she was all over him like a duck on a bug. I don't think she ever looked back when she left me, but I didn't sleep for weeks, wanting her. I still want her, from time to time." He sighed roughly. "And now she's coming back, she and Bob. They're going to be in town for a few weeks while he gets rid of all his investments. He's retiring, and he wants to sell me his racehorse. Hell of a gall, isn't it?" he muttered coldly.

She felt his pain and didn't dare let him see how much it disturbed her. "Thanks for untangling me," she said breathlessly, to divert him, and started to get up.

His hand stayed her. He looked studious and calculating. "Don't. I want to try something."

His fingers went to the snaps of his chambray shirt and he unfastened it all down his chest, pulling the shirttail out of his jeans as he went. His chest was broad and tanned, thick with hair, powerfully muscled.

"What are you doing?" she whispered, startled.

"I told you. I want to try something." He drew her up on her knees, and unfastened the remaining buttons on her shirt. He looked searchingly at her expression. She was too shocked to protest, and then he pulled her close, letting her feel for the first time in her life the impact of a man's seminudity against her own.

Her sharp breath was audible. There was wonder in her eyes as she lifted them to his in fascinated curiosity.

His hands went to her rib cage and he drew her lazily, sensuously, against that rough cushion of his chest. It tickled her breasts and made the tips go harder. She grasped his shoulders, biting in with her nails involuntarily as all her dreams seemed to come true at once. His eyes were blazing with dark fires. They fell to her mouth and he bent toward her.

She felt the hard warmth of his lips slowly burrow into hers, parting them, teasing them. She held her breath, tasting him like some rare wine. Dimly she felt his hand go between them and tenderly caress one swollen breast. She gasped again, and his head lifted so that he could see her eyes.

His thumb rippled over the hard tip and she shivered all over, helpless in his embrace.

"Yes," he whispered absently, "that's exactly what I thought. I could lay you down right here, right now."

She barely heard him. Her heart was shaking her. His fingers touched her, teased her body. It arched toward him, desperate not to lose the contact.

His eyes were all over her face; her bare breasts pressed so close against him. He felt the touch all the way to his soul. "I want you," he said quietly.

She sobbed, because it shouldn't have been like this. Her own body betrayed her, giving away all its hard-kept secrets.

But there was a hesitation in him. His hand stilled on her breast, his mouth hovered over hers as his dark eyes probed, watched.

"You're still a virgin, aren't you?" he asked roughly.

She swallowed, her lips swollen from the touch of his.

He shook her gently. "Tell me!"

She bit her lower lip and looked at his throat. She could see the pulse hammering there. "You knew that already." She ground out the words.

He didn't seem to breathe for a minute, then there was a slow, ragged exhaling of breath. He wrapped her up in his arms and sat holding her close, rocking her, his face buried in her hot throat, against her quick pulse.

"Yes. I just wanted to be sure," he said after a minute. He released her inch by inch and smiled ruefully as he fastened her blouse again.

She let him, dazed. Her eyes clung to his as if they were looking for sanity.

Her mouth was swollen. Her eyes were as round as dark blue saucers in a face livid with color. In that moment she was more beautiful than he'd ever known her to be.

"No harm done," he said gently. "We've learned a little more about each other than we knew before. It won't change anything. We're still friends."

He made it sound like a question. "Of...of course," she stammered.

He stood up, refastening his own shirt and tucking it back in as he looked at her with a new expression. *Possession.* Yes, that was it. He looked as if she belonged to him now. She didn't understand the look or her own reaction to it.

She scrambled to her feet, moving them to see if anything hurt.

"The wire didn't break the skin, fortunately for you," he said. "Those jeans are heavy, tough fabric. But you need a tetanus shot, just the same. If you haven't had one, I'll drive you into town to get one."

"I had one last year," she said, avoiding his eyes as she started toward Bess, who was eyeing the stallion a little too curiously. "You'd better get Cappy before he gets any ideas."

He caught Cappy's bridle and had to soothe him. "You'd better get her out of here while you can," he advised. "I didn't think you'd be riding her today or I wouldn't have brought Cappy. You usually ride Toast.''

She didn't want to tell him that Toast had been sold to help settle one of her father's outstanding debts.

He watched her swing into the saddle and he did likewise, keeping the stallion a good distance away. The urge to mate wasn't only a human thing.

"I'll be over to see you later,'' he called to her. "We've got some things to talk over.''

"Like what?'' she asked.

But Hank didn't answer. Cappy was fidgeting wildly as he tried to control the stallion. "Not now. Get her home!''

She turned the mare and galloped toward the ranch, forgetting the fence in her headlong rush. She'd have to come back later. At least she could get out of the sun and get something cold to drink now.

Once she was back in the small house, she looked at herself in the bathroom mirror after a shower and couldn't believe she was the same woman who'd gone out into the pasture only this morning. She looked so different. There was something new in her eyes, something more feminine, mysterious and secretive. She felt all over again the slow, searching touch of Hayden Grant's hard fingers and blushed.

There had been a rare and beautiful magic between them out there in the field. She loved him so much. There had been no other man's touch on her body, never another man in her heart. But how was he going to react when he knew the contents of her father's will? He didn't want to marry again. He'd said so often enough. And although he and Dana had been friends for a long time, he'd drawn back at once when he made her admit her innocence. He'd wanted an affair, obviously, but discovered that it would be impossible to justify that with his conscience. He couldn't seduce an innocent woman.

She went into her bedroom and put on blue slacks and a knit

shirt, leaving her freshly washed and dried hair loose around her shoulders. He'd said they would talk later. Did that mean he'd heard gossip about the will? Was he going to ask her to challenge it?

She had no idea what to expect. Perhaps it was just as well. She'd have less time to worry.

She walked around the living room, her eyes on the sad, shabby furniture that she and her father had bought so many years ago. There hadn't been any money in the past year for re-upholstery or new frills. They'd put everything into those few head of beef cattle and the herd sire. But the cattle market was way down and if a bad winter came, there would be no way to afford to buy feed. She had to plant plenty of hay and corn to get through the winter. But their best hand had quit on her father's death, and now all she had were two part-time helpers, whom she could barely afford to pay. A blind woman could see that she wouldn't be able to keep going now.

She could have wept for her lost chances. She had no education past high school, no real way to make a living. All she knew was how to pull calves and mix feed and sell off stock. She went to the auctions and knew how to bid, how to buy, how to pick cattle for conformation. She knew much less about horses, but that hardly mattered. She only had one left and the part-time man kept Bess—and Toast, until he was sold—groomed and fed and watered. She did at least know how to saddle the beast. But to Dana, a horse was a tool to use with cattle. Hayden cringed when she said that. He had purebred palominos and loved every one of them. He couldn't understand anyone not loving horses as much as he did.

Oddly, though, it was their only real point of contention. In most other ways, they agreed, even on politics and religion. And they liked the same television programs. She smiled, remembering how many times they'd shared similar enthusiasms for weekly series, especially science fiction ones.

Hank had been kind to her father, too, and so patient when a man who'd given his life to being a country gentleman was suddenly faced with learning to be a rancher at the age of fifty-five. It made Dana sad to think how much longer her father's life might have been if he'd taken up a less exhaustive profession. He'd had a good brain, and so much still to give.

She fixed a light lunch and a pot of coffee and thought about going back out to see about that downed fence. But another disaster would just be too much. She was disaster-prone when Hank was anywhere near her, and she seemed to be rapidly getting that way even when he wasn't. He'd rescued her from mad bulls, trapped feet in corral fences, once from a rattlesnake and twice from falling bales of hay. He must be wondering if there wasn't some way he could be rid of her once and for all.

It was nice of him not to mention those incidents when he'd rescued her from the fence, though. Surely he'd been tempted to.

Tempted. She colored all over again remembering the intimacy they'd shared. In the seven years they'd known each other, he'd never touched her until today. She wondered why he had.

The sound of a car outside on the country road brought her out of the kitchen and to the front door, just in time to see Hank's black luxury car pull into the driveway. He wasn't a flashy sort of man, and he didn't go overboard to surround himself with luxurious things. That make of car was his one exception. He had a fascination for the big cars that never seemed to waver, because he traded his in every other year—for another black one.

"Don't you get tired of the color?" she'd asked him once.

"Why?" he'd replied laconically. "Black goes with everything."

He came up onto the porch, and the expression on his face was one she hadn't seen before. He looked as he always did, neatly dressed and clean-shaven, devastatingly handsome, but there was still a difference. After their brief interlude out in the pasture, the atmosphere between them was just a little strained.

He had his hands in his pockets as he glanced down at her body in the pretty ruffled blue sundress.

"Is that for my benefit?" he asked.

She blushed. She usually kicked around in jeans or cutoffs and tank tops. She almost never wore dresses around the ranch. And her hair was long and loose around her shoulders instead of in its usual braid.

She shrugged in defeat. "Yes, I guess it is," she said, meeting his eyes with a rueful smile. "Sorry."

He shook his head. "There's no need to apologize. None at all. In fact, what happened this afternoon gave me some ideas that I want to talk to you about."

Her heart jumped into her chest. Was he going to propose? Oh, glory, if only he would, and then he'd never even have to know about that silly clause in her father's will!

Chapter 2

She led the way into the kitchen and set out a platter of salad and cold cuts and dressing in the center of the table, on which she'd already put two place settings. She poured coffee into two mugs, gave him one and sat down. She didn't have to ask what he took in his coffee, because she already knew that he had it black, just as she did. It was one of many things they had in common.

"What did you want to ask me, Hank?" she ventured after he'd worked his way through a huge salad and two cups of coffee. Her nerves were screaming with suspense and anticipation.

"Oh. That." He leaned back with his half-drained coffee cup in his hand. "I wondered if you might be willing to help me out with a little playacting for my ex-wife's benefit."

All her hopes fell at her feet. "What sort of acting?" she asked, trying to sound nonchalant.

"I want you to pretend to be involved with me," he said frankly, staring at her. "On this morning's showing, it shouldn't be too difficult to look as if we can't keep our hands off each other. Should it?" he asked with a mocking smile.

Everything fell into place; his odd remarks, his "experiment" out there in the pasture, his curious behavior. His beloved ex-wife was coming to town and he didn't want everyone to know how badly she'd hurt him or how he'd grieved at her loss. So Dana had been cast as his new love. He didn't want a new wife, he wanted an actress.

She stared into her coffee. "I don't guess you ever want to get married again, do you?" she asked with studied carelessness.

He saw right through that devious little question. "No, I don't," he said bluntly. "Once was enough."

She grimaced. Her father had placed her in an intolerable position. Somehow, he must have suspected that his time was limited. Otherwise why should he have gone to such lengths in his will to make sure that his daughter was provided for after his death?

"You've been acting funny since your father died," he said suddenly, and his eyes narrowed. "Is there something you haven't told me?"

She made an awkward motion with one shoulder.

"Did he go into debt and leave you with nothing, is that it?"

"Well..."

"Because if that's the case, I can take care of the problem," he continued, unabashed. "You help me out while Betty's here, and I'll pay off any outstanding debts. You can think of it as a job."

She wanted to throw herself down on the floor and scream. Nothing was working out. She looked at him in anguish. "Oh, Hank," she groaned.

He scowled. "Come on. It can't be that bad. Spit it out."

She took a steadying breath and got to her feet. "There's a simpler way. I think...you'd better read Dad's will. I'll get it."

She went into the living room and pulled out the desk drawer that contained her father's will. She took it into the kitchen and handed it to a puzzled Hank, watching his lean, elegant hands unfasten the closure on the document.

"And before you start screaming, I didn't know anything about that clause," she added through her teeth. "It was as much a shock to me as it's going to be to you."

"Clause?" he murmured as he scanned over the will. "What clause... Oh, my God!"

"Now, Hank," she began in an effort to thwart the threatened explosion she saw growing in his lean face.

"God in heaven!" He got to his feet, slamming the will back on the table. His face had gone from ruddy to white in the space of seconds. "What a hell of a choice I've got! I marry you or I end up with a stock car racetrack on the edge of my barn where my mares foal! Moving the damned thing would cost half a million dollars!"

"If you'll just give me a chance to speak," she said heavily. "Hank, there may be a way to break the will—"

"Oh, sure, we can say he was crazy!" His black eyes were glittering like diamonds.

She flushed. He was flagrantly insulting her. She might love him, but she wasn't taking that kind of treatment, even from him. She got to her own feet and glared up at him. "He must have been, to want me to marry you!" she shouted. "What makes you think you're such a prize, Hank? You're years too old for me in the first place, and in the second, what sane woman would want to marry a man who's still in love with his ex-wife?"

He was barely breathing. His anger was so apparent that Dana felt her knees go wobbly, despite her spunky words.

His black eyes slewed over her with contempt. "I might like looking at your body, but a couple of kisses and a little fondling don't warrant a marriage proposal in my book."

"Nor in mine," she said with scalded pride. "Why don't you go home?"

His fists clenched at his side. He still couldn't believe what he'd read in that will. It was beyond belief that her father, his friend, would have stabbed him in the back this way.

"He must have been out of his mind," he grated. "I could have settled a trust on you or something, he didn't have to specify marriage as a condition for you to inherit what's rightfully yours!''

She lifted her chin. ''I can hardly ask what his reasoning was,'' she reminded him. ''He's dead.'' The words were stark and hollow. She was still in the midst of grief for the passing of her parent. Hank hadn't considered that she was hurting, she thought, or maybe he just didn't care. He was too angry to be rational.

He breathed deliberately. ''You little cheat,'' he accused. ''You've had a crush on me for years, and I've tolerated it. It amused me. But this isn't funny. This is low and deceitful. I'd think more of you if you admitted that you put your father up to it.''

''I don't give a damn what you think of me,'' she choked. Her pride was in tatters. She was fighting tears of pure rage. ''When you've had time to get over the shock, I'd like you to see my attorney. Between the two of you, I'm sure you can find some way to straighten this out. Because I wouldn't marry you if you came with a subscription to my favorite magazine and a new Ferrari! So I had a crush on you once. That's ancient history!''

He made a sound through his nose. ''Then what was that this morning out in the pasture?'' he chided.

''Lust!'' she threw at him.

He picked up his hat and studied her with cold contempt. ''I'll see what I can do about the will. You could contact your mother,'' he added pointedly. ''She's wealthy. I'm sure she won't let you starve.''

She folded her arms across her breasts. ''I wouldn't ask my mother for a tissue if I was bleeding to death, and you know it.''

''These are desperate circumstances,'' he said pointedly, a little calmer now.

''My circumstances are no longer any of your business,'' she said in a voice that was disturbingly calm. ''Goodbye, Hank.''

He slammed his hat over his eyes and went to the front door, but he hesitated with the doorknob in his hand and looked over his shoulder. She was pale and her eyes were shimmering. He knew she was grieving for her father. It must be scary, too, to have her inheritance wrapped around an impossible demand. If he didn't marry her, she was going to lose everything, even her home. He winced.

"Goodbye," she repeated firmly. Her eyes startled him with their cold blue darkness. She looked as if she hated him.

He drew in a short breath. "Look, we'll work something out."

"I'm twenty-two years old," she said proudly. "It's past time I started taking care of myself. If I lose the ranch, I'll get a grant and go back to college. I've already completed the basic courses, anyway."

He hadn't thought that she might go away. Suddenly his life was even more topsy-turvy than before. Betty was on her way back to town, Dana's father had tried to force him into a marriage he didn't want and now Dana was going away. He felt deserted.

He let out a word that she'd never heard him use. "Then go, if you want to, and be damned," he said furiously. "It will be a pleasure not to have to rescue you from half a dozen disasters a day."

He slammed the door on his way out and she sank into a chair, feeling the sudden warm wetness of the tears she'd been too proud to let him see. At least now she knew how he felt about her. She guessed that she'd be well-advised to learn to live with it.

The rest of the day was a nightmare. By the end of it, she was sick of the memories in the house. Grief and humiliation drove her to the telephone. She called Joe, the oldest of her two part-time workers on the ranch.

"I'm going away for a couple of days," she told him. "I want you and Ernie to watch the cattle for me. Okay?"

"Sure, boss lady. Where you going?"

"Away."

She hung up.

It only took her a few minutes to make a reservation at a moderately priced Houston hotel downtown, and to pack the ancient gray Bronco she drove with enough clothes for the weekend. She was on her way in no time, having locked up the house. Joe had a key if he needed to get in.

She spent the weekend watching movies on cable and experimenting with new hairstyles. She drifted around the shops downtown, although she didn't buy anything. She had to conserve her money now, until she could apply for a grant and get into college. On an impulse she phoned a couple of colleges around the area and requested catalogs be sent to her home address in Jacobsville.

The runaway weekend had been something of an extravagance, but she'd needed to get away. She felt like a tourist as she wandered around all the interesting spots, including the famed San Jacinto monument and the canal where ships came and went into the port city. Heavy rain came on the second day, with flash flooding, and she was forced to stay an extra day or use her Bronco as a barge, because the streets near the hotel were too flooded to allow safe travel.

It was late Monday before she turned into the long driveway of her ranch. And the first thing she noticed as she approached the farmhouse was the proliferation of law enforcement vehicles.

Shocked, she pulled up and turned off the ignition. "What's happened? Has someone broken into my home?" she asked the first uniformed man she met, a deputy sheriff.

His eyebrows went up. "You live here?" he asked.

"Yes. I'm Dana Mobry."

He chuckled and called to the other three men, one of whom was a Jacobsville city policeman. "Here she is! She hasn't met with foul play."

They came at a lope, bringing a harassed-looking Joe along with them.

"Oh, Miss Mobry, thank the Lord," Joe said, wringing her hand. His hair was grayer than ever, and he looked hollow-eyed.

"Whatever's wrong?" she asked.

"They thought I'd killed you and hid the body!" Joe wailed, looking nervously at the law officers.

Dana's eyes widened. "Why?"

"Mr. Grant came over and couldn't find you," Joe said frantically. "I told him you'd gone away, but I didn't know where, and he blew up and started accusing me of all sorts of things on account of I wouldn't tell him where you were. When you didn't come back by today, he called the law. I'm so glad to see you, Miss Mobry. I was afraid they were going to put me in jail!"

"I'm sorry you were put through this, Joe," she said comfortingly. "I should have told you I was going to Houston, but it never occurred to me that Mr. Grant would care where I went," she added bitterly.

The deputy sheriff grinned sheepishly. "Yeah, he said you'd had an argument and he was afraid you might have done something drastic…"

She glared at him so furiously that he broke off. "If that isn't conceit, I don't know what is! I wouldn't kill myself over a stuck-up, overbearing, insufferable egotist like Mr. Grant unless I was goofy! Do I look goofy?"

He cleared his throat. "Oh, no, ma'am, you don't look at all goofy to me!"

While he was defending himself, Hank came around the side of the house to see where the search party had disappeared to, and stopped when he saw Dana. "So there you are!" he began furiously, bare-headed and wild-eyed as he joined her. "Where in hell have you been? Do you have any idea how much trouble you've caused?"

She lifted her chin. "I've been to Houston. Since when is going to Houston a crime? And since when do I have to inform you of my whereabouts?"

He snorted. "I'm a concerned neighbor."

"You're a royal pain in the neck, and I left town to get away from you," she snapped. "I don't want to see you or talk to you!"

He straightened his shoulders and his mouth compressed. "As long as you're all right."

"You might apologize to poor Joe while you're about it," she added pointedly. "He was beside himself, thinking he was going to jail for doing away with me."

"I never said any such thing," he muttered. He glanced at Joe. "He knows I didn't think he'd done you in."

That was as close as he was likely to come to an apology, and Joe accepted it with less rancor than Dana would have.

"Thanks for coming out," Hank told the deputy and the others. "She was missing for two days and I didn't know where she was. Anything could have happened."

"Oh, he knows that," the city policeman, Matt Lovett, said with a grin, jerking his thumb at the deputy sheriff. "He and his wife had an argument and she drove off to her mother's. On the way her car died. She left it on the river bridge and caught a ride into town to get a mechanic."

"Matt...!" the deputy grumbled.

Matt held up a hand. "I'm just getting to the best part. He went after her and saw the car and thought she'd jumped off the bridge. By the time she got back with the mechanic, the civil defense boys were out there dragging the river."

"Well, she might have been in there," the deputy defended himself, red-faced. He grinned at Hank. "And Miss Mobry might have been eaten by one of her young steers."

"Or carried off by aliens," Matt mused, tongue in cheek. "That's why our police force is always on the job, Miss Mobry, to offer protection to any citizen who needs it. I'd dearly love to protect you at a movie one night next week," he added with twinkling green eyes. "Any night you like. A good movie and a nice big burger with fries."

Dana's eyes were twinkling now, too.

Hank stepped in between her and the policeman. "I think she'll need some rest after today's excitement, but I'm sure she appreciates the offer, Matt."

The words didn't match the dark threat in his eyes. Matt had only been teasing, although if he'd really wanted to take Dana out, all the threats in the world wouldn't have stopped him.

"You're probably right," Matt agreed. He winked at Dana. "But the offer stands, just the same."

She smiled at him. He really was nice. "Thanks, Matt."

The law enforcement people said their farewells and went off to bigger tasks, leaving Dana and Joe and Hank standing aimlessly in the front yard.

"I'll get home now, Miss Mobry. So glad you're all right," Joe said again.

"Thanks, Joe," she replied. "I'm sorry for all the trouble you had."

"Not to worry."

He ambled off. Dana folded her arms over her breasts and glared furiously at Hank.

He had his hands deep in his pockets. He looked more uncomfortable than she'd ever seen him.

"Well, how was I to know you hadn't done something desperate?" he wanted to know. "I said some harsh things to you." He averted his eyes, because it disturbed him to remember what he'd said. In the few days Dana had been missing, he'd done a lot of remembering, mostly about how big a part of his life Dana was, and the long friendship he'd shared with her. He'd had no right to belittle the feelings she had for him. In fact, it had rocked his world when he realized how long he'd been deliberately ignoring them. He was torn between his lingering love for Betty and his confused feelings for Dana. It was an emotional crisis that he'd never had to face before. He knew he wasn't handling it very well.

Dana didn't budge an inch. "I've already decided what I'm going to do, in case you had any lingering worries," she told him coolly. "If you can find a loophole, a way for us to break the will, I'm going to sell the place and go back to school. I have catalogs coming from three colleges."

His face went rigid. "I thought you liked ranching."

She made an amused, bitter sound. "Hank, I can't even use a fence tool. I can't pull a calf without help from Joe or Ernie. I can feed livestock and treat wounds and check for diseases, but I can't do heavy lifting and fix machinery. I don't have the physical strength, and I'm running out of the financial means to hire it done.'' She threw up her hands. ''If I even tried to get a job at someone else's ranch, with my lack of skills, they'd laugh at me. How in the world can I run a ranch?''

''You can sell it to me and I'll run it for you,'' he said curtly. ''You can rent the house and stay here.''

''As what?'' she persisted. ''Caretaker? I want more than that from life.''

''Such as?'' he asked.

''Never you mind,'' she said evasively, because a ready answer didn't present itself. ''Did you talk to my lawyer?''

''No.''

''Then would you, please?''

He stuck his hands into his pockets. ''Listen, Dana, no court in Jacobsville is going to throw out that will on the grounds that your father was incompetent. His mind was as sound as mine, and he knew business inside out.''

Her heart fell. ''He might have been temporarily upset when he inserted that clause.''

''Maybe he was,'' he agreed. ''Maybe he'd had some chest pain or a premonition. I'm sure he meant it as a way to make sure you weren't left alone, with no support, after he was gone. But his reasons don't matter. Either you marry me or we both stand to lose a hell of a lot of money.''

''You don't want to marry me,'' she reminded him with painful pleasure. ''You said so.''

He drew in a long, weary breath and searched her wan little face. ''God, I'm tired,'' he said unexpectedly. ''My life is upside down. I don't know where I'm going, or why. No, Dana, I don't want to marry you. That's honest. But there's a lot riding on that will.'' He moved his shoulders, as if to ease their stiffness. ''I'd rather wait a few weeks, at least until Betty's visit is over. But there's a time limit as well. A month after your father's death, I believe, all the conditions of the will have to be fulfilled.''

She nodded miserably.

''In a way, it would suit me to be married right now,'' he reflected solemnly. ''I don't want Betty to see how badly she hurt me, or how much I still want her. I might be tempted to try and break up her marriage, and that's not the sort of man I want to be.''

''What about her husband?''

''Bob doesn't care what she does,'' he replied. ''He's totally indifferent to her these days, and he's no longer a financial giant. I don't think it would take too much effort to get her away from him. But she left me because he had more money, don't you see?'' he added pointedly. ''My God, I can't let myself be caught in that old trap again, regardless of what I feel for her!''

She felt sorry for him. Imagine that. She linked her hands together over her stomach. ''Then what do you want to do, Hank?'' she asked quietly.

''Get married. But only on paper,'' he added deliberately, his dark eyes steady and full of meaning. ''Despite the physical attraction I felt for you out in the pasture that day, I don't want a physical relationship with you. Let's get that clear at the outset. I want a document that gives you the right to sell me that land. In return, I'll make sure the figure you receive is above market price, and I'll put you through college to boot.''

It sounded fair enough to Dana, who was wrung out from the emotional stress. ''And I get to stay here, in my own house,'' she added.

''No.''

Her eyebrows shot up.

''I'll want you to stay up at the homeplace with me,'' he replied, ''as long as Betty and Bob are in town. Even though this is a legal marriage, I don't want Betty to know that I'm only a paper husband.''

"Oh, I see," she replied. "You want us to pretend that it's a normal arrangement."

"Exactly."

She didn't want to agree. He'd hurt her feelings, made horrible remarks, insulted her and embarrassed her with today's woman-hunt. But she needed to be able to sell the ranch. It would be her escape from the emotional poverty of loving where there was no hope of reciprocation.

"Okay," she said after a minute. "Will we have to get a blood test and a license at the courthouse?"

"We'll fly to Las Vegas and get married out there," he told her. "As soon as we've completed the legal maneuvers and Betty is safely out of my hair, we'll get a divorce there, which will be just as easy."

Easy marriage. Easy divorce. Dana, with her dreams of returned love and babies to raise, felt the pain of those words all the way through her heart.

"An annulment will spare you any hint of scandal afterward," he continued. "You can get your degree and find someone to spend your life with. Or part of it," he added with a mocking smile. "I don't think anybody has illusions about marriage lasting until death these days."

Her parents had divorced. Hank had divorced. But Dana had seen couples who'd stayed together and been in love for years. The Ballenger brothers with their happy marriages came instantly to mind.

"I'm not that cynical," she said after a minute. "And I think that children should have both parents while they're growing up if it's at all possible. Well," she added, "as long as it isn't a daily battleground."

"Was your family like that?" he asked gently.

She nodded. "My mother hated my father. She said he had no ambition, no intelligence, and that he was as dull as dishwater. She wanted parties and holidays all the time. He just wanted to settle down with a good book and nibble cheese."

She smiled sadly, remembering him, and had to fight the easy tears that sprang so readily to her eyes.

"Don't cry," he said shortly.

She lifted her chin. "I wasn't going to," she said roughly. She remembered him holding her at her father's funeral, murmuring comforting words softly at her ear. But he had little patience with emotion, as a rule.

He took a deep breath. "I'll set everything up and let you know when we'll go," he said.

She wanted to argue, but the time had long passed for that. She nodded. He waited, but when she didn't say anything else, he went back to his car, got in and drove away.

Chapter 3

Las Vegas sat right in the middle of a desert. Dana had never been there, and the sight of it fascinated her. Not only was it like a neon city, but the glitter extended even to the people who worked at the night spots. Dana found the way women dressed on the streets fascinating and almost fell out the window of Hank's hired luxury car trying to look at them. It wasn't until he explained what they did for a living that she gave up her surveillance. It was interesting to find that what they did was legal and that they could even advertise their services.

"Here we are," he said gruffly, stopping at one of the all-night wedding chapels.

It looked flashy, but then, so did the rest of them. Hank offered her an arm but she refused it, walking beside him with her purse tight in her hand. She was wearing a simple off-white suit. She didn't have a veil or even a bouquet, and she felt their omission all the way to her toes. It was so very different from the way she'd envisioned her wedding day.

Hank didn't seem to notice or care. He dealt with the preliminaries, they signed a document, he produced a ring that she didn't even know he'd bought. Five minutes later, they were officially married, ring, cool kiss and all. Dana looked up at her husband

and felt nothing, not even sorrow. She seemed to be numb from head to toe.

"Are we flying right back?" she asked as they got into the car once more.

He glanced at her. She seemed devoid of emotion. It was her wedding day. He hadn't given her a choice about her wedding ring. He hadn't offered to buy her a bouquet. He hadn't even asked if she wanted a church wedding, which could have been arranged. He'd been looking at the whole messy business from his own point of view. Dana had deserved something better than this icy, clinical joining.

"We can stay at one of the theme hotels overnight, if you like, and take in a show."

She didn't want to appear eager. The only show she'd ever seen was at a movie theater in Victoria.

"Well," she said hesitantly.

"I'll introduce you to the one-armed bandit," he added, chuckling at her expression.

"If you think we could," she murmured, and that was as far as she was willing to commit herself. "But I didn't pack anything for an overnight stay."

"No problem. The hotel has shops."

And it did. He outfitted her with a gown, a bag and everything in the way of toiletries that she needed. She noticed that he didn't buy any pajamas, but she thought nothing of it. Surely they'd have separate rooms, anyway.

But they didn't. There were too many conventions in town, and they got the last suite the hotel had—one with a king-size bed and a short sofa.

Hank stared at the bed ruefully. "Sorry," he said. "But it's this or sleep on the floor."

She cleared her throat. "We're both adults. And it's only a paper marriage," she stammered.

"So it is," he mused, but his dark eyes had narrowed as they assessed her slender, perfect figure and he remembered the sight of her in the pasture with her blouse open and the feel of her breasts pressed hard into his bare chest.

She glanced up, meeting that hot, intent stare. She flushed. "I'm not having sex with you, Hank," she said shortly.

His eyebrows went up. "Did I ask?" he drawled sarcastically. "Listen, honey, the streets are full of prime women, if I'm so inclined."

Her eyes blazed at him. "Don't you dare!" she raged. "Don't you dare, Hank!"

He began to smile. "Well, well, aren't we possessive already?"

"That's not the point. You made a vow. Until we have it undone, we're married." She stared at her shoes. "I wouldn't go running to some gigolo on my wedding night."

"Of course you wouldn't." He moved closer, his hands finding her small waist, and brought her gently to him. His breath feathered her forehead. "I can hear you breathing," he whispered. "Nervous?"

She swallowed. "Well...yes...a little."

His lips brushed her hair. "There's no need. It's a big bed. If you don't want anything to happen, it won't."

She felt disappointed somehow. They were legally married. She loved him. Did he really not want her at all?

He tilted her face up to his dark, curious eyes. "On the other hand," he said softly, "if you want to know what it's all about, I'll teach you. There won't be any consequences. And you'll enjoy it."

She felt the words to the very tips of her toes. But she wasn't going to be won over that easily, even if she did want him more than her next breath.

"No dice, huh?" he mused after a minute. "Okay. Suppose we go downstairs and try our luck?"

"Suits me," she said, anxious to go anywhere away from that bed.

So they went the rounds in the casino and played everything from the one-armed bandits to blackjack. The glittery costumes of the dancers on stage fascinated Dana, like everything else about this fantasy city. She ate perfectly cooked steak, watched the shows, and generally had a wonderful time while Hank treated her like a cherished date. In fact, that's what it was. They'd never been out together in all the years they'd known each other. During that one evening they made up for lost time.

They returned upstairs just after midnight. Dana had gone overboard with piña coladas, the one drink she could tolerate. But she'd underestimated the amount of rum the bartender put in them. She was weaving at the door, to Hank's patent amusement.

He slid the coded card into the slot and when the blinking green light indicated that it was unlocked, he opened the door.

"Home again," he murmured, standing aside to let her enter.

She tugged up the strap of her black dress that had slipped off her shoulder. Like the rest of her abbreviated wardrobe, it was the result of the afternoon's quick shopping trip. In addition to the knee-length cocktail dress and hose, she had a far too revealing black nightgown and no robe. She hoped Hank was agreeable to letting her undress in the dark.

"You can have the bathroom first," he invited. "I'll listen to the news."

"Thanks." She gathered her gown and underwear and went into the bathroom to shower.

When she came out, Hank was sitting on the edge of the bed. He'd removed everything except his slacks. He got up, and she had to suppress a shiver of pleasure at the sight of him bare from the waist up. He had muscular arms and a sexy dark chest with a wedge of curling black hair running down it. His hair was mussed and down on his forehead. He looked rakish because he needed a shave.

"Good thing I packed my razor," he mused, holding up a small pouch that had been in the attaché case he always carried when he traveled. "I have to shave twice a day." His dark eyes slid over her body in the abbreviated gown, lingering where her arms were crossed defensively over the thin fabric that didn't quite cover her breasts from view. "We're married," he reminded her. "And I've seen most of you."

She cleared her throat. "Which side of the bed do you like?" she asked shyly.

"The right, but I don't mind either one. You can have first pick."

"Thanks."

She put her discarded clothing on a chair and climbed in quickly, pulling the covers up to her chin.

He lifted an eyebrow. "Stay just like that," he coaxed, "and when I come out, I'll tell you a nice fairy tale."

She glared at him through a rosy haze. "I'll probably be asleep. I haven't ever had so much to drink."

He nodded slowly. "That may be a good thing," he said enigmatically, and went into the bathroom.

She wasn't asleep when he came out. She'd tried to be, but her mind wouldn't cooperate. She peered through her lashes and watched him move around the room turning out lights. He had a towel hooked around his hips and as he turned out the last lamp on his side of the bed, she saw him unhook the towel and throw it over the back of the vinyl-covered chair.

She stiffened as he climbed in beside her and stretched lazily.

"I can feel you bristling," he murmured dryly. "It's a big bed, honey, and I don't sleepwalk. You're safe."

She cleared her throat. "Yes, I know."

"Then why are you shivering?"

He rolled over and moved closer. She could feel the heat of his body through her thin gown. She trembled even more when his long leg brushed against hers.

"Shivering," he continued, moving closer, "and breathing like an Olympic runner." He slid a long arm under her and brought her sliding right over against him. "I haven't forgotten the signs when a woman wants me," he whispered as his hands smoothed the gown right down her body. "And you want me, Dana."

She started to protest, but his mouth was already covering hers. He turned and pulled her to him, so that she felt his nude body all the way down hers. He was warm and hard, and even in her innocence she was aware that he wanted her badly.

His lean hands smoothed over her flat belly, tracing down to the juncture of her long legs. His thumb eased between them and he touched her softly in a place that she hadn't dreamed he would.

She jerked.

"No," he said gently. "Don't pull back. This isn't going to hurt. It's only going to make it easy when I take you." His fingers were slow and sensual and insistent. She shivered, and the pressure grew. His mouth teased over her parted lips while he taught her body to yield to building pleasure.

"Does it feel good?" he whispered.

"Yes," she sobbed.

"Don't fight it," he breathed. His mouth slid down to her breasts and explored them in a silence that grew tense as the movement of his hand produced staggering sensations that arched her body like a bow.

He was doing something. It wasn't his finger now, it was part of his body, and he was easing down and pushing, penetrating…!

"It hurts," she whispered frantically.

"Here," he whispered, shifting quickly. He moved again, and she shivered, but not with pain. "Yes, that's it," he said quickly. "That's it, sweetheart!"

She was unconsciously following his lead, letting him position her, buffet her. She felt his skin sliding against her own, heard the soft whisper of it even as the sensations made her mind spin. She was making sounds that she didn't recognize, deep in her throat, and clinging to him with all her strength.

"I…wish…!" she choked.

"Wish what?" he bit off, fighting for breath. "What do you want? I'll do anything!"

"Wish...the light...was on," she managed to say.

"Oh, God..." he groaned.

He tried to reach the light switch, but just at that moment, a shock of pleasure caught him off guard and bit into his body like a sweet, hot knife. He gave up any thought of the light and drove against her with all his might, holding her thrashing hips as she went with him on the spiral of pleasure. He heard her cry out and thanked God that she was able to feel anything, because his only sane thought was that if he didn't find release soon, he was going to die...

"Dana!" he cried out as he found what he craved, shuddering and shuddering as he gave himself to the sweetness of ecstasy.

Her hands soothed him as she came back down again, shivering in the aftermath. She stroked his hair and his nape, pressing tender kisses on his cheeks, his eyes, his nose.

"It was good," she whispered. "It was so good, so sweet. Oh, Hank, do it again!"

He couldn't get enough breath to laugh. "Sweetheart, I can't," he whispered huskily. "Not just yet."

"Why? Did I do something wrong?" she asked plaintively.

He turned his head and kissed her soft mouth. "A man's body isn't like a woman's," he said gently. "I have to rest for a few minutes."

"Oh."

He kissed her lazily, stretching his strained muscles and drawing a deep breath before he laced her close against him again and sighed.

"Did it hurt very much?" he murmured drowsily.

"A little, at first." She stretched against him. "Heavens, it's just like dying," she remarked with wonder. "And you don't care if you die, because it's so good." She laughed wickedly. "Hank, turn on the light," she whispered.

"I thought you were a prude," he taunted.

"No, I think I'm a voyeur." She corrected him. "I want to look at you."

"Dana!"

"And don't pretend to be shocked, because I know you aren't. I'll bet you want to look at all of me, too."

"Indeed I do."

"Well, then?"

He turned on the light and peeled the covers away. She looked at him openly, coloring just a little at the sight of his blatant nudity. He didn't blush. He stared and stared, filling his eyes with her.

"God, what a sight," he murmured huskily. He held out his arms. "Come here."

She eased into them, felt him position her and lift her, and then bring her down over him to fit them together in a slow, sensual intimacy.

"Now," he whispered huskily, moving his hands to her hips. "Let's watch each other explode."

"Are we...going to?" she whispered back, moving slowly with him.

He nodded, because he couldn't manage words. His black eyes splintered as the sensations began to build all over again. His last sane thought was that he might never be able to get enough of her....

He was distant the next morning. Dana had expected a new and wonderful closeness because of their intimacy in the night, but Hank was quiet and reserved in a way he'd never been before.

"Is something wrong?" she asked worriedly.

He shrugged. "What could be wrong?" He checked his watch. "We'd better get a move on. I have an appointment in the office late this afternoon, and I can't afford to miss it. Got your stuff together?"

She nodded, still a little bewildered. "Hank...you aren't sorry about last night, are you?" she asked uneasily.

"Of course not!" he said, and forced a smile. "I'm just in a hurry to get home. Let's go."

And so they left and went home.

Chapter 4

Dana peered again at the thick gold wedding ring on her hand. They'd been back in Jacobsville for two weeks, and she was living in his big sprawling brick mansion now. The housekeeper, Miss Tilly, had been with Hayden for a long time. She was thin and friendly and secretly amused at the high-handed manner Hayden had managed his wedding, but she didn't say a word. She cooked and cleaned and kept out of the way.

Dana was uneasy at first. Her brand-new husband didn't wear a wedding band, and she didn't like to suggest it to him for fear of sounding possessive. But it made her uncomfortable to think that he didn't want to openly indicate his wedded state. Surely he wasn't thinking of having affairs already?

That was a natural thought, because despite his ardor in Las Vegas on their wedding night, he hadn't touched her since. He'd been polite, attentive, even affectionate. But he hadn't touched her as a lover. He was like a friend now. He'd insisted on separate bedrooms without any explanations at all, and he'd withdrawn from her physically to the point that he wouldn't even touch her hand. It wore on Dana's nerves.

His behavior began to make sense the next morning, however, when Tilly went to answer the doorbell and a strange couple entered the house as if they belonged there.

"Where's Hank? He saw Bob at the bank and invited him to lunch," the woman, a striking brunette, announced flatly. "Didn't he say he'd be back by this time, Bob?" she asked the much older, slightly balding man beside her. He looked pale and unhealthy, and he shrugged, as if he didn't much care. He glanced at Dana with an apologetic smile, but he seemed sapped of energy, even of speech.

"I don't know where he is. I just got home," Dana said. She was very conscious of her appearance. She was wearing jeans and boots and a dusty shirt, because she'd been down to her own place to check on her small herd of cattle. She smelled of horses and her hair wasn't as neat in its braid as it had started out.

"And who are you, the stable girl?" the woman asked with a mocking smile.

Dana didn't like the woman's attitude, her overpolished look, or the reek of her expensive perfume that she must have bathed in.

"I'm Mrs. Hayden Grant," she replied with curt formality. "And just who do you think you are, to come into my home and insult me?" she added for good measure, with sparks in her blue eyes.

The woman was shocked, not only by the name she'd been given, but by that quick hostility.

She fumbled her words. "I'm Betty Grant. I mean, Betty Collins," she amended, rattled and flushed. "I didn't know Hank... had remarried! He didn't say anything about it."

"We've known each other for years, but we've only been married a few weeks," Dana replied, furious at Hank for putting her in this position so unexpectedly. He hadn't said anything about his ex-wife paying a visit. "Tilly, show them into the living room," she told the thin housekeeper. "I'm sure Hank will be along," she added curtly. "If you'll excuse me, I have things to do." She spared the man a smile, because he hadn't been impolite, but she said nothing to Betty. Her feelings had been lacerated by the woman's harsh question.

She walked to the staircase and mounted it without a backward glance.

"She isn't very welcoming," Betty told her husband with a cold glance toward the staircase.

"She wasn't expecting you," Tilly said with irritation. She'd never liked the ex-Mrs. Grant and she liked her even less now. "If you'd like to wait in here, I'll bring coffee when Mr. Grant comes."

Betty gave the housekeeper a narrow-eyed look. "You never liked me, did you, Tilly?"

"I work for Mr. Grant, madam," she replied with dignity. "My likes and dislikes are of concern only to him. And to Mrs. Grant, of course," she added pointedly.

As the blood was seeping into Betty's cheeks, the housekeeper swept out of the room and closed the door. She went down the hall to the kitchen and almost collided with Hayden, who'd come in the back door.

"Whoa, there," he said, righting her. "What's got you so fired up?"

"Your ex-wife just slithered in, with her husband," she said grimly, noticing the pained look the statement brought to his face. "She's already had a bite of Mrs. Grant, which she got back, with interest," she added with a smile.

He sucked in his breath. "Good Lord, I forgot to phone and tell Dana I'd invited them. Is she very upset?"

"Well, sir," Tilly chuckled, "she's got a temper. Never raised her voice or said a bad word, but she set Betty right on her heels. Betty asked if she was the stable girl."

His face grew cold and hard. "How does she look?"

"Dana?"

He shook his head. "Betty."

"She looks very rich, very haughty and very pretty, just as she used to." She frowned. "Sir, you aren't going to let her knock you off-balance again, are you?"

He couldn't answer that. The memory of Betty in his bed had tormented him ever since the divorce, despite the ecstasy Dana had given him that one night they'd had together.

"No," he said belatedly. "Certainly I'm not going to give her any rope to hang me with."

"Might think about telling Dana that," Tilly mused. "She won't take kindly to the kind of shock she just got. Especially considering the sleeping arrangements around here."

He opened his mouth to reply hotly, but she was already through the door and into the kitchen. He glared after her. Tilly's outspokenness was irritating at times. She was right, which didn't help the situation.

"Bring a tray of coffee to the living room," he bellowed after her.

There was no reply, but he assumed that she heard him. So, probably, had half the county.

He strolled into the living room, trying not to think about how it was going to affect him to see Betty. He wasn't as prepared as he'd thought. It was an utter shock. She'd been twenty when she left him, a flighty girl who liked to flirt and have men buy her pretty things. Ten years had gone by. That would make her thirty now, and she was as pretty as ever, more mature, much more sensuous. The years rolled away and he was hungry for this woman who'd teased him and then taken him over completely.

She saw his reaction and smiled at him with her whole body. "Well, Hank, how are you?" she asked, going close.

With her husband watching, she reached up and kissed him full on the mouth, taking her time about it. She laughed softly when he didn't draw back. She could feel the tension in him, and it wasn't rejection.

He hated having her know how he felt, but he couldn't resist the urge to kiss her back. He did, thoroughly. His skill must have surprised her, because he felt her gasp just before he lifted his head.

"My, you've changed, lover!" she exclaimed with a husky laugh.

He searched her eyes, looking for emotion, love. But it wasn't there. It never had been. Whatever he felt for her, Betty had never been able to return. Her victorious smile brought him partially back to his senses. Ten years was a long time. He'd changed, so had she. He mustn't lose sight of the fact that despite her exquisite body and seductive kisses, she'd left him for a richer man. And now Hank was married. Dana was his wife, in every sense of the word.

He blinked. For the space of seconds he'd kissed his ex-wife, Dana had gone right out of his mind. He felt guilty.

"You look well," he told Betty. His eyes shifted from her to his friend Bob in the distance. He held out his hand. "How are you, Bob?" he asked, but without the warmth he could have given the man before the divorce.

Bob knew it and his smile was strained as he shook the proffered hand. "I'm doing all right, I guess," he said. "Slowing down a little, but it's time I did. How've you been?"

"Prosperous," Hayden replied with a faint, mocking smile.

"So I've seen," the older man said congenially. "You've made quite a stir among breeders, and I hear one of your two-year-olds will debut this year at the track."

"That's the long and short of it. How's the poultry business?"

"I've divested myself of most of my holdings," Bob said. He grimaced. "I was so busy traveling that I didn't realize I'd lost control until there was a proxy fight and I lost it," he added, without looking at Betty. "Then I had a minor stroke, and even my shares weren't worth the trouble. We're living comfortably on dividends from various sources."

"Comfortably is hardly the word," Betty scoffed. "But we've got one prize possession left that may put us in the black again. That's one reason we're here today." She smiled flirtatiously at

Hank, who looked very uncomfortable, and deliberately leaned back against his desk in a seductive pose. "When did you get married, Hank? When you heard we were moving back here?"

His face hardened. "That's hardly a motive to get married."

"I wonder. Your new bride is frightfully young, and she seems to prefer the great outdoors to being a hostess. She wasn't very friendly. Is she the little farm girl whose father just died? She's not even in your league, socially, is she?"

"Oh, I wouldn't say that," came a voice from the doorway.

Hank turned his attention to his wife and didn't recognize her. Her blond hair was down around her shoulders, clean and bright, and she was wearing a silk sundress that even made Bob stare.

She was wearing just enough makeup, just enough perfume. Hank's eyes went down to her long, elegant legs and he felt his whole body go rigid as he remembered how it felt to kiss her. His face reflected the memory, to Betty's dismay.

Dana walked in, her body swaying gracefully, and took Hank possessively by the arm. She was delighted that she'd bought this designer dress to wear for Hank. The occasion hadn't arisen before, so she'd saved it. "I thought you'd forgotten the invitation," she said idly, glancing at Betty. "We're so newly married, you see," she added with indulgent affection.

Betty's face had flushed again with temper. She crossed her legs as she leaned back further into the desk. Her eyes narrowed. "Very newly married, we hear. I was just asking Hank why the rush."

Dana smiled demurely and her hand flattened on her stomach. "Well, I'm sure you know how impetuous he is," she murmured huskily, and didn't look up.

The gesture was enough. Betty looked as if she might choke.

Hank was surprised at his wife's immediate grasp of the situation, and her protective instincts. He'd been horrible to her, and here she was saving his pride. He'd been set to go right over the edge with Betty again, and here was Dana to draw him back to safety. Considering his coolness to her since their marriage, and springing this surprise on her today, it was damned decent of her.

His arm contracted around her waist and he smiled down at her with genuine appreciation. "A child was our first priority, but we sort of jumped the gun," he added, lying through his teeth as he helped things along. "We're hoping for a son."

Bob looked wistful while Betty fumed. "I'd have liked a child," he told them. "It wasn't on the cards for us, though."

"Children are a nuisance," Betty murmured. "Little irritations that grow."

"Aren't you lucky that your mother didn't have that opinion?" Dana returned smoothly.

Betty stood up. She'd been expecting a pushover, and she was getting one until the venomous child bride walked in and upset her cart. Things weren't going at all according to her plan. "Has Bob asked you about the racehorse? He hoped you might be willing to come down to Corpus Christi with us and take a look at him, Hank," she said, getting straight to the point. "He's a proven winner, with good bloodlines, and we won't rob you. We'll make you a good price."

Why hadn't he realized that Betty might have had an ulterior motive when Bob had all but invited himself and Betty for lunch? He'd thought she'd put Bob up to it because she wanted to see him again, perhaps because she'd regretted the divorce. But it was just like old times. She was after money and saw him as a way to feather her nest—and Bob's. Her body had blinded him again. Angrily he drew Dana closer. "I don't think Dana would feel up to traveling right now," Hank replied, continuing with the fiction of pregnancy.

"We don't have to take her with us," Betty said curtly.

Bob laughed. "Betty, they're newlyweds," he said with noticeable embarrassment. "What are you trying to do?"

"That would have been *my* next question, Mr. Collins," Dana replied quietly. "Although I'll tell you right now that my husband doesn't travel without me.'' She caught his hand in hers, and he was surprised at how cold it was, and how possessive.

"Oh, you don't surely think *I'm* after your husband,'' Betty scoffed. "I...we...only want to see our racehorse placed in good hands. Nobody knows thoroughbred horses like Hank.'' She shifted her posture, for effect. She had a perfect figure and she didn't mind letting it show whenever possible, if it was to her benefit. "You must be very insecure in your marriage, dear, if you don't trust your husband out of your sight with a married woman and her husband. And that's rather a sad statement about your relationship.''

Dana flushed. She could tell that Hank was suddenly suspicious. He looked down at her with narrowed eyes, as if he'd taken Betty's taunt to heart. And his hand was dead in hers, as if he felt nothing when he touched her.

Dana felt his withdrawal. She drew her fingers away. So much for the pretense, she decided. "Hank and I have only been married for two weeks,'' she said.

"Yes, dear, but if you're pregnant, it hardly means you've only been sleeping together since you married, or can't I count?'' she asked pointedly.

Which put Dana between a rock and a hard place. She couldn't admit that she and Hank had only slept together since their wedding, unless she wanted to make herself a liar about the pregnancy. She glanced at Hank, who'd started the fabrication, but he wasn't helping her now. In fact, he looked as if he hated being tied to her when Betty was within his grasp. Her husband didn't seem to be jealous at all. It was a frightening thought to a woman in love with a husband whose motives for the marriage had been suspect from the start, and who had admitted that he still felt something powerful for his ex-wife. He'd said, too, that he had no love to offer Dana; only affection.

"Besides, it isn't as if I'm trying to break up your marriage,'' Betty continued. "Bob and I are in terrible financial shape. That's one reason we're having to give up our holdings all over Texas and our racehorse. Even if Hank doesn't want to buy the horse, he might be able to help us find someone who'll want him. Surely you don't begrudge us a little advice, for old times' sake? It's only Corpus Christi, after all, not some foreign country. It would only mean a night away from home.''

Hank was wavering, so Betty advanced on Bob and draped herself against him with a seductive smile, as if she was making him an offer. ''Tell him, honey,'' she drawled seductively.

Bob's face burned with color as he looked at her and he shifted restlessly. ''Come on, Hank,'' he said. ''The stable where this horse is kept is right down the road, about ten miles from where we live. We've got plenty of room. You can spend the night and come back tomorrow.'' He smiled weakly. ''We really can't afford to wait any longer. I've had some health problems, so I have to get this settled now. We were good friends once, Hank.''

You're being suckered, Dana wanted to scream. *She's using him to get to you, she's bribing him with her body to coax you down to Corpus Christi so she can seduce you into buying that horse.*

Hank felt Dana's tension. His eyes narrowed as he looked down at her and recognized the jealousy, the distrust. He was feeling much too threatened already by Betty, and he was puzzled by the stormy indecision his own feelings brewed inside him. He felt trapped between two women, one whom he wanted to the point of madness and the other who'd discarded his heart and now seemed to want him again—despite her husband.

He glanced from Dana's set, angry face to Betty's coaxing one and felt himself wavering.

''Your wife doesn't have you on a leash or something, does she?'' Betty asked pointedly.

That did it.

Chapter 5

Male pride asserted itself. "I can spare a day or two," Hayden told Bob with a meaningful glare down into Dana's flushed face. "After all, we're civilized people. And the divorce was years ago. It's stupid to hold a grudge."

Betty beamed. She'd won and she knew it. "What a nice thing to say, Hank. But you always were sweet."

Dana felt left out. The other two took over the conversation, and in no time, they were recalling old times and talking about people Dana had never met. She poured the coffee that a disgruntled Tilly had brought on a tray, with cake, and served it to the guests. But she might have been invisible, for all the attention Hank paid her. After a few minutes she excused herself and left the room, without being really sure that he'd even noticed her absence.

Tilly was headed toward the kitchen with her tray right ahead of Dana's retreat, muttering to herself about men who couldn't see their own noses. Normally Tilly amused Dana by talking to herself, but she was far too preoccupied today to notice.

She went up the stairs to the room she occupied alone and began to pack. If Hank was going away, so was she. She'd had enough of being an extra person in his life, in his house. If she'd had any hopes that he might one day learn to love her, they'd been killed stone dead with the arrival of his ex-wife. Anyone could see how he still felt about her. He was so besotted that he hadn't even noticed Dana once Betty flashed that false smile at him. Well, let him leave with his ex-wife, on whatever pretext he liked, and good luck to him!

It took her ten minutes to pack. She threw off the sundress and put on jeans and a knit top and her boots. She braided her hair and looked in the mirror. Yes, that was more like it. She might have been a society girl once, but now she was just a poor rancher. She could look the part if she liked, and Hank surely wouldn't miss her if she left, not when Betty was ready, willing and able.

Apparently it didn't matter at all to Hank that Betty was still married, avaricious, and only using Hank to make a profit on that horse. God knew he could afford to buy it, and the woman looked as if she wouldn't mind coming across with a little payment in kind to reimburse him.

She was going through drawers to make sure she hadn't left anything when the door opened and Hank walked in.

He'd expected to find her crying. She had a sensitive nature and he'd been unkind to her, especially downstairs in front of their guests. Betty's remarks had made him feel like a possession of Dana's, and he'd reacted instinctively by shutting Dana out. Now he was sorry. His conscience had nipped him when she walked out with such quiet dignity, without even looking at him, and he'd come to find her, to comfort her, to apologize for making her feel unwelcome. But apparently it was going to take a little more than an apology, if those suitcases were any indication of her intentions.

"Going somewhere?" he asked politely, and without a smile.

"I'm going home," she said with quiet pride. "You and I both know that this was a mistake. You can get a divorce whenever you like. The will only required a paper marriage. The property is now mine and I promise you that I won't sell it to any enterprise that might threaten your horses."

He hadn't been prepared for this. He stared at her with mixed feelings.

"It's a big house," he said, because he couldn't think of anything else to say.

"You and Tilly won't miss me. She's busy with domestic things and you're never here, anyway." She didn't meet his eyes as she said that, because she didn't want him to see how much his frequent absences had made her feel unwanted. "I thought I might get a dog."

He laughed coldly. "To replace a husband?"

"It won't be hard to replace a husband who won't even sleep with me...!" She stopped dead, cold, as she realized that the door was standing open and Betty was right there, listening.

Her abrupt cessation of conversation and her horrified gaze caused him to turn, too.

Betty wasn't even embarrassed. She smiled victoriously. "I was looking for a bathroom. Sorry if I interrupted anything."

"The bathroom's down the hall, as you know, third door on the right," Hank said shortly.

"Thank you, darling." Her eyes swept over the suitcases and Dana's pale face, and she smiled again as she left them.

Hank's face had no expression in it at all. Dana picked up her suitcase. "I'll take this with me. If you wouldn't mind, could you have one of the men drop off the rest of my things? I've still got my Bronco in the garage, I hope?"

"I haven't done anything with it."

"Thanks."

She walked past him. He caught her arm, feeling the stiffness, the tension in her.

His breath was warm at her temple. "Don't," he said through his teeth.

She couldn't afford to weaken, to be caught up in some sordid triangle. Betty wanted him, and he'd always loved her and made no secret of it. Dana was an extra person in his life. She didn't fit.

Her dark blue eyes lifted to his brown ones. "Pity isn't a good reason to marry. Neither is breaking a will. You don't love me, any more than I love you," she added, lying through her teeth, because she'd always loved him. Her eyes lowered. "I don't want to stay here anymore."

His hand dropped her arm as if it was diseased. "Get out, then, if that's what you want. I never would have married you in the first place except that I felt sorry for you."

Her face was even paler now. "And there's the way you feel about your ex-wife," she returned.

He stared at her blithely. "Yes. There's Betty."

It hurt to hear him admit it. She went past him without looking up. Her body was shaking, her heart was bursting inside her. She didn't want to leave but she had no choice, it had been made for her. Even as she went down the staircase, she could hear Betty's softly questioning voice as she spoke to Hank.

Dana headed for the front door, and a voice called to her from the living room.

"Good Lord, you aren't leaving, are you?" Bob asked, aghast. "Not because of us?"

She stared at him without expression. "Yes, I'm leaving. You're as much a victim as I am, I guess," she said.

His mouth opened to refute it, and the sadness in his eyes killed the words. He shrugged and laughed shortly. "I guess I am. But I've lived with it for ten years, with taking Betty away from Hank with my checkbook. Funny how life pays you back for hurting other people. You may get what you want, but then you have to live with it. Some choices carry their own punishment."

"Don't they just?" she replied. "So long."

"She doesn't really want him," he said softly, so that his voice didn't carry. "She wants a way to live as high as we used to, on an unlimited budget. I've lost my bankroll so I've become expendable. It's his money she wants, not the man. Don't give up if you love him."

She lifted her chin. "If he loved me, I'd stay, I'd fight her to my last breath," Dana replied. "But he doesn't. I'm not brave enough to have my heart torn out by the roots every day of my life, knowing that he looks at me and wants her."

Bob winced.

"That's what you've done for ten years, isn't it?" she continued perceptively. "You're much braver than I am, Mr. Collins. I guess you love her so much that it doesn't matter."

"It isn't love," he said coldly, with the most utter self-contempt she'd ever heard in a man's voice.

She sighed. The needs of men were alien and inexplicable to her. "I guess we're both out of luck." She glanced toward the staircase with eyes that grew dark with pain. "What a fool I was to come here. He told me he had nothing to give me. Nothing except wealth. What an empty, empty life it would have been."

Bob Collins scowled. "Money means nothing to you, does it?" he asked, as if he couldn't comprehend a woman wanting a poor man.

She looked at him. "All I wanted was for him to love me," she said. "There's no worse poverty than to be bereft of that, from the only person you care about in the world." She made a little face and turned away. "Take care of yourself, Mr. Collins."

He watched her go, watched the door close, like the lid on a coffin. *Oh, you fool*, he thought, *you fool, Hank, to give up a woman who loves you like that*!

Dana settled back into her house without any great difficulty, except that now she missed more than just her father. She missed Hank. He hadn't been home much, probably because he was avoiding her, but at least he'd given her the illusion of belonging somewhere.

She looked at her bare hands as she washed dishes. She'd left the rings behind, both of them, on her dresser. She wondered if he'd found them yet. She had no reason to wear wedding rings when she wasn't a wife anymore. Hank had married her because he didn't want Betty to know how he felt about her. But his ex-wife was so eager to have him back that a blind man could see it. He'd never made any secret of his feelings for Betty. What an irony, that his wife should come back now, of all times, when Dana might have had some little chance to win his heart. Betty had walked in and taken him over, without a struggle. She wondered if she could ever forget the look in Hank's dark eyes when he'd stared at his ex-wife with such pain and longing. He still loved her. It was impossible not to know it. He might have enjoyed sleeping with Dana, but even so, he'd never shown any great desire to repeat the experience.

She put away the dishes and went to watch the evening news. Her father had liked this time of the day, when he was through with work, when they'd had a nice meal and he could sit with his coffee and listen to the news. He and Dana would discuss the day's events and then turn off the television and read. She'd missed that at Hank's elegant house. It was empty and cold. The television was in his study, not in the living room, and she'd never felt comfortable trespassing in there to watch it. She had none of her own favorite books, and his were all about horses and live-stock and genetics. He read biographies, too, and there were some hardcover bestsellers that looked as if they'd never been opened at all.

Hank didn't make time to read for pleasure, she supposed. Most of his material seemed to be business-related.

She curled up in her father's armchair with tears stinging her eyes. She hadn't given way to tears in all the time she'd been married, and she wasn't going to cave in now, either, but she felt entitled to express a little misery while there was no one to see her.

She dabbed at tears, wondering why Hank had tried to stop her from leaving since he'd said he didn't want her anymore. Maybe it was the thought of ending their brief marriage so soon. It would be hard on the pride of a man like that to have failed more than once as a husband.

After a while, she got up and turned on a movie. It was one

she'd seen half a dozen times but she only wanted the noise for company. She had to consider what she was going to do for the rest of her life. At this point, she was certain that she couldn't go on trying to keep the wolf from the door while she fought to maintain the small cattle ranch. She didn't have the working capital, the proper facilities or the money to trade for more livestock. The best way to go would be to just sign the whole thing over to Hank before it bankrupted her, and use the trust fund her mother had given her to pay for a college education. With that, she could find a job and support herself. She wouldn't need help from anyone; least of all from a reluctant husband. There was no alimony in Texas, but Hank had a conscience and he'd want to provide for her after the divorce. She wanted to be able to tell him she didn't want it.

Her plans temporarily fixed in her mind, she turned her attention to the movie. It was nice to have things settled.

Hayden Grant didn't have anything settled, least of all his mind. He was on the way to Corpus Christi with Bob and Betty, only half listening to the radio as he followed behind the couple, they in their Mercedes, he in his Lincoln.

He could have gone in the car with them; something he thought Betty was secretly hoping for. But he wanted to be alone. His ex-wife had fouled everything up with her untimely reappearance. Her taunts had caused him to be cruel to Dana, who'd had nothing from him except pain. He'd forced her into marriage whether she wanted it or not, seduced her in a fever of desire, and then brought her home and literally ignored her for two weeks. Looking back, he couldn't explain his own irrational behavior.

Since the night he'd been with Dana, his only thought had been of how sweet it was to make love to her. He hadn't dreamed that he could want anyone so much. But his feelings had frightened him because they were so intense, and he'd withdrawn from her. Betty's intervention had been the coup de grace, putting a wall between himself and Dana.

But desire wasn't the only thing he felt for his young wife, and for the first time he had to admit it. He remembered Dana at the age of sixteen, cuddling a wounded puppy that some cruel boy had shot with a rifle and crying with anger as she insisted that Hank drive her to the vet's. The puppy had died, and Hank had comforted the young girl whose heart sounded as if it might break. Dana had always been like that about little, helpless things. Her heart embraced the whole world. How could he have hurt her so, a woman like that?

He groaned out loud. He wondered if he'd lost his reason with Betty's return. He'd dreaded it because he thought he was still in love with Betty. He wasn't. He knew it quite suddenly when he saw Dana with tears in her eyes and her suitcase in her hand. Dana had lived with him for two weeks, and he hadn't even touched her since their wedding night. He thought of it with incredulity. Now he realized what his behavior had masked. He'd been afraid of falling so deeply in love with her that it would be as it had been with Betty. Except that Dana wasn't mercenary. She wanted him, and seemed to be ashamed of feeling that way. But she had a tender heart, and she'd cared about him. If he'd tried, he might have made her love him. The thought, once dreaded, was now the essence of heaven.

It was too late, though. He'd let her leave and he wouldn't be able to get her back. He'd lost her. What the hell was he doing driving to Corpus Christi with two people he didn't even like?

As he thought it, he realized that they were already driving into its city limits. It was too late to turn back now. He'd do what he'd promised, he thought, but after that, he was going home to Dana. Whatever it took, he was going to get her back.

If only it had been that easy. They'd no sooner gotten out of the car at the Collins's white brick mansion when Bob groaned and then fell. He died right there on the green lawn before the ambulance could get to him, despite Hank's best efforts to revive him. He'd had another stroke.

Betty went to pieces and Hank found himself in the ironic position of arranging a funeral for his ex-wife's second husband; and his former friend.

Back home, Dana heard about Bob Collins's death; it was all over the radio. He'd been a prominent man in the state's poultry industry and was well-known and liked. His funeral was very big and many important people attended it. Dana saw newspaper clippings of Hank supporting the grieving widow. She couldn't imagine that cold-eyed woman grieving for her husband. If Betty was crying, it was because Bob's life insurance policy had probably lapsed.

Dana chided herself for her uncharitable thoughts and threw the newspaper into the trash. Well, one thing was certain, Hayden Grant would be asking for a divorce so that he could remarry the woman he really loved. If Betty was what he wanted, he should have her. Dana remembered what she'd said to Bob Collins about not wanting to eat her heart out for the rest of her life with a man who wanted someone else. Poor Bob, who'd done exactly that, steadfastly, for ten long years. Dana offered a silent prayer for him. At least now perhaps he would have peace.

Two long weeks passed, with no word from Hank. The next morning, Dana went to see the family lawyer and asked him to initiate divorce proceedings. It would mean dipping into her small trust fund to pay for it, but that didn't matter. She wanted Hank to be happy.

"This isn't wise," the attorney tried to advise her. "You've been upset and so has he. You should wait, think it over."

She shook her head. "I've done all the thinking I care to. I want the deeds made up for my signature and delivered to Hank, along with the divorce papers. I'm throwing in the towel. Betty's free now and Hank deserves a little happiness. God knows he's waited long enough to get her back."

The attorney winced as he looked at the vulnerable, pale woman sitting in front of him. She'd suffered, judging by the thinness of her face and those terrible shadowed blue eyes. He couldn't imagine a man crazy enough to turn down a love that violent and selfless. But if she was right, that's exactly what Hayden Grant had already done. He sighed inwardly. Talk about throwing gold away in favor of gloss! Some men just didn't know their luck.

"I'll have everything ready by tomorrow morning. You're absolutely sure?"

She nodded.

"Then consider it done."

She thanked him and went home. The house was very empty and she felt the same. There would be a new life ahead of her. She was closing a very firm door on the old one, starting tomorrow. That thought was fixed firmly in her mind until the morning came and she began to throw up as if she were dying. She made it to the attorney's office to sign the papers, but she was too sick to travel.

Fearful that she had some virus that would prevent her plans to move, she made an appointment to see Dr. Lou Coltrain, a newly married member of the local medical community.

Lou examined her, asked pertinent questions and began to whistle softly while Dana looked at her with horror.

"It must have been some wedding night," Lou said, tongue in cheek, "because you've only been married a month and I know Hayden Grant. He wouldn't have touched you until the ring was in place."

"Lou, you're awful!" Dana groaned, flushing.

"Well, I'm right, too." She patted the younger woman on the shoulder. "It's two weeks too early for tests to tell us anything positive. Come back then. But meanwhile, you watch what medications you take and get plenty of rest, because I've seen too many pregnancies to mistake one. Congratulations."

"Thanks. But you, uh, won't tell anyone, right?" Dana asked gently.

"Your secret is safe with me." The doctor chuckled. "Want to surprise him, I guess?"

"That's right," Dana said immediately, thinking what a surprise it would have been.

"Come back and see me in two weeks," Lou repeated, "and I'll send you to Jack Howard up in Victoria. He's the best obstetrician I know, and it's a lot closer than Houston."

"Thanks, Lou."

"Anytime."

Dana went home in a cloud of fear and apprehension and joy. She was almost certainly pregnant, and her marriage was in tatters. But she knew what she was going to do. First she had to find her way to Houston, get an apartment and find a job. She'd handed the deeds to her father's property and the divorce petition over to the attorney for disposition. Presumably, he'd have already forwarded them to Hank in Corpus Christi in care of the bereaved Mrs. Collins. She'd burned her bridges and there was no going back.

Unaware of what was going on in Corpus Christi, Dana set out for Houston the next morning, painfully working out a future without Hank while a tall man with shocked dark eyes was served a divorce petition and cursed her until he went hoarse.

Hank jerked up the phone, oblivious to Betty's shocked stare, and dialed the phone number of the attorney, who was also a friend of his.

"Luke, what the hell's going on?" he demanded, shaking the divorce papers at the receiver. "I didn't ask her for the deeds to the ranch, and I sure as hell don't remember asking for a divorce!"

"There, there, old fellow, calm down," Luke said firmly. "She said it was the best thing for both of you. Besides, you're going back to Betty anyway."

"I am?" he asked, shocked.

"That's what Dana told me. See here, Hank, you're throwing over a good woman. She never thought of herself once. It was what you wanted, what you needed to make you happy that she considered when she arranged all this. She said it would give you a head start on all the happiness you'd missed out on ten years ago, and she was glad for you.''

"Glad for me." He looked at the papers and glanced irritably at Betty, who'd been practicing bereavement for two weeks while trying to entangle Hank in her web again. She hadn't succeeded. He was untangling Bob's finances for her, and they were in one major mess. It had taken time he didn't want to spend here, but for Bob's sake he'd managed it. Now he only wanted to go home and reclaim his wife, but he was holding proof that she didn't want to be reclaimed.

"She knew you'd be happy to have the matter dealt with before you came back," he continued. "Listen, if you don't contest the divorce—and why should you, right?—I can get it through in no time."

Hank hesitated, breathing deliberately so that he wouldn't start swearing at the top of his lungs. The words on the pages blurred in his sight as he remembered the last time he'd seen Dana. He mentally replayed the cruel, hateful things he'd said to her. No wonder she was divorcing him. She didn't know how he felt; he'd never told her. She thought he hated her. What a laugh!

"Can you hold it back for a few weeks?" he asked the attorney. "I've got some things to untangle down here for Bob's widow, and I can't get back home for a week, possibly longer."

"I can, but she won't like it," Luke said.

"Don't tell her."

"Hank..."

"Don't tell her," he repeated. "Leave it alone until I get back."

There was a heavy sigh. "If she asks me, point-blank, I won't lie to her."

"Then make sure she doesn't have the opportunity to ask you."

"I'll try."

"Thanks."

He hung up. He felt sick. God, what a mess he'd made of his life!

Betty sidled close and leaned against his arm, wearing a wispy

negligee. "Poor old dear, is she leaving you?" she asked softly.
"I'm sorry. Why don't you come upstairs with me and I'll kiss
you better?"

He looked at her as if he hadn't heard correctly. "Betty, your
husband was buried week before last," he said.

She shrugged. "He'd run out of money and he was barely able
to get around by himself." She smiled in a shallow, childlike way,
and he realized that she was just that—childlike. She had no depth
of emotion at all, just a set of wants and needs that she satisfied
the best she knew how, with her body. He'd lived with her for
two years, ached for her for ten more, and he'd never known the
sort of person she really was until he became involved with Dana.
Now he could see the real difference between the two women.

He removed her hand from his arm. "I have some things to
finish," he told her. "We'll talk later. Okay?"

She smiled. "Okay, lover."

Chapter 6

It took all of another ten days for Hayden to wrap up the odds and ends of Bob's life and get his affairs safely into the hands of a good local attorney. Bob had an attorney, but the man had been evasive and almost impossible to locate. Finally it had taken the threat of litigation to get him to turn over needed documents. And afterward, the man—who had a degree in law from an interesting but unaccredited law school overseas—had vanished. It was no wonder that Bob had lost most of his money. The charlatan had embezzled it. Fortunately there would be enough left, added to the life insurance, to keep Betty fairly secure if she was careful.

It was only as he explained things to her and she realized that he wasn't going to propose marriage that she came apart for real.

"But you love me," she exclaimed. "You always have. Look at how quickly you married that child just so I wouldn't think you were carrying a torch for me!"

"It might have started that way," he replied quietly. "It didn't end that way. I can't afford to lose her now."

"Oh, she's got money, I guess."

He frowned. "No. She hasn't a dime in the world. Do you always ascribe mercenary reasons to every decision?"

"Of course I do," she said, and smiled faintly. "Security is the most important thing in the world. I didn't have anything when I was a child. I went hungry sometimes. I promised myself it would never happen to me.'' She made an awkward gesture with her shoulder. ''That's why I left you, you know. You were heading into debt and I was scared. I did love you, in my way, but there was Bob and he had a lot of money and he wanted me.'' She smiled. ''I had no choice, really.''

''I don't suppose you did.'' He was remembering that Dana had nothing, and she was giving him the only thing of worth in her possession, those deeds to the land, so that he wouldn't face the threat of some dangerously noisy neighbor. He could have kicked himself for letting her walk out of the house in the first place.

''I felt sort of sorry for her,'' she added thoughtfully. ''She isn't sophisticated, is she? She was afraid of me.'' Her eyebrows met. ''Why won't you sleep with her?''

He averted her eyes. ''That's none of your business.''

''It is, in a way. You won't sleep with me, either. Why?''

He grimaced. ''I don't want you,'' he admitted reluctantly. ''I'm sorry.''

''You used to,'' she recalled. ''You wanted me all the time. I thought it was going to kill you when I walked out.''

''It damned near did. But things have changed.'' His eyes were sad and quiet. ''I am sorry, Betty. For your loss, for everything.''

''Bob wasn't a bad man,'' she said. ''I was fond of him. I guess I'll miss him, in a way.'' She looked up. ''You're sure about not wanting me?''

He nodded.

She sighed and smiled again. ''Well, that's that. At least I'll have enough money to make ends meet, thanks to you. And I'm still young enough to make a good third marriage!''

On that note, he said his goodbyes and went back to the motel where he'd been staying. It felt nice to have the weight of Betty's disastrous finances off his shoulders, although he'd enjoyed untangling the mess. Now he was going to go home and work on his own problems.

He looked at the divorce petition and the deeds and his eyes narrowed. Dana had wasted no time at all turning over the ranch to him. He began to frown. Where was she going to live without her house?

He picked up the phone and dialed the attorney's number, but he was told that Luke was in court on a case and couldn't be reached. Really worried now, he dialed the Mobry ranch number. It rang twice and the line was connected. He started to speak. Just as he did, a mechanical voice informed him that the number had been disconnected.

Frustrated and worried, his next call was to his own house, where he found Tilly.

"All right, what the hell's going on? Where did Dana go?" he demanded without preamble.

"She wouldn't let me call you," Tilly said stiffly. "I begged, but she wouldn't budge. I gave my word. Couldn't break it."

"Where is she?"

"She's left," came the terse reply. "Said you had the deeds and that Joe and Ernie would keep watch over the place until you made other arrangements, but you'd have to pay them."

"Oh, to hell with the ranch!" he snapped. "Where is she?"

"Took a cab to the bus station. Got the bus to Houston. I don't know where she went from there."

Hope raised its head. "Houston! Tilly, you're a wonder!"

"There's, uh, something else. The nurse who works for Dr. Lou Coltrain is a cousin of mine. Seems Dana went to see Lou before she left town. If you don't find her pretty soon, you're going to be looking for two people instead of one," she said, and hung up.

He stared at the telephone blankly and felt all the blood draining out of his face. Dana was pregnant? He counted back to their wedding night and realized that neither of them had even thought about precautions. His Dana was going to have a baby, and she'd left him! What an idiot he'd been!

He called the airport. Houston was a good place to start, thanks to Tilly, who'd saved him hours of tracking. But it was a big city, and he didn't even know where to start. He cursed himself for every painful thing he'd ever said to her. It couldn't be too late to convince her how much he cared, it just couldn't!

He soon realized how impossible it was going to be to locate Dana in Houston. She had a little money, but it would soon run out if she didn't get a job. He had to find her quickly, so he went straight to one of the better-known Houston detectives, and told him everything he knew about Dana including a description.

"Do you have a photo of your wife, Mr. Grant?" Dane Lassiter asked the man across the desk from him. A former Texas Ranger, Dane had built his agency from scratch, and now it had a fine national reputation for doing the impossible.

The question startled Hank, who hadn't expected it. He looked uncomfortable. "No," he said.

The other man didn't comment, but his eyes were steady and curious. No wonder, because the table behind Lassiter's desk carried a family photo of the detective, his attractive wife and two young sons who looked just like him.

"We're newlyweds," Hayden felt constrained to explain. "It was a quick marriage."

Dane didn't say a word. He was busy writing things down. "Did she run away, Mr. Grant?" he asked suddenly, and his black eyes pinned the other man.

Hayden took a sharp, angry breath. "Yes," he said through his teeth. "I did something stupid and I deserve to lose her. But I don't think I can stand to, just the same." He leaned forward and rested his forearms on his splayed legs in a defeated position. "And she's pregnant," he added through his teeth.

Hank's predicament sounded very familiar to Dane Lassiter. He knew all about pregnant women who ran away.

"We'll find her," Dane told the man, not so distant now. "You've given us some good leads, we'll check them out. Where can I reach you?"

Hayden gave the name of a local hotel. "I'll be here until I hear from you," he added, and he had the look of a man who planned to stay there until the turn of the century if that's how long it took.

"Okay. I'll get right on it." He stood up and shook hands. "Women need a lot of tenderness. They get hurt easily, and they keep secrets," he said surprisingly. "But if it helps, you learn how to cope with it after a while."

Hayden smiled. "Thanks."

Dane shrugged. He smiled back. "I've been married a long time. Nobody starts out in paradise. You sort of have to work up to it."

"I'll remember that. I hope I get the chance to find out first-hand."

It took two days for Dane to track Dana to a small boarding house outside Houston. During that time, Hayden lost sleep and thought torturously of all the things that could have happened to his errant, pregnant wife. It didn't improve his temper, or his heartache.

When Dane called, he was over the moon. He wasted no time at all getting to Mrs. Harper's Boarding House, but when he pulled up at the front steps in the Lincoln he'd rented at the airport on his arrival in Houston, he didn't know quite what to say. He stared at the big white house with longing and apprehension. His wife was in there, but she didn't want him. She'd tried to divorce him, had moved here and she'd made a good effort to erase her presence from his life. She hadn't even said a word to him about her pregnancy. How did he talk to her, what did he say to cancel out all the hurts he'd dealt her?

He got out of the car and approached the house slowly. His steps dragged, because he dreaded what was coming. He went up and rang the doorbell. A plump, smiling elderly woman opened the door.

"May I help you?" she asked politely.

"I'm Hayden Grant," he said in a subdued tone. "My wife lives here, I believe. Her name is Dana."

"Miss Mobry is your wife?" she asked, puzzled. "But I'm sure she said she wasn't married."

"She's very much married," he replied. He removed his cream-colored Stetson, belatedly, and let the hand holding it drop to his side. "I'd like to see her."

She gnawed on her lip, frowning. "Well, she's not here at the moment," she said. "She went to see that new adventure movie playing at the shopping center. With Mr. Coleman, that is."

He looked vaguely homicidal. "Who's Mr. Coleman?" he asked shortly.

"He lives here, too," she stammered, made nervous by the black glitter of his eyes. "He's a very nice young man…"

"Which shopping center and which movie?" he demanded.

She told him. She didn't dare not to.

He stomped back to his car, slammed into it and skidded on his way out the driveway.

"Oh, dear, oh, dear," Mrs. Harper mumbled. "I wonder if I shouldn't have mentioned that David is eleven years old…"

Sadly unaware of the age of Dana's "date," Hank drove to the shopping center, parked the car and went straight to the theater. As luck would have it, the feature was just ending, so people were pouring out of three exits. He stood, glaring, until he spotted Dana.

She was talking to a small boy in a baseball cap, her face animated, smiling. His heart jumped as he watched her come out of the big building. He loved her. He hadn't known. He honestly hadn't known. His heart accelerated wildly, but his eyes began to glow from within, quiet and watchful and adoring.

Dana was too far away to see his expression. But she spotted him at once and stopped dead in her tracks. The boy was saying something, but she wasn't listening. Her face was stark white.

Hank approached her, alert to any sudden movement. If she tried to run, he'd have her before she got three steps.

But she didn't run. She lifted her chin as if in preparation for battle and her hands clenched the small purse she was holding against the waist of her denim skirt.

"Hello, Dana," he said when he was within earshot.

She looked at him warily. "How did you find me?" she asked.

"I didn't. A detective agency did."

She looked paler. "I signed all the necessary papers," she told him curtly. "You're free."

He stuck his hands deep into his pockets. "Am I?"

Dana turned to David and handed him a five-dollar bill. "Why don't you go back in there and play the arcade machine for a minute or two while I speak to this man, David?" she asked.

He grinned. "Sure, Miss Mobry, thanks!"

He was off at a lope.

"So you came with the boy, not with some other man," Hank murmured absently.

She flushed. "As if I'd trust my own judgment about men ever again! David's mother is at work, so I offered to treat him to a movie."

"You do like kids, don't you?" he asked, and his eyes were very soft as they fell to her waistline. "That's fortunate."

"That isn't what I'd call it," she said stubbornly.

He sighed. He didn't know what to say, but this certainly wasn't the ideal place to talk. "Look, suppose you go fetch the boy and we'll go back to your boarding house? Did you drive here?"

She shook her head. "We got a city bus." She wanted to argue, but he looked as if he was going to dig his heels in. She couldn't understand why he was here, when Betty was free. Perhaps that's what he wanted to explain. She seemed to have no choice but to do as he said, for the time being, at least.

"A city bus!" he muttered, and in her condition! But he didn't dare mention that he knew about her pregnancy. Not yet. "Get the boy," he said shortly. "I'll take you home."

She went to find David, and Hank drove them back to the boarding house. David thanked her and deserted her. Mrs. Harper hovered, but a hard glare from Hank dispatched her soon enough.

He closed the door behind her and sat down in the one chair in Dana's room, while she perched on the bed a little nervously.

"Where's Betty?" she wanted to know.

"In Corpus Christi, I guess," he said. "I'm alone."

"You won't be alone for long," she reminded him. "You're getting married again."

"I'm already married," he said quietly. "I have a young and very pretty wife."

She flushed. "I divorced you."

He shook his head. "I stopped it."

"Why?" she asked miserably, her eyes eloquent in a face like rice paper. "You don't have to stay married to me now that she's free!"

He winced. He reached over and touched her cheek, but she jerked away from him.

He averted his face and stared down at the floor. "I don't want to remarry Betty."

She stared at his averted features, unconvinced. "You've never gotten over her, Hank," she said sadly. "You said yourself that part of the reason you married me was so she wouldn't know how you'd grieved since she divorced you."

"Maybe it was the old story of wanting what I couldn't have, or the grass being greener on the other side of the fence," he ventured.

She drew in a long breath. "Or maybe it was just that you never stopped loving her," she added, and the eyes that searched his were wistful and sad. "Oh, Hank, we can't love to order. We have to settle for what we can have in this life." Her eyes went to the floor. "I'll go back to school and work toward my degree and I'll be happy."

His eyes slid up to hers. "Without me?" he asked bluntly.

She wasn't sure how much he knew. She blinked and gathered her scattered wits. "Doesn't Betty want to marry you?" she asked suspiciously.

"More than ever," he affirmed.

"Then what's the problem?"

"I told you. The problem is that I don't want to marry her."

"I don't understand," she said uneasily.

He smiled wistfully. "I used to envy other men taking their sons on camping and fishing trips with them. I never thought I might have one of my own. But a girl would be nice, too. I guess girls can fish and hunt as well as boys can, if they're so inclined." His eyes lifted to hers. "You like to shoot, as I recall."

"I don't like to hunt," she replied, uneasy at the way he was talking about kids. He couldn't possibly *know*...

He shrugged. "I'll teach you to shoot skeet."

"Okay, but I won't cook them."

He chuckled. "Concrete won't tenderize."

"I know what a skeet target is made of." She drew in another breath. The way he was touching her made her toes tingle. "Betty might change her mind about having a child."

He shook his head. "And even if she did, she wouldn't want it, or love it. You will. You'll want our kids and spoil them rotten if I don't watch out." His eyes lifted. "Tilly's already looking forward to it. She's bought a food processor so she can make fresh baby food for him."

She flushed. "She's jumping the gun."

"No, she isn't," he said with a grin. "Tilly's kin to Dr. Lou Coltrain's office nurse."

"Oh, my God!" she said in a burst.

He shrugged. "So I know. The world won't end because you didn't tell me." His eyes darkened. "I'm sorry that I made it so rough on you that you didn't feel you could tell me."

She glared at him. "I'm not going back."

His shoulders seemed to fall. "I know I've made a lot of mistakes," he said. "You have to make allowances. Until a couple of weeks ago, I thought I was still in love with my ex-wife. I had to get to know her again to realize that she was an illusion. The reality of Betty was pretty harsh, after you."

"I don't understand."

"Don't you?" He sighed. "Well, Dana, I suppose I made an idol of her after she left. The one that got away is always better than anything that's left."

"You didn't act like someone who wasn't in love with his ex-wife," she reminded him as all the painful things he'd said to her returned in a flash of anger.

"All it took was two weeks in Corpus Christi to cure me," he returned. He leaned forward with his forearms resting on his knees and stared at the floor. "She's shallow," he said, glancing at Dana. "Shallow and selfish and spoiled. And I'd been away from her so long that I forgot. It cut the heart out of me when I realized that you went away because you thought I wanted Betty instead of you. I'm sorry for that."

"You can't help wanting someone else…"

"I want you, Dana," he said with a quizzical smile.

She clasped her hands hard at her waist. "You're just making the best of it, aren't you? You know about the baby and how I feel about you and you're sorry for me."

His heart jumped. "How you feel?" he prompted.

"You know that I'm in love with you," she said, avoiding his penetrating gaze. "That I have been since I was seventeen."

His heart wasn't jumping anymore, it had stopped. He barely could breathe. He certainly was robbed of speech.

She jerked one shoulder as she assumed his silence was one of regret for her sake, because he had nothing to give her. "Shameful, isn't it? I was still a kid. I couldn't even let boys kiss me, because I kept thinking about you. I've lived like a nun all these years, waiting and hoping, and it has to happen like this…you have to be forced into marriage just when your ex-wife is free again."

He hadn't known that she loved him. He'd known she wanted him, which was a very different thing altogether. He was stunned for a moment, and then overwhelmed, overjoyed.

"I'm sorry," she said on a long breath. "I guess we're both trapped."

''You'll need some maternity clothes,'' he remarked, clearing his throat. ''Things to wear when we give parties. After all, I'm a rich man. We wouldn't want people to think I couldn't afford to dress you properly, would we?''

She frowned. ''I'm not coming back...''

''We can turn that third guest room into a nursery,'' he continued, as if she hadn't spoken. ''It's next door to the master bedroom, and we can leave the door open at night. I'll get a monitor, too,'' he added thoughtfully. ''So if the baby has any problems at night, it will set off an alarm next to our bed. Or we could get a nurse for the first month or two. Would you like that?''

He'd made her speechless with plans. ''I haven't thought about any of that,'' she stammered.

''Don't you want a settled life for our baby, with a mother and father who love him?'' he persisted.

He cut the ground right out from under her with that last question. What could she say? Of course, she wanted a settled life for their child. But if Hank still loved Betty, what kind of life would it be?

Her eyes mirrored all her worries. He touched her cheek, and then smoothed back her disheveled hair. ''I was trying to live in the past because I didn't have much of a present, or a future, unless you count making money. That's no longer true. I have something to look forward to now, something to challenge me, keep me going.'' He smiled. ''I guess Tilly will make me miserable for a week, paying me back for the way I treated you. I won't be allowed to forget one rotten thing I said to you, and she'll burn the banana pudding every time I ask her to make it.'' He sighed. ''But it will be worth it, if you'll just come home, Dana. Tilly's all aglow at the thought of having a baby in the house.''

''We've already discussed this,'' she began.

He bent and drew his lips tenderly across hers. ''Not really,'' he murmured. ''Open your lips a little, I can't taste you like this.''

''I don't wa...''

"Ummm, that's it," he whispered gently, and deepened the kiss.

She forgot what she was trying to think to say to him. Her arms curled up around his neck and she let him lift her over his legs, so that he could hold her gently across his body. He was gentle and slow, and very thorough. When he finally lifted his head, she couldn't think at all.

"I'm going to like being a father," he assured her. "I won't mind sitting up with you when he's teething or giving bottles or changing diapers."

"That's nice."

He smiled. "Do you have a lot to pack?"

"Just a few skirts and blouses and shoes. But I haven't said I'm going with you."

"What's holding you back?" he asked gently.

"You haven't explained why you don't want Betty back."

"Oh. That." He shrugged. "I don't love her. I'm not sure I ever did. I wanted her, but there's a big difference in lust and love."

"Are you sure?"

"Considering the sort of man I am—and I think you know me pretty well by now—do you think I'm capable of making love to one woman when I'm in love with someone else?"

She searched his eyes. "Well, no, I don't think so. You're pretty old-fashioned like that."

He nodded. "So how could I have made love to you so completely that one time if I'd really been in love with Betty?"

"I'm sure most men wouldn't have refused something that was offered."

"We're talking about me. Would I?"

She grimaced. "No."

"That being the case, making love to you was something of a declaration of my feelings, wasn't it?"

It was. She caught her breath. "Oh, my goodness. I never considered that."

"Neither did I until I was well on my way to Corpus Christi," he admitted. "I called it guilt and remorse and misplaced emotion, I denied it to you and myself. But in the end, I came back because I loved you. And you weren't there." He smiled sadly. "I thought you'd fight Betty. I never expected you to run."

"I didn't think you wanted me. Women only fight when they know they're loved. I didn't." She searched his eyes, fascinated. "I don't guess you'd like to…say it?"

He grimaced. "Not really."

"Oh."

"But I could. If it matters that much." He looked down at her stomach. "I guess kids like to hear it, too, don't they?"

She nodded. "All the time."

He cleared his throat. "Okay. Give me a minute to get used to the idea."

She smiled with excitement and growing delight. "You can have as much as you need."

"Okay. I…love you."

Her eyebrows rose.

"I love you," he repeated, and this time it sounded as if he meant it. He stared down at her with wonder. "By God, I do," he whispered huskily. "With all my heart, Dana, even if I didn't realize it."

She moved closer and slid her face into his hot throat, curling into him like a kitten. "I love you, too, Hank."

He smiled crookedly, staring past her head to the door. He hadn't expected it to be so easy to confess his deepest emotions. He'd never done it before, not even with Betty. His arms contracted. "I guess we're not the first people who ever fell in love."

"It feels like it, though, doesn't it?" she asked drowsily. "Oh, Hank, I wish my dad was still alive, so he'd know."

His hand smoothed over her hair. "He knows, Dana," he said at her temple, his voice deep and quiet and loving. "Somehow, I'm sure he knows."

She curled closer. "Perhaps he does."

Chapter 7

The baby was born at two o'clock in the morning. Tilly sat in the emergency room cubicle in her robe and slippers, her hair in curlers, glaring at the disheveled man across from her who was sitting up, pale-faced, on the examination table thanking the doctor for his new son.

"It's a boy!" he exclaimed when the doctor moved out of sight. "And Dana's fine! I can see her as soon as they bring her out of the recovery room!"

"You saw her already," she muttered at him and cocked an eyebrow at his red face. "Just before you fainted..."

"I never!" he said. "I tripped over that gown they made me wear in the delivery room!"

"The one that only came to your knees?" she asked knowingly. "Dana was laughing so hard, she didn't even have to push. The baby just popped right out."

"I've had a hectic night," he began defensively.

"Sure, denying that it was labor pains, right up until her water broke. 'It's just false labor, sweetheart, you're only eight months and three weeks along,' you said. And there we were, rushing her to the hospital because you were afraid to wait for an ambulance, me in my nightgown, too! And then we no sooner get her into the delivery room when you see the baby coming out and faint dead away!''

He glared at her. ''I didn't faint, I tripped...!''

She opened her mouth to argue just as a nurse peeked around the corner. ''Mr. Grant, your wife is asking for you.''

''I'll be right there.''

''Are you feeling all right now?'' she asked.

''I tripped,'' he said firmly.

The nurse and Tilly exchanged amused glances, but he didn't see them. ''Yes, sir, I know you did, but we can't overlook any fall in a hospital.''

''Sure. I knew that.''

He followed the nurse down the hall until she stopped at a private room and stood aside to let him enter.

Dana was sitting up in bed with their son in her arms, tears of pure joy in her eyes as she watched the nurse stuff Hank into a gown and mask.

''Hospital rules,'' he muttered.

''Yes, sir, but all for baby's protection, and we know you don't mind,'' she replied with a grin.

He chuckled. ''Of course not.''

She tied the last tie and left him with his small family.

''Are you okay?'' she asked.

He nodded. ''Just a little shaky, and I did not faint,'' he added.

''Of course you didn't, darling,'' she agreed. ''Come see what I've got.''

She pulled back the flannel and exposed a perfect little boy. His eyes weren't even open just yet, and he looked tiny.

''He's going to grow, isn't he?'' Hank asked worriedly.

''Of course he is!''

He touched the tiny head, fascinated. The baby was smaller than he'd expected, so fragile, so new. Tears stung his eyes as he looked at his very own son.

Seconds later, the tiny mouth opened and began to cry. Dana chuckled as she fumbled with the gown and got it off one shoulder, exposing a firm, swollen breast. While Hank watched, spell-bound, she guided the tiny mouth to a hard nipple and caught her breath as he began to suckle.

Flushed, she looked up to find an expression of pure wonder on her husband's face.

"I know we talked about bottle feeding," she began.

"Forget we said a word," he replied. He stood over her, his eyes so full of love that they sparkled with it. "I hope you can do that for a year or so, because I love watching it."

She laughed a little self-consciously. "I love feeling it," she confessed, stroking the tiny head. "Oh, Hank, we've got a baby," she breathed ecstatically. "A real, live, healthy little boy!"

He nodded. He was too choked for speech.

"I love you."

He took a steadying breath. "I love you, honey," he replied. His eyes searched hers hungrily. "With all my heart."

"My paper husband," she murmured.

"Remembering?" he teased. "Me, too. But I feel pretty flesh and blood right now."

"You look it, too." She drew him down and kissed him through the mask. "Have you forgotten what day it is?"

He frowned. "Well, in all the excitement..."

"It's your birthday!"

His eyebrows arched. "It is?"

"Yes, it is." She grinned at him. "Like your present?" she added, nodding toward the baby feeding at her breast.

"I love it," he returned. "Do I get one of these every year?" he teased.

"I won't make any promises, but we'll see."

"That's a deal."

Tilly joined them minutes later, still in her gown and robe with her hair in curlers.

"Good Lord, haven't you gone home yet?" Hank asked, aghast.

She gave him an amused grin. "How?"

"You could..." He pursed his lips. "No money for a cab, and you can't drive."

"Got it."

He looked sheepish. "I'll drive you home right now." He bent and kissed Dana and his child. "I'll be back as soon as I drop off Tilly. Anything you want me to bring you?"

She nodded. "Strawberry ice cream."

"I'll be back in a flash!"

And he was. For years afterward, the small hospital staff talked about the day young Donald Mandel Grant was born, when his proud dad satisfied Dana's craving for strawberry ice cream by having a truckload of the most expensive made delivered to the hospital. Dana said that it was a shame their baby was too young to enjoy it, but Hank promised that he wouldn't miss out. Hank had just purchased an ice cream company, and he was waiting for their son's first birthday party with pure glee!

* * * * *

July 2001
COWBOY FANTASY
#1375 by Ann Major

August 2001
HARD TO FORGET
#1381 by Annette Broadrick

September 2001
THE MILLIONAIRE COMES HOME
#1387 by Mary Lynn Baxter

October 2001
THE TAMING OF JACKSON CADE
#1393 by BJ James
Men of Belle Terre

November 2001
ROCKY AND THE SENATOR'S DAUGHTER
#1399 by Dixie Browning

December 2001
A COWBOY'S PROMISE
#1405 by Anne McAllister
Code of the West

MAN OF THE MONTH

For over ten years Silhouette Desire has been where love comes alive, with our passionate, provocative and powerful heroes. These ultimately, sexy irresistible men will tempt you to turn every page in the upcoming **MAN OF THE MONTH** love stories, written by your favorite authors.

Available at your favorite retail outlet.

Silhouette®
Where love comes alive™

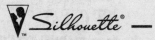

Coming in January 2002 from Silhouette
Books...

THE GREAT MONTANA COWBOY AUCTION

by

ANNE McALLISTER

With a neighbor's ranch at stake, Montana-cowboy-turned-
Hollywood-heartthrob Sloan Gallagher agreed to take part
in the Great Montana Cowboy Auction organized by
Polly McMaster. Then, in order to avoid going home with an
overly enthusiastic fan, he provided the money so that Polly
could buy him and take him home for a weekend of playing
house. But Polly had other ideas....

Also in the Code of the West

A Cowboy's Promise (SD #1405)
A Cowboy's Gift (SD #1329)
A Cowboy's Secret (SD #1279)
The Stardust Cowboy (SD #1219)
The Cowboy Crashes a Wedding (SD #1153)
The Cowboy Steals a Lady (SD #1117)
Cowboy Pride (SD #1034)
The Cowboy and the Kid (SD #1009)
Cowboys Don't Stay (SD #969)
Cowboys Don't Quit (SD #944)
Cowboys Don't Cry (SD #907)

Available at your favorite retail outlet.

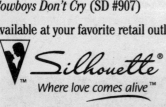

Silhouette®

Where love comes alive™

SOME MEN ARE BORN TO BE ROYALTY.
OTHERS ARE MADE...

CROWNED HEARTS

A royal anthology featuring,
NIGHT OF LOVE, a classic novel from
international bestselling author

DIANA PALMER

Plus a brand-new story in the MacAllister family series by

JOAN ELLIOT PICKART

and a brand-new story by

LINDA TURNER,

which features the royal family of the upcoming
ROMANCING THE CROWN series!

Available December 2001 at your favorite retail outlet.

Where love comes alive™

Visit Silhouette at www.eHarlequin.com

PSCH-TR